AFTER DARK

VOLUME 1

AFTER DARK
Volume 1

Edited by Aaron Crocker & Linette Kasper
with additional assistance by Mark Mackey
Cover Design by Leslie Safford
Formatted by KH Formatting

TABLE OF CONTENTS

Dear Reader,

Campfires have provided heat, safety, and a place of togetherness and community for around two million years, as evidenced by recent archaeological findings in Southern Africa's Wonderwerk Cave.

I will challenge you all to ponder, what comes to mind when you think of the word 'campfire'? I'm sure if we could compare, the answers would be as diverse as the flecks of color inside each individual flame.

Growing up in a small town in Southwestern Missouri, "campfire" reminds me of camping with family, summer camp, and more specifically, campfire stories—and even when there was no campfire, I had Grandma's front porch, where I would sit with one of my oldest childhood friends and share…or twist…small town gossip into something far darker and more sinister than reality. Needless to say, some nights I had trouble sleeping. And it is through this nostalgia, a desire for togetherness, community, and just good old-fashioned horror storytelling that the name "Campfire Publishing" came about.

The name wasn't enough. I searched for a "why"; the obvious being my love of horror and commitment to giving back to the genre everything it offered me from a young age. And my, what an extensive genre horror is, from thriller to slasher to psychological, gothic, zombie, dark fantasy, containing elements of shadows, ghosts, demons, poltergeists, and you guessed it, dear reader—werewolves and vampires, two of the genre's most beloved creatures.

What I've found throughout my personal artistic journey, while speaking to fellow enthusiasts is that some don't prefer slasher; but they enjoy zombies, or perhaps someone who doesn't prefer gothic horror enjoys psychological horror or—well, I'm certain you get the picture. And it's because of this, that Campfire Publishing strives to publish a gamut of horror subgenres, each one in its own collection and each collection containing several volumes.

Our campfire is a community— it is a sense of togetherness where we strive to be non-judgmental, safe, genuine—where we support and encourage a range of artistic voices from expert to novice, where readers can easily find organized collections of stories that fall within their preferred category of horror subgenres.

So it is, with the utmost gratitude to the authors, our editors, those who relentlessly encouraged me to continue with my vision despite personal difficulties, and an equal amount of thankfulness and humility to you, our readers, that I present our inaugural collection, "After Dark, Volume 1".

The "After Dark" collection features tales of both werewolves and vampires, beginning with Richard Beauchamp's "The Gnashing", Volume 1's singular werewolf tale—I apologize in advance for the imbalance of Vampires vs Werewolves, and ensure equilibrium in upcoming volumes.

Compiling the edited manuscripts into this anthology, I noticed a theme which I hesitate to allude to in this letter for fear of biasing the reader. Instead, I'll subtly nod to the idea of "journey"; the realization of such so poignant—to me— I placed our powerful, historical pieces at both ends of this volume.

It is my hope that within this, our very first collection, you are entertained. If we do our jobs right, you'll be frightened, unsettled, maybe you'll chuckle, or a tear will form. Most of all, above any of these, maybe you'll feel empowered, emboldened. Maybe just one story, one paragraph, one sentence was sewn together by one of our talented authors in such a way that it becomes exactly what you need to read when you need it the most.

Before I close this letter, I want to say thank you to all our authors for their professionalism and for sharing their talents, immense gratitude to Linette Kasper for her assistance in editing, and to Mark Mackey who stepped up and offered help with a bit of our edits. Certainly not least, I'd like to thank you, our readers, for your support, readership, and contribution to independent arts.

Best Wishes,
Aaron Crocker

THE GNASHING

BY RICHARD BEAUCHAMP

CHAPTER ONE

"You hear that?" Holloway asked.

"I don't hear nothin," replied Maler, who was busy cleaning his musket.

"Exactly, dead silent. Weren't like that a minute ago."

"Keep your fuckin' yap shut then. Listen," came lieutenant Boswell's voice, a baritone rasp.

The three men listened. The night air hung pregnant with silence, whereas only moments ago the world around them was alive with the scream of cicadas, the keen of crickets, and owls occasionally speaking their mind on the matter.

Holloway looked towards camp, towards the distant blur of the campfire some half mile away, its wavering orange light occluded by the many limbs of trees between them. He suddenly felt very alone out here in this corner of the woods, though a company of some hundred men sat just across the small hollow. He hated picket duty, especially out here. Ever since they'd setup camp on the bluff, he'd gotten a tight, suspicious feeling that nestled into the back of his neck and refused to leave, and that feeling did not abate the longer they stayed. The abrupt silence magnified that feeling a thousandfold.

"Christ, what're we doing out here in this shithole anyway? Shouldn't we be garrisoning in Buck's Point? Making sure the rebels don't take that little berg from us too?" Maler whispered, all of them defaulting to that hushed tone of voice.

"You heard the colonel. We're to keep a low profile until we can confirm the jayhawkers and rebels are in the area. Now shut the hell—"

The lieutenant was cut short as they heard a branch break somewhere nearby. In the abyssal silence it carried the weight of a gunshot.

Holloway didn't realize he'd been holding his breath until another branch broke, and he'd let it out with a gasping whoosh.

"Whose there! Show yourself!" Lieutenant Boswell barked out into the night, his revolver wavering slightly as it caught the last vestiges of moonlight before it disappeared behind the clouds, robbing them of that small precious bit of illumination. The thicket of white oak that surrounded them now took on an impenetrable quality, and the campfire felt like it was a whole nation away.

"Probably just a deer." Maler said, though he'd loaded his musket with a full charge and now stood by the lieutenant, the octagonal barrel swiveling slowly from left to right.

"Weren't no deer that took private Benji," Holloway said.

"Ain't nothin took him. Just a no good yellowbelly deserter. Ran off in the night. Now shut your goddamn—"

There came a sound then, what could only be described as a bestial grunt. A low, bassoon exhalation of air that sounded like it'd come from a large, tunneling throat; another branch breaking, this time off to the right.

The sound of the lieutenant's hammer being drawn back on his revolver was a small comfort. Holloway tried to grow some spine with that sound. They were the federal army, the best armed, best trained military force in the whole country. Whatever was making those stealthy sounds of inquiry would be of no threat to them. Rebel irregulars and jayhawkers be damned. They should be the ones who were feared, not—

Movement then. Shadows darting through the dark, barely discernable, the sounds of feet against forest undergrowth unmistakable.

"Oh fuck this, I—" Maler began, but his words were cut off with a blast of wind and the sound of meat slamming into meat. His musket fired, but the shot went wide, the minie ball caroming off trees with a splintering crack far off in the distance.

Halloway's ears immediately began to ring with a high atonal screech, the flash of light from the muzzle blast momentarily blinding him as he sensed huge bodies moving past him. He caught whiffs of gun smoke, and another, more musty miasma beneath this. He heard the lieutenant screaming, his pistol going off very close to his ear.

And then an explosion of pain. A vice made of knives had clamped onto Holloway's leg, and he was aware of being ripped off his feet and dragged across the ground, sticks and leaves and mud finding its way into his open, gaping mouth as he tried to scream. He heard distant shouts, heard men from the camp coming to investigate, but already he was in the tree line, whatever was dragging him pulled his body with the ease of a child pulling along a ragdoll. He tried to claw at the earth, to arrest his journey deeper into the woods, but his fingers only found yielding mud, for that was all there was up in these godforsaken foothills. Rocky mud, constant fog, shifty and suspicious town folk whose allegiance to the great war was unclear.

And now, this.

Sometime later they stopped dragging him, and just as Halloway rolled over, intent on fighting for his life, intent on making his last stand, adrenaline temporarily usurping the fear, he was aware of a hot blast of fetid breath bathing his face. He lashed out, struck something inhumanely solid, and was about to scream out some profanity, some insult, but teeth had ripped the words from his throat as pain exploded across his shoulder.

Teeth. So many goddamned teeth.

Then gun shots. The shouts of men. The frustrated grunts of things feral and monstrous. The teeth went away, but the pain remained.

Chapter Two

"Shoulda just left him to die."

"Aye, he's in real bad shape. Bastard Jayhawkers I bet it was. Striking from the shadows like cowards."

"Look at him. Rebel nor Jayhawker did what was done to that man. Pieces torn out of him. Some of the men said they saw something huge running through the woods when they started firing."

"Black bear? We don't have wolves up here. Christ, you think—"

"It doesn't matter what you all think." Colonel Arnold Mayhew said as he entered the triage tent. All of the men stood up, saluted upon his entering. He was tall, his slicked back brown hair nearly scraped the squat tent's fabric roof as he walked over to where private Daniel Holloway lay among two other wounded, these men convalescing from their most recent scrape with the confederate irregulars who were entrenched in the region like rotten teeth in sore gums.

The field surgeon sweated as he worked, attempting to close up a nasty crescent valley of gore that interrupted the swell of Holloway's bicep. There were several other similar wounds to his thigh and buttocks, the fattiest parts of the man's lean body. Clearly the work of an animal or someone wildly deranged. Mayhew would've interrogated the poor man, asked what had happened, but his sweat slicked visage was slack with shock, the eyes heavy lidded, breathy whispers escaped his mouth.

"We do not leave our brothers in arms in the field. We aren't savages like those heathens who hit and run at us from the woods. Tell me, doctor, will he make it?" Mayhew asked the sawbones.

"Well, hard to say Colonel. I've managed to arrest his hemorrhaging, but the fever has taken to him something fierce, and I'm runnin low on laudanum. If we don't get resupplied soon, I'm gonna be treating these folks with backwoods poultices and a whole lot of faith," Doc Tomlin said, bushy eyebrows crushed together as one giant gray roof over which wire-rim spectacles presided.

"Do your best then. I'm still working on the resupply problem." Mayhew sighed and retired to his quarters.

***

Their camp stood on an elevated plateau that overlooked the small, isolated berg that Mayhew had been dispatched to occupy. Nothing more than a smattering of farmhouses and a few colonial holdovers from when the first Dutch settlers had moved here. The large wooden structure at its center was obviously a trading post of sorts. One road led into town, and it was the same road out of it. There was no through.

It was first light, and the sun crested the low green humps that hemmed the village in on all sides. The gentle, rolling slopes of the Saint Francois mountains, though truly they were more like foothills, squat knobs of karst and galena filled soil, rolled on until horizon's end like waves in a viridian ocean, occasionally punctuated by cliffs and bluffs like the one he stood atop now. Fog hugged the tree line and sunk into those many hollers and holes and gave the township of Buck's Point an almost mystical, ethereal quality, a town floating in the heavens.

Were it not for the last two nights of harassment from some unseen foe, Mayhew would've found the township idyllic in its isolation. But as he stared at the disproportionately huge farmstead at the rear of the town, with several acres full of cattle, hogs, and chicken pens, he couldn't help but feel a keen sense of alienation. He knew these simple hill people would not be happy to see him, and the feeling was mutual. Mayhew was far from the front lines of the war, on his own, having to blaze a path for the union army so that they could extend the rail lines from Kansas to Arkansas. He was the spearhead here. A spear in a very lonesome, very deep patch of woods.

He was Colonel Mayhew, the 'Mouth of The Lion', a name he garnered for leading general Lionel's men into Missouri in the first place, riding bravely into battle, commanding his battalion from the front lines while grape shot tore his men asunder and minie balls whizzed past his head like an agitated nest of hornets. Once one of the most esteemed colonels in the federal army, having stomped out several treasonous pockets of rebel activity forming in the heavily contested state in many successful skirmishes, he'd failed miserably at the battle for Wilson's Creek some fifty miles away, allowing himself to underestimate those goddamn confederate guerillas. He'd lost almost an entire regiment of men that day to a fighting force nearly half that size, the rebels knowing these woods better than he ever could, and making him look like a fool because of it.

He'd lost his prestigiousness that day, and to make him pay for embarrassing the union war effort, Lionel had sent him out here, to the middle of nowhere, as a means of clearing a path for an auxiliary railway. And with a sorry company of green eared recruits to boot.

This was low work, and Mayhew presumed that was the point.

"Should we just ride in then? Make ourselves comfortable? Sir?" First Lieutenant Giles Evans asked. Though he was Mayhew's subordinate, he was the highest-ranking man in the company besides the colonel and one of the most competent. Squat and wide like a cypress stump, an unruly tide of red curly hair usually pulled back in a fiery horsetail, and cut from surly Irish stock, he was Mayhew's righthand man.

"No. We need these people's cooperation. We can ride in, take their food, sleep in their beds, but then we'd have to sleep with one eye open. This is to be a friendly occupation. Otherwise, we may as well kill them all. Then as soon as we leave, the rebels will just take it from us. We need these people to trust us."

"Trust ya… Yeah. You know these people probably don't even know there's a war going on. Being this isolated. We're not gonna know whose side they're on."

"It's to be a friendly occupation, Lieutenant." Mayhew said, looking down at Giles. Being one of the shortest men in the 3rd Missouri Infantry, with the colonel being one of the tallest, the lieutenant had to crane his thick neck very far to meet that steely gaze. Blue eyes met hazel.

"Aye sir. I'll tell the men to be on their best behavior."

As lieutenant Evans went to muster the men and tell them of the conditions of garrison, Mayhew continued to stare at that pasture, with that cornucopia of livestock that could feed a town twice, no, three times the size of Buck's Point. Surely, he could strike some kind of trade bargain with the townsfolk. His men needed food, badly. Word had still not come of the supply wagons that were supposed to be headed this way. His head throbbed with last night's libations, and the thought of having to go without his bourbon in these conditions was almost too horrible to fathom.

He made sure his men looked presentable, then tended to himself, straightening his uniform, scraping the mud from his boots, shellacking his hair back, his mustache primmed. It was important these people saw distinguished military officers, gentleman at arms, and not the ragged wild mountain men with their beards and squirrel guns and rebel whoops.

CHAPTER THREE

Holloway was sure he was in hell. His whole body blazed with an internal conflagration that cooked him alive. Ghastly visages loomed before him, his vision showing him a world that was not his own. He shut his eyes against them, where a pulsing red aura blotted out the horrors. Pain tore his body asunder from the inside out. He felt his blood simmering in his veins.

He tried to think of his family. His wife, whom he'd left when the call to arms came to him from the humble berg of Van Buren, where he was a fisherman before the war, making his living on the banks of the Current River providing the town with all the fresh walleye, spotted bass, and catfish they could eat. He longed for his familiar foothills, for the many caves that were the demesne of talented mountain men who could brew some of the finest shine in the state, for the clear and cold stream of the Current, for the warm, tender embrace of his wife.

The private howled in pain then as some terrible demon with four eyes and hair sprouting out of his head like silver horns poked and prodded at his body.

"Easy son, I'm trying to help." The demon said, his voice low and monstrous, his face vaguely familiar. He tried to move, but he was lashed down, helpless, left to this vile monster's evil ministrations.

Chapter Four

One by one they filed out of their homes and farms, coming to look at the wave of cobalt that marched towards them. Mayhew expected fear, confusion to be present in all those white eyes that stared at him. Instead, he saw a sort of forlorn suspicion, as if though they'd dealt with his like before, and begrudgingly they would deal with them again, like a recurring infestation of fruit flies in one's larder.

A few people caught in the act of various rural industry: a man tanning hides in his front yard, a woman instructing her son how to skin a rabbit, did not even pause in their duties as the men marched past in neat double rows, their weapons at port arms, thoroughly nonplussed by the colonel and his uniform and his big white quarter horse and his men marching in step. He noticed that a disproportionate amount of people were missing hands, feet, whole limbs sometimes. He knew it was common for these hill folk to go without an eye or a finger here, eking out a living in the highlands was hard, sometimes dangerous work. But Jesus, if he had to assume, at least one in five of the folks he saw was an amputee of some sort.

"Excuse me sir," Mayhew said, his mount casting a long shadow over a man who'd come out of his small shack holding an ear of corn, his trousers and hands soiled by dirt, his body with all of its parts. "I'm colonel Mayhew of the 3rd Missouri infantry battalion, state militia, company C. This is the township of Buck's Point, I presume?" He asked, doing his best to sound jovial, going so far as to dismount from his horse, so he didn't loom over the man so much as meet him at eye level.

The man only nodded, his hands working at the ear of corn, shucking it from its green cocoon.

"Is there a mayor I can speak to? Or some other leader, a constable perhaps?" Mayhew asked. The man grinned, revealing mostly pink gums and a few lonely specks of ivory.

"Ain't got no mayor. Reverend Meyer is our steward. You can speak with him, if he'll have you," the man said, his accent strange. It had the lilting roll of the hill people but was clipped with Germanic undertones. The word *Meyer* immediately informed Mayhew that this was a Dutch settlement, which bode well for him. The rebels in this part of the state hated the Dutch with a passion, for they were some of the first of the immigrant groups to join the Missouri State Militia when Lincoln declared war.

The man had raised a dirt speckled finger towards one of the colonial homes that stood apart from the rest which were all clustered around the muddy thoroughfare that cut through the town like a brown vein. Nicer than the others, the structure featured a brick façade and gabled roof, compared to the amalgamations of wood and pitch that comprised the other houses, it had the air of a palace.

"Thank you. Good day sir." The colonel said and led his horse by the reigns through town, nodding amicably at the various townsfolk he passed, keeping an eye on his men as they maintained formation, until he found himself in front of the large house. Delicious smelling meat smoke poured from the chimney of this supposed Reverend's house, and the colonel's stomach, usually in a perpetually sour state from his bourbon breakfast, roiled with hunger.

"Hold!" He barked in his most authoritative battlefield baritone. The thudding tempo of the march halted immediately. He had warned the men, anyone caught outside of formation, or trying to fraternize with the townsfolk would be punished severely. He looked back at his men; they stood still as statues. Satisfied, he turned back towards the house.

He was about to knock when he paused, noticing the deep scoring that marred the bricks, as if someone had been hacking away at the walls with an axe. Not only that, but the front door looked brand new, unwarped by the relentless humidity that plagued this region in the summer months. As if recently the place had been laid siege.

He noted these peculiarities as he knocked, wondering what sort of man would be behind the door, or, if he'd find himself being greeted by a colored servant. That was the other peculiarity of this town. He'd yet to see a single slave, though he'd heard that people in this region didn't kin to that particular system, given that there were no massive acres of agriculture to tend to or large plantation houses in evidence to house them.

If he was pious, fine. Mayhew was no longer a man of God, his faith jaded from years of battlefield depravity and the two-faced snakes he'd been forced to deal with during his time as a governor on the Saint Louis legislative counsel, but he could put on a convincing act. He knew his scripture, his verses.

As Mayhew waited for the door to open, he glanced further upon the townsfolk, who'd resumed their banal activities. Upon hearing a reverend led this small village, and given their Dutch origin, he thought perhaps he was dealing with a sect of Mennonites. But their garb was utilitarian and unceremonious, and the women, who were taught to downcast their gaze in the presence of men, glared boldly at these armed interlopers. Not only that, but some of them, he realized, bore a strange looking tattoo. He'd only caught a glimpse, not wanting to stare, he knew his gaze was intimidating. Two triangular black staves with a circle below it. He'd seen it on at least three of the townsfolk. He noted he'd yet to see any of the amputees with the symbol.

The door opened, and Colonel Mayhew was face to face with a man of equal stature and height to himself. Rare was the moment when he could look a man in the eyes without having to tilt his eyes downward.

The man before him had long, raven black hair that was unrestrained by horse tail or shellack. A thick beard equally as dark furred his cheeks, splitting open at the lips to reveal a smile that presented a surprising amount of healthy-looking teeth.

"Hello stranger."

"Hello. Would you be the reverend Meyer, by chance?"

"It just so happens I am." Meyer said, his smile warm, inviting, making the lines in his face deepen. He was in his late fifties, early sixties perhaps. Despite his advanced age however, time did not stoop his spine or diminish the spark in his eyes.

His exposed forearms were vascular and very hairy; he stood straight, shoulders broad and pulled back. Mayhew hoped he could age this gracefully one day.

"And what brings a—" the reverend paused for a moment, examining the colonel's uniform, eyes flitting to the two embroidered bars on his shoulder that had stitched within each a facsimile of an eagle. "Colonel, to my doorstep? To my humble warren of a town?" he asked.

"I…" Mayhew was taken aback. To the average citizen, military uniforms all looked the same. Only a fellow soldier could differentiate the subtle distinctions in rank. "I'm here, to inform you, Reverend Meyer, on behalf of the United States Federal Army, that we will be garrisoning within your township for the foreseeable future. This is not a hostile occupation, but rather, a temporary bivouac within your town."

"Is that so?" the reverend asked, his tone still bright, conversational, but the friendly glint in his eyes altered slightly. Ever so slightly. "And what on God's good earth does your military see of strategic value in my town? As you can see, we're rather…insulated," he said with a laugh, waving a gnarled hand outwards to encompass the wall of trees that hemmed the town like palisades in a feudal village. "My people, my land, have stayed insulated from the greater conflicts of the country. We have no side to take."

"I understand that, sir, and I will personally do my best to make sure our occupation in this beautiful little hamlet doesn't disrupt too much of your usual goings on. I'm afraid I must insist however, that we setup in your township, and that your people cooperate with mine in finding them shelter. The union rail lines are currently being built, and aim to cut through these hills and head south, towards Arkansas. Securing this area would be another stepping stone to making sure we stay supplied on the ever expanding front line. Your people can be of great help in this regard, and it would behoove the town to be in the union's favor," the colonel said.

He tried to keep the authoritativeness out of his voice. He'd heard of the forced occupations going on in other places throughout the state. Both union and confederate soldiers confiscating land and house carte blanche, using their new found military powers to take what they wanted with little regard for the people caught in the middle. He was sure this man, who could spot a colonel by his bars, knew as well. Perhaps these people weren't as insular and naïve as he thought.

"I see…" The reverend said. He sucked his teeth, gray eyes slowly roving over the rows of men on his door step, as if sizing them up, and then nodded, stepping aside. "Come in Colonel. Let us break bread then, if we are to be sharing such intimate quarters together."

The savory aroma emanating from the house was invitation enough.

Mayhew entered, his mouth watering and his stomach cavernous.

Chapter Five

Mayhew was expecting all manner of religious effigies and décor. What he got instead was a rather spartan furnished house, the walls blank save for various farming implements tacked to the walls, which looked wholly out of place in this clean hallway. He paused momentarily before a particularly wicked looking harvester's scythe, its long silver blade untarnished by rust or wear. In fact, the tool looked like it'd never threshed a single grain in its life.

"Sorry, I prefer to keep my tools close at hand. It rains so much up here, anything made of metal rusts so soon in the elements." The man said as he beckoned the colonel into a cozy kitchen, where the smells of simmering meat and bread nearly drove Mayhew out of his mind.

Their supply wagons were coming at irregular intervals, either being stalled by the rough terrain of the Saint Francois foothills they had to cross through to get to their position, or were lost to those goddamn bushwackers, killing the stagecoach and taking their weight in food and other provisions. The colonel and his men had had to make do with wild plants such as honeysuckle and boiled cat tail chutes, and the odd game, mostly rabbit and squirrels, and with no seasoning upon which to flavor the gamey, stringy meat.

"Sit, please." The reverend said, gesturing towards a small wooden table in one corner, facing a window that looked out over the large pasture that marked the rear of the town. He took a moment to stir a simmering pot of stew. Mayhew could see glistening chunks of red meat, beef probably, in the brown broth, and he almost wept. Then the reverend opened up a cabinet, produced a brown bottle and two wooden cups. "Do you partake?" He asked, pouring a clear liquid into one of the cups.

"I do," the colonel said, identifying by smell alone the potent tang of high strength corn mash. The Reverend nodded, poured a finger into the other cup, and slid it across to the colonel. He knew he shouldn't. Ever since his humiliation at Wilson's Creek, the colonel made sour mash a part of every meal, breakfast included. But it was rude to turn down such an offer in one's own home, wasn't it? And he was to wear his most diplomatic face if he were to see this occupation through smoothly. He took the cup, and raised his own when he saw the Reverend raise his cup in salute.

"To amicable relations." The reverend said and knocked back his drink.

The colonel nodded his ascent, gulped the firewater.

For a moment he couldn't breathe. He was used to the smooth burn of bourbon. This was an all-consuming hellfire that scorched a path down his throat and hit his chest with a blazing fist. Meyer grinned as he swallowed the liquid lava like it was water.

"Sorry, we don't get many outsiders. I forget to warn them. We're used to it I suppose," he said, and while the colonel was busy finding his voice, feeling the immediate warm flush spread across his whole body, the reverend began to ladle the delicious looking soup into large wooden bowls. "You know, you aren't the first military force to try and occupy Buck's Point. The secessionists were here first," he said nonchalantly, handing the colonel a spoon.

Despite the comforting flush coursing through his body and loosening his aching limbs, his guard immediately went up at the mention of rebels.

"Is that so? And did you aid them?" The colonel asked, his voice hoarse as he immediately went at the soup, not caring that it burned his still-tingling mouth. For a moment his suspicions were arrested as he savored the delicious, hearty flavors filling his mouth. God, it was like ambrosia, the meat tender, fall off the bone. The potatoes and carrots were soft and salty.

"Not really, no. They did not stay long. Just a few of those bushwackers. They did not find our location… suitable to their needs."

"When was this? Are you telling me there's rebel activity in the area?" Mayhew asked, his mustache dripping with soup broth, his eyes fixing the reverend, letting his gaze harden. He forced himself to stop shoveling the soup in his mouth long enough to inquire.

"Rest easy Colonel," the reverend said with a laugh, pouring them both another finger of the fire water, "the only thing looming in these woods you should be weary of are loons and bears," he said. Mayhew thought about telling the reverend about their attacks on the camp, of the man he found mauled and mutilated. And the three who were never found. He decided not to though.

"We should discuss arrangements for my men," he said over another spoonful of soup.

"Yes, we should," Meyer said and raised his cup for another toast. The colonel returned it.

"We'll need food. Shelter. I'd be willing to trade, within reason, for such commodities."

"No offense Colonel, but I got a look at your men. Aside from the weapons you carry, you don't seem to have much to offer."

"We can offer protection from further rebel incursion. Tell me about your livestock. You have far more than your people need. There a trade route that come through here?"

"Protection?" Meyer asked and grinned again. The smile was a little less friendly this time. He said the word like it was the silliest thing he'd ever heard. "That is something we don't need."

"You didn't answer my question. You have more livestock and provender out there than a town twice, no… three times your size would have. This tells me you do commerce with someone." The colonel said. He felt a tension begin to settle over the room like nimbus clouds poised to erupt with lightning.

"No, no commerce. Winter is upon us Colonel. We are an isolated people, as you can see. Once the snow comes, there is no way in or out for several months. Our crops are not abundant, the soil here shallow and foul with rock. I believe in staying well prepared. Meat is what see's us through the winter. And eggs." The reverend said, but he stared at his bowl of soup while he said it.

"Must be incredibly well stocked larders then. I spot, what, sixteen head of cattle? Ten dozen pigs? Twice as many flocks of chickens?" The colonel asked, looking out the window, taking visual inventory. "Gods man, you could feed a whole regiment with that. Surely you won't mind if we—"

"No." The response came abruptly and with a sharpness the colonel wasn't expecting. "I'll house your men, and feed them to the best of my ability, but the livestock remain untouched. That condition is immutable." He said, the jovialness gone.

"Reverend, I'm trying to be polite here. I want no animosity between our people. I—"

"And my people want no part of this war, Colonel. You said you offer protection, but you cannot protect us."

"Protect you from what? Are you in danger? You said the rebels steer clear of this area." The colonel said, not understanding the man's sudden turn in mood.

"We will hold a town council meeting tonight about making arrangements for your men. I ask you leave us unmolested until we convene on how to handle this. Perhaps you may retire back to your bluff that you'd huddled upon over the last fortnight, staking us out like wolves stalking a kill."

The colonel, for a brief second, floundered for words, the conversation was deteriorating rapidly; the moonshine was some strong stuff. It made his mind slow to adapt to this escalation.

"Really, sir, I do not ask much of you. Your supply of meat is bordering on excessive, we—"

"No. If anything it is just barely enough. You have no idea, but it is not my place to enlighten you. Now, I have invited you into my own home, broken bread with you, shown you hospitality. I hope you return such kindnesses upon us. Please Colonel, leave me be. There is much work to be done. Someone will send for your men when we are ready," he said, standing, and began to clear the table.

"I hope it does not come to this, but I reserve the right to declare any provision or tool I see as materiel for the army. Martial law. If I want to, I can simply take what I need from your pasture. Any resistance will be seen as abetting an enemy and will be met with lethal force. Please do not make me force my hand." The colonel said, hating that the conversation had devolved to this, but growing increasingly frustrated at the man's strange obstinate disposition towards his animals.

"You do that, and you kill us all." Meyer said. Sagely gray eyes, a shade colder than Mayhew's own, bore into him with a knowing weight of someone who's witnessed grave and terrible things. "Now leave, please. Give us a few hours to convene." The reverend said, and handed the colonel the large brown bottle of shine. "Take this, as a symbol of good faith."

On his way out, Mayhew caught sight of a strange thing. Sticking out of one wall-lined shelf was an odd wooden contraption, vaguely cruciform in nature. Weeds and other detritus were interwoven into the little wooden device. It struck Mayhew as oddly pagan in nature.

Chapter Six

"Well? Were you well met?" Lieutenant Giles asked, trying to control his horse as they rode at the head of the march. It would've been comical, watching the squat man struggle, if Mayhew's own quarter horse wasn't acting surly herself. Something in the woods or in the air spooked them.

"Hostilities were minimal. We make our way back to camp and wait. They will send for us when they are ready." The colonel said, taking a small nip off the moonshine before forcing himself to put the bottle in the saddle bag. It didn't burn so much on the fourth swig.

"Colonel, sir, I do not mean to speak out of turn, but the seasons are changing. The night's grow long and cold. We are the federal army. We can just march in there and—"

"We can, but we *won't*. We need the people of this nation to support us, Lieutenant. We are long from home and these woods could hold surprises. I'd rather endure them with a sympathetic populace than one who would slit our throats in our sleep. I give them a day and a night. If they've not sent for us by then, I will switch tactics. Speak no more of it."

"Aye sir." The lieutenant said as they began to climb the steep tract that crawled up the side of the bluff where they'd spent the last few nights.

With grumbles and mumbled protestations that were abruptly silenced as the colonel rode through camp, the 3rd infantry setup their cloth tents and made small fires, again. The detachment left behind with the triage tent reported no suspicious activity while they were gone. Some good news, at least.

"Have our best marksmen do a patrol of the area. Shoot what game they can find." He told Lieutenant Evans. While the men tried to secure some food, he went to see the doctor, and check the status of the private. If he was beyond saving, Mayhew would put the man down himself. The sawbones, a veteran surgeon named Augustus Tomlin who served

Mayhew faithfully for two full scale engagements, was overburdened as it was with his failure to save so many broken men. Even the hardiest of souls could shatter with such a burden.

He entered the tent, and despite it being relatively empty, only three of the ten beds occupied, a thick, heavy effluvium hung in the air, as if it were a full plague triage. A profound rot that assaulted the nose and churned the stomach.

The doctor, perpetually exasperated when his charges were on the decline despite his best efforts, loomed over private Holloway, a cloth mask over his face, wire rim spectacles amplifying his blood shot eyes and making him look particularly ghastly.

Holloway on the other hand, was a tragic sight. His cot was soaked through with fever sweat, his skin the color of goat's milk left to congeal in the high Missouri sun. His eyes revealed only blood shot sclera.

"How is he?" Mayhew asked softly, knowing not to get too close when the doc was like this.

"I don't get it, Colonel. Never seen someone deteriorate so quickly. If only I had my goddamn laudanum! This fever will be the death of him." Doc Tomlin barked, his voice ragged. "Lest the animal that attacked him carried some disease, he has no reason to decline like this. I've tried *everything* I could Colonel. Bloodletting, bourbon, hell, I'd trepan him if my goddamn trephine wasn't duller than a halfwit!" he beat the ground with a fist caked with blood and pus.

"You've done good work doctor. I think he's in the lord's hands now." The colonel said, daring to put a comforting hand on the doctor. "Go see what the men are cooking up. Get yourself some of the moonshine I procured. It does a body good. Go on now, your work is done." The colonel said.

The doctor gave a noncommittal grunt and stomped out of the triage tent. Holloway didn't thrash or writhe anymore, only his lips moved in a continuous pantomime of words, his head swaying gently from side to side.

Colonel Mayhew sighed as he undid the lashings tying the dying man to the bed. His stomach roiled with the miasma of rot boiling off this man, but he forced himself to bear it. Not wanting to soil the cot any further or damage it with what he was about to do next, he gently rolled Halloway off the cot and onto the ground, where he knelt beside the man.

Mayhew took out the silver crucifix from the breast pocket of his colonel's jacket, he kept it more as a good luck talisman than some true sign of his faith, and lowered it towards that stinking, sweating body. He noticed the puckered lips of Halloway's wounds, where catgut pushed his flesh together, wept a yellow sebum that made his stomach lurch to look at, and shuffled a little farther away from the man, lest he have some contagion.

Mayhew began to cite the lord's prayer, making the sign of the cross before taking out his revolver, setting it on the ground beside him.

Mimicking what he once saw a southern Baptist preacher do to his mama on her death bed, giving her last rites, Mayhew took the cross and placed it on that ashen plain of flesh between eyebrow and hairline.

The reaction was so violent, so sudden, that Mayhew didn't have time to react. A scream, no, a bestial *wail* erupted from Halloway's throat, a howl of agony so loud it pushed at the colonel's ear drums the way a howitzer volley did. Holloway twitched violently as the cry abruptly cut off, followed by the sound of bacon hissing in a pan as smoke rose from the crucifix, no, from Holloway's *forehead* where the crucifix made contact.

Then he was on hands and knees, looking around wildly, eyes still rolled up to look inside his skull, but all the same, he bolted, tearing through one flimsy canvas wall of the triage tent, loping, not running, out of it, his banshee wail continuing and fading as he moved with incredible speed. The colonel heard branches breaking in the distance, leaf litter being disturbed, a wild animal darting through the forest. Except that wild animal was one of his soldiers.

"What the hell?! What—" Doc Tomlin erupted into the triage tent, looking down at the colonel, who still kneeled, crucifix dangling where only a moment ago a man's head was. "Where in the hell is Holloway?"

Chapter Seven

He was a man afire. A man asunder from the inside out. He moved through the blur of brown and green like some ephemeral spirit moving through the plains between this world and the next, his feet barely touching the ground.

Over the pain that encompassed his body, the one sense that rose above it all was his smell. Halloway's nose was an entity in itself now, detecting scents so complex, so profound his eyes watered, and his breath hitched as he ran. He did not know what these smells were, but one in particular stood out. It was a *good* smell. That was all his brain could do to categorize the overwhelming olfactory sensory assault it was being fed. *Good* smells and *bad* smells.

He ran towards the good smell. A comforting smell. It tickled that primal baser instinct deep in his brain, a smell associated with comfort, familiarity. He always smelled lavender on his wife's skin during intimate moments. That smell set off the same deep tingling in his brain because it was what he smelled as a babe when his mother took him to breast because his mother used lavender soap as well. Swaddled in all that soft flesh, warm, life-nourishing milk spurting into his mouth. What he smelled wasn't lavender, but had the same effect. It was the smell of safety, of home. Of nirvana.

His pale body shot through the woods towards it, at some point going from a loping bipedal run to a more animalistic locomotion, hands and feet kicking up dirt as he ran. He tried to outrun the boil in his veins, the invisible tidal pull straining at his flesh, at his very nerve endings, telling him he needed to shed this body.

Soon he came upon a small wooden house, engulfed by poplar and white oak. He circled it, unaware of the tongue lolling, slavering nature he presented. He reached for the door, faintly remembering how doors worked but unable to grasp the handle all the same, so he simply clawed at the pane of wood, the pain lost to him as his nails were pried from their beds.

***

Soon the door opened, and a woman appeared. She did not at all seem shocked by the pale, slobbering man-thing on her doorstep, not recoiling in terror but leaning forward with grave curiosity.

"Oh my." She said, kneeling down, the concern on her face growing. Without fear or reservation, she held the man, who began to softly gabber and grunt now, like words were starting to form on his tongue, but died as unintelligible vocalizations on his lips. "Shhh. Shhh. It's confusing, I know. Gods. Who did you run into, hmm? This should not be. This should not be…" The woman said, trailing off, nostrils flaring as she took in his scent, eyes glazing over as she inhaled him, leaning a head towards his wounds, the stitches burst in his wild journey here, weeping freely blood and a clear, mucus-y substance.

All she could smell were smells of men though- cleaning agents, alcohol. This man had been tended too recently, burning away all identifying traces of saliva and other secretions that would've told her who was responsible for this mistake.

"Shhh. You poor thing…" She cooed as the man began to whimper now. The sleeve of her simple deerskin smock rode up, and a black tattoo showed itself as she held the man like a giant infant, her face torn deep with sorrow and genuine sympathy, as if she knew exactly what the man was going through, and armed with the terrible knowledge that it would get so much worse for him.

Chapter Eight

The colonel nipped at the shine while he added wood to the fire. The past few nights he'd ordered his men to keep the fires small and spaced out, keep the bushwackers from fixating on an exact location, but Giles was right, the nights were starting to grow teeth with which to nip at a body, the damp chill a slow, insidious thing that worked through clothes to get one's flesh cold and the joints raw. He ordered the fires to burn large tonight. He knew the picket he'd sent Giles on would be next to fruitless, this land preternaturally denuded of all the fauna that should roam in abundance in such an isolated swath of sylvan desolation, but he had to do what he could to boost morale.

He skipped on a helping of soup, guilt gnawing at the warm brick in his belly where the reverend's stew had pleasantly sat, and watched as his men slurped demurely at their meager broth of tubers and cat tail roots. A few men had found wild berry bushes interspersed among the unending walls of trees and their mouths were smeared with red and black as they ate.

"You're telling me he just… got up, and ran out?" The doctor had asked for the third time, the colonel's report beggaring credulity.

"I told you goddamnit, yes. Never seen anything like it in my life before. Poor bastard's probably lying dead out there, becoming coyote steak." Mayhew said as he watched the brown bottle of shine passed around by everyone sitting around the main pyre, forcing himself to share, though he wanted nothing more than to drown his anxieties in that anesthetizing fluid. He hoped there would be a few swallows left by the time the bottle came back to him.

The sun was just beginning to hide behind the knobs and trees when Giles and his squadron arrived back at camp. Mayhew saw the two small hares dangling from Giles's belt. He tossed these to the colonel.

"Bounty of riches this forest contains." He said sarcastically. "Goddamn woods are as barren as a widower's cunt. That's not all though." He said, gesturing for one of the men, private Elias Richards, to come forward. He had in his hands a soiled but still identifiable brown wool shell coat. Faded but still visible were the double golden bars of a first lieutenant. "Found a whole platoon of uniforms, all rebs. Most of 'em were torn to pieces, but a few like that we found whole. No bodies though. Just cloth scraps and a few squirrel guns. And this." He said, and handed the lieutenant colonel a gun whose wide flared barrel was the size of a trumpeter's horn. It was a scattergun, a goddamn big one too.

"Was loaded with this. Whoever owned it never had a chance to fire." Another one of the soldiers, Mayhew's shine-soaked mind couldn't recall the name, said, handing him a palmful of silver shot. The small metal balls scintillated in the firelight. The colonel blinked. He'd never seen silver shot before.

"Weren't no bushwackers that came through here, sir." Giles said, his voice serious now. "You know they don't attach an officer with such a high ranking to some half-assed irregular guerillas. Must've been a full-sized detachment come through here. Found a few cannons mired in the mud up yonder as well. Big enough to have an artillery battery. Something wiped those men out, Colonel, and left nary hide nor hair of them."

Mayhew studied the lieutenant's jacket for a long time.

It made no sense.

Just a few bushwackers. They did not find our location… suitable to their needs. The reverend's deep, calm voice came back to him, with its odd combination of Germanic clip and foothill lilt.

"Tell me, did that reverend send for us yet? Or has he left us to freeze on this cliff, sir?" Giles said, daring to speak in such a way to the colonel. Half drunk from the shine, Mayhew was about to dress down his first lieutenant when there came a short, clipped blast from a bugle at the edge of camp. The picket's had spotted something.

"Ho there!" One of the men called, raising his rifle. The colonel did a rough shambling jog over to where the picket was hailing, and saw a lone figure coming up the hillside, from the direction of Buck's Point. At first all Mayhew could see was a glowing blob of firelight, reminding him of the spook lights the hill folk swore populated these squat mountains. But then it grew closer, and an arm, then a shoulder, then a face grew out of the torch's glow.

The wavering firelight aged Reverend Meyer's face preternaturally, the shadows deepening the arroyos of flesh around his face. His eyes were unreadable as he approached the colonel. Mayhew didn't know if he should be relieved or on guard. What Giles found in the woods changed everything.

"Colonel Mayhew."

"Reverend." The colonel said, and they shook hands. The reverend's was like a granite statue, cold and unyielding.

"Apologies for the wait. I've convened with the townsfolk. They've agreed to let you shelter in our town. This arrangement is conditional though."

"Conditional? Who are you to—" Giles began but the colonel shot him a look, and his mouth snapped shut.

"What are these conditions?" The colonel asked.

Chapter Nine

The barns were a step up from canvas tents, and Mayhew supposed he should be grateful they were given shelter at all, though he did not like being separated from his men. The lower ranking men, privates and corporals, were allowed to stay in the three large barns that bordered the farmland containing the vast swath of pasture and the animals that grazed upon it. Rudimentary straw beds were made for them, though they were warned to check for brown recluse and wolf spiders among the hay pallets before bedding down.

The wounded were allowed to stay with Miss Tilda Bayer, whom the reverend informed them was their *defacto* doctor, a medicine woman who had the stature of Giles, short, squat, a prodigious bosom that gave her the air of a stout German milkmaid. The two remaining men from the triage tent were carried down on caissons, and the doctor insisted on staying with his men. Upon exiting the old woman's home, having deposited the convalescing men within, the doctor pulled colonel Mayhew aside.

"She's a witch doctor, Colonel. Her house is full of jars of homemade nostrums, fetid poultices and god knows what else. I'll warn you right now, sir. She tries any of that hoodoo hogwash on my patients, I'll throttle her." He hissed under his breath.

"At ease, son. They're just making due with what they have. Mountain medicine is all you're seeing. I'm sure she won't touch your men." The colonel said, though the woman, who had a protruding snaggle tooth that made her grin rather unfortunate and a sort of insane glint in her eyes, unsettled the colonel for reasons he could not specify.

The colonel, first lieutenant Evans, sergeant major Anderson, cavalry sergeant Wallace, and quartermaster Unger, were all put in homes. The colonel was to shelter with the reverend, while the other three stayed with a woman named Hannah Caldwell, who was a recent widow, her son and husband both lost when the rebels had incurred on their land, or least that's what the reverend had said. Colonel Mayhew silently noted she was one of the ones with the black brand on her arm. She was a thin, quiet woman whose eyes never met his, and who took the news of sheltering the officers with a mirthless nod, as if she'd just been told it was her job to clean the stables tomorrow.

On the matter of stables, Mayhew saw the people of Buck's Point had a robust equestrian population that rivaled even their livestock when the few cavalry mounts they had were led to one of four fully stocked stables. Mostly quarter horses such as his own but with a smattering of saddle horses and even a few appaloosas. The saddle horses bothered Mayhew. He'd captured enough of the damned things to know they were the preferred breed of the confederate cavalry.

"They'll be properly fed and watered, hell, our stablemaster will even clean their shoes for you if you want. We believe all life is sacred and to be treated with respect even if their fate is to fill our bellies." The reverend said when he saw the colonel's appraising gaze. Indeed, all the horses he saw looked well fed, well groomed, their manes and tails free of matts and detritus, unlike his own, which were rough and hard rode.

With the matters of shelter arranged and the men seen to their new quarters, the reverend informed them there was to be a large communal feast in the morning to commemorate their new guests and that they should turn in early, for tomorrow would be the start of their work. He was quite adamant in marshalling the men towards their sleeping quarters, saying the women needed peace and quiet to prepare for tomorrow's culinary largesse.

"If you don't mind, Reverend, I would like to have a quick palaver with my subordinates before turning in. There is also the matter of setting up a picket. Surely you cannot expect my men to not stand guard. They shall be quiet in their duties." The colonel said as the reverend ushered him towards his house. The reverend stopped, regarded the colonel with a thin smile.

"Yes, of course. How easy it is to forget this land is a contested one," he said, "Do not be too late, I have more soup ready for you; it doesn't hold up well to the cold." Meyer said and headed towards his house.

***

"Something's not right. For being a piss ant farming burg, they're stocked like kings." Quartermaster Unger said quietly. As old as Mayhew and with enough battlefield experience to have a keen judgement, his appraisal validated the colonel's suspicions.

"You think they had something to do with what we found in the woods? There's maybe thirty full grown men capable of fighting and twice that many women and children in this place. Rest are all missing bits and pieces. Goddamn lot of them too. The rebels may be as sharp as a butter knife, but I don't think they'd let a farming village best them. They had an artillery battery for Christ Sakes!" Giles said, his voice low, conspiratorial.

The five men were huddled on the very outskirts of the township, a small detachment of corporals brought with them to stand guard where open land abruptly met the thick wall of trees that closed them off from the rest of the world.

"They met their end somehow. And the stables have at least ten saddle horses within them," Mayhew said, smoking a pipe, trying to let the tobacco clear his shine-haze and let him think clearly.

"A rebel captain's favorite horse." The cavalry sergeant said bitterly. They all nodded at that.

"Sleep with your weapons at your side, and with one eye open. You lot—" The colonel said, gesturing towards the five men standing sentry by the small wooden fence, quite unnecessary really given the nearly impenetrable thicket that closed the town in, "You see anything suspicious at all, you come straight to me. Don't call out alarm."

"Sir?" One of the men asked, his face gaunt, an undercurrent of fear clear on all of them. So reluctant were they to pull picket duty that the colonel had to force the men to draw straws when no one volunteered.

"You heard me. Be quiet about it. Or, if it looks like we're under siege, if it's an *emergency*—" he said, emphasizing this last, he handed one of the men the bugle. "You blow this. Three short blasts. Understood?"

They'd lost their designated bugler during the battle for Wilson's creek, and so men had to take turns practicing their embouchure technique, ensuring that most of them were competent enough with the instrument to signal basic field commands in an improvised engagement.

"Yes sir," they all said in tandem.

The colonel nodded and looked back towards the direction of the village. He could see candles burning in several of the homes, and saw more than a few faces peering out them as an obsidian veil cloaked the town, the darkness out here absolute with the heavy cloud cover obscuring the moon and stars.

"Be wary, men," he said to his ranking officers as he made his way back towards the reverend's house. Now that dark was fully upon them, he felt even more reticent to leave his men separated like this. But he supposed he had no choice. The 'conditions' that the reverend laid out specified that, among other things. The requests were odd, but not altogether egregious, and the colonel was obliged to meet these conditions lest he turn his men out into the cold.

As he walked through the town, its one street completely empty, he saw far off to the east, atop a bluff similar to the one he'd occupied in the days before, he saw a small fire burning.

Condition number one: the men of the 3rd infantry were expressly forbidden from exploring the land to the east. When the reverend pointed in the direction the colonel was now looking, he noted to himself that that was the direction in which Halloway had taken off. Again, odd, but the land to the east looked particularly rugged and unforgiving, and they were incurring south, into rebel territory, so it wouldn't have been a problem anyway. He stared at the fire a minute longer, assuming it was perhaps the blaze from a shiner's still. It made sense, considering the bounty of firewater the reverend had.

Upon entering the reverend's house, he saw a fire blazed in the hearth, and a single bowl of soup left out on the kitchen table, along with a cup of shine.

"Forgive me, Colonel, but I rise with the sun and set with the moon. I'll be retiring promptly." The reverend said from down the hall, and made an appearance in a long night shirt that went down to his knees. The colonel noted a litany of scars marring his calves and his now visible forearms. "Hope your dinner is to your liking," he said, gesturing towards the bowl of soup.

The colonel nodded and thanked him, digging in without ceremony.

"Before you retire, Reverend, one question," the colonel said around mouthfuls of soup.

"Yes?"

"What is to the east?"

The reverend paused for a moment, taking in a deep breath before speaking.

"A burial ground. Buck's Point is small but it's been around since the first settlers came to this land, back when the Shawnee still considered this their land. Many generations lie in those hills, and we wish them to be undisturbed. We consider it hallowed ground up yonder," the reverend said, and without another word turned to retire to his bed chambers.

Mayhew ate in silence, considering this. Should he tell the reverend what happened to his man? What he found in the woods?

His gut told him no. His gut told him that the people of Buck's Point were not what they seemed, and that subterfuge would be required to see his men through this occupation safely. Things were not being told that he should know, and so, in turn, he would hold his cards close to his chest. Tomorrow, perhaps, he would inquire further into the reverend's cryptic statements about protection and the animals. Why it seemed a life or death imperative to maintain their excessive populations of livestock.

And the horses.

He ate. And he drank. He looked at the scythe on the wall, the silver blade. Then remembered the scattergun with its silver shot.

Why silver? He wondered.

His bed was a small hay and feather pallet hugging one wall of the foyer. He noted there were several rooms within the house that appeared unoccupied, and he wondered why he'd been put out in the foyer. He had clear view of the silver scythe as he let the shine lull him into a torpid stupor.

He knew silver was viewed by some as a magical metal, its properties in repelling certain germs and other medical esoterica beyond Mayhew's understanding that he'd overheard in various bars and taverns in various cities. His mind floated away on such matters, his dreams bringing him visions of the woods becoming alive, of trees moving together as sentient beings to block his men from escape. Of things with teeth and claw coming out of those impenetrable sentinels of timber to tear him apart.

He awoke sometime in the middle of the night, the house still, his body drenched in sweat, a heavy silence permeated by a distant wail. A scream, really. But so far away, so barely audible that he at first thought it was the residual phantoms of his nightmare. But he heard its distinct decay into nothingness. A loon perhaps, or a coyote.

The sound did not come again.

Chapter Ten

Bound, again. The fire had come back, worse somehow, though he did not understand how he could burn hotter than he already was. There was a great, roaring creature in his belly, a monstrous thing whose hunger physically hurt him. Not hunger pangs, no, not that crampy discomfort that takes root in one's belly, but a great ripping *need*. He could feel his stomach twisting in on itself, the digestive juices trying to breakdown its own corporeal container in an abhorrent attempt at auto-cannibalism. It was as if a thousand little teeth gnawed at his gut.

He'd even went at his own tongue, biting it off at its root and chewing the gristly tough organ, only the faintest trace of copper tang speckling what few functioning taste buds he had in his mouth. He swallowed this and then tried to wiggle the remaining ragged stump of flesh around, moving it side to side, trying to gnaw off what he could with his molars. Anything to fill the cavernous, volcanic void in his stomach.

The woman watched over him, and there were others now too. All dressed like primitive people, the men wild and unkempt, the women only slightly less so. They had that good smell to them, that smell of familiarity, of an unknown bond of blood, and yet they only watched, talking amongst themselves.

"We should kill him before he turns. We cannot add another to our ranks. We cannot spare even more food."

"We can't. He's one of us."

"Not yet he ain't."

One of the men approached, a knife blade glinting in the candlelight, its silver blade brilliantly diaphanous like a thousand suns in Halloway's painfully sensitive eyes. A bad smell came off the blade, a smell of poison, of lethal metallic agents that burned his nostrils when inhaled. The man handled the knife as if it were a feral creature just barely kept at bay, his hand clad in several layers of cloth to protect it from the blade, the weapon thrust far out in front of him, a pained expression on his face.

The woman, his savior, now his captor, stopped him though.

"It's upon him, look." She said, and at that Halloway felt his face begin to split open, the agonizing headache that cooked his brain like stew over a bonfire coming to its apex as he felt his skull literally splitting open, his body changing, bones grinding out of place, teeth being pushed out to make room for other, more primal dental wear.

***

She closed her eyes and set her jaw against the scream. The scream that was really a howl, a primal modulation between man and beast, a yell and a caterwaul, a wail and a screech. She knew the cry could be heard for miles. She knew soon The Others would come to investigate. No one had admitted to attacking this man. No one wanted to, she knew, for that meant a violation of the truce. And if The Others suspected the truce was violated, there would be war. Each of them had family with The Others. Each of them knew the stakes if the truce was rendered null.

"We tell them." She said once the scream had concluded.

"*What?*" They all said in unison, their eyes peeled away from the hideous amalgam of man and beast roiling on the bed. His constitution must've been strong, for he fought back against the change, his forms shifting back and forth. It would've been easier if he just accepted the thing trying to captain his body. But they always fought it.

"If we get out in front of this, they might make an exception. The nation is at war. These are exceptional times. This man was an interloper, he is not one of them, and we know they now occupy the village. Perhaps he will—"

"He will not, and you know it. Christ. Should've just slaughtered them all when we had the chance. *We* are the predators here. We can just—"

"Elias, they have your son. You know what happens if there is provocation." She cut him off.

Silently, they regarded the man as his teeth gnashed the air, blood crusting his lips and chin. She knew the hunger he felt. She would feel it soon herself. It pained her to see someone going through it. She wished she could offer him food, but her own house was barren. Their hunting grounds had to keep expanding, the forest's local system could not keep up with their bottomless stomachs. They had to travel miles now for their food. Risk being spotted by men. Risk becoming the hunted.

They were faster, stronger, harder to kill, but man was innumerable, and cunning. The men in gray and brown who'd marched on their hunting grounds a few months ago bore weapons of a fearsome variety, great mounted barrels that could fire dozens of rounds in the space of seconds. Some fired huge lead projectiles that could tear them in half, giving even their miraculous healing properties a true test of mettle. They'd lost two of their pack during that attack. There were simply too many men and too many guns. Though they fed well from the slaughter, they paid a heavy toll for their feast. The Others did not intervene for this fight, instead hoping one would cancel out the other.

There were even more men this time around, and these looked better equipped, better trained.

Exceptional times, indeed.

Chapter Eleven

The meal laid out before them was a very spread from the heavens. Cathead biscuits, thick cut bacon, red skin smashed potatoes, scrambled eggs, fried squirrel, and gallons of chicory coffee. The colonel, whose head pounded and his stomach an acidic cauldron, eagerly dove in, all one hundred and fifty of his men silent save for the occasional grunt or smacking of the lips.

"I know we've yet to be formally introduced, so I just wanted to take this time to welcome the soldiers of the 3rd infantry company to Buck's Point," the reverend said from atop a wooden stage that sat at the head of the endless rows of tables laid out before the town square. "Colonel, if you would join me, please," he said.

Reluctantly Mayhew left his plate, hastily mopping up the last bits of bacon grease with the remainder of his biscuit before making his way to the stage. He did not feel like speaking; he did not feel like playing into this man's game, but now was the time for diplomacy. If he was to redeem himself in the eyes of Major Lionel, he would have to make sure this operation was a success, and for it to be a success, he had to play nice with these peculiar hill folk.

"Thank you, Reverend. Thank you all for being so kind as to house us in this time of great uncertainty! And this food, mercy!" The colonel's voice cracked and he cleared it, using his projecting battlefield baritone to address both his men, and the citizens of Buck's Point, who ate at their own segregated area off to the right, and noticed those with the black brands were further segregated from them. He'd also noticed that those with the tattoo were the very last to be fed, mostly women and children, and the occasional ancient, they had to scrape the remainders from the giant stewpots and skillets. Judging by their silent, solemn demeanor as they scraped and searched for scraps , this was an established routine.

"However, we do not wish to be freeloaders, or parasites! And so, starting today, each man from my company will be assigned certain chores that are to be done throughout the village. We need to make sure this area is clear for when the union railroad comes through, and not only that, we need to make sure that the fine, gracious people of Buck's Point are not put out by our being here. We will earn our keep, and we will not abuse our host's generosity. That being said, listen closely. Labor will be divided by squadron and their assigned sergeants. Sergeants Colefield and Maxton, you'll be helping with animal husbandry duties. Sergeant Morrel, your men will be working at the lumber camp, which is just south of town."

There came assorted grumbles at this.

"Didn't come here to be no fuckin' baby sitter."

"What was that, sergeant Danforth?" The colonel snapped, knowing that goddamn voice from anywhere. Danforth was a big man, rotund as he was tall, and was one of those draftees who were as eager to serve the union as a cat was to take a bath. The fat man had been sitting at the front most row of tables, close to the stage, his uniform speckled with bits of egg and cream as the colonel made him stand up, plump cheeks blossoming red as he did so.

"Nothing, sir."

"*You*, Danforth, along with your men, will be in charge of stable duty. Lots of animals on that pasture, I believe you'll be in your element, sergeant, among heaping piles of bullshit," the colonel said to a mixed smattering of groans and laughter. He went on, assigning the remaining three squadrons to the tasks the reverend had laid out for him.

Mayhew could tell by the end of his little speech that his men were not thrilled. But they stayed their complaints, their bellies full, their base needs met. Still, he felt his stomach churn his hearty breakfast with nauseating gurgles as he prepared himself to lay out the other rules handed down by the reverend, who looked at him expectantly from across the stage, his eyes seeming to say, *yes, go on then.*

"Finally, there are some ground rules set forth by the reverend and his people, and I expect you all to abide by them. Men who are caught violating these rules will be recorded and court martialed upon return to the nearest township with a legislative body. They are as follows: You are not to fraternize with the women of the village. You are not to leave your sleeping quarters come sundown unless you've been assigned picket duty. You are not, for any reason, to head east, over yonder bluff—" He said, pointing towards the large outcropping of tan rock that jutted from the hillside like a lone tooth, where only last night, he'd seen the small fire blazing. "And lastly, you are not to hunt or harvest any animal you see among Buck's Point town limits, livestock or game," he said. He put up a hand at the immediate uproar this caused. "The reverend assures me he will have enough food to see us through our occupation!" He bellowed, speaking over the uproar.

"I would also like to add in one week, Samhain will be upon us, and Buck's Point will be engaging in a very special ceremony, a long standing tradition of…ours…" The reverend began but his voice trailed off when he caught sight of the three wild-looking folk who came in from the eastern border.

"At ease, men!" Colonel Mayhew yelled as he saw some of the men standing from their tables, muskets fixing on the haggard looking interlopers.

The denizens of Buck's Point, who were thoroughly nonplussed by the speech and its ensuing volatile reaction, all froze in the act of eating when they too saw the three folk who were dressed in animal skins and whose hair was matted and dappled with forest matter. Two men and one woman. The colonel studied them closely, reminded of certain folk he'd encountered years ago.

They called them the Arkansas wild men. The colonel had come across them some twenty years ago when he'd first moved to Missouri, crossing over Crowley's ridge, which marked the geographic border between the Ozark uplift and the alluvial plains of the Mississippi river valley, to stake a land claim in that flat, fertile soil. They were once farmers and simple minded god fearing folk whose lives had been completely ruined and uplifted, sometimes quite literally, by the great 1811 earthquake. Folks who escaped into the hills, traumatized from what they thought was a biblical reckoning, and lived on in these isolated knobs and low lying mountains, going feral and living like Neanderthals.

But these folk, despite their wild appearance, seemed to conduct themselves with a modicum of civilized being. All the same, the colonel saw the Reverend's façade of joviality evaporate like morning mist in a high sun upon their appearance. He quickly left the stage, approached them at a brisk walk, and then ushered them towards his house, looking over his shoulder as he did so, as if hoping no one else noticed this odd intrusion. They quickly disappeared inside.

"Get to it men!" Mayhew barked, and there was a great shuffling as each squadron formed up, met by each of the townsfolk responsible for overseeing their various duties.

He approached the reverend's house, noted the door was ajar. He stood just outside of it, listening.

"They're not part of the town, this shouldn't be considered a prov—"

"It damn well is, and you know it. Whoever did it left him alive for a reason. One more of those goddamn things we have to worry about now. Trying to build your numbers, aren't you?"

"Reverend, it was an accident, a—"

"Colonel, sir—"

Mayhew's heart kicked against his chest like a mule and whirled to find Lieutenant Evans looking up at him.

"Christ man, address me from the front next time!" He whispered as he pulled the stumpy man away from the doorway. "What is it?" He asked, realizing he hadn't seen Giles at all this morning.

"We just received word from our scouts. Another supply wagon-train was hit. The army doesn't know when we will be resupplied next. The fighting is heavy in Tennessee right now, materiel is being rerouted to the front lines…" he said, his face tense, knowing the last thing Mayhew needed was this news.

"Christ, those fucking bushwackers… Can't fight us like men…" He said, shaking his head.

"That's the other thing sir… There's been a company spotted heading this way. Looks like a detachment from McCullough's division."

Mayhew felt a cold, burning weight settle in his stomach and agitate the food within it. Before he could wallow too deeply in his own despair, he heard the crowd approaching from inside the reverend's home, and quickly pulled Giles behind the house, putting a hand over his mouth.

"We have only a few days until the harvest moon is upon us. You want to keep the truce? Then kill these god forsaken interlopers and leave the animals be when the time comes. Keep your fucking mutts in line."

They both heard the reverend's voice in a harsh rasp as the wild-folk were rudely ushered from his abode, his Germanic clip very present now given his agitation. Mayhew peered around the side of the house and caught a brief glimpse of them with their dirt crusted bare feet and grimy skin, and being this close, he detected the unmistakable whiff of wet dog.

"And if you show up unannounced again, I'll kill one of the pups," the reverend said, his voice so thick with venomous hatred the colonel almost didn't even recognize it. His lieutenant regarded him silently as Mayhew took his hand away from that greasy mouth. He peered around the corner of the house once more, making sure the reverend was out of ear shot.

"Surrounded by enemies." The colonel said in a soft voice.

"For being a man of the cloth he sure does speak a lot of filth," Evans said.

"I don't think the religion he heralds is altogether a holy one. Find four of your best men, take them off whatever bullshit detail they've been assigned. Meet me on the eastern border of the woods come lunch time." Mayhew said.

"Sir?" Giles said, not understanding.

"I think Halloway is over yonder. I think those wild folk got something to do with what harassed us at the camp. Make sure no one follows you," he said and ran off after the reverend.

Chapter Twelve

He exploded across the forest, and god did it feel good. His muscles screamed for movement, for exertion, his snout tingled and twitched as it inhaled this overwhelming palette of smells. He could smell the hawks flying high ahead, their lean sinewy flesh making his mouth water. He could smell the ancient puddles of piss deposited around the forest, the piss from his pack. He could smell the voles and moles deep underground, and wished he could burrow down there to eat them. He smelled men too, and though their rich fatty aroma enticed him, he could also smell gun oil and steel and gun powder, smells he recognized from his human mind, which was there but rapidly diminishing. The animal in his head slowly eating away at it.

He could smell the pack after him, they did not think he could escape, but he did, and he would not be captured again. The forest was a blur as he raced towards the faint but hearty smell of a doe in estrus, some miles away, a singular point of fixation. He locked in on it and bound up the steep bluffs and zig zagged through the trees like a mountain stream flowing smoothly over every surface and channel, easily finding the path of least resistance.

Then something was slamming into him, and he had just enough time to register the heady aroma of the head bitch, her coat slimed with mud as she slammed into him like a cannon ball. She had covered her scent, rolling around in one of the many bog-hollows that lined the low mountains, having blind sided him completely.

They rolled and tumbled over each other, maws snapping, bassoon growls sounding over the otherwise preternatural quiet of the forest. He had vitality on his side, the others in the pack were underfed and lethargic with starvation, but the bitch had the youthful vitality too, even more so than he, and coupled with that, skill. She'd grown long accustomed to her wolf form, while he, despite his graceful charge through the forest, still had much to learn about using his new body. With traces of man still in his mind, he wanted to swing and strike with hands but instead pawed pitifully with back legs.

His muzzle crinkled up in a snarl as the bitch had him pinned to the ground, her teeth buried in his scruff, her size, much bigger than he, negating his energy. Still, he managed to break free, ignoring the swath of flesh torn from between his shoulder blades as he darted off towards the smell of that doe, her scent growing fainter, she was running now, so far away.

He skidded to a halt in the leaf litter then as abruptly the pack surrounded him. He whirled, trying to find a gap in the flanks, there were ten of them and they closed in rapidly. Two of them were big, their coats darker and thicker than the rest, scars marred their muzzles, one had a clouded over eye.

In a last desperate move, he leapt high into the air, trying to go over instead of through, but they could leap just as high, if not higher, than he, and caught him by his tail and back feet. In an instant a thousand snapping muzzles were upon him, pinning him down. He began to piss and shit out of fear of being eaten alive, for he could smell the hunger on them.

He began to howl with pain and frustration as they tore at him, snapping at those within muzzle distance, and soon the howls turned into high pitched yips of pain. He began to feel himself changing back, the slow grinding agony of bones reforming and skin stressing to the point of tearing, fur receding painfully back into the dermis and resprouted as course pubic hair, his muzzle being crushed back into his face in place of the inferior human nose.

Then a gun shot, followed by the whine of a minie ball. The nearest of the gnashing muzzles exploded in a shower of red and white as teeth splinters erupted from the sundered snout. More gun shots. They barked, he heard a warning in that call, he didn't know how he knew but he understood perfectly well: *Scatter.* The pack spread, leaving him a twitching, bleeding half formed abomination.

An indeterminate amount of time later, he heard footsteps, men's voices. Drawing closer. He could only lay there and twitch in his own mess at their approach.

Chapter Thirteen

"You sure about this, Colonel?"

"I'm not sure about anything, that's why we're doing this." Mayhew hissed at his lieutenant as they stalked through the woods.

They were about a hundred paces in, deep enough that any passerby's from Buck's Point wouldn't see them. He knew they had an hour at the most before someone noticed their absence, and so they moved as stealthily as they could at best possible speed. Mayhew, Evans, and four handpicked men, all of them trackers and expert huntsman before the war, proceeded without another word.

The woods were mercilessly thick, tangles of Virginia Creeper devoured the copses of white oak and short pine and made passage through them a miserable, disorienting job. Vestigial tinges of anxiety pulled at the colonel as he was reminded of his nightmare in the reverend's house, of a forest animated with insidious life, sentient. He was wholly out of his element, his mind thought in formations and battle maps. Give him a wall of sweating, reloading meat to hurl at the enemy, and he could give you a victory.

This was different. The many layers of deceit between himself and the reverend, if he really was a reverend, grew to an almost palpable tension. And now he was breaking one of those apparently cardinal rules.

What happened prior to his ingress into the woods only furthered suspicions. He'd chased Meyer down to inform him that he'd be going on a patrol with his men and to not expect them for lunch, and to also, in a casual aside, ask after those strange folks who smelled like a mutt gone to mange. The man's response to the colonel's inquiries regarding those wild folk was as obstinate as it was coy: Savages, natives from across the valley they occasionally did commerce with. Did he think the colonel that stupid? For they were not red skinned, nor did they bare any of the native tribe garb aside from their rough-hewn deerskins. They were as white as the iron men that jangled in his pocket.

Then there was the matter of this supposed "festival" the reverend spoke of. Mentions of the autumnal equinoxes by their pagan appellations and great ceremonies surrounding them reeked of witchcraft to the colonel, who'd seen his fair share of backwoods hoodoo during his time in the Boston mountains down south. The reverend, who was suddenly quite industrious and did not have time for the colonel's questions, only gave non-committal grunts and dismissive answers.

"Just a simple harvest ceremony. A few tithes to the ones above so our bounty may be aplenty," he'd said. No mention of Jesus Christ. In fact, the colonel had not seen anything even resembling a cruciform object since they'd entered buck's point.

Except for that strange wooden sculpture in the reverend's house.

They went on perhaps a half mile, or maybe it was only a quarter, the lush, unending wall of viridian made it hard to decipher distance. But other than the unchanging primordial condition of this forest, it was unremarkable. No gravestones spotted. No burial plots cleared.

They continued on, the miserable trek making one's legs and feet ache as they proceeded up a steep hillside, having to do an odd shambling walk to clear the mud and vines that pulled at one's brogans and boots like a thousand little incessant, yearning hands. The colonel remembered the fire atop the bluff and did his best to keep their point of egress aimed towards that sign of human activity.

He had no idea if he'd wondered off course though, until he'd realized he was standing atop a stone plateau, and directly behind him he could see Buck's Point, realizing he was looking down from the mirror opposite end of the town compared to where they'd first made camp.

"Sir!" One of the tracker's hissed. Mayhew snapped forward and saw the man was pointing to something on the ground. He walked over, saw it was a blood trail. Silently the man rubbed the bright red ichor between his fingers, showing without saying how fresh it was. Mayhew also noticed a few white things glinting in the morning sun, and stooped to pick one up, and understood immediately it was a piece of a tooth. The colonel nodded to the tracker, signaling for him to follow it. Just as this silent bit of communication terminated, Evans, whose squat form did not permit him to move with anything resembling grace in this unforgiving terrain, exploded through a thicket of twisted together branches and vines, his face shining and scarlet.

"Christ on a cross that—" But the colonel rushed him, putting a hand to his mouth and a finger to his own lips. *Quiet, you goddamn fool.* Giles's eyes went wide, but he nodded his understanding. He held up a hand to the other three who came up behind him, and they all froze at once, instantly understanding. *God bless competent men*, Mayhew thought quickly before he followed after the man, a man named Robert Murtaugh from Lordell, who apparently trapped cougars and coons with great proficiency up in his slice of the Ozarks before uncle Sam directed his crosshairs to long haired rebels instead of surly mountain lions.

Mayhew saw the expert tracker coming out, the man fixing on even the slightest alterations in the barely discernable path that lead through the woods, which were blessedly thinner now that they were atop the bluff. The blood trail ebbed and flowed, from great splashes to small, easy to miss droplets that this Murtaugh fella fixed on like a blood hound.

They moved quick, and the colonel estimated they were two miles deep into the wood now, the bluff long behind them. They crossed several shallow gorges, and the colonel began to see the makings of game trails as they followed the trail.

The tracker abruptly stopped, pointed. The blood trail grew thicker in one spot, and next to it the colonel spotted a secondary source of blood splatter. He knelt down, saw more of the shattered bits of teeth, no, *fangs,* among the clumps of fur that clung to the blood spattered leaf litter at odd intervals.

"Right around here, he went from running to being dragged. Something hunted him down and got 'em," Murtaugh said in a whisper.

Mayhew felt his testicles shrink into raisins and his bowels quake with hot waste. He thought of Halloway's body, how ravaged it was. Yes, wholly out of his element he was. He looked around briefly, imagining things predatorial and vicious hiding behind every bit of vine clusters and thick trunk.

The trail continued for another quarter mile before they all froze at the lip of a shallow valley. Below they saw what Mayhew first took to be perhaps a small native village. But he knew the Shawnee and Osage had long been driven from this area. Smatterings of huts and things that, in the most liberal sense of the word, could be considered houses, dotted the trough of dirt and leaves. Was this where those wild mountainfolk lived?

Two things immediately stood out to Mayhew. One was the heaping, stinking piles of dung that seemed to line the perimeter of the camp. He could see in a nearby mound ivory hunks of bone and tufts of hair among the roiling horde of flies. The other was the overwhelming smell of animal urine. Canine, judging by the heady ammonia reek of it. *Wolves? Did they have wolves in the Ozarks?* He didn't think they did.

Robert signaled for him and pointed towards a nearby tree. The pale trunk of the white oak bore a splintered wound, and upon closer inspection the colonel could see a handful of bird shot embedded within. He was so fixated on seeing if the shot was silver or not that he did not realize Giles was tackling him until he hit the ground and felt the wind ripped from his lungs. They fell in a heap behind one of these hideous amalgams of wood and mud that was supposed to pass for shelter.

"Scout." The lieutenant breathed, hot and wet into his left ear. He clumsily got off the colonel, and when he raised his head, he saw Robert and one of the other men were hiding behind thick oak trees, rifles hugged vertically to their bodies, trying to make themselves invisible.

"Christ a'mighty it *stinks* up in here!" Came a voice, heavy with mountain drawl.

"Shut your goddamn yap. Found that sumbitch bare assed yank over this way. Could be Feds afoot."

What followed were sounds of inquiry, the crunch of leaf litter and small branches trampled underfoot spreading out in all directions. Mayhew didn't hear a horse, surprised a scouting party would be unmounted. But then he remembered the skittish way their own horses acted, barely controlled for want of their own fear. *The animals sense it. Whatever's in these hills. The men probably had no choice.*

He dared a glance around the side of the hut; he needed to know what numbers he was dealing with.

He saw two men from his field of vision, saw their Enfields. Not bushwackers with varmint guns, these were ranked men. Bushwackers didn't wear cadet gray jackets and slouch caps. He saw the blue chevron of an infantry sergeant among them.

Field scouts. Field scouts on foot meant the main company couldn't be more than ten or so miles away. If they'd captured Halloway, then he might've dropped the shoe on their location. But no, he remembered that rictus of dazed agony, the insane glint in his eye before the private darted off naked into the woods. That was a man whose mind was ruined by illness. What they found had to be a stark raving lunatic, unable to give them anything of strategic importance.

But how would they know he was one of us? He wondered. He heard footsteps coming towards the shelter they used for cover.

Unlike most union colonels, Mayhew did not carry a saber. He found the damn things antiquated and unyielding, the weapon of a man who did his commanding from the safety of the rear ranks. For Mayhew, who was always in the thick of it, not letting his rank spare him from the hellscape of battle, he preferred an eight inch bowie knife, engraved with the insignia of West Point Academy at the blade's tang. The blade had found it's way into the bellies of six rebels so far, and the silver edge sang for more secesh blood.

Despite his tall, lank frame, the colonel could move viper quick when he wanted to, reflexes honed from the brutal trench charges of the early battles. Fixed bayonets, blood gouts and having life and death be the difference of a split second decision to bob instead of duck. The second he saw gray coming around the corner, he grabbed for the scout, pulling him to the ground behind the house and plunging that knife into the bearded throat.

The man's incredulous grunts soon took on a liquid rasp as his jugular was sundered. Mayhew kept his hand fastened to the man's furred lips, feeling hot blood leak into his uniform, the copper tang of it temporarily usurping the feral smells of animal waste. He let his emotions go numb, though he couldn't help but feel dirty for this. There was no forward charge, no looking the man in the eye as he killed him, no valor. Just stealth and self-preservation here. He hugged the man to him until his body stilled in its twitching protestations, the blood hot on his hands.

"Hey, what the—" He heard one of the scouts say, and Mayhew saw in that molasses dilation of time that only comes with a massive adrenal surge as Robert came out from behind the tree, leveling his Spencer and taking aim. The rifle cracked, and soon was answered by a volley of shots. Mayhew saw a bright crimson blossom erupt from Robert's shoulder, but still he reloaded and fired, his semi-shot rifle giving him the advantage as he knew within the next few seconds the scouts would be reloading… unless they'd looted repeating carbines from the supply wagons that were supposed to be for Mayhew's men.

He soon got his answer when he heard the steady three second interval pops of a man well trained with the spencer. Robert fell, his skull blossoming outward in a sickening fashion towards the back, a red crater magically appearing in his forehead.

Drawing out his own pair of Colt revolvers, the colonel and Evans both appeared from the side of the houses, Evans with his two shot flintlocks already breathing dragon smoke, not taking time to aim, just firing.

Mayhew took his time though, his eyes taking in six gray bodies, one of which was breaking off from the rest and heading east at a sprint.

The revolvers kicked in his hands as he aimed in the general direction of the men, who were busy firing on the other two from his small squadron, not realizing the colonel and lieutenant were flanking them until two of their men fell in a dancing jig. Their rifles turned on Evans and the colonel, who retreated behind the house. The trees around them exploded with splinters and gouts of dirt. The shelter shuddered as it absorbed rifle fire.

"We got you outnumbered. Surrender and we'll show mercy!" A man bawled from somewhere across the universe. Even over the shrill ringing in his ears, battlefield deafness creeping in, Mayhew could make out the high pitched, distant warble of a bugle being sounded. All of McCoullough's detachment was about to be hot on his trail.

In a last desperate bid to show courage, to avenge his fallen men who'd died because they followed him unquestioningly into this verdant hellhole, he leaned his body out from the knotted logs of poplar and oak and emptied the rest of each cylinder, eight shots total, into their general direction.

He cried out as he felt a bullet kiss the side of his head and leave a molten trail in its wake. He turned to tell Giles to make a run for it when he looked over just in time to see the man's thick neck bulge outwards before a corona of red exploded from the back of his neck.

"Christ almighty." He breathed as he sprinted for the tree line, hoping the tight packed walls of foliage would provide enough cover to lose them.

He ran for his life, hearing the occasional whine of a passing round fly by his head, until these too stopped. He could tell he was approaching the bluff once more as the trees began to cluster in tighter, the creeper vines gradually thickening like a festering infection. He tripped once, twice over those goddamn infernal growths but got up each time and kept running. He dared look to his right as he caught movement out of the corner of his eye, and nearly tripped and fell again when he saw a huge brown blur keeping pace with him through the woods.

Branches and switches whipped at his eyes and face, and occulted the full view of the thing stalking him, but its sight was enough for him to remain fixed forward, legs burning with his exhaustive sprint to safety. Whatever it was moved with an eerie silent grace despite its size, and he thought he saw a brief flash of yellow in those eyes before he had to look forward once more.

Then he saw the opening of the bluff, the plateau of rock. He didn't even pause, hoping the densely coiled vines and trees would break his fall below as he hurled himself off the forty-foot cliff.

Chapter Fourteen

The elder was incensed upon her return to camp, which stunk of men and the singed exhalations of their firebreathers. Not only was her mood fouled by their failed attempt at diplomacy with the others, she learned that her own pack had let the pup slip free under their care.

"He'd been shifting all day, we kept having to retie his bindings so he couldn't slip loose. Then all quick like he went over completely," her pack mate had said, snapping grimy fingers to show how quick the change occurred. "Haven't ever seen a pup turn like that before. Slipped out, nipped Josiah a good one on the cheek 'fore he lit out," he said, gesturing towards young Josiah, a runt of the litter, his pale cheek scabbed over with fresh scar tissue. They'd changed recently she realized.

"Tried to chase after ma. We had 'em pinned down. But the men came. Two groups of 'em. They was fightin' one 'nother. You said if ever we can't get the drop on 'em we run," Josiah said.

"We could've taken 'em. But you all shit and run 'fore I could flank them. I had the little shit pinned down," the oldest of the litter, Lya, said. She was on the cusp of womanhood and her eyes were bright with feral energy and need. Of them all, she was the most fearsome in her true form. She was the most vital of them all, her life force was strong, and so when she shifted, her form was massive, truly indicative of the strong soul who commanded it. Despite her small human frame in light of the males, she cast a spiteful gaze upon them for their cowardice and they downcast their eyes in submission to her knowing she was right. The others were too scared to fight. They still remembered the men with the thunderous iron snakes that could rip them in half. They did not yearn to let blood like she did. They simply wanted to feed.

"What do we do?" Lya asked, looking to her elder for guidance.

She thought long and hard. This war was something she and The Others had not accounted for. The Others. Those goddamn cunning interlopers from across the great water who'd invaded her land and figured out their one weakness. Who'd held her own litter hostage and demanded a sanctimonious coexistence with them. Forced them to eat their cattle and other low life forms, which sustained them, but barely.

The viscera of hens were but diluted skillet gristle compared to the succulent ambrosia of man flesh. A truce was struck with The Others when they began trapping and sterilizing the pups, putting an end to the natural progression of their bloodline, promising to stop and allow a true hunt with every full cycle of the moon in exchange for them to stop picking off their hunters and loggers at every turn. The Others offered a single tribute of the two legged variety on the night when the moon drove them mad that lasted all of thirty minutes before the pack ate it down to the bone while The Others hid in their fortified domains. All this measly tribute did was ignite their blood lust without actually satisfying it.

She swore he did it to torture them.

Perhaps this war could work to their benefit. Enough of The Others get caught in the crossfire, the pack could go in and pick off the remainder. Rescue their mutilated litter. Try to rebuild the life that once was when this wood was theirs and they were the head of the food chain. They would just have to remain hidden, and hope by the time the blood moon came and ripped the beast from their veins, it would be opportune to strike. Otherwise, they faced annihilation.

"We wait. We let them fight each other. We don't have the numbers to fight on two fronts," she said. "We eat the stragglers, same as before. And we don't leave them *alive*," she said this last with acid, her old gray eyes drilling into each face of her pack. "Now the men have the pup. They don't know what he is. He goes wild, starts nipping off them, we'll have an outbreak on our hands."

"Good. Let's rise up, like the old days, when *they* feared *us*," Lya said with a sneer.

"There'll never be enough of us to turn the tide. Man is a plague upon this land now. All it would do is strain the food supply. Make those of the outside world aware of us. And once that happens, you're gonna see a lot more of those cannons. And guns."

"Canin? Wassat?" Josiah said. Lya made a boom motion with her mouth and threw her hands wide. The young male understood immediately, and fear clouded his eyes.

"I'm hungry," the elder said, all this thinking and strategizing made her stomach growl and her head ache.

"That's one good thing that came of all this. They kill each other real well. Josiah, get ma that meat. Left some for ya," her pack mate said, and her stomach growled despite the fuming rage she was in. She knew she smelled blood, freshly spurted, but assumed there would be no body to accompany it.

Josiah dragged in a leg, thick and hairy, the leg itself short and squat, the course red hair standing out in contrast to the pale flesh of thigh and calf, into their den. Immediately they all began to drool, eyes dilated at the sight of that succulent thigh meat.

She did not thank Josiah, for it was to be expected that they provide for their elders. The elders may not have the strength and veracity of the newer generation, but their sage wisdom in dealing with their hominid neighbors was what truly kept the pack alive.

She changed in a matter of seconds, she the original progenitor of this clan, the wild genes flowed old in her veins when the original settlers came here, scaring off the fierce Osage, whose brave warrior spirit quaked even at the sight of her in her prime.

The others changed too, some of the younger ones unable to help it, like a yawn that spread. She knew the blood moon would soon be upon them, and with it, *none* of them would be able to help it.

She snarled and snapped at them, protecting her food as she devoured the leg in minutes, occasionally spitting out lead balls, powerful molars cracking the thick bone and lapping the marrow within. She licked her chops as she had her fill, leaving the others to fight over the remaining gristle. She retired to her den, her pack mate following. He tried to initiate coitus, but she snapped at his extended red proboscis, enough warning for him to leave the hut dejectedly. The rut was not upon her. She had much to consider. She slept in her beast form, hoping to find further enlightenment in those old predatorial genes.

Chapter Fifteen

"How in the hell—"

He became ephemerally aware of his body.

"Have the frame of a goddamn scarecrow—"

The horde of aches that assailed him, all bleeding into one big throb.

"Fall forty goddamn feet and don't break a single goddamn bone—"

He recognized that voice. He pushed air through his throat. Tried to speak. It came out a monosyllabic groan.

"He speaks!" The voice rasped, heavy with sarcasm.

He tried to blink, managed to crack one eye open. The other feels sealed shut. Gummy.

A face colored with gin blossoms and slicked with sweat looks down at him; mole's eyes stare out at him from dirty glass panes of wire rim glasses. The white hair shot out wild in all directions, the way it did when Doc Tomlin had been pulling on it, which he did when he was stressed. The man was often stressed.

He then took in the room around him. He was in some candle lit subterranean stone dwelling; he could smell raw earth and wet rock. Flag stone rock wall boxed him in. He craned his head, which felt like it had a howitzer shell fastened to one side, and saw a few rows of cots, their once white fabric now a dirty crème color with various darker occultations to show where hands had tried unsuccessfully to wash the blood from the cloth.

He heard heavy feet approaching from somewhere.

"Go on you old cuss, I know you can say something. A 'thank you' might be in order. Or maybe you can tell me the name of the guardian angel assigned to watch your old ass when you decided to swan dive off a goddamn *cliff*. Christ amighty Colonel, what the hell was that about? Found you in a heap of limbs and covered in blood. Not your own, apparently," Doc Tomlin said, keeping his voice low but still hissing with exasperation. His eyes were wild; he kept casting glances over his shoulder.

"Doc—"

"There's something not right here Colonel. These people are strange. Men said they seen stone dungeons in these peoples' houses. They've been erecting these… things, these infernal sigils made of wood, all over town—"

"Doc—"

"And that goddamn *woman*, if you can call her that, she practices the *hoodoo*. I seen her down here with some of the folks with the black tattoos, and she… She was down here, citing some incantation over 'em. Put 'em in a spell. These ain't holy people colonel, they—"

"Tomlin, *goddammit!*" Mayhew barked, trying to use the last of his strength to push through the doctor's apoplectic tirade. He pulled himself up, felt something liquid grind in his torso. He meant to say something, but pain made the words in his mouth evaporate. He heard the protestation of wood under great strain as someone came down the stairs to the right.

"Oh now you done it goddamnit. That reverend wants your hide. She been waiting hand and foot to see when you wake up—" The doctor whispered, eyes going wide as the colonel tried to sit up right. "You sprained a rib, don't you be trying to sit up just yet, you—"

"The rebels, doc," Colonel Mayhew breathed. "The rebels are coming. Full detachment. McCollough—" He tried to say more, but each breath brought with it a molten stitch, an invisible bayonet spearing him through his side with each ragged inhalation.

"*What?!*" The doctor said, his eyes, somehow, bulged a fraction bigger than they already were, the bloodshot sclera amplified in his spectacles. A door opened to the basement. The doctor's eyes squeezed shut.

"He wake? Man awake?" A woman asked in a thick German clip.

"Be gone woman! Let him rest!" Doc Tomlin snapped.

The woman, Mayhew couldn't remember her name, approached, her massive frame making the bones quake in Mayhew's body with each step. A round face peered down at him, her prolific bosom crushing his right side painfully as she leaned over and adjusted something on his head. Pulpy things slopped and slurred as she tenderly touched the side of his head with the bad eye. Abruptly he smelled the earthy tang of wet foliage, and understood she'd applied a poultice of some sort to his head.

"Very good. You no move. I get Herr Meyer," she said, her ghastly smile not reaching her eyes. She went away, her heavy tread growing steadily quieter.

"What's this about McCollough?" Doc asked when the crone was gone.

"Ran into... Scouting party... Tried to find... Halloway."

"You found—"

"Shut up. They. Have Halloway." He hated this breathy stilted speech. Time was of the essence, and he was speaking like a one-legged man doing jumping jacks. He took a moment to compose himself, though urgency wished he could just blurt it out. "Have Halloway. Scouts found us. Giles gone. They're coming. Need to get... ready."

"Sweet jumping Jesus. The rebels are coming *here*?" Doc shot up from the bed, gnarled hands pulling at his hair. He took a moment to control himself, then sighed and rummaged somewhere out of Mayhew's field of vision. He returned with a small brown bottle. He produced a dropper top from the bottle and squirted amber fluid into his mouth, hissed. Mayhew immediately recognized the sharp heady tang of laudanum. He reached out a hand longingly for the blessed mixture of cannabis, morphine, and ethanol. The doc nodded.

"Keep mum on this. It's my last bottle. Didn't think I'd need to use it so soon. That's it Colonel, take a you a snoot." He said, pouring the bottle to the colonel's lips, not bothering with the dropper at all. The colonel took a pull far bigger than any saw bones would advise.

Gasping, a smacking of the lips as earthy, bitter fire flooded his mouth. The throbs ebbed immediately. A warm wave washed over him. Ethereal hands caressed his body and unleashed the tension boiling within. He settled deeper into the cot. He longed for the reverend's shine, wicked man though he was.

"How long have I been out?" He asked, finding he could speak easier now, the hot blade in his side receding slightly. He felt his face scratchy with stubble.

"A day and some change. When you reckon the rebels will get here, Colonel? Who do I need to speak to? Spread the word? No no, you gotta rest old boy." He said, his high-strung demeanor dialed back as the laudanum took hold, and gently pushed the colonel back down into the cot when he tried to get up again. The colonel sighed. His mind fuzzy with the potent pharmacopeia, he tried to make a mental audit of his remaining highest-ranking men. The most competent. His heart abruptly kicked when he remembered Evans being shot in the throat. Christ, his best man, even if he was a tad scatterbrained.

"Second Lieutenant Ashford. Cavalry sergeant Wallace. The Quarter Master. Tell them to enact garrison procedures immediately," he said, his voice suddenly feeling disembodied, as if he were reduced to mere soul and circumstance, his aches gone. He put his head back on the clump of rags in place of a pillow. God, he was floating on a cloud. He just wanted to sleep now. Sleep till the rebels came.

"I'll tell 'em. Christ you better heal fast. We need you, you goddamn big dumb galute," the doctor said as the colonel succumbed to the soporific waves pulling him deeper into something beyond sleep but not quite death.

***

Voices came to him from the ether. Some spoke German. Some were harsh. Their words all gibberish. He refused to listen to them, instead letting his body remain in that comatose state, a pupae within it's chrysalis, soon ready to emerge anew.

But then rough hands were pulling him out of the stupor.

"Come off it you old sonofabitch. I know you're not concussed. Wakey wakey." A familiar voice very close to his face, breath thick with smoke and coffee. When he only moaned, a firm hand clapped his face, the slap loud and jarring. He felt the poultice slough off with the impact. Air cooled the side of his head where a vague tingling took hold as air tickled exposed, healing tissue.

The colonel came awake, and the haggard bearded visage of Reverend Meyer filled his view.

"Good, you're awake. There's someone here to see you. Someone with a lot of guns and pissed off men. Help me get him to his feet, Tilda."

Mayhew turned and saw the rotund medicine woman had been sitting on Doc Tomlin.

"Don't you... Touch him..." he wheezed, coughed, groaned, gave up, went limp as Tilda heaved herself off him. Mayhew wouldn't be surprised if the doc had sprained ribs of his own now to contend with.

Powerful bodies wrenched him to an upright position; the whole world tilted sickeningly and his legs trembled as dormant muscles were forced awake. A sharp stitch took hold in his side, the sprained rib speaking to him, but aside from that and the huge swathes of tender bruising that still ached across his body in places, he felt okay. He managed to support himself against the reverend and the one named Tilda.

"Good, you can stand. Answer for your blunders, of which there are many to atone for. But let's deal with this one first," the reverend said, and together they practically dragged him up the stairs. He took note of the many jars containing anonymous viscera and plant matter lining the walls, and other things he had no classification for. He saw strange wooden effigies hanging from the ceiling of the woman's home as they rushed him through the front door.

Sunlight stabbed at his eye, the left one, which he'd managed to peel open a crack, the lid gummy with whatever Tilda had smeared on his head, and winced as he blinked tears away.

Soon, his eyes adjusted to the high noon sun, and standing before him was a wave of mismatched gray, and at the front, a single naked man, his neck bound in a leash, hands bound behind his back.

Chapter Sixteen

"Is that *Arnold Mayhew*? Excuse me, I believe the full title is Colonel Arnold 'The Mouth of the Lion' Mayhew? Jesus wept." The only man on a horse said. He approached, his mount a huge quarter horse whose nostrils flared and eyes wide, blinders affixed to its head. The man spurred his horse forward, it went reluctantly, it's body visibly wired with tension, looking as if anything louder than a cough might set it to bucking.

Mayhew saw the double stars of a Lieutenant Colonel. He didn't recognize the man who appraised him like an interesting clump of shit on one's boots. He had a full flowing brown beard and sweaty long hair tied back in a horse tail, as was the secesh custom. Mayhew didn't say anything; his eyes flitted from the colonel to Halloway, who trembled and twitched, his feet covered in mud.

Mayhew stared at his body. Saw the vicious bite wounds were gone. No suture lines, no puckered lip wounds. Just the faint patches of scar tissue here and there. It made no sense.

"This is the man that took out an entire regiment of my men? With *this*?" The lieutenant colonel said, gesturing towards the scatters of company C who stood at port arms, clearly unsure of what to do. "Christ, you really must be in league with the devil. I didn't believe it 'till I heard reports of the beasts. And *this*—" he said, nodding towards one of the huge wooden contrivances of wood, fashioned in such a manner to resemble a stick figure, a man with his arms raised in exaltation. Fastened to the warped planks and boards was dried creeper vine, which was also used to lash various skulls to the wooden appendages. The colonel looked long and hard at the skulls, could not define their genus or species except to say they were vaguely canine. But god... also somewhat human.

"You *must* be in cahoots with the devil to pull that off son. You look like ten pounds of shit stuffed into a five-pound sack. I can't imagine my men being bested by... you."

"Rest assured, sir, our small town has no league with the federals. They came here and forced occupation upon us. We want no part in this war, we have no allegiance," the reverend said, thrusting the colonel forward. "If it means getting all of you out of here, you can take him."

The lieutenant colonel let out a guffawing laugh. The men in rank with him shifted uneasily on extremely worn boots.

"The mighty colonel Mayhew, famous dealer of dixie death, offered up on a silver platter by some backwoods hoodoo preacher? Phew, that's a kick in the head. You think I give a shit about your people, son? You got anything to do with these unholy effigies?" The reverend didn't respond to that. "In that case, shut your goddamn mouth. You're all culpable here. I'd blow this town to smithereens even if the federals didn't shit here purely for the blaspheme I see on display. And that's colonel Marshall Smith to you. 1ˢᵗ regiment, Missouri State Guard. Here under General McCollough."

"A full brigade of Lionel's men is headed this way as we speak," Mayhew finally bluffed. "If you mean to take this town for yourself, you better take it quick, Lieutenant."

The colonel blew a raspberry, but despite the dismissive gesture, the gloating look in his eyes changed.

"I doubt that. I heard you got whooped up at Wilson's Creek and they sent you out here to be rid of your sorry ass. Don't you want your man here back?" He said, and one of the men shoved Halloway forward.

"Private Halloway?" Mayhew asked. Halloway looked vaguely in his direction but the vacuous gaze on his face remained. He muttered something unintelligible, and he drooled all over himself. Christ, the man was of no use to him, callous though that thinking was. He then turned his attention to the lieutenant colonel. "Listen Colonel, it wasn't I who slaughtered your men. Theres's things in these woods, these people," he said, shouldering the reverend hard, "are in cahoots with them somehow."

"That so? Awful convenient these beasts only prey on good old southern men then. Don't think I haven't heard the reports. Had a full company head this way not even a month ago and never heard from them again. Heard the stories about the beasts in these woods, how goddamn fearsome they are." The colonel spat. "Your boy here, pretty sure he's turning into one of 'em. You can have him back, by the way, gesture of good faith. Watch him though, he's a mind to bite. Feral sumbitch he is."

"Is this a raid, then? Get on with it," Mayhew said as one of the men cut loose Halloway's leash and kicked him hard in the ass. He stumbled forward and fell face first in the mud.

"No. I'm a man of god, a man of mercy. I don't believe in burning whole villages to the ground and killing every got damned farmer and seamstress I suspect of abolitionist skullduggery, unlike *some* navy blue boys I know," he said with a sneer. "So I'll give you some terms, and I'll give you a day and a night to ponder it. You surrender to me, let me have Buck's Point without all this needless bloodletting, and I'll make sure you get a meal and a cot up at Camp Morton. See if we can't do an exchange with you yankees. You be a stubborn mule about it though, think your valor and honor is gonna save you from my wrath, then I'll raze this entire god forsaken mud hole to the ground. Think on it, son. Long and hard. Behind every tree in this forest is a man ready to ventilate your noggin," he said, and with a cautious canter wheeled his horse around. He looked over towards the pasture. "Them some fat hogs you got Reverend. Can't wait to make me some bacon. Got damn I haven't had bacon in an age!" He whooped.

"Look what you got us into, you sonofabitch," the reverend hissed behind the colonel. He whistled and a young man with a scar running across his face came over, stick thin arm branded with that off black symbol, which upon further recognition the colonel realize was a two dimensional facsimile of the wooden lattice symbols erected all over town. "I need you to send a message to the mongrels. An emergency meeting," he said.

"Colonel, you okay?" It was sergeant Wallace who came to him as he wavered on his feet. There was too much to take in, too many developments. He felt himself losing control of the situation, which sobered him significantly. He put a hand on the sergeant's shoulder. Giles Evan's words came back to him. He'd been right all along. A flame of indignant righteousness flooded him. They outnumbered these simple country folk three to one, and he let them walk all over him in some pedantic show of diplomacy. No more.

"Initiate martial law. Round these heathens up. Subdue the reverend. Make sure no one leaves or enters. Make sure every able-bodied man in my company is either fortifying houses or digging trenches. Get the townsfolk, those able bodied enough, to help you, even if they gotta do it under the gun," he said, marshalling his last bit of strength into commanding. "And make sure the doc see's to Halloway, but also tell him to prepare for mass triage."

"Yes sir. Good to have you back Colonel. Was it true what you said about Lionel—"

"No. But that doesn't change things. You think we surrender they'll actually take us alive? No. I've killed too many of their men. I'm sorry son. We stand our ground and we fight. We repel them or die trying," Mayhew said, forcing himself to meet the young man's eyes.

"I'd be honored to die by your side, sir," Wallace said, snapping a salute before he began shouting orders.

The reverend saw the sea change happening around him, and quickly made for his house, but went down kicking and screaming as three men marshalled him into restraints. It was time Mayhew got some goddamn answers.

Chapter Seventeen

"You're going to get us all killed. I hope you realize that," Tobias Meyer growled as he was lashed to a chair in his own house. Next to him was the young man, a boy really, the one he'd told to send word to 'the mongrels'. He looked terrified. Outside, the muffled shouts of men shouting orders, the grinding of wagon wheels as men made use of the many horses crowded in the stable, a lot of *hyas!* as men struggled to control the skittish animals.

"You are to explain to me what religion you practice, Reverend, for I know it is not our lord and savior Jesus Christ that holds dominion over this land," the colonel said as he turned the kitchen upside down looking for alcohol. He found two large gallon bottles of the shine and brought them out, setting them on a counter. Alongside the bottles was one of the man-shaped wooden figures, doll sized compared to the seven-foot abominations outside. He grabbed this and threw it at the reverend's face when he did not answer, then promptly took a swig of the shine. "And you're to tell me what in god's green earth those things are."

The reverend laughed, shaking his head.

"What I teach is not a religion but a weapon to be used against an evil that's as ancient as the lead in these hills. Fight fire with fire, and all that. You wouldn't understand—"

"Enlighten me, then," the colonel said, shambling his way over to the table, wincing as he sat across from the two bound men, rubbing his side where his rib sang a steady, painful song. The wound on his head itched something fiercely, and it took a concerted effort not to scratch at the massive scab covering the side of his head.

"*Werewolves* I believe is the common term. We prefer lycanthropes. Does more justice to what they really are," the reverend said.

The colonel started to laugh but then remembered the shape that kept pace with him in the woods. The glint of yellow eyes. The sheer size of it. The way his pickets were picked off. Halloway's injuries.

"You mean men that turn into wolves on a full moon? Christ, that old wive's tale?" Mayhew asked. Quartermaster Unger shook his head in silent awe as he cleaned and loaded each of the colonel's weapons.

"You'll want those bullets to have silver in them. Otherwise, it'd be like throwing a pebble at a bear," the Reverend said. He then turned his gaze to the colonel, his eyes grave. "The tales are wrong. Not men masquerading as beasts. The other way around. The wolfen abominations the moon pulls from their blood is their real form. For some reason though, they revert to human when not on the hunt. This thing beside me looks like a boy, but he is not, I assure you."

The young man did not react to this accusation. He kept his eyes downcast, glazed over.

"If that's true, why not kill them outright?" The colonel asked, studying the boy closely. "Why keep them among your ranks? And why the small commune in the woods?" The colonel asked. "I saw your palaver with them. The wild folk." Meyer smirked at this.

"You found their camp, huh? No surprise I guess." He sighed and nodded toward the moonshine. "Can you at least give me a nip? Might as well enjoy my last night alive," he said.

"You speak as if your death is a sure thing," the colonel remarked as he tilted the bottle to that questing mouth. Meyer gulped, grimaced, smacked his lips.

"It is. You came here and upset the order. You see, we've been fighting them for years. Generations have passed, thousands have died at their pogroms and hunts. We learned their ways, learned to combat them. But they are cunning, and on certain nights, they are flat out invincible. My home village in Stugart was completely wiped out by them. I fled, came across the sea, hoping to start a new," he said with a defeated sigh.

"Instead, I found more land blighted by the lycanthrope scourge. I understood they were everywhere; there was no escaping them. Others like me learned to fight them. Powerful magic to keep the beast at bay. Certain substances can harm them. Pure silver is the most effective. Certain plants inhibit the beast form as well. Wolf's Bane, Night shade. When I came here with a rightful claim to this land, I found a small, but very active enclave of them living in these woods. I had to decide then if I was to wage war once more or find a way to live among them. I chose the latter," he said.

"You cut our balls off with silver!" The boy abruptly yelled. Despite appearing in his late teens, perhaps early twenties even, he had a child's high pitched keen. He was trembling now. "You took us from our families!"

"Oh, come now. It was either that or wholesale slaughter," the reverend said with annoyance, and noted the confused look in the colonel's eye. "See, besides silver, that is their one other significant weakness. Not of the *body* but of the *heart*. Their pack is everything to them. You will meet a clan none more loyal than a blood bound lycanthrope. They'd do anything to preserve the pack. And so, I used this to my advantage. We have a truce with them. We give them meat to feed. We keep their litter—our hostages—alive. In exchange, they don't hunt the people of Buck's Point. There are three exceptions to this truce, and they coincide with the three significant lunar phases our planet is enthralled too each year. The nearest of them, the harvest moon, is tomorrow. When the moons are at their peak closeness to the earth, it imbues them with a sort of juggernaut madness. They cannot control the change. Even our most powerful incantations and nostrums are ineffective against this lunar phenomenon. They go on a blood frenzy."

The colonel forced himself to take small sips from the shine. What this man was saying was complete madness, but he saw the clear intelligence in those eyes, the unwavering conviction as he talked. This man was either telling the truth or was convinced absolutely that what he said *was* the truth.

"You want my advice? Find all the ones who are branded, we did that part for you. Each house, even the clapboard ones, have underground cellars we built to hide from the pack during these full moons. They can also be used as prisons, I guess. I don't think any of them would hold out against them forever, but you can throw them down there when they start to show the signs. Tomorrow morning they'll all be hysterical and prone to seizing. That's how you know the moon will be upon them. Barricade the door. That would at least buy you some time to run. Especially your man, the one they gave back. You should just kill him now, before he becomes an unstoppable killing force. The freshly turned are always the most fearsome. The most unpredictable. You cannot let them spread, Colonel."

"I'm not running," the colonel said. He could, sure, and then what would he tell his superiors? The thought of going before major Lionel and reporting he'd surrendered the contested land he'd been ordered to occupy because it was infested with werewolves made him want to laugh and cry in equal measure. No. It would be career suicide.

"Then god help us all. Give me another snort of that shine colonel. You just sentenced my whole town to death. It's the least you can do," he said bitterly. The colonel obliged.

"Witchcraft. Werewolves. Jesus," the colonel said with a laugh.

"He's lying sir. Man's plumb mad. All them pagan folks is. Madness awaits those who consort with Satan, his mind is corrupted." The Quartermaster spoke as he handed the colonel his carbine and revolvers, all freshly cleaned and oiled.

"You haven't seen what I saw, Unger."

"That may be, but I recognize insanity when I see it. If you'll excuse me sir, I must see to the men, take stock of our weapons and ammunition."

"You still have that old scattergun Lieutenant Evans found in the woods?" The colonel asked before the quartermaster made for the door.

"Yes sir," he said.

"When you're done taking stock, bring it to me. Make sure the silver shot is still in there."

The quartermaster sighed. It was a very tired sound. "Yes sir." He left the colonel with the two bound men.

With the quartermaster gone, Mayhew began exploring the rest of the reverend's house. He searched each room, eager to see if the reports could be verified of these stone rooms the reverend spoke of. He remembered the stone cellar he'd convalesced in, how thick the walls were. They could make good defensive positions if some of them bore portals of any kind, windows or view holes perhaps.

"Christ." He inhaled as he opened up the first room he came upon and was faced with something akin to a taxidermist's workshop. Pelts lined the walls of the small room, all of them distinctly wolfish, with bristly gray coats and their splayed-out profiles suggesting they once clad to a canine frame. A skull sat floating in a jar of some amber fluid. The skull, identical to those bleached white ones he saw lashed to the effigies was distinctly canine but bulged out around the cranium, as if the brain housed within were much bigger than that of the typical dog brain. Then there were the teeth, which seemed disproportionately huge to the jaw from which they sprouted. Fearsome serrated ivory blades that curved inwards.

Even timber wolves and other feral, predatorial species had molars and small front teeth. Not this breed. Each tooth was uniform in size and wickedness. He remembered Halloway's wounds, the clean crescent valleys of gore sheared from his body. He shuddered, exited the room.

"Terrifying, aren't they?" the reverend called from the kitchen. Mayhew ignored him as he searched the other rooms. In another, he found the makings of the effigies, logs of white oak sheared and planed into uniform size among piles of wood shavings, clumps of creeper vines laid out to dry, skulls, not just the strange canine hybrids but possum, raccoon and cougar skulls lined a shelf on the wall. "Used to be all kinds of wildlife that roamed these hills. Black bears. Cougars. Elk. That's all gone now. The hills are denuded. They ate them all. Hence our prodigious collection of livestock."

The colonel found what he was looking for in the next room. Stairs went down into darkness. He quickly returned to the kitchen, grabbing a lit candle off the dining table and purposefully not looking at the reverend as he did so, and ventured down below. He was met with a thick oak door that was reinforced with steel bars on the other side. He remembered the brand-new door on the reverend's house. The gouge marks on the outside.

The door opened with a screech of rusted iron hinges, and the wavering firelight revealed a room clad solidly in stone. Granite and dolomite packed layer upon layer against their earthen foundations, as thick as the walls of Fort Davis. There were two small square portals towards the back and the side wall, thick iron bars embedded within it so no more than a six-inch gap was permitted between each. One looked out over the dense wall of trees lining the back of the reverend's yard, the other had a view of the thoroughfare. Down here he found a rudimentary crossbow, not the modern kind with the winding attachment for quick reloading, but a relic from the seafaring era, a distinctly European model with the emblem of some foreign military engraved into the wood stock. A silver tipped bolt was already loaded within it.

Yes, these would indeed make fine defensive positions. He hoped the reverend wasn't lying about these being in every house. If that was so, he might have a chance at making it out of this alive. His mind began to strategize, trying to figure out the best way to fight these rebel bastards. He was grossly outnumbered, but if he could draw them out, make them come to him instead of them picking him off from the tree line, hemming him in on all sides, then he might—

Someone was pounding on the door above.

"Colonel! Colonel Mayhew!" One of his men was shouting. He sounded urgent. He sighed, made his way back upstairs. *What now, for Christ sake?*

Chapter Eighteen

He headed back towards the small house where'd he spent an unknown amount of time convalescing in a laudanum haze, and, he suspected, some hallucinogenic panacea Tilda had slipped into his food. He saw his men were making good progress with the trench ruts, which would prevent the dixie bastards from doing a full-on cavalry charge through town, if they could even get their horses to cooperate in such a fashion. He also saw that the two howitzers they had in their company were placed at the start of these trenches. Rough wooden palisades were in the process of being erected around these.

"It's Halloway sir. Doc says you gotta come see it. He's… I don't know. It's madness, sir." A private whose name escaped him rambled on as he followed him to Tilda's home. *Oh, I'm sure it is*, he thought numbly. He was loathe to go back down into that cellar, with those jars and evidence of witchcraft. But he did anyway, morbid curiosity pushing him down there, forcing him to bear witness to the terrible secret he'd uncovered lurking in these hills.

Chapter Nineteen

He hungered for them. He hated them. He yearned for their flesh. The devil woman was splashing something on him that made his powerful nose burn with its scent, until all he could smell was fire. Before she sprayed him with that godawful acidic goop, he could smell the fat on her, the salt of her sweat, wanted to plunge his muzzle into her stomach, to burrow and chew and swallow all that delicious marbled meat. But he did not have a muzzle. This body felt strange to him, yet oddly familiar. He wanted the other body. The one he felt truly right in, truly free. But he could not will it. As hard as he tried, he stayed in this gangly, awkward form, this weak hairless vessel. Rage flooded him. He wanted not only to eat now, but to kill. To destroy those which put him in this position.

Chapter Twenty

"Colonel, dear lord in heaven. Halloway, he's possessed by something. I saw him… I saw him…"

"Is wolf," Tilda said nonchalantly, cutting off the wheezing doctor as she stood over Halloway, now barely recognizable from the meager, wide eyed private Mayhew had first set eyes upon when he was reassigned to this unit. Halloway was tied down to the same cot the colonel himself only recently vacated, pouring sweat as if he were in hell's own furnace. He snapped at the plump woman as she dashed some strong-smelling dark fluid against his skin like a preacher anointing someone with holy water, his teeth audibly clicking together. She deftly avoided the snapping ivory, going about her job in a perfunctory manner that spoke of performing this particular ritual innumerable times before. "He battle wolf. Wolf always win. This help. Keep wolf from him a little longer," she said with a shake of her head. She then uttered some thick, heavy voweled phrase in Dutch speak. Mayhew assumed it was an incantation of some sort.

"I tried to put him out of his misery colonel. A cut to the femoral and carotid arteries. Let him bleed out, it was the most merciful way I could think of… But he… He just healed right back up. It don't make no goddamn sense colonel!" The doctor said, his voice cracking, wavering. The colonel could tell the man was on the brink of losing it. It was simply one trauma too many. The empty laudanum bottle spoke to the man's fragile mental condition.

"Need silver. Cut deep," Tilda said, dragging a finger across her flabby throat. "We have silver. You want me to—"

"No, I'll do it." The colonel sighed, and withdrew his bowie knife, which he knew was cast from mostly pure silver with a steel core. The instant the knife was out of its sheath, Halloway went berserk.

For a moment the colonel had a flash of disorienting deja… what did the French call it? Something. He was back at their base camp, looking over the same sweating, insane man when he first got bit. A sickening repeat of this nightmare.

The wood creaked and began to splinter under the man's thrashing.

"Jesus, that's a solid oak frame, how—" The doctor gasped, but Mayhew was moving, the knife flashing in candlelight.

He plunged the knife straight into Halloway's sternum, he felt the blade punch through the bone plate, the silver scraping against bone with a horrible gritting sensation, and then he felt the blade's tip piercing something that yielded and shuddered against the knife.

The effect was almost instantaneous. Blood boiled out of the wound, not wept but *erupted* from the sundered flesh and bone, and the body of Private James Wright Halloway began to change. Silver-gray hair began to erupt over his body. His arms and legs contorted violently with the sickening tree-branch cracking of bones bending to their breaking point.

Mayhew backed away, watching in stunned awe as the legs snapped back at the knees, the legs and arms shortening, skin bulging and ripping in some spots before quickly sealing shut. The head began to bulge outward as Halloway let out a shrieking call, it was the same modulated caterwaul that awoke the colonel from his nightmare, except it was no longer distant, it was all encompassing and deafening and mind-shattering. A protrusion of bone erupted out from where the nose was. There came the audible grinding of bone plates shifting, the devil's own mortar and pastel at work.

He watched the ears slide up the distorted skull and grow outwards into triangular protuberances of cartilage.

And then there were the teeth.

Mayhew couldn't move. Paralysis rooted him to the stone floor as what was once Halloway sprang to his feet, clawing at the hilt of the knife protruding from a huge barrel chest with horrible malformed hands whose knuckles were shrinking and turning into the stubbed digits of paws.

He then let out a full-throated howl, a sound so primal and feral it harkened back to the days when men were but hooting and hollering primates in caves, and beasts ruled the world. The abomination turned its yellow eyes to Mayhew, and it fell upon him, pushing him to the ground.

Mayhew tried to scream, but every ragged inhalation tore at his side with hot telescopic pinpoints of pain. His long arms saved him as he managed to keep those gnashing ivory scythes at bay, the teeth coming together with such violent force they chipped and splintered and fell onto his face and into his beard along with gossamer runners of hot drool.

But then finally, his strength ebbed, red pushed at his temples, and his arms, trembling, gave way. A great hot, furry weight, reeking of canine musk fell atop him. He felt the teeth rip into his shoulder, a bright hot corona of pain, a second sun blossoming in his scapula as he felt teeth scrape bone as the beast immediately began to feast. He could hear the sound of his own flesh being rendered between those hideous primal weapons.

And then there was a heavy impact, a crunching thud as something slammed into the beast. The golden eyes abruptly went wide with shock, and its mouth opened wide, revealing a long lolling tongue smeared in red, and again Mayhew was afforded another of those adrenaline dilated moments where everything slowed to a snail's crawl, and he could see bits of his shoulder caught in those teeth, could see the articulated ridges of it's pallet, the long, cavernous pink cave of it's throat.

Mayhew braced himself for another burning explosion of pain as the beast made to bite him again, when it abruptly shuddered, a torrent of black blood erupting from its mouth to splash hot and stinging against the colonel's face, before going limp. The sharp stitches of pain in his side erupted once more and met with the searing agony in his shoulder, rendering him speechless as the heavy beast crushed him with its dead weight.

Then the sweating, red face of Tilda was looming over him, and he found he could breathe again as she shoved the beast off him. Mayhew wanted to crawl away from the thing which was changing again, more of those godawful snapping and grinding noises as the bones within the meat moved and transformed in impossible ways.

What he witnessed was a very aberration to the laws of nature, an affront to the laws of god. It was a thing that should not be, and yet, within the space of a few minutes that felt like whole glaciers could've melted and reformed, Halloway, or the thing that looked like Halloway, had returned. He lay in a heap on the ground, his pale skinny limbs akimbo, a silver mace stuck out of the back of his head.

Tilda wrenched the weapon from the skull with the same sound an axe cutter makes when removing a hatchet embedded within a tree. Tilda then turned her gaze on the colonel, the dripping mace with its tufts of matted fur and bone stuck in its head pointed accusatorily at him.

"Bite, you bite now!" She said, her eyes locked on his shoulder. Dazedly, Mayhew turned, saw the neat little 'U' of flesh gouged out of his shoulder, the fabric of his colonel's uniform cleanly torn there to show white bone surrounded by weeping red borders of flesh. Understanding slammed into him then as the wound burned with the knowledge of the abhorrent venom that at this very moment spread through his veins.

"Oh god. Oh sweet Jesus," he said to himself. "There's got to be a way to stop it. Can't you… Can't you do something with all that goddamn mountain medicine you practice!?" He asked, his voice raw. Already he could feel a faint heat radiating from the wound site and spreading through his body.

Tilda took another step closer, the mace slowly being raised. Her mouth was crushed into a thin, grave line.

"No… You bite now. You danger to us. You spread wolf. You cut or you die!" She said, shaking her head slowly as the mace continued its foreboding arc upward, one finger pointed at his wounded shoulder. "You cut! Is only way!" She bellowed.

"What're you doing you crazy bitch? Drop that goddamn thing!" Doc Tomlin yelled. The private who escorted him here didn't know what to do, his brain probably shocked to numbness at what just happened, his musket was aimed in their general direction but his eyes were unfocused, kept flitting to the naked man with the caved in skull.

Tilda came closer.

"Is only way. You cut arm or you die. Not like that one." She said, head tilting slightly to indicate Halloway.

"No. Not yet. I have an army to lead goddamnit," he said, and fumbled for his revolver, not quite sure what she was trying to say, the holster getting all tangled up in the struggle with Halloway.

Tilda charged just as the heavy gun was free of its holster. He'd never shot a civilian before, and he hesitated slightly as the mace's bloody head scintillated in the candlelight.

God spoke in that tiny stone basement as the revolver roared, the explosion bouncing off the reverberant stone walls and transforming into a thunderclap from the heavens. Tilda jerked and her swing went wide, the mace slamming into the wall, showing the power this woman could generate as stone chips went flying.

She pitched forward, her blue denim smock growing a ragged red hole in the back as she collapsed, letting out a muffled death gasp that the colonel barely heard. He felt the world swimming away, and he stumbled forward, needing to be out in the open air, needing to get to his men. Needing to be away from this goddamn madness.

"Colonel!" Tomlin said, going to him, but the colonel threw him aside. He needed the moonshine. Yes. That was what he needed. He needed to burn this sickness out, he needed that anesthetizing succor. He left the stone chasm beneath that infernal woman's house and walked in a deliberate but wobbling daze back towards the reverend's house. All of his men moved with studious industry, all them understanding what must be done. They all paused in their fortifying of positions and trench digging to look at their colonel as he passed though, his wound suppurating, his eyes wild and shifty, a man on the precipice of madness. He barely noticed the folks with missing arms and legs looking at him with knowing terror in their gazes.

He kicked open the door to the reverend's house, went straight to the bottles of moonshine left on the table. A man stood guard over the reverend, who saw the colonel and his bite mark, and shook his head woefully.

"Colonel Mayhew. You poor fool. You poor goddamn fool," the reverend said, eyeing the man as Mayhew stumbled over to the counter, grasped the moonshine bottle, and tipped the brown jug up and drank deep. "You're gonna need to get that arm cut off Colonel. Otherwise—"

"Shut your *GODDAMN MOUTH!*" Mayhew roared, spittle and shine flying from his lips as he brought the revolver up with his other hand. "Killed your goddamn mountain witch and I'll kill you too," he hissed. He stumbled over to the reverend, revolver thrust outward, which still had back splatter from Tilda on its cold steel barrel, and shoved it into Tobias Meyer's mouth, the barrel cracking off teeth as he forced it in all the way to the back of Meyer's throat. He gagged and spluttered around the barrel. The colonel grabbed a handful of that thick black hair and forced the man to stop struggling. Their eyes met. "One more word out of you. One more goddamn word," he said—his voice had an unfamiliar wavering edge to it now—and pulled back the hammer to finish the rest of his sentence.

The reverend said nothing more, nor did the branded boy, who began to squirm in his seat, his skin shined with sweat. Satisfied, he pulled the gun from the reverend's mouth and went back to his shine.

The colonel studied the haggard looking young man, wondered if he too would soon turn into one of those god-awful things. He decided not to ponder such things, his mind was already falling over the edge into madness. He could feel it in his unwavering voice and the crooked smile that kept wanting to pull at his lips, a lunatic's grin. He took the bottle he'd been drinking from, braced himself against the counter, and tipped the mouth of the jug over to his shoulder, meaning to clean the wound out.

"Colonel, I wouldn't—" But the reverends gentle protestation was lost to the sound of screaming, followed by the shatter of glass. The colonel's world exploded in sights and sounds and colors never known to him, a profound sense of burning so strong he was sure he'd taken the jump straight to hell, before abruptly a black curtain fell over his eyes.

Chapter Twenty-One

"Colonel… Sir…"

"Husmahfuckin—"

"Colonel!"

Hands were shaking him violently. He lashed out, opening his eyes, saw a wall of blue surrounding him. He looked up, saw the quartermaster looking at him with grave concern.

"They're here sir. Waiting for your reply," the quartermaster said softly. "I know I'm in no position to lead, but sir… You look awful. Perhaps maybe we should—"

"No…" the colonel said, acutely aware of the burning in his arm. He looked down at his shoulder, the edges of flesh around his wound no longer red but black, weeping a foul yellow pus. He tried to move it, found it was numb save for a deep, throbbing burn that coursed up his shoulder and into his neck with every labored beat of his heart. The smell of spilled alcohol was strong in the air, and he saw with heartbreaking sadness that one of the jugs had exploded on the floor when he'd lost consciousness.

They pulled him to his feet, the world felt like he was walking up hill though the ground was flat. His sprained rib was all but forgotten as his arm now blazed with a hot internal inferno. His whole body did, really. He stripped off his colonel's jacket as he went outside.

"Make sure the men are all barricaded," he told the quarter master in a voice that was all shaky gravel and grit as they made their way down the thoroughfare, which was deserted save for the four cavalrymen at the edge of town.

"Already are sir. They've been waiting for your command," the quartermaster said.

Mayhew noted it was early morning and realized he must've slept through the night. Normally a good night's rest like that would do him good, but he felt more tired than ever, his boots seemed filled with pounds of Ozark mud. His muscles were wound taught and he shivered with fever heat as he stumbled towards the line of men. He saw steam coming from their mouths, realized the trees and grass around them tinkled with frost caught in the morning sun, and yet he felt as if he were standing in the middle of a July heat wave.

"The colonel will hear the terms of your surrender!" A man called from his mount. He was a cavalry sergeant if Mayhew's eyes didn't betray him.

The colonel stared at them for a long time, not saying anything. He met each of their eyes, remembering their faces. Besides the cavalry sergeant speaking to him now, sent as an envoy, the others were but corporals.

"What say you, sir?" The sergeant asked.

"You tell that colonel…" He said through gritted teeth, he felt his jaw spasming and wanting to clench convulsively, "That I'll see him in hell," he said and raised his revolver in his good arm. Though his arm shook, and though his vision was blurred at the edges, the last remaining bit of soldier's intuition, of that West Point training took over, and he fired. The sergeant's head exploded, his slouch cap flying before any of the rebel soldiers could react. Before he even had time to fall off his horse, the others nearly lost control of theirs as their skittish mounts were thrown into a frenzy. The men were too busy trying to retreat and corral their scared horses to return fire.

The colonel turned and began to march back towards the Meyer house, where if he recalled correctly, another bottle of shine awaited him.

"Sir… About the townsfolk. The branded ones. They're starting to act piqued sir. Should we lock them somewhere?" It was his own cavalry sergeant, his men seemed to blur into and out of existence now, materializing out of the ether as he wandered towards the reverend's house, his fever addled mind focused on one singular thing: the moonshine. "I think that reverend might've been right sir…"

"Oh, he was right," the colonel breathed, biting back an unhinged laugh as he stopped to look up at the bright blue sky. It was the last day of October, and the frost was fully here now, though the colonel didn't feel it. He knew they could see the tendrils of steam rising off his body with the fever heat, but no one dared say anything. He looked up and saw the ghostly face of the moon in the sky. He knew come nighttime it would hold dominion over their heads with a deep red glow. In his most recent fugue, visions came to him. Tattered confederate uniforms. A silver loaded scattergun. Abandoned confederate armaments gone to seed in the woods. In these bleary kaleidoscopic visions, he found revelation. He found a way out. "Let them free. March them to the tree line. And give them your jackets and uniform shirts as you do."

"Sir?" The sergeant asked.

"You heard me. Get 'em outta here, the marked ones. Make sure not a one with the tattoo is left in this town, and make sure they're wearing our colors. For the others, the unbranded, put a gun in their hand, and tell them to fight. If they don't, tell them they're officially considered traitors of the United States and shoot them on sight. The amputees…" he said, staring at an old woman who was missing her left leg below the knee, she propped herself on a gnarled walking stick and glared at the colonel with unhidden contempt, "Just make sure they don't get in your way," he said, and marched off towards Tobias Meyer's house.

***

"What are you doing?" Meyer asked as Mayhew took out his silver knife, the blade still fouled with that terrible black blood, and went behind the boy's chair.

"What's your name son?" The colonel asked as he cut the sweating, writhing boy free. He fell to the floor, panting on his hands and knees.

"…Roland…" The boy gasped.

"Roland. What a good Christian name. Run along Roland. You're free. Run to your people up yonder," the reverend said, and sat heavily in the seat the boy previously occupied.

"What? What in god's name are you planning? Don't you understand you fucking idiot? The harvest moon is tonight! They'll slaughter you all, they'll—"

The colonel withdrew his revolver while the man ranted and raved, and casually shot him in the head mid-sentence. Brain and skull and rich black hair clung to the wall on the other side of the reverend's head. He slumped in his chair, feet drummed lightly on the floor, and then came the unmistakable sound of bowels being voided before the reverend finally stopped moving.

"Christ. They always gotta shit themselves," the colonel groaned. He then noticed the boy was still there. "I said go on son!" He barked at the wide-eyed thing, who'd only went on staring in disbelief as if unable to accept his newfound emancipation, hands and feet poised to move but unable. The colonel leveled his barrel at him and that got the young one moving; he loped out of the door, the way Halloway loped out of camp, like a man who's forgotten to run and thinks he's a dog. He went over, grabbed the remaining bottle of shine, and went to work at it. "They probably will kill us all. But they'll kill the secessionists too. And *that*, mister Meyer, I consider a tactical victory," he said to the corpse, still tied in its chair, its drawers full of waste.

He drank.

CHAPTER TWENTY-TWO

He drank, and he watched from the doorstep as his men went about hastily evicting those with the tattoos. They were scared, confused, unsure of this new coup as they were marched off to the eastern border. In the distance, through the trees that began to shed their leaves and permit the colonel a view into that primeval wood, he could see the rebels and their mismatched gray uniforms, tiny little dots like ants moving along the hillside, in between the trees. They were coming down from the same bluff his men had only recently vacated a few days prior. He noticed the eastern hillside where the wild folk lived was devoid of the gray diaspora. Perhaps they too knew of what lurked and bit and howled in those woods.

Or perhaps they knew not to fight a two-sided engagement. Too much risk of friendly fire. Notoriously bad shots, those pig farmers and drunks and convicts that made up the treasonous gray scourge.

He searched among the men, only a few of which still had their coats and uniforms on, many marched in their sweat stained white under shirts. He did manage to spot a sergeant though, he'd been marshalling one of the branded families to the eastern front, all of them looked comical in oversized union coats that billowed around them, like a child trying on their daddy's work shirt.

"Sergeant. Make sure my men are hold up in cellars with viewing ports to the west. Move 'em quick, keep out of sight when possible. I want these inbred traitors to think we left with our tail between our legs."

"Yes sir. We're almost done evacuating these folks and I'll put out the move order," the anomalous sergeant said. Mayhew saw doubt in his eyes and knew his current condition made up a ghastly sight, he was sure. But he was still the colonel. He was to be obeyed.

In the distance, he could hear the blat of bugles as men got into position, the horns sounding like the baleful mating call of an elk. Despite his mild inebriation, the colonel could feel the thick electricity in the air, the palpable sense of impending violence on a grandiose scale. It made his bristly arm hair straighten and his beard itch and his neck hairs bristle. That heavy, invisible fog had haunted him over every battlefield he'd presided, but this was different. With the presence of those creatures, those abominations, that unknown factor increased the tension considerably.

His feverish state didn't help. His muscles felt as wound tight as bow strings, and though he was halfway deep into the gallon jug of shine, he felt only a mild, ephemeral inebriation, as if his body burned through the shine faster than he could pour it down his gullet.

He watched his men darting between houses, many scrambling to get into position as musket and scattergun barrels poked out through the bars.

"Pull those goddamn barrels in! Don't let 'em see ya! Wait till they're right up on us. In the streets! You fire on my mark!" The colonel said, his head pounding as he tried to project his voice. His battle-baritone was long gone, replaced with a rasping, unsteady croak, but he heard men quietly relaying the order through town and watched as barrels slowly receded, and soon all of Buck's Point appeared deserted.

The colonel looked up once more and blinked. Somehow two hours must've slipped by, for the sun had shifted considerably in the sky, slowly being beaten out by the ever-growing moon. Halloway's monstrous form stirred behind his eyes, that deafening howl that came out of the malformed mouth. Those teeth.

Christ, those teeth.

Softly, he closed the door to the reverend's house. He walked down the hall, grabbing the silver scythe off the wall, holding it in his good hand while he had a tenuous grasp on the shine bottle in his left, which was no longer numb but now tingled and spasmed, but through sheer force of will he held onto the bottle. He nodded to the dead man as he walked past, giving him a wide birth so as to not smell the shit percolating in his drawers.

"Sorry about this, Mr. Meyer. No other way I'm afraid," he said to no one as he receded downstairs. He pulled down the two metal barricades that would keep the door in place, and nearly tumbled down the stairs as he turned with scythe and shine in hand.

He stood near one wall, his height allowing him to be at eye level with the rectangular portal outside. With the bars on the window and the thick rock walls surrounding him, he felt truly imprisoned, ready to face judgement. What had that 'reverend' said?

Answer for your blunders, of which there are many to atone for.

He laid the scythe by his musket, and the scattergun loaded with silver, which he'd ordered the quartermaster to make sure was loaded and brought to the house. He doubled checked both anyway, saw they both had full charges. He refilled both cylinders of his revolvers, those wonderful innovations in destruction. He saw the day being washed away on a deep hued red tide and felt the blood boil in his veins. He ground his teeth audibly now, his left arm spasmed uncontrollably.

It felt as if he had a million little fish hooks embedded in his skin, all of them being pulled upward, towards the moon. Like the moon itself was trying to pull something out of him.

He could feel and hear the rebel wave converging upon them. Move orders were called by harsh voices thick with Appalachia drawl. Horses neighed. On the other side of town, the cattle lowed mournfully. Mayhew had almost forgotten about the animals, how he had such big plans to harvest them. For many days hunger eluded him, his body only craved the anesthetizing firewater that filled his belly. But now, at the thought of all that juicy, succulent beef made him groan aloud with hunger. He pictured raw, red meat. Not cooked, not some medium rare porterhouse, no, the thought of destroying that precious flesh with heat was horrible.

Mayhew began to drool as he thought of ripping it right off the cow's body. The only heat the meat needed was the blood that kept it warm and alive. Visions of his teeth rending flesh and filling his stomach with warm, fresh blood assailed him, his eyes rolled to his head. He continued to drool.

It wasn't until the first volley came that Mayhew snapped out of it. The percussive cacophony of a hundred rifles firing at once pulled him from his carnivorous fantasies. A second later the sound of a hundred musket balls peppering roofs and wood walls sounded. He heard the whine of a ball strike off one of the iron bars, and that was enough to ground him into the here and now. He receded into the shadows of the cellar, praying he wouldn't hear return fire from his men.

He didn't, thank god.

A few seconds of pregnant silence, and then another volley as ranks were changed out. Wood splintered, the whine of balls tearing air, the thuds of lead slamming into dirt and wood.

Still no return fire.

There was a longer interval this time, and the colonel waited for the thunderous roar of artillery. Just when he thought the rebels would not volley, they did. Thunder rolled and he felt the percussive *whoomp* in his chest. A split second later the whole world exploded in noise. He felt Meyer's house shudder as grape shot tore through the building. Dust rained down on him, but the floor did not collapse.

Still, no return fire. He dared a glance out his portal, saw the house directly across the thoroughfare was completely gone, a ruin of wood, but he could see the whites of eyes glinting at him from the recessed barred portal across from him. He nodded, and the face nodded back.

There was a long silence then. No more volleys were fired. Mayhew was sure the rebel boys were thoroughly confused now, wondering if they were wasting their ammo on empty claptrap houses.

Soon he could hear voices, the great subtle rustling of men in uniform coming to inspect the carnage, sure that the reports of blue coated men running into the woods and the conspicuous absence of ranks or return fire confirming their thoughts that the town was abandoned.

They came closer. He could hear individual snatches of conversation now.

"Colonel acted all tough, but in the end he ran, yellabelly sumbitch."

"You get a look at the bastard? That old cuss looked nuttier than a squirrel turd."

"You think them hogs is still alive? Boy I could go for a pork steak."

The colonel's molars ground audibly like gravel crunching underfoot. He looked out the portal, and could see filthy brogans and boots and sometimes bear feet wholly caked in mud. It was now or never.

He took out one revolver with his good hand, and took his time taking out the other, letting his twitching hand, the veins bulging and turning black in his forearm, unsteadily take out the other shooting iron. He rested them both against the concrete relief of the barred window. He took aim at the nearest of the pair of legs, saw there was a cluster of ten of them right in front of him. He flexed his trigger finger in his left hand slightly. Shaky, barely in control of the muscle fibers there, but he could muster enough tension to pull the trigger, if he really put his mind to it.

He tried to say a quick prayer, but his fever addled mind kept tripping over the first line of the lord's prayer, unable to remember the rest. *Dear god, who art in heaven, hallowed be thy name.*

Hallowed be thy name.

Hallowed be thy—

"Hey, what the hell—" One man said, and, realizing he had no time to pray, Mayhew opened fire.

CHAPTER TWENTY-THREE

His world erupted in flashing strobes as his revolvers spat fire and gun smoke, fingers convulsing on their respective triggers. Somewhere far away he could hear someone yelling *ambush! Ambush!* In a thick Virginia drawl before this got cut off with a liquid screech of pain. Through the thick tang of gun smoke and hot iron he could smell it. Fresh blood, hot blood, the coppery offal of exposed innards. It was maddening, that smell. More maddening than the savory aroma of the reverend's delicious stew after he'd been marching on nothing but tuber soup and rabbit legs for four days. Normally the battlefield high included a complete negation of hunger, thirst, all peripheral bodily needs, being replaced instead with preternatural focus, but now his stomach roared with a battle cry of its own. It took every ounce of his will power not to stick his head out and jut his tongue forth to lap what spilled on the ground just outside.

He dropped down from the view hole just as musket balls chipped away at the rectangular portal, his left hand now a twitching claw that could not hold anything. His heavy Colt revolver clattered on the stone floor, smoke oozing lazily from the barrel. He tried to reload his other one, but found he was out of ammo.

Mayhew screamed in frustration, but then this was abruptly cut off as his body began to violently contort. It felt as if some mad god-like puppeteers were yanking invisible strings on his body, those fish hooks pulling to all compass points now, his body no longer in his control.

The fire blazed within him. Sweat poured off of him, made his shirt suction to his body. He collapsed, contorting on the floor, legs and arms akimbo, his own muscles betraying him. He did not know how long he lay like this, but when he was finally able to open his eyes again, to come back into the moment, the cellar was a dark monochrome of varying grays, outside the ghostly illumination from the harvest moon cast long shadows through the bars.

He could hear new sounds now in the absence of all that cacophonous gunfire.

"Retreat! Retreat! Re—" Someone bellowed, before their call was truncated cleanly with a snarl. A feral, animalistic grunt. Men were screaming now. The screams didn't last long. There came the sound of flesh rending and popping, and god, how beautiful it sounded to his ears.

Except, no, that wasn't right. He was always mildly deafened after battle, the high-pitched screech that accompanied him on long quiet nights and was most loudest after a large engagement was completely absent now. His ears were tuned in acutely to everything going on outside, he couldn't remember ever hearing this well, even when he was a young man and his ears virgin to the deafening roar of war. The rattling moans of men in their death throes. The heavy, husky breathing of large, bestial animals. Gurgling groans as throats were torn asunder. The lapping of tongues against wet viscera.

He blinked then, his eyes feeling as rough as the grain on his musket stock, and saw that a large shadow temporarily occulted the light coming in through the concrete portal, passing slowly from the first viewing hole to the next. Mayhew saw the bristling furred forepaws of something massive. The paws weren't like normal wolves though, they appeared aberrant with too many knuckles, the claws curved up and inward at a wicked angle.

A huge, blocky head lowered itself into the eastern most hole. Mayhew saw saucer sized eyes that scintillated against the crimson moonlight, giving it the appearance of a specter. It let out a low growl, and suddenly Mayhew's nose took in something that completely overpowered the savory waves of blood coming at him from all directions. A potent, heady musk that was equal parts musty and astringent. He found his nostrils involuntarily flaring at the scent. He felt goosebumps prickle his wracked body. It hit him like a gun butt to the face, and his eyelids fluttered and he absurdly felt himself growing erect, as if though the thing had scented him with potent, primal pheromones, the way deer hunters would cut out the excretory glands of does and douse themselves with its scent to attract the bucks.

Then it was gone, leaving him in a trance that was equal parts hunger, lust, and terror as his body struggled to cope with all these new intrusions of its various systems. He was beginning to lose his sense of self, his humanity, and he began to feel things shifting in his body.

"Nuh….Nuhnoo…" he gasped as he thought of Halloway. That would be him, his body hideously transmogrifying into some hideous wolf being, his flesh housing an inner turmoil between two beings, his body forever a corrupt vessel for the poison that now flowed through him.

He forced himself to reach out with his right hand, trying to grab the scythe. He couldn't look at it, the silver hurt his eyes though it cast no light, but the barest glint made bolts of pain shoot through his head. Having the silver scythe anywhere near him caused immediate bouts of nausea, but he fought these, taking the wooden shaft in his hand. He would not turn into one of these beasts. He would die in battle the way god had intended.

Mayhew heard the groan of wood being stressed to its breaking point upstairs. The door, freshly replaced from the last pogrom. Would they break it again?

He had his answer a minute or so later when he heard the corporeal thuds of bodies slamming repeatedly into the frame. The house, already damaged from the fusillade of cannon and small arms fire, shuddered violently under the repeated blows, until finally, with a crackling squeal he heard the door buckle. Dread welled up in his abyssal cavern of a stomach as he heard the clack of canine nails against wood. The footsteps were heavy too, as if though a heavyset man walked upstairs, his nails overlong and hitting the floor with each step.

The door was double barred. Surely they couldn't come to him down here.

Still, a sense of urgency overcame him as he tried, in vain, to bring the scythe's blade to his neck. Every time the silver got within a foot of his throat it was like sticking his face into the searing radius of glowing coals. He was making strange, throaty moaning noises now as he did this, desperate to end his life but unable to. He heard more wooden wrenching now as industrious beasts began to pry away the wood planks of the door. They knew it was double barred, for they did not attempt to slam into it. Christ, for beasts they were smart, cunning.

He remembered the shotgun then, and reached for it, scrabbling in an abhorrent version of a spider crawl to the weapon, its silver charge screaming at every sensory input he had. He hugged the weapon to his chest as more wood was ripped away upstairs. He could hear the scrape of teeth as they sunk into the wood and pulled. He could hear heavy panting, growling, chuffing. Mayhew was whimpering now as he tried to reach for the shotgun's trigger, but the stock was too long; he would have to fire the trigger with a toe if he hoped for complete annihilation of his head.

But soon the searing waves of poison from the silver was too much, and he had to push the gun away, his blood feeling like it was simmering in his veins now. Soon he heard one of the heavy iron bars clatter down the stairs as the thick oak door was slowly, methodically destroyed. He tried to wrench off his boot, but he barely had control of his legs; all his limbs felt possessed by another being within him, one that only wanted to thrash and kick and betray his every move.

"Mmmmguh," he moaned through locked jaws as his boot scraped uselessly against the concrete as he tried to slip it off, the second bar clattering down the stairs with a clang. The musk was overwhelming now, physical waves of primal need in all things assailed him. He switched tactics then, his arms trembling so bad the shotgun's barrel wavered like a divining rod over a wellspring as he heard soft taps as they came down the stairs. He pulled himself against one wall, panting heavily as he laid the shotgun across his trembling legs, trying to steady it. "Nuhhh…No!" He hissed as he waited for that huge vulpine head to appear, waiting for the ghostly glint of those yellow eyes.

The instant he saw them, he flexed his finger. For a horrifying second, he couldn't muster the strength to pull the rusted mechanism, but with a final gasp of effort he did.

Thunder boomed and it felt as if his ear drums imploded as his sensitive ears took the brunt of the blast. He heard a high pitched canine whine and smelled smoking flesh under the musk. A moment later he was being tackled, sharp teeth digging into him.

"No!" He cried out as he felt himself pinned to the ground. He tried to reach for the scythe, but a heavy furry weight settled on his spasming arm. He half hoped they would tear him to shreds. Horrible though that death would be, it would be a far better fate than turning into one of them. Again, harrowing visions of Halloway flooded his mind.

But they did not rend him to gristle and marrow as he had hoped. Instead, they began to drag him upstairs. A few whined for their fallen pack member, its head a smoking ruin from the gun blast, and then turned to snap at Mayhew, as if in anger for what he had done.

His body thumped rigidly against the stairs as he was carried by the back of his neck, like a kitten being scruffed by its mother. He saw two of the wolfs had completely dismembered the reverend. They were not eating him though. Instead they took turns defiling the corpse, one squatted, it's bushy tail curved upwards as it deposited a coiled mound of scat atop the man's sundered torso. The lower half was soaked in urine as a wolf with one eye and a scar going down its muzzle hiked a leg. Mayhew understood immediately.

Retribution for what the reverend had done to them.

Then he'd been dragged out of the house, and the destruction before him was almost biblical in scope and savagery. Body parts were strewn haphazardly across the mud tract that cut through town, great swathes of dark red mixing with the tan clay mud. All the houses were gone, reduced to splinters and anomalous heaps of wood and stone. The rich scent of offal and exposed gore was so potent now it overrode the musk that had enthralled him. He reached out feebly towards the occasional gray coil of intestine or for an arm still clutching a gun, but the beast transporting him refused his appetite.

Dixie and Yankee blood ran in intermingling tributaries upon the uncaring earth as he was dragged through the foul mud. Once or twice he stuck his face into the occasional puddle filled with crimson, lapping at what he could, silty mud-blood getting into his mouth, he savored the bitter tang that coated his tongue.

Soon, in his barely cognizant state, Mayhew realized he was out near the great pasture now where a bounty of meat from hoof to horn once lay. He no longer heard the blat of goats or the lowing of cows or the gobble of a surly rooster. All was quiet save for the sounds of mastication.

The beast dropped him on the ground before an unidentifiable red mass of meat. With a snout he was flipped over and saw the night sky before him, saw the huge red sphere in the sky, his eyes dilating instantly to take in that beautiful crimson titan.

Mayhew felt his blood actually begin to boil now, felt a wave of fire crash through his body in pounding waves. He bucked and writhed, but they pinned him there, one pinning his head to the ground by his hair, making sure he stayed within full sight of the moon.

The change was fully on him now. He felt his bones elongate and shorten simultaneously, joints and vertebrae ground and disintegrated and reformed with a profound agony. He felt himself be pulled apart and put back together, felt the last vestige of humanity eek away as the moon tore the wolf out of him.

Soon they let him go, his true form now upon them. They left him to feast among the others, who were busy reducing the cattle and hogs into vague masses of glistening red as he immediately turned and burrowed his entire head into the cavernous maw of what was once a prize-winning Holstein's chest cavity. He ate until his stomach cavity could not hold anymore, and then continued to eat even after the membranous sac ruptured and he felt his newfound body begin to tingle and tickle as it began to repair itself almost instantly. On and on this cycle went, his hunger uncontrollable and all consuming.

Despite the ache in his jaws, he continued to chew, swallow, chew, swallow, until his yellow eyes caught a glint of something, and his gluttony ceases for the briefest of moments. Blue in color where the blood hadn't soaked through, with golden embroidered bars at its ragged edges, smeared in gore and gobbets of gristle yet still clearly visible.

The sight of those golden bars triggered something deep within him, penetrating the primal pull that now dominated his mind, but ultimately, it becomes a meaningless prickle compared to his hunger. What finally snaps him out of out of his ravenous frenzy is the large, commanding body of *her* walking by. Her musk strong and her coat beautiful, her presence immediately calling forth simple, lustful needs that usurped whatever stirred in him at the sight of that piece of cloth. Eager to be in her wake, to bask in her carnal heat as she sought a mate to commemorate this grand feast, he follows after.

THE CIRCLE

BY FRANCIS VERELLE

The neighbourhood looked a lot different from the way it used to be. He didn't recognize any of the buildings.

He knew he'd been here before only recently. He also felt a vague sense of purpose which must have led him here. He'd been on his way somewhere, but he couldn't quite recall where he'd been headed, so he just continued walking.

The houses were tall and the city was noisy. It was past midnight already and yet the sound of passing cars echoed through the streets, these speeding vehicles that often scared him with the suddenness with which they approached. The city never seemed to sleep at all anymore.

His head was buzzing with the slight pain right behind his eyes that hadn't left him for decades now. The nights were too bright. It wasn't just the streetlights and neon signs, but also general light pollution. He had read about that somewhere lately; he couldn't recall where. It didn't get properly dark anymore, not the way it used to. People were worried about the effects on the ecosystem, but no one knew how it affected him, how it affected the creatures of the night.

Back in the day, the gas lamps had created islands of brightness in a dark sea of night that he'd wandered through undisturbed. The buildings had been small, leaving room for the black night sky above, and it had been quiet while he was on the hunt. The night hadn't been a shared space yet; it had belonged to him and his kind.

He hadn't felt properly rested since the turn of the 20th century.

He remembered the olden days better than the recent years. He could still picture the roads of his old hometown, the old Heimat, vividly. Everything had been so dark and quiet. You could see the stars clearly at night. The streets hadn't been paved properly, not as neatly and evenly as the ground underneath his feet now. The world had smelled different, too.

He wished he could recall how he'd ended up in this part of town. The name of the city was on the tip of his tongue, but it kept slipping away like a reflection on stirred water.

His memory let him down more and more often lately - people, places, things seemed to tumble through his mind like they'd been shaken loose, and he couldn't always name them correctly. Whole centuries filled up his brain, and it was getting too crowded inside his head. There wasn't enough space for him to store all the information.

He needed to feed.

He'd feel better afterwards, his body would be stronger again and his memory sharper. The effect never lasted long; instead, the intervals at which he needed to consume seemed to grow shorter. Once he fed, the migraine would subside a little and he might be able to find his way back home.

He couldn't recall where home was.

The last thing he recalled clearly was a small suburban house furnished in the mid-century style, but that didn't seem right, that must have been decades ago. It didn't fit this neighbourhood either. The buildings here were tall, and there was no free space between them. The apartments inside were probably tiny. He didn't think he'd ever been inside one of these buildings. He'd never even been to this neighbourhood before. Everything looked unfamiliar.

"Hey!" someone called out to him. "Old bum!"

He turned his head. A group of five boys on the edge of adulthood had gathered in front of an apartment building on the other side of the street. Two of them were sitting on the stairs. They were holding beer cans. He could smell the metal of the cans and the stench of alcohol even from where he was standing. They smelled heated, too, angry and ready to pick a fight. Humans always smelled different depending on their emotions. The smell of anger made him hungry. It was probably a natural instinct, his body encouraging him to feed on the potential threat first before they could attack.

He pulled up his shoulders and quickened his steps. He often got called names, insulted, and even shoved around when he walked the streets at night. Something about his looks seemed to upset people. His clothes were always dirty, coming apart at the seams. He couldn't recall the last time he'd taken a bath. It might have been recently; he just couldn't remember. The smells all around were too overwhelming to take notice of his own body odour underneath them.

His kind had fallen. They used to be respected and even feared by the daywalkers, but nowadays it was becoming harder and harder to provide for a living when no one knew of their existence and the lines between night and day had become blurred. He wasn't smarter than the average human being, didn't know what markets to invest in or which paintings would go up in value eventually. No fortune had been passed down to him. He'd been a simple farm boy once. He'd risen with the sun and worked on the fields to make his living. He remembered the smell of hay. And today, he still had to work for his money but was stuck to the night shifts. With his increasing memory lapses, even simple tasks were getting difficult. Maybe he didn't even have a home. Maybe he was living on the streets. But where did he go once the sun came up? Where did he hide?

"Hey!" one of the boys shouted again. "We're talking to you!"

There were only five of them; he could easily take them out, even in his weakened state. He'd grab one of them and sink his teeth into his throat. Warm blood would fill his mouth, delicious and nutritious. The others would probably attack or run before he could drain the first one. He'd have to snap some necks; that would be the most efficient way to go about it - kill three of them quickly and precisely, maybe stop the fourth one from running by breaking his legs and save him for later. The kid would probably scream, but if he emptied the first one quickly enough, no one would come running. In the cities, people screamed all the time these days. It would be a waste of three deliciously fresh meals, though. He couldn't drink from corpses, even while they were still warm. He always had to watch out for the moment their heart stopped beating.

"Hey!"

He started running. Five dead bodies for two meals weren't worth it. Five dead bodies multiplied the risk of getting caught by five. Five times as many friends and family members who wanted justice, five times as many people who wouldn't stop digging. One missing person might fly under the radar, but five murders would warrant a thorough police investigation. His head started pounding with every step. He was so hungry, he nearly turned around and threw caution to the wind. He wasn't sure when he'd last fed. It must have been a while.

He rounded a corner. No one had followed him. It seemed they hadn't been that angry after all, just bored.

He'd hoped to recognize the street, but it looked exactly as alien to him as the last one. He tried to read the street name at the corner, but his vision was turning blurry. He wondered why it was only his eyesight getting worse. He could still smell and hear everything too intensely, with the heightened senses of a predator. The noise of the cars was getting to him. Everything reeked of fumes.

Killing had been easier back in the days, too. You'd think the cities would work in his favour with their anonymity, but everyone was registered somewhere and easily identified. Forensics had improved drastically over the last fifty years. He'd heard they could tell all kinds of things about a person just based on their teeth.

And humans were crawling everywhere like vermin. He remembered being able to drag a corpse into a deserted part of the woods and being able to count on the fact that no living soul would pass by. The world today was too small and filled with too many people. There were no hidden corners left. And the wars, oh, the wars had been a blessing. No one had wondered where people disappeared to. He could leave the remains of his meals on the side of the road without a second thought. They'd been at war for thirty years, shortly after he'd been turned. Those thirty years had been truly glorious. Even war wasn't the same anymore. People blew each other up and it was too dangerous to hide out in a warzone during the day. So he simply had to roam the cities and frequent the kinds of neighbourhoods where people went missing all the time. Maybe he had come here to feed. The area seemed shady enough, but he wasn't sure if it actually was. He couldn't tell a good neighbourhood from a bad neighbourhood anymore. It smelled dirty everywhere.

He was scared that one day he'd just forget to take precautions, that he would simply feed whenever he got hungry, like an animal, and that a hunter would track him down. Or that he'd forget that the sun would burn him, that he would just go out in broad daylight like he had during his childhood, and that it would melt the flesh straight off his bones.

The only way to prevent that would be to stay well-fed at all times, but hunting had become so difficult in these modern times. Maybe he should have killed one of the boys. Let the other four get away, for all he cared, or track them down later to silence them.

One of these vehicles, cars - that was what they were called, the term had escaped him momentarily, there had been no cars when he was young - pulled up to him. He'd been able to hear its approach for the last minute or so, but he'd misjudged the distance, so its sudden appearance made him flinch. With everything being so noisy, it was hard to judge an object's distance by sound alone.

The car window was rolling down. The electric whirr of the mechanism dazed him. A girl sat behind the steering wheel. She had curly hair that made her head seem bigger than it really was.

He took a step backwards. It was too tempting. If he killed her, he'd have to get rid of the car somehow. He couldn't just leave it out in the streets. He didn't even know how to drive.

She smiled at him. Her teeth looked very blunt. He checked for her canine, even though he could already smell that she was human. She smelled delicious.

He had never seen this girl before in his life.

"Ansgar," she said.

The name brought back vague memories. "Ansgar, komm rein!" - that was what his mother used to shout. He remembered her clearly, a brash woman with hands that were always red and never still because there was always work to do. She had seemed old to him while growing up, but looking back from this point of his existence, he realised she'd basically still been a child. He'd had three older siblings, two of which had died before his birth.

How did this girl know his name? He had never seen her before in his life.

"Did you get lost again?" she asked. "Get in, I'll take you home."

So she knew where he lived. She knew his name and knew his home, yet he couldn't place her face as he dug through his memory. Maybe he had seen her before, he wasn't sure.

The thought that she knew him was scary. It put him at a disadvantage. He knew nothing about her.

"It's me, Celia," she said. "Get in the car, Ansgar, it's alright."

He hesitated but figured he had nothing to lose by getting into the car. If anything, he was the menace. He could kill her in an instant. And he was lost after all. He rounded the car and got in on the passenger side.

"Celia," he repeated her name to pretend that he had recognized her. He felt like he'd said that name many times before, but he couldn't recall a single occasion. It rolled off his tongue easily.

Ansgar didn't want to let on that he had no idea who the girl was. Although she didn't seem like a threat, openly displaying weakness was always a bad idea. There were plenty of people who were out to get him. Hunters, relatives of humans he had killed. Being a creature of the night wasn't easy. You were hated, everyone was out to get you. No one ever showed him kindness anymore. No, there was one person. One person recently, who had helped him, someone important in his life. Their name and face were gone. Maybe they were already dead.

He checked on the girl briefly, although he didn't need to watch her to be aware of her presence. Her smell filled the confined space of the vehicle. She was calm, not scared, not on guard. Her blood smelled sweet. He heard her breath and the sound caused by her fingers on the steering wheel whenever she adjusted her grip. He could hear her heartbeat, too. Underneath it all was the constant roar of the car engine. It made his head hurt even worse.

She was in her thirties at most, probably even younger. Ansgar remembered how strong and naïve he'd been at that age. He remembered it more vividly than anything that had happened since the Great War. Time seemed to run in circles. The beginning was closer to the end than anything that had happened in between.

"You shouldn't go out by yourself anymore. You keep getting lost," Celia said. "This is the second time this week."

Ansgar didn't remember the first time. She could be lying to him. Maybe she wanted to confuse him, weaken him by making him doubt himself, while she lured him into a trap.

He turned to look out the window. The buildings were passing by fast, and he focused on the inside of the vehicle again. How was he supposed to recognize anything with the buildings rushing by like this? Of course, he couldn't memorise anything with the humans forcing him to speed through the streets like this. This means of transportation wasn't natural.

"The neighbourhood looks so different these days." His voice sounded cracked, like that of an old man. "Nothing looks the same anymore."

The buildings were all so tall and cars and people moved everywhere, the city constantly seemed in motion around him. It was confusing when everything kept changing. It had been different in his hometown. The nights had been darker, the sky had been clear enough to see the stars. The roads weren't paved evenly yet. It'd been quiet at night.

"You just took a wrong corner, that's all. We're still close."

That meant he'd been going somewhere after all. He wondered how that had happened, that his memory had just deleted the information halfway through his journey. There was just so much on his mind. He remembered growing up in the countryside in Deutschland. He remembered the war. He remembered churches and priests and how scared people had been of his kind. He remembered the superstitious staking of regular corpses, just to make absolutely sure they wouldn't come back. He remembered the ship that had brought him across the ocean. He even remembered how badly it had smelled below deck. He remembered how everything had seemed possible in this new country and how people had turned out to be even more religious here. They shunned him for not attending Sunday's church, but they didn't remember the old legends, not as clearly at least, not after a generation or two. He remembered Clarissa. He remembered that it was the smallpox that had killed her. How was he supposed to memorise anything more? His mind was full.

The scent of blood seemed to grow stronger with every passing moment. The heating was turned on, and Celia's body warming up made her smell all the more alluring. Her blood would taste rich, a little metallic around the edges, salty and sweet at once. Every human being tasted slightly different.

Ansgar considered draining her. In that case, he'd never find out where she was taking him. But a good feeding would bring back his memory and he'd find his way back home on his own. He'd avoid the risk of walking into a trap, too. But he couldn't drive the car. He was so hungry that he could barely think straight. It wasn't just a hunger that gnawed at the pit of his stomach. He felt hungry with his entire body. He felt old.

The car stopped.

"Here we are," Celia announced. She got out of the car, and Ansgar hesitantly followed her example. The motions came to him naturally, undoing the seat belt he didn't recall fastening, opening the door. His muscle memory took over as if he had ridden this vehicle countless times before, though the whole concept still felt strange and novel to him.

Once his eyes fell onto the house in front of them, he was flooded with a sense of relief. Of course, this was Richard's house, the blue paint, the wooden front porch. In this country, houses always looked new.

He followed Celia up the steps. The neighbourhood looked different here, even though it had only been a short car ride. He couldn't estimate the physical distance they'd crossed. The vehicle had been going so fast. The buildings on this street were smaller, but the houses were still large enough to accommodate several families. It felt unreal that they were meant only for one household. Humans had gotten greedy and spoiled, with their indoor toilets and electric lights and DNA tests at crime scenes.

He hesitated when Celia unlocked the door, briefly unsure if he'd really been here before, or if he still needed an invitation to be able to enter.

"Come on in," Celia said gently. She put her hand on his back like a nurse guiding a patient. The touch felt warm even through his clothes. Ansgar could sense the blood throbbing in her veins. But this was Celia, he couldn't feed on her, he had to remember that. He had to remember that. He was scared that he would forget.

As he removed his shoes, he realised he wasn't wearing a coat. He didn't really get cold outside, but his body was always freezing. He should take better care to stay warm, it kept the ingested blood circulating a little longer. Not that he'd ever cared about measures like that in the past. Not too long ago, he still used to feed whenever he got hungry.

"Just go right on through, I'm going to make a quick call to let him know I found you. I bet he's out there looking for you right now."

Ansgar didn't know of whom she was talking about, but he didn't want to give himself away by asking. Instead, he went into the living room, surprised that he knew which door to pick. He wanted to sit down, let his weary body rest for a while, but a sudden sense of dread forced him to stay upright and alert.

He looked around the room. The place seemed entirely unfamiliar to him. A large bookshelf covered most of the left wall, the blinds in front of the windows were shut. There were two dark grey couches, a large wooden desk and a sideboard with framed photographs on it.

He'd never been here before. He had no idea how he'd ended up in this place. He felt trapped. He had to leave this stranger's home, but first he had to find out what he was doing here to begin with. There had to be a reason why he was in this room right now. Someone had to have invited him in.

He went over to the bookshelf and scanned the titles, hoping they'd give away some clues about their owner. Most of the volumes seemed to be about European folklore, at least two of the books were exclusively about his kind. He had to lean in closely to read the titles on the spine.

Maybe he'd been captured by a hunter. He didn't know why else someone would put in all that research. If this house really belonged to a hunter, it meant he was in danger.

Listening closely to make sure he was still alone, he went over to the window. He heard footsteps in the other room, but they sounded light. The only other person in the house had to be rather light, so they probably didn't pose a serious threat to him, and they weren't wearing any shoes.

He considered climbing out through the window. Using the door might be too dangerous; his captor would expect that. But he could probably make it out through the window.

He opened it, only to be faced with the closed blinds. He tried to push them open, but they were shut tight. There was no string or anything similar to pull them up. It had to be the house of a hunter. Who else would barricade their windows like that? Or maybe it belonged to another creature of the night, who had sealed their home shut to keep out the sunlight. He liked the idea. If his memory ever let him down so much that he forgot he had to stay out of the sun, he could just lock himself in. But it hadn't come to that yet; his mind was still sharp enough. In the meantime, he'd have to find another way out of here.

Leaving the window open, he crossed over to the sideboard.

If there was another night creature living in this house, that didn't necessarily mean he was safe, either. They usually stayed out of each other's way and didn't engage in fights, but there were always exceptions. Some creatures defended their hunting grounds. If too many humans disappeared within the same area, it raised suspicion and created an unnecessary risk of being found out. Killing the competition was the obvious solution to that problem, and he was easy prey these days, feeling disoriented most of the time.

He scanned the photographs on display. Most of them were family pictures, showing a man who looked vaguely familiar and a girl with curly hair. A few of the photographs showed a woman too, but in the majority of them, it was just the man and the girl. He wondered if he'd ever seen these people before. They had to be the inhabitants of this house.

"Ansgar, what are you doing? Just sit down."

He turned around, feeling caught. The girl with the curly hair had entered the room; she just looked older than in the pictures. Ansgar now remembered that she was the one who had driven him here. He even knew her name, though his mind was temporarily drawing a blank.

She went over to the window to close it.

"How are you feeling?"

"Good," he said, trying to keep it vague. He couldn't let her know what was really going on, how much he was struggling to remember the context of this situation. But he was convinced that he would be able to fool her as long as they kept their conversation superficial.

"I know you need to feed," she admitted.

Ansgar tried not to let his instant panic show on his face. She knew he had to feed, which meant she had to know what he was. But she didn't seem scared, and that wasn't right. Her heart should be racing, being alone in this big house with a killer like him. She either trusted him for a reason he couldn't recall, or she was up to something. Maybe backup was on the way, maybe she was a trained hunter and kept a wooden stake hidden under her shirt, ready to end him as soon as he let his guard down. Her clothes seemed too tightly fitted to hide any weapons, but that might be a trick to lure him into a false sense of security.

She had to be human. The smell of her blood was strong.

The girl stepped towards him and placed her hand on his shoulder again to guide him over to the couch. She touched him as if she wasn't scared of getting close to him at all. Her pulse created a throbbing sound pounding in his ears. He couldn't block it out.

He felt scared because he didn't know what was going on. If he drained her, the confusion would subside. He was so hungry, his body felt hollow. The space beneath his ribs seemed to be completely empty, as if no flesh and no organs and no blood were filling it at all.

"Just sit down. You look exhausted."

Ansgar felt as if she was trying to lure him in. He was indeed tired, but he couldn't just give in to that weariness. He couldn't just let himself relax and take down his defences. He had to stay alert for a potential attack. Being a creature of the night wasn't easy. Everyone was out to get you all the time, everyone feared you, everyone wanted revenge.

He sat down despite himself. The couch was soft, and it seemed easy to just sink into it. It felt like just another trick. He tried to keep his eyes on the room, but his vision was too hazy, so he listened closely to make up for it. There were these godforsaken cars driving by on the streets, the overall noise of the city making it hard for him to focus on anything specific.

The girl sat down on the other couch, watching him attentively. He wondered what she was doing up around this time of night, anyway. But humans these days never slept. Back when he'd first been turned, people worked out in the field all day. They needed the daylight and adjusted their sleeping schedule to it. With these electric lights everywhere, everything was turning into a mess, upsetting everyone's natural rhythm. Maybe that was why his vision was so poor, his eyes were constantly strained. He wondered if the girl was tired. There were shadows around her eyes, but it rather looked like they had been painted on with coal, like the women who sold themselves on the streets.

"What were you doing out anyway?" she asked, clearly worried. He hadn't been supposed to be out, that was good to know. He could work with that. Maybe she had indeed tried to lock him up and he had managed to escape. Maybe he'd just been captured again. "You are lucky I was out with Imani tonight, otherwise I wouldn't have found you."

She pronounced the name as if she was talking about a person he was supposed to know. Imani sounded foreign to him. He couldn't imagine knowing a person with such a name.

"I was hungry," he said. His voice still sounded dry and cracked, like it hadn't been used in centuries. Someone had called him old today already. A kid on the street, they had called him an old bum. He had to seem old. He felt old. The hunger made him age. He hadn't been thirty yet when he had been turned, or at least that was what he assumed. Back then, no one had kept track of their age all that accurately.

The girl winced slightly. It was rather a sharp inhale, but he could hear it clearly anyway, as if she was breathing straight into his ear. He wished she would have told him her name.

"You can't feed in the immediate neighbourhood," she pointed out, as if that was another thing he was supposed to remember. "And you know we have been looking for someone. I'm sure we'll find the right person soon."

"Looking for someone?" he inquired. He couldn't let that one slide, not if it was about feeding. He needed to feed.

"Yes, you know, a bad person. Or someone who is about to die soon anyway. Like a cancer patient or something. We agreed on that, remember?"

He frowned, trying to recall if they had ever talked about such things before. All he could think about was how bad a cancer patient would taste. It wasn't just the sickness that spoiled the taste, but also the medication. He must have drunk from a person dying like that before. He remembered the taste, stale and artificial, blood that had lost all its flavour, because it was barely alive anymore.

"An ill person will be missed just as much," he said. He pictured sneaking into a hospital to drain someone in the ER. There would be doctors and nurses and patients and relatives and the corpse would be sent to autopsy straight away, raising questions. He was quite sure he'd done it before, or he wouldn't be able to picture all the obstacles so clearly.

"I mean for moral reasons," Celia said. He couldn't really see her face. He didn't like it when it was this plastered with makeup anyway. But he could hear her nails on her bare skin as she scratched her elbow. The gesture was nervous, uncomfortable. Her blood smelled a little sharper now. "It wouldn't be so bad to kill if the person was dying anyway. We agreed on that. Don't you remember?"

Ansgar did remember it now: the experiments with blood bags, that got him sick, and the draining of living animals that had made his stomach churn while he vomited gushes of blood, all in the name of a moral conduct. He had done it for their sake, to appease the two of them, and because he'd hoped that it would make things easier. There was no risk of getting caught, if no one went missing, if there were no dead bodies to be found. But it simply didn't seem feasible. Night creatures like him just couldn't survive on substitutes, they needed the blood of humans to stay alive.

He could have chosen his own death time and time again, could have starved himself, walked out into the sun or taken a stake to the heart. But the truth was that Ansgar didn't want to. He wanted to live, and he only went along with schemes like these to be liked, to receive help, because it was difficult to survive on his own nowadays. Not just because of the troubles with feeding, but because he needed money and he needed papers to rent a place or to do literally anything.

During the war, he had fed freely. The years right after being turned had been the most blissful ones of his existence. Mercenaries went missing all the time, whole villages were slaughtered. Sometimes, he had fed up to three or four times a night to satisfy his hunger. It hadn't just been a means of survival; it had been a source of pleasure. Even the blood had tasted richer back then.

The memory caused his stomach to stir. Maybe he could sneak out again after Celia had gone to sleep. She was human. She would have to sleep eventually. But her upright posture indicated that she would stay with him until Richard came home. They pretended to be helpful, but really, they were keeping him in check, forcing him to keep his violent nature under control to soothe their fragile human conscience. In a way, they were indeed keeping him trapped.

"Of course, right, I wouldn't just want to kill at random," he said, just to pacify her. "Do you remember the last time I fed? I've lost track."

Her heart rate slowed down again. He seemed to have chosen the right words to calm her.

"It hasn't been quite two weeks or so since the last time, I think." Her voice was strained again. She wasn't nervous, but the memory was unpleasant to her. Ansgar couldn't recall what had happened. He couldn't recall how exactly he knew Celia either, he just knew they were acquainted. "That homeless guy. It was needed."

So he had killed someone not because they were dying anyway, but because they most likely wouldn't be missed. The plan to find him morally suitable victims didn't seem to be going well. Ansgar had no recollection of draining a homeless guy whatsoever.

"Two weeks," he repeated. That wasn't nearly long enough. He shouldn't be feeling this starved after only two weeks. During the 18th century, he had experimented with dry spells and gotten up to about six weeks. Usually, he feasted about twice a week. He wasn't sure if it was necessary, or if he just lacked self-control. He had never liked to deny himself anything, and he wasn't very good at it. Since his kind kept to themselves, he didn't know other night creatures he could ask for their experiences. They kept their distance from each other, so as not to compromise their hunting grounds.

"Just a little while longer, it will be alright," Celia soothed him.

Ansgar turned his head to look around the room. He had trouble seeing as far as the opposite wall and it bothered him that he couldn't inspect the space properly. It made him feel unsafe not to know his surroundings precisely. He didn't like new places at all.

"I should probably head home soon," he said. "Before the sun comes up."

Not that he'd know where to go. He vaguely remembered a mid-century style house; he just didn't know how to find it. He wasn't quite sure which year it was, either.

"Ansgar," the girl said softly. She seemed to be playing on time. Apparently, she didn't want him to leave. "You're staying here with us. You are home."

"No," he said firmly. She seemed to believe he was that far gone already, but he had to make it clear that she couldn't just tell him anything. He knew that he'd never been to this house before. "I'm going home."

"But you are home. Look around you. You've lived here for the past fifteen years."

It was obviously a trick, but he looked around the room anyway to see if anything seemed familiar. Only now did he notice that there were photographs put up on a sideboard close by. The people in the pictures were strangers to him. Naturally, Ansgar himself wasn't in any of the photos since his reflection couldn't be caught on camera. Still, you'd think that during those fifteen years he'd have left his traces around the house, and yet, everything looked entirely unfamiliar to him.

But there had to be a reason why the girl wanted him to stay. As soon as the sun came up, he'd be trapped inside this building at least until nighttime. Even now he was still stronger than the average human being, but during the day he was practically defenceless. If she had backup, they might be able to overpower him during the day, since he couldn't flee anywhere. He had to get out of the house before dawn, just to make absolutely certain he wouldn't get caught.

He could defeat this child without lifting a finger. He'd have to prevent her from alarming someone after he left, though, and he also needed to feed to remember where to go, or at least clear his mind enough to find a hiding spot before sunrise. All it would take was draining her, and his problems would solve themselves. It was so simple.

Yet there was the faint possibility that she wasn't lying to confuse him. His memory had gotten worse recently, and the past couple of years might very well have slipped his mind. What were a few years in the grand scheme of things, anyway? A decade or two could go missing occasionally. She might be someone he cared for, maybe even someone he loved. Immortality was lonely. He had grown to care about humans before, though only in the way one grew fond of a pet. You might get attached, but you always expected them to be gone before you.

He couldn't risk killing someone dear to him, and he couldn't risk getting stuck in this house during the day. It was a stalemate.

He imagined sinking his teeth into her neck. It wasn't as aesthetic as people believed it to be. Back in his childhood, they had still known, they had still feared his kind; the night creatures hadn't been romanticised yet. He'd rip the flesh right off in a large chunk, opening the luscious vein. The thick, white scars on his own neck were still visible even to this day. The blood would splash into his mouth as he cupped the open wound. He didn't like the expression of sucking blood since it got the process all wrong, in his experience. All you had to do was swallow because the heart kept pumping the blood through the veins and each beat provided another gush that you only had to drink up. Eventually, the heartbeat would slow down and you had to be careful to find just the right moment to stop feeding. If you drank from a lifeless body, you'd get sick, awfully sick. But if you stopped too soon and there was still a spark of life left inside of them, you risked them coming back, stronger and most likely angry. Ansgar had always prided himself on his perfect timing.

His entire body clenched with need as he thought about the blood filling his mouth. The girl smelled so inviting, and after all, what did it matter? If a pet died, you could always get yourself a new one.

"I want to go home," he repeated, still hoping she would just let him go. If she did, she probably had his best interest at heart and it was better not to kill her. He could find someone on the street. He'd walked past a delicious group of kids earlier. They had called after him aggressively, even though he didn't remember what it was that they had said. They probably deserved to die. "And I need to feed. I'm starving."

The girl shook her head. He heard the rustling of jewellery around her neck. He wondered if she was wearing a crucifix to protect herself. People used to do that. The best crosses were made out of silver, offering protection against his kind and other kinds.

"You are not starving. You lasted for almost three weeks the last time around."

Now Ansgar knew that she was lying to him. Six weeks, he had managed to last up to six weeks before, he knew that for a fact. He had experimented with starvation somewhere during the 18th century. He couldn't figure out why the girl was lying to him about this. Or could it be that age was wearing him down and he needed to feed more often to maintain his strength? Or maybe it hadn't been six weeks in the first place.

If she was trying to confuse him, it was working. He felt very insecure. Maybe he remembered incorrectly. The 18th century had been quite a while ago. He needed to feed badly. He needed to clear this fog that was obscuring his thoughts.

"Maybe you want to lie down, go to sleep already. You could save your energy that way. I'll take you down to the basement, to your room."

So the basement was where she wanted to lure him. He was quite certain that he'd never been to this house's basement. He hadn't even known there was a basement. Clearly, she was up to something. Maybe there was someone waiting for him down there, wooden stake already in their hand. He couldn't hear anything, but the city noise floating in from the streets made it hard to pick up specific sounds.

"I'd rather not," he said. Even if her suggestion was genuine, he couldn't risk going to sleep this early during the night. It would mess with his entire sleep schedule. He might wake up during the day and in one of these recurring moments of disorientation, he might just walk outside, unaware of the hour. He might end up burning himself alive.

"Sure, we can also just sit here and talk," the girl agreed. Her voice sounded a little strained, but it could have been simply because she was tired.

"You can go to sleep," Ansgar suggested. "I'll keep myself company." It was smart of him to act so casual. If she believed he could be trusted, she might just go to bed, offering him the chance to escape. He could kill a random person on the street, drinking up their richly flavoured blood. He'd just leave the body on the sidewalk. At this point, he had already stopped caring. Even if he was a bit careless, what were the odds of him getting caught, really? It wasn't like people nowadays knew what to look for. They would try to pin it on a freaky serial killer before they consider the obvious.

"No, really, it's no trouble. I'm not tired anyway. And I enjoy talking to you." She was slurring the words towards the end of the sentence, barely audible for the human ear. She was lying. She didn't want to leave him unobserved. Yet her blood still smelled sweet, not panicked, not frightened. Humans tasted best when they didn't see it coming.

"You know what I am, don't you, kid?" Although he couldn't recall the girl's name at the moment, he felt a certain kind of fondness towards her that he couldn't explain rationally. Whatever their relationship was, he felt that his feelings towards her were positive. He felt like he needed to warn her. "They have a name for us in pretty much every language, and they all sound similar. Vampire, Vampir, Vampyr, that's what they called us in der alten Heimat. It's surprising they forgot the truth to a myth that was so popular. They still talk about us today, but no one believes the stories anymore."

He tossed the old word around in his mind - Vampyr. It made him feel nostalgic.

"My mother always warned me to not stay out after dark. Bei Sonnenuntergang you had to be home. People still knew that. They knew it was dangerous to stay out in the dark. We had a lot of forests. Everything is different nowadays. Everything looks different."

It felt good to get the words out. His memory stretched back so far, he knew so many things that he had to share with the world, he could enrich the lives of everyone around him. Oh, the stories he had to tell.

The girl seemed unimpressed. She nodded, making her curls bob.

"Yes, I know that, Ansgar. You've told me about your childhood in Germany before, many times, remember?"

That couldn't be true; the memories had only been resurfacing recently. The images were vividly clear, they had come back to him as he'd wandered through the city tonight. He remembered the uneven ground of unpaved roads beneath his feet and how quiet the world had been at night. He could still recall the smells, too.

"Then came the war. It was a delicious time. There were rivers of blood. Everything was in bloom because the earth was soaked with blood. Battlefields had the best soil because of all the rotting flesh, but they only benefitted from that years later. That's the natural course of things, you know? Blut ist Leben. It keeps us all alive, you and me and the earth we walk on. The world was beautiful back then."

Her blood smelled different now, slightly more unpleasant. It wasn't the smell of fear, not yet, but his words seemed to be making her uncomfortable. Humans didn't like to think about death, even though it was so close for them at all times, with their lifespan this short.

"There were difficult times as well, of course," he carried on.

It was nice to delve into these memories after such a long time, realising how clearly he still recalled them. Battles were usually fought during the day when he hid out in the woods, but the whole country had been filled with an atmosphere of violence. People had been scared and angry, their blood was constantly heated and it had made him hungry all the time. His stomach had been like a deep pit that couldn't be filled fast enough. And no one had cared for a few more dead bodies on the roadside. He'd fed freely several times a night.

"The religious days were hard on my kind, you know?"

The girl didn't try to interrupt him. She just nodded and leaned further into the cushions of the couch, as if she was mentally tuning out. It made him angry, but he tried not to pay it any mind. The memories were distracting him from the hunger hollowing him out.

"Everyone still listened to what the church said. People knew their prayers and wore their crucifixes. We were feared, but the superstitions also had their disadvantages. Today, no one bothers to protect themselves anymore, but things were different back then. It was somewhere during the 17th century that people started leaving the country, so I decided to join them. I thought there'd be more freedom here. That people would be less wary of the old night creatures, the Vampyre and Werwölfe and Hexen. But it wasn't easy here, no, it wasn't easy here either."

He paused, trying to gather his thoughts for a moment. He remembered the ship and how troublesome it had been to hide under deck during the day. It had smelled awful down there, too, and the waves had created a deafening noise when they splashed against the hull.

There were more memories related to his early days in America, but he wasn't sure if those dated all the way back to his arrival or had taken place sometime later. At first, he'd had trouble with the language. It took him a long time to learn, since he rarely conversed with anyone. The nights had still been quiet, too, back then.

"I was rich, for a while," he said. He remembered a fancy house, and a maid who was only allowed in at night so she wouldn't snoop around while he was asleep and defenceless. These had to have been the very early days in the new country.

He remembered killing someone on the ship, a wealthy gentleman travelling alone who looked similar enough to him in age. He'd tossed his drained body over the railing into the dark sea at night. He'd taken his papers to register upon his arrival and had spent his money as his own.

"I had a beautiful home. I wore the fanciest clothes. I had a tailor come to my house at night. Nobody cared I was being extravagant. With money, you can do anything."

Prior to that, he'd run around in rags for years, unable to walk into a shop during the daytime and therefore being forced to live with the ill-fitted clothes he stole from the dead.

"But the money ran out eventually. Quite fast, actually."

He could have been a little more frugal, but he'd never been the type to deny himself anything. And people would have wondered why he didn't seem to age after a decade or two, anyway.

"I moved around the country a lot. I've seen most of it by now, different states, different landscapes. I don't like the cities much, but they offer more food. I've seen a lot of cities by now."

It shocked him to realise that he couldn't remember most of them clearly. He still remembered the travelling, remembered it like a tale from his childhood that'd been told to him over and over again until it felt like something he could actually visualise himself even though he'd still been too young to recall it properly. He still remembered the story of his life, but the places that belonged to it were mostly gone.

It filled him with panic, made him feel helpless, and he hurriedly continued talking. He had to focus on the things that he did remember, these were the important things. He had to retell them to himself, so they wouldn't slip away like the rest of his memories.

"I killed people and took over their identities, living their lives for a while before moving on. It's hard to do that nowadays, there's all these papers you need to identify yourself with. And corpses get identified so easily, too. Back in the day, you could just leave them in a ditch and no one would find out who they'd once been. Sometimes it was bachelors, sometimes I just killed the whole family, the wife and kids. Sometimes the grandparents, too."

He only became aware of the girl again because the smell in the room changed. For a moment, he had forgotten that he wasn't just talking to himself. There was a sharp, almost spicy edge to the smell of her blood now, as if the story was starting to scare her after all.

He wondered why he was even telling her all of this. He'd never been one to toy with his food, and the way it was going, he was only about to spoil the taste of her blood.

"I had a family of my own for a while, too." A very hazy memory flashed up in his mind. There had been a woman, that much was for sure. He couldn't recall her face. He didn't know if she'd been one of his kind and if not, why he hadn't turned her. "I had a wife."

"Clarissa," the girl said.

The name sounded familiar. He still couldn't recall the face that belonged to it, but there was a sharp pain inside his chest, as if someone had staked him but missed the heart by just a few centimeters.

The girl shouldn't know that name. That name was something private and hidden, something that belonged only to him. He couldn't imagine sharing it with anyone.

"How do you know that name?" He spoke sharply, expecting his voice to scare the girl, but instead she seemed to calm down. The cushions on the couch rustled as she leaned forward, getting even closer to him as if she was completely unaware of the danger she was in.

"You've told me about her. Your wife, Clarissa. She was a seamstress. She came to your place at night to take your measurements. You were surprised that it wasn't a man. You only knew her last name then. Don't you remember? You used to tell me that story all the time when I was younger. She had dark hair and blue eyes."

He shook his head, trying to fight off her words. They were too precise. It sounded like something he was supposed to remember, and yet his mind couldn't quite catch up as she spoke. He remembered a pair of blue eyes, but that was all. The rest of the story was completely new to him.

"You shouldn't know about that," he said. "No one can know about that."

He would never have shared these precious memories with anyone. They kept escaping even him by now, so this complete stranger shouldn't possess them. She'd obviously found out about his past another way. She must have looked into it, tracked him down with her research somehow, and then lured him here. She was the enemy, probably a hunter, and she'd just given herself away.

"It's alright, Ansgar," she said and for a moment he thought she would reach out to touch him again. Her hand lingered right above his knee for a moment, and he could sense the heat her body radiated, but she changed her mind at the last second, either to not startle him, or because leaning over that far would have been awkward for her. "You told me those things. We're friends. We're your friends, Ansgar."

He tried to settle down and make himself comfortable again. He'd tensed up, his canine teeth sharply digging into his lower lip. He always became more aware of them when he was hungry.

Maybe she was speaking the truth. If she knew things this personal about him, it might be because he'd trusted her enough to share them. Maybe she was his friend after all. The memory lapses were making him paranoid. In all these past centuries, no one had ever tracked him down. A hunter who had stumbled across him through dumb luck had tried to kill him once, but Ansgar had snapped his neck before he'd even had time to draw his stake. He couldn't recall during which century that had been.

"You are right," he mumbled. "I must have told you about Clarissa. She was very beautiful, wasn't she?"

Even though he couldn't picture her face, he had this vague feeling that he'd loved her more than he had ever loved anyone else. She must have been beautiful to him.

He remembered another girl from his hometown; fair-haired and young, someone he had planned to marry before he'd been turned. But the memories of that time were mostly overshadowed by the taste of blood. The experience of feasting every night had been so ecstatic, it had overwritten most other recollections from that time period.

"She was, you always said that, too." Celia nodded and suppressed a yawn. He suddenly felt a little worried about her. Humans weren't supposed to stay up this late.

"You should go to sleep soon, Cee," he said. She smiled a little at the nickname, although he had just chosen to shorten it instinctively.

"It's fine. I might make myself a coffee though, if you promise to stay put."

"Where would I go?"

He gestured across the room to indicate that he was right where he was supposed to be, but the sight only filled him with dread. It all looked so strange. He knew that he'd been here before, he simply knew it. Yet he couldn't recall anything about the house. It was scary to lose orientation like this. He really didn't know where he would go if he managed to leave. He didn't know where he was. If he stepped out the door, everything would look alien again. And there were people out to get him. It wasn't easy when you were a creature of the night. You were always hated for the lives you took.

"Alright, I'll be right back."

The girl got up from the couch and walked over to the door. Her footsteps sounded light on the floorboards. Only now did he notice that she wasn't wearing shoes.

He watched her form from behind. Her scent still hung heavily in the air. There was a hint of sweat and perfume and alcohol on her skin, but compared to the smell of her blood, it was hardly noticeable.

He didn't understand why she was leaving him. He didn't want to be alone. This room was so unfamiliar, and he might forget about her as soon as she was out of sight. Besides, it was dangerous out there. You couldn't just go outside.

"Geh nicht," he said. She stopped short in the doorway and turned back to him, seemingly confused. "Es ist gefährlich. Es ist doch Krieg. Draußen ist Krieg. Krieg." He repeated the word urgently, hoping that she would understand. There was a word for it in another language that she would understand for sure. Another word in English, but he'd had a hard time learning that language to begin with. It hadn't been that long since he had left his homeland. The trip had been awful. All that bad smell below deck and the sound of the crashing waves. He remembered it so vividly, it couldn't have been long ago.

"War," he finally said, his tongue nearly stumbling over the word. The first letter sounded too harsh coming out of his mouth, he couldn't get it to sound soft enough. Krieg was a better word. It sounded more like the thing it was referring to. "There's a war outside."

"The war is over, Ansgar," the girl said. The name Ansgar sounded familiar. It was what his mother used to call him. "It's been over for a long time already."

But he knew something that the girl hadn't learned yet because she was still too young. War was never just over, it kept coming back in waves, switched on and off like a defective device. There was always a war going on somewhere.

"Be careful, Clarissa," he begged. He wasn't sure if that was her name, but it had to be. It sat on his tongue loosely, as if he had used it countless times before. They knew each other, didn't they?

"Celia," she corrected him gently.

"Celia," he repeated and nodded as if he had known that all along. He was pretty sure that he'd never heard the name Celia before.

"I'll be careful. I'm just going to make myself a cup of coffee. I'll be right back."

She left the room and Ansgar wondered if she was about to get her backup. They would come back as a group to attack him. Even though she had seemed friendly enough, he knew the truth. And he knew that everyone hated him, that everyone wanted him to pay for what he'd done. He had killed so many people. He didn't remember any of their names.

He got up from the couch, feeling restless. He wasn't sure how he had ended up in this house. This wasn't his place. Someone must have taken him here. Someone must have invited him in.

He could leave through the door, but there were footsteps in the next room. He could hear them loudly and clearly, although they were light as if the person walking around was barefoot. It would be safer to make his way out through the window. At least he should check if it was possible to open the blinds.

Even just walking the short distance over to the window exhausted him. His body felt so weak, he probably hadn't fed in weeks. It was so difficult to hunt without being caught these days, but he was about to reach the point where he would stop caring about safety altogether. He needed blood. He needed to fight off this tiredness and this constant headache, because it was so bright everywhere, even at night, and he needed to get his memory back on track. Every recollection felt jumbled and confusing. Sometimes he recalled events without being able to place them within the time frame of his life at all. The war might have been recent.

He reached out to open the window, but stopped short, because the footsteps were getting louder behind him. Not only that, but the smell of blood grew stronger too. It wasn't the sharp smell of someone who was scared, it was the sweet scent of someone completely at ease. Apparently, he wouldn't have to go out to eat. There was food in the house.

He spun around.

A girl was standing in the doorway. Her curly hair made her head look much bigger than it was. She was holding a steaming mug. The smell of coffee mixed in with the smell of blood, but it was much fainter. He was so hungry, the space beneath his ribs felt hollow. His headache was turning into a throbbing pain that seemed to match a pulse he didn't have.

"What are you …?"

She didn't even finish the sentence before he was already at her side. He felt extremely weak, but his movements were still faster than that of any human being.

He grabbed her upper arm to hold her in place and reached into her curly hair with the other hand. His hands looked like claws, not in the way that an animal had claws, but the way old people's hands turned weirdly bony. The flesh seemed to have melted off his bones, making them look skinny and his fingers too long and thin in proportion. His veins stood out visibly, as if the only blood left in his body was too thick and flowing too slowly.

Her curls felt soft on his skin. He could smell her body underneath the scent of blood more clearly up close. Chemicals in her hair, sweat on her neck, cigarettes on her shirt, as if someone had blown smoke in her direction earlier tonight.

He yanked her head back by the hair, forcing her to expose her throat. She was tall, he barely had to lean down to access her neck. People had been shorter when he'd still been alive.

She shrieked with pain, and something shattered on the floor. The smell of coffee intensified, as if she had set it free by dropping the mug.

Things had happened so fast, she must have been feeling disoriented still, because the smell of her blood had hardly changed yet. Her heart was racing, so loudly he could practically feel her pulse vibrating in the air, but she hadn't grown scared yet. It had happened too fast for her to realise she was in danger.

Ansgar had never been one to relish the moment. He assumed that some vampires liked to drag it out, play with their food and raise the anticipation as their victim's heartbeat became quicker and quicker. But he had never enjoyed their fear, only the taste of their blood.

The girl whimpered, reminding him that he was holding on to an actual person who might start fighting back any time. For a moment, she had turned into nothing but a blood-filled vessel to him. He didn't remember how she had gotten into his arms, how he had come across her or where he was in the first place. The hunger was so all-consuming that the hollow sensation took over his entire body, leaving no room for thought.

He bared his fangs and sunk them into the girl's throat. The skin there was soft. It had always struck him as a design flaw that the thick veins inside the human body were not better protected, but instead ran so close to the surface.

He tore away again, his teeth cutting through the skin and tendons and muscles, ripping out a large chunk of flesh. Blood started gushing from the tattered wound immediately, streaming down her shoulder and soaking her dark shirt. The metallic smell was dizzyingly strong.

Not wanting to waste any more of the precious liquid, he pressed his mouth to the hole in her neck, letting the blood flood his mouth. The first gulp was heavenly. He'd been abstinent for far too long; it must have been weeks. The room around them disappeared, he was completely absorbed in the taste. Just as he had imagined, her blood was sweet.

The girl was screaming. That part was always ugly. He wanted to cover her mouthbut decided to keep his hand in her hair to hold her steady instead. She started struggling, but her movements were already becoming less energetic, and he was much stronger than her to begin with.

The blood was so hot that he felt it streaming down his throat and filling his stomach with a warm sensation. He was already regaining strength, the pain in his joints disappearing and the throbbing in his head beginning to cease.

The girl, on the other hand, was rapidly weakening. The whole process of feeding rarely took more than a few minutes. She leaned onto him more heavily, he could feel her full weight against himself. It was always awkward to drain someone while they were standing, he remembered that now. He'd had the presence of mind to kick the knees of the homeless guy he had drained last week, so he had fallen down before Ansgar had gone for his neck. He had dragged his body into a narrow side street and covered him with a dirty blanket, so it looked as if he'd died of hypothermia or malnutrition or something else that no one would feel compelled to look into any further. That had been good thinking on his part.

The girl's legs gave out, and since he was only grabbing her by the arm, he couldn't hold her upright in spite of his renewed physical strength. He tried to guide her body so that she fell to the side, his mouth glued to her neck the whole time. He didn't want to waste another drop; she was almost fully drained anyway. He could hear her heartbeat slowing down significantly already. It was easier to filter the sounds now, he could tune out the noises flowing in from the street, focusing only on what he needed to know.

He had sunk to his knees beside the girl, his motions fluent and precise again. He bent over her body; the blood being pumped into his mouth more slowly now.

He brushed back her hair that was getting into the way, tickling his face. The dark curls reminded him of Celia.

He swallowed again. When he'd first been turned, he'd had trouble with that. Swallowing while keeping your mouth pressed to an open wound that kept oozing blood wasn't an easy task; it took practice. His chin and his clothes had always been drenched in blood, but during the long war, no one had cared. Those had been the dark days. He had lived like an animal, feeding several times a night because he'd had no self-control yet, killing without a second thought even when he didn't have to. He felt disgusted with this inhuman night creature he'd once been, that didn't even deserve to be called a person.

The girl's heartbeat was very faint now. A few seconds more only, another two or three heartbeats and he'd have to pull back before it could turn him sick.

The curls brushed his forehead again and he wanted to push them down when a frightening apprehension spread through him. He needed to pull back, but he didn't want to. He didn't want to look up and see her face. He wasn't prepared for what he might find.

Her heart stopped beating.

He swallowed one last time, knowing instantly that he would regret it.

Ansgar released her neck from his lips, keeping his eyes downcast. All he saw was her hair. It looked painfully familiar, those dark curls, now partially sticky with spilled blood. But he couldn't have done that, he simply couldn't have. Sure, he was getting a little forgetful, but he wouldn't have forgotten something this important.

He sat up and looked into Celia's face. She was pale in death, completely drained of blood. The dark eyeliner stood out even more sharply in contrast to her ensanguined skin. Her neck and shoulder were completely covered in blood though. A small puddle was forming beneath her body, where it was still dripping from the wound, now smelling stale and unappealing to him. The blood on the floor was mixing with coffee that someone had spilled earlier.

He started gagging, his stomach cramping painfully. He couldn't tell if it was because of the realisation of what he had done or because of the mouthful of lifeless blood he had accidentally swallowed. It hadn't been enough to poison him, just enough to make him feel sick.

Still retching he spit out onto the floor, the splatters looking darker than the rest of the puddle, as if his body had somehow transformed the blood into something else already, something that was no longer life-giving but toxic and deadly.

He tried to breathe through his nose to calm himself, but it only made him very aware of the smell in the air. The rotten, spoiled smell turned his stomach even more.

"Celia," he said and touched her shoulder. Her body was cold. Usually, it took a while for corpses to cool down, but with most of their blood drained, the process was sped up. His own skin felt warm for the first time tonight. "Cee."

He listened for a heartbeat, hoping that he hadn't quite finished the job, although he already knew better. After all, he wasn't an amateur. But he still hoped that she might come back, even though he didn't wish that on her. It was a horrible life, lonely, and filled with self-loathing. He had to live with all the things he'd done. Now he'd have to live with this, too. If he wasn't so cowardly, he'd have ended things a long time ago. But he had killed so many people already, one more death never really seemed to add to the guilt all that much. Some deaths were more painful than others, though.

He'd seen Celia grow up. She'd been twelve years old when Richard had found him. He'd been working on his post-doctoral thesis; his wife had already died, of a cause completely devoid of the supernatural. Ansgar had been struggling to find his footing in this modern age, although his memory loss hadn't become an issue yet. He'd told Celia bedtime stories every evening after getting up. In summer, when the sun set late, she'd always stayed up past her bedtime to listen to one of his stories. His life had been long, he'd had a lot to tell. He'd always left out the gruesome parts, his stories had never been about the killing, never about the war.

"I'm sorry," he whispered, brushing the curls from her face one last time. He wanted to memorise her face. He wanted it to be one of the few things he wouldn't forget. She had trusted him so much, she hadn't even worn the crucifix Richard had given her a while ago, just in case. Maybe she had only taken it off for the club tonight. Her favourite colour had been green, and she had always drunk her tea with milk in it, although that wasn't very common in this country. As a teenager, she had played the guitar for exactly 65 days before giving up again. She had loved winter and reality tv, maybe because Richard had never allowed her to watch it growing up. Her favourite song had been "Thriller", mostly because her mother had loved it too. Soon, Ansgar would forget about all of this. Even if he kept feeding to preserve his memory, all the little details would disappear over time, just like they always did. If you lived long enough, every person you had once loved became just a name and a face at best, with all of their individuality erased by the relentless passing of time.

He needed to grieve Celia properly while he still could, but he would only find the leisure for it later. First, he had to get rid of the body.

Richard would be home soon. For all Ansgar knew, Richard had gone out to look for him. Since Celia had called him to let him know they were both home again, he was surely on his way back by now. It was the middle of the night, after all; he had nowhere else to be. Ansgar didn't know what Celia had told him about the state he was in, but there was a chance he'd be on his guard.

And Richard wasn't as unprepared as his daughter had been. He was a professor of European cultures, specialising in folklore and mythology. He'd researched and published about vampires; he knew all there was to know, and the things he hadn't found in his research, Ansgar had told him.

More than just a historian, Richard had been smart enough to keep an eye on local murder cases as well as digging through the library archives. He hadn't so much believed in vampires as he had tried to find the origins of the myth, assuming that some form of killing technique must have inspired the rumours of bloodsucking night creatures in the first place. With his research, he had intended to prove that the roots of these myths could still be found today, but that they didn't spark the same superstition anymore, since more scientific explanations could be given these days. What he'd found instead was Ansgar, and his sheer existence had proven his entire theory wrong.

Since the researcher in him had been too curious to keep his distance, he'd approached Ansgar. Upon realising how difficult it was for vampires to survive unseen in this day and age, he had taken him in, risking the life of his own daughter in search for answers. And he'd gotten his answers, late at night as they'd sat together and talked after Celia had gone to sleep. They'd discussed the myths from the old country and what the creatures of the night were really like. They'd talked about the war and the start of a new life here in America, they'd discussed love and loss and what it meant to be cursed to take lives just to stay alive yourself. More than once they'd stayed up all night, causing Richard to run late for his university lectures, and somewhere along the lines, they had become friends.

Richard had been the first person in a long time to show Ansgar any kindness. He was the living being who knew him best in this world, the closest and dearest friend he had.

Of course, Ansgar would have to kill him now.

He knew too much, knew too much about Ansgar himself and his species in general. He knew how to track him down, and he most certainly knew how to kill his kind. Ansgar had drained his daughter, the one person whose life he valued more than their friendship. He had let the other murders slide, though Ansgar knew that the knowledge had always tormented him, but he had accepted it as the price it took to secure his friend's survival. Celia, however, was a price too high to pay. And Ansgar wasn't in good shape. He remembered everything clearly now, and his thoughts stayed on track. But with the speed his memory had been declining lately, he'd have forgotten everything that had happened tonight within the span of a few days. He wouldn't remember that he was being hunted, which would make him easy prey. He needed to strike first, and he needed to do it quickly, before Richard could grow suspicious and before Ansgar could forget about the task at hand.

It pained him that he would have to kill his friend. It would haunt him for centuries to come, every time he'd manage to remember. But the equation was simple: Richard would have to die regardless, and Ansgar didn't. Richard had maybe about thirty years left. Ansgar could live forever, as long as he kept feeding. It didn't matter if it was a cancer patient or a young, healthy woman like Celia, every human being was destined to die eventually. Ansgar was just shortening their time on earth by a few decades and in the great scheme of things, a few decades weren't really all that much.

But he had to get to work. The place needed to be at least reasonably clean before Richard got home.

For a moment he considered what the best course of action would be in this case. He could drag Celia's body across the floor or lift her up in his arms. Carrying her wasn't a problem with his renewed physical strength, but it would definitely get bloodstains on his clothes. He debated whether it would be easier to change clothes or scrub the floor. He'd have to drag her all the way through the kitchen, too.

So he lifted her in a bridal carry instead. Her body was cold and stiff. The blood loss should have made her lighter, but she felt surprisingly heavy, with all the tension gone from her muscles. The weight didn't really bother him, but he could sense it in his arms like a reminder that she wasn't just a lifeless doll but a dead human being, made of flesh and organs and bones.

Ansgar carried her out of the living room and into the kitchen, where he had to put her down in order to open the door that led into the small garden. He would bury the corpses, both hers and Richard's. It definitely wasn't a great way to let a body disappear, but it would at least buy him some time. Unfortunately, their disappearance would be noticed soon. Someone would start looking for them when they didn't show up for work. That meant he wouldn't be able to stay here, which was a shame, because the house was very nice and it had been his home for many years. But it wouldn't feel the same without Celia and Richard here to keep him company, anyway.

He gently laid Celia's body down on the grass outside. Obviously, she couldn't feel anything anymore anyway, but he still believed that the dead deserved to be treated with dignity. In his early, barbaric days as a killer, he had just left his victims by the roadside like everyone else. But over the years he had learned to appreciate the gift of life they kept granting him. The least they deserved was his respect.

He'd still have to mutilate the corpse, though. He'd have to slice her throat, opening up the wound on her neck further and hope that no one would look into it too deeply. Nowadays, the forensic team would be able to tell the cut had been added postmortem, but it would offer an explanation at least for how she had bled out, though they might wonder where all the blood had disappeared to. No one would believe she'd been attacked by a wild animal within the safety of her own house. Or maybe they would believe that. Maybe that was what they would write into the report, because humans tended to find explanations for everything they didn't want to acknowledge.

But he'd get to the cutting and the burying later. First, he needed to clean the living room. Richard wouldn't check the garden when he came home, but he'd see the living room. The living room at least had to be clean.

Ansgar went back inside, closing the door behind him. He could still make out the body outside in the dark when looking through the window, but like most beasts of prey, he had extremely sharp eyes. Things weren't blurred anymore the way they'd been when he was hungry. The intervals at which he needed to feed were getting shorter and shorter; it was really quite worrying. He had been able to justify killing once a month to stay alive, but where was the line? When did one life stop being worth the lives of many others? Was it when you had to kill every week? Every night? Twice a night?

Not knowing where to find a bucket, he got out a large plastic salad bowl and filled it with water. He grabbed a sponge along with several towels. He'd cleaned away blood before, this time was hardly any different. In the past, he used to dispose of his victims' bodies, sanitise the crime scene and move into their homes.

Except this time, he felt sick. He wasn't sure if it was because of the mouthful of stale blood he had consumed, that was still circulating through his system, or if it was Celia's pale, dead face that kept haunting him.

Back when he used to kill people in their own homes, he hadn't experienced any moral scruples at all yet. He'd felt like he was just taking up his natural place in the food chain. Things had only changed when he met Clarissa.

She'd come to his house to take his measurements for a couple of suits he had meant to purchase. The maid he'd sent out with his special request for a tailor to come to his mansion at night had only mentioned a last name, and he'd expected a man, not the seamstress who had shown up instead. Women's businesses hadn't been all that established yet. But Clarissa hadn't cared much for convention, and she hadn't been afraid to come to his mansion alone at night in spite of what that might do to her reputation, or her life for that matter. Her eyes had been very blue. After the first night, she had kept making up excuses to return. And after the fourth night, they had stopped bothering with excuses altogether. Ansgar had known right away that he was in love with her.

They'd built a life together, with a lot of setbacks and plenty of moving around at first because of his reckless feeding habits, but he'd learned to keep his hunger in check for the sake of stability. The murders themselves had never bothered Clarissa too much; she was unconventional in many ways. She had been better with money than Ansgar, and eventually they had settled down in a nice house that was luxurious without being opulent. The townspeople had talked about the strange husband, who was never seen during the day, but Clarissa had always found enough excuses to keep the peace. They had never officially been married, since he couldn't enter a church nor receive a sacrament, but she had been his wife in every way that mattered. She had taught him what it meant to love a human being. He had watched her grow older and waste away quickly once she got sick. When he had offered to turn her, she had declined. Her death had been the first one he had truly mourned and the one that had taught him about the importance of human life. Because even if it was short, every moment of it mattered with the people you loved. That realisation was what had turned him from a mere night creature into something resembling an actual person.

He had already cut back on his feeding habits after he'd met Clarissa, simply because being reckless increased the risk of being discovered and ending up with a stake through the heart, and he didn't want to put her in danger by association. A stake through the heart killed humans, too. But after her death, he had gone from killing only once a week to holding out for up to two months. He had felt guilty for every life he took and tried to single out his victims more carefully. He'd targeted people who wouldn't be missed that much, old women without a family, men who beat their wives and children, known criminals who terrorised their surroundings. He'd tried to be better. He'd tried not to be a monster.

Ansgar went over to wipe the blood off the handle of the backdoor. He had left bloody handprints while unlocking it. He felt sick again, dizzy, almost as if he was still hungry, but he couldn't let that get the better of him now.

His memory loss was slowly turning him back into the compassionless night creature he had once been, monstrous and cruel, the thing he had never wanted to be again. He wasn't ageing backwards. Instead, he seemed to jump straight back to the beginning, as if time really was a circle, blurring together the end and the beginning.

But still, he couldn't let himself be killed, couldn't let Richard stake him or walk out into the sunlight. Because if he gave up now, it would turn all of his reasoning so far invalid. If he died now, all the people he had murdered would have died for nothing. He wouldn't have traded an inevitable death for eternal life, he'd only have sacrificed them all to selfishly delay the end of a monster. He had to stay alive to justify his own existence. He had to stay alive to honour the people he had already killed.

The only way to not become something unforgivable was to keep feeding often enough to stay in control so that at least he could choose his victims wisely. He'd have to kill more often, but it would be alright, if only he picked people who wouldn't be missed all that much. Celia had been a mistake. Celia was what happened if he didn't feed often enough.

There was blood on the kitchen floor too, even though he had carried her in his arms. It must have kept trickling down from her neck.

He knelt down to scrub the floor, following the trail of blood that led back to the living room. The police would still find traces of it if they investigated. They would be able to tell that Celia had been killed in the living room. Ansgar himself could still spot the stains where the floor had changed colour ever so slightly even after the blood had been wiped away. But he didn't have to fool the police, only Richard, with his inadequate human eyesight.

Once he reached the living room, the smell of dead blood hit him like a wave. It was unpleasantly metallic, and he wondered if Richard would be able to smell it, too. Ansgar was sensitive to the smell of blood, but he wasn't sure if it was as obvious to humans. The entire room seemed stuffy and heavy with it though, like red fog hanging in the air. It felt weirdly humid to him.

Ansgar fought down the urge to gag again. He couldn't vomit any more blood. He had to keep it down, so he would be able to keep functioning properly. If he lost too much of the freshly consumed blood, he'd grow weak again too soon and his memory would fail him once more.

He wiped up the blood, soaking the towel in his hand completely. He tried to wash it clean in the water, but the towel stayed red, and the water changed colour, too. He felt like he'd never get anything clean again, not this fabric, not this house, not his hands. He wondered how there was still so much blood when he had swallowed the majority of it.

His motions were turning frantic. Even if he got rid of the bloodstains everywhere, the smell would betray him. He'd have to open the window at least. He had to get rid of all the evidence. He tried not to think of Celia's laughter. Of how she'd leaned into him when he told her bedtime stories as a child, and how she had never hesitated to touch him. She was always quick to put her hand on his shoulder or take his hand in hers to guide him and calm him down when things had gotten more difficult recently. She'd never shied away from him, even though his skin was unpleasantly cold to the touch. She'd done it because she had loved him. Celia had been like a stepdaughter to him, the closest he had ever gotten to having a child in all these centuries.

He got up to open the window. He could still see the stains on the floor. The wood looked darker where the puddle had been, even though the floorboards were varnished and the blood shouldn't have soaked into them. If he focused hard enough, Ansgar could still make out the shape of a body on the ground.

With the window open, it was rapidly growing cold. Ansgar could sense the change in temperature more clearly with fresh blood circulating through his veins. He listened closely, now easily able to distinguish between the sounds around him. He had to stay alert for a car pulling into the driveway, but so far, all the cars were driving past in the next street over. Still, he knew Richard could be back any moment.

He went back to the kitchen to pour out the water. He left the soaked towels in the sink. Richard wouldn't check the kitchen sink. Why would he check the kitchen sink? The formerly white fabric was now stained red.

Ansgar needed to change out of his clothes. They were black, which made it easier to fade into the dark of night, and the blood wasn't all that visible, but you could still see the wet stains on the front of his shirt and even on his right thigh and his knees where he had knelt on the floor. It looked as if he'd bathed in blood.

He'd have to go down to the basement for a change of clothes, since that was where he kept his personal belongings. He went over to the door and down the creaking flight of stairs. He didn't bother to switch on the lights. His night vision was excellent, and the bright electric lights only ever blinded him anyway. The basement was the darkest room of the house, which was why he had taken up residence down here. He could have had a proper room, but he preferred the basement with its small windows close to the ceiling that were easy to cover up.

There was a bed in the centre of the room though, which might become an issue. Once the police searched the house, they would realise that a third person had been living here. They would go looking for him, but at least his DNA wouldn't tell them anything. His fingerprints weren't in any database; in fact, he wasn't registered anywhere. He'd miss sleeping in a bed, though. He would have to make do with breaking into mausoleums again, the way his kind had always handled these things. It was the only shelter where they could be sure to sleep unbothered during the daybecause the living didn't like to disturb the dead's rest. The old stone coffins offered a solid protection against the sunlight as well. You could steal money from your victims and check into a hotel these days, but the flimsy curtains were hardly a good shield against the sun. It felt ridiculous to Ansgar that after all these centuries, he still hadn't come up with a better solution than the old-fashioned coffin. It was where Richard had found him about fifteen years ago as well, in a tomb at the local cemetery.

Ansgar skimmed through his clothes. There weren't a lot of options to choose from, since he didn't earn money himself and disliked depending on Richard's charity any more than was absolutely necessary. All of the clothes were black.

He changed pants and when he stripped the shirt over his head, he realised that the blood had soaked right through the fabric. Blood was sticking to his pale skin. It was already beginning to dry. Unfortunately, he wouldn't have time for a shower — the luxury of showers was another thing he would miss when he returned to the streets — so he just tried to wipe himself as best as he could with the dirty shirt. The metallic smell of stale blood that radiated off his body was disgusting.

He grabbed a hoodie that would cover most of his skin. He didn't really have a plan, he just knew that he needed the element of surprise on his side.

He heard a car pulling up somewhere nearby. It could be Richard, or it could be the next door neighbour. But Ansgar doubted that anyone else was out this late anymore.

He rushed up the stairs faster than any human being could, reaching the living room before the engine died.

He pulled the hood over his face as far as possible and tugged at the sleeves to get them down to his knuckles. His hands no longer looked bony and claw-like, but like the hands of a healthy young man in his twenties. If Richard looked at him closely, it would be very evident that he'd fed only recently.

The front door was unlocked and then it fell shut again. There were steps in the corridor, heavy and not pausing. Richard hadn't taken off his shoes, which meant he was already alarmed. Ansgar wondered once more what Celia had told him over the phone.

"Cee!" Richard called out. "Ansgar?"

Ansgar turned towards the door, flinching slightly as if he'd been startled.

"Yes," he said, keeping his voice low to not draw attention to the fact that it no longer sounded cracked at all.

Richard entered the room, a sturdy looking man in his late fifties, clean shaven and wearing a blazer even now as if he had gone out for a lecture instead of forming a one-man search party.

"Ansgar," he said, visibly relieved. "You're home."

Ansgar tried not to give too much of a reaction. When he was confused, he usually stuck to short and general replies to keep up his cover, so it was probably best to do that now as well, to give Richard the impression that he was still suffering from memory loss.

Richard scanned the room. His eyes darted across the suspicious spot on the floor where Celia had bled out as if he couldn't see it at all. The air was still heavy with the smell of blood.

"Where's Celia?" Richard asked. He already sounded calmer, yet still not entirely at ease. He had no reason to suspect what had happened, though. Ansgar had lived with them for fifteen years. Richard trusted him.

"Who?" he asked.

Richard frowned. Ansgar hadn't been able to read his expression this clearly since the last time he'd fed. He could see the lines on Richard's forehead and the smaller wrinkles around the corner of his mouth. He could even count the seventeen white hairs on his left temple that were showing in his otherwise dark hair. He could have counted his eyelashes too if he had wanted to, even though they stood several feet apart. Richard wasn't wearing glasses. He only wore them for reading while crouching down over his research at the desk. Ansgar thought that he would miss watching him. He'd miss their conversations, too, and Celia's laughter. He'd miss everything about this life.

"Celia," Richard repeated and then paused as if he realised that Ansgar might indeed have forgotten whom he was talking about. He pointed towards the photographs on the sideboard. "My daughter. The girl in the pictures. She's older now."

Ansgar took a step towards the sideboard. He'd moved a little too fast and tried to make up for it by staring at the pictures intensely as if he could hardly recognize them.

"Yes, yes, the girl," he finally said quietly. "She was here. A very nice girl. I think I've met her before. Said she would go to sleep. This is a very nice house, too. But I'd like to go home now."

Richard's expression softened. "I can take you to your room. Don't you want to take off the hood?"

Ansgar reached up to touch the black hood as if he had completely forgotten that he was wearing it.

"The lights," he mumbled. "They're too bright. The electric lights. They hurt my eyes."

"That's right." Richard sounded even more relaxed now. He had the typical voice of a professor, which had something to do with his intonation that was hard to pin down. He sounded like he was used to speaking in front of an audience. "You haven't fed in a while. You must be sensitive to the lights."

The fact that Ansgar was still hungry obviously soothed him.

"We'll find someone for you soon. For now, let's get you to the basement. You should rest, especially when you are hungry."

"No, no," Ansgar said and tried to wave the offer aside, still keeping the sleeves of his hoodie down to his knuckles. "I want to go home."

Richard took a step towards him, holding out his arm.

Ansgar quickly scanned him over. He wasn't carrying any visible weapons on him, no wooden stake at least. A quick, physical overpowering was certainly the easiest way to kill him. Ansgar knew that he could rely on his superior strength and that he had nothing to worry about. He was the born predator. The only reason he hesitated was that he liked Richard. He was his friend. But sadly, his death was inevitable.

Richard took another step forward and he gently took hold of Ansgar's arm to guide him towards the door. He flinched back as soon as he touched him, though. Even through the thick material of the hoodie, the blood in his veins must have given him away.

"You are warm," Richard observed, and then Ansgar dove in. He couldn't give Richard time to realise what that meant. His blood still smelled sweetly calm, not tainted with sharp fear yet. He smelled less sweet than Celia, his blood not as young and full of life anymore. To his own surprise, Ansgar realised that he was still hungry. Dieting for whatever reason just wasn't healthy for his kind. By the laws of nature, they were meant to feed to their heart's content.

He sunk his teeth into Richard's neck. Up close his shave wasn't all that clean, and a light stubble scratched against Ansgar's chin. His canine teeth pierced the skin easily. Before he could rip the wound open though, a sharp pain burned his cheek.

He cried out with his lips still pressed to Richard's throat, the first blood already trickling into his mouth, making it harder to focus on anything that wasn't blood and pain. His voice came out muffled. He tried to pull away. Richard was taller than him and the angle was awkward. He tore open the wound but not as deeply as he had intended to. Blood was trickling down Richard's neck onto the collar of his button-down shirt, the sight making it hard for Ansgar to keep his distance.

The scent of blood filled the room again, and it wasn't stale blood, but a fresh, delicious smell that made his stomach clench.

He had to force himself to back away in spite of his instincts. In his hand, Richard was holding a cross the size of his palm, attached to a rosary. He must have carried it in his pocket, easily accessible.

Ansgar had assumed he would be somewhat prepared. He hissed. It sounded animalic and pained.

Richard tried to back away towards the door, keeping his eyes on Ansgar while still holding up the cross. Ansgar's cheek was still burning where the crucifix had made contact with his skin. The hood of his shirt had fallen back.

The blood kept running down Richard's neck. The wound Ansgar had inflicted on him was by no means small, and he'd punctured a large artery. Richard was already turning paler. It was easy to tell that he was in pain, the hormones transmitted through his blood smelled differently now. He reeked of fear, too, but it wasn't the panic humans usually emitted in a life-or-death situation. Richard wasn't scared for himself.

Ansgar could have told him that Celia was already dead, but the anger and despair would only spoil his blood further. He kept his eyes fixed on Richard's bleeding neck. All this blood going to waste while he tried to decide on his next move was truly a shame. This was going to be a messy kill, not very energy efficient either. Ansgar would have to fight, and a lot more blood would go to waste in the meantime. It would end up being a sparse meal. He didn't want to have to kill his friend, but if he was going to do so anyway, it should at least be worth his time.

Conflicting instincts fought inside him. A part of him wanted to leap forward to keep drinking without thinking about the risk of further pain at all. It was the animal part of him that only cared about his hunger. The other part of him wanted to run away and curl up somewhere. His cheek still hurt as if someone had burned him with fire, and vampires were cowardly by nature. They didn't have a lot of natural enemies, so the feeling of pain was unfamiliar to them and activated their flight mode. That part of him was animalistic, too.

But the part of Ansgar that'd once been human knew that he had to finish this. Because if he didn't, there was a chance that Richard would survive. Since he had already bitten him, he might even turn if he managed to push through, making him an even stronger enemy. And after what Ansgar had done to his daughter, he would hunt him down to the ends of the earth. So Ansgar couldn't succumb to his instinct. He had to be more than an instinct-driven night creature; he had to be an actual person, who followed the voice of reason.

Crouching down, he lunged at Richard's legs, crashing into him with his full weight and toppling him. The crucifix brushed his temple, sending another shock of burning pain through his body, but he held on as they both tumbled to the floor.

He quickly crawled up to pin Richard down, grabbing his wrist. The chain of the rosary touched his hand, but he forced himself to not let go. He was a person, after all. He was stronger than his instincts, stronger than his pain.

He slammed Richard's hand down on the floor repeatedly and forcefully until he heard something crack, a bone snapping under his grip. Richard howled, finally losing his hold on the rosary.

Ansgar covered his hand with his sleeve and pushed the crucifix away, making it slide across the floor and out of their reach. Even through the fabric, the touch still stung.

Richard twisted underneath him, trying to shove him off, but Ansgar kept him pinned down with his body weight. He'd had a far better grip on Celia, her long curls had been the perfect handle to expose her throat. Richard was a lot bigger, and stronger, too. In his formerly weakened condition, Ansgar might not have been able to defeat him at all. It had definitely been different when he still used to feed a lot more frequently. He'd been able to overpower even armed soldiers with ease.

He bent down, sinking his teeth into the open wound again. The blood already tasted a little stale where it was coating the skin. Richard screamed. It was already getting easier to hold him still. From this angle, Ansgar also couldn't see his face and the pain in his voice made it barely recognizable. That made it easier, too. Ansgar could have been killing anyone.

He tore out a large chunk of flesh, because his teeth had managed to go in extraordinarily deep into the already established wound. In fact, the opening was a little too large now; blood kept gushing out of it, and Ansgar couldn't fully cover it with his mouth. Blood kept running past the corner of his mouth, down onto the floor. He wished he could save it, but you had to drink it freshly from the body, or the blood turned bad. He swallowed greedily. Beneath him, Richard had already stopped thrashing.

His heart was still beating quite steadily, though. The blood filled Ansgar's stomach and instantly made him feel better. The burning of his cheek turned to a dull, throbbing pain. It would take time for him to heal, time and more blood, presumably. He'd been burned before by religious symbols, though that had been long ago, as they had gone out of fashion over the centuries. Back then, he had still healed more quickly in general, because he'd fed more frequently.

The touch of the crucifix had also made him feel a little feverish. He could drain another man after this, although he shouldn't, definitely not anywhere close by when he was already leaving the corpses behind in this house.

Richard's heartbeat was slowing down more and more. He had gone completely limp, too. He still had a few gulps left in him, and Ansgar wanted nothing more than to keep feeding, but he didn't dare to take the gamble. He'd already been weakened by their fight, and he couldn't risk swallowing another dose of dead blood. His system would surely take it badly.

So he sat up and wiped his chin with the back of his hand. There was blood everywhere. He'd have to get changed again before leaving the house. He wondered if he should leave straight after cleaning or risk waiting out another day in the basement.

The chances that someone would barge in looking for Richard and Celia tomorrow already were very slim. There would be a few worried phone calls at most. The early morning hours were already approaching, and Ansgar had no idea where to go yet. If he didn't find an adequate hiding spot before sunrise, it would mean his death. Staying seemed like the better option, but the effect of the blood seemed to wear off more and more quickly. He wouldn't be completely disorientated by tomorrow yet, but maybe a little bit confused already. It might be safer to go looking for a new hiding space while his mind was still as sharp as it could be.

He looked down at Richard. His breath was coming very faintly, but Ansgar could hear it clearly nonetheless. It sounded loud and ragged to his sensitive ears. He obviously couldn't leave him breathing.

He reached down, cupping Richard's face with both hands in a last tender cradle. His friend was looking up at him, but Ansgar doubted that he could still see him. His eyes looked vacant and broken. He couldn't smell anything noteworthy in his blood anymore either, no fear or confusion, no sadness or regret. Richard was too far gone to still experience any complex emotions. That burden was all Ansgar's now.

He twisted his hands sharply, snapping his friend's neck. Without his strained breathing, the living room suddenly fell very quiet.

Ansgar stared down at the body. He should get going. There was still so much to do. He had to cut their throats, though with the way he had torn Richard open, he had no idea how a simple cut would cover up the wound. He'd never been good at covering his traces. He'd only survived until now because he kept moving a lot and because no one ever suspected a vampire attack. He considered setting the house on fire. Maybe the corpses would be burned beyond recognition. He didn't know if you could still diagnose the blood loss of a burned corpse.

All things considered, Ansgar wasn't very good at being a vampire, and he wasn't very good at being a killer. If he'd had the choice, he wouldn't have wanted to get turned. If he'd had the choice, he would still have liked to live forever, though.

He forced himself to get up. His knees felt extremely weak. He tried not to think about what Clarissa would have said, if she could see him now. She had loved him in spite of the killing, but he'd tried to be better for her. Richard had been the human being closest to him since she had died. With the way Ansgar kept regressing lately, he might have killed Clarissa, too.

He bent forward to stabilise himself. It had to be the injuries from the rosary that were making him feel so dizzy. The throbbing in his cheek was the worst, but his temple and his hand still hurt as well.

Richard's face was pale and smeared with blood. The shadow of his stubble shone through more clearly in death, as if his skin had become thinner due to the blood loss.

This felt different than looking down at Celia had felt. With her, it had been an accident, plain and simple. But killing Richard had been a choice. Ansgar didn't know if that made him more human or less than one. His head was spinning.

His breath was coming fast. He didn't even need to breathe; it was just a force of habit. His stomach clenched. It felt as if his body was rejecting the blood; he didn't know if this was an actual sickness or just the feeling of guilt.

Something hit his knees, and it took him a moment to realise his legs had given out and he was back on the floor. His stomach clenched again, and stale blood rose in his throat like bile. He tried to fight it down, but it had already reached his mouth. He bent forward, clenching his revolting stomach as if he could somehow soothe it from the outside.

He vomited onto the floor, black liquid splattering everywhere. It wasn't just a mouthful like it had been before. The sight made him retch all the more, and he seemed to empty out his entire stomach next to the dead body. It didn't even look that gross, it was just dark liquid which mixed in with the blood that had already spilled out on the floor. Only the shades looked slightly different. It made him feel helpless, though, and the taste that filled his mouth was disgusting. The blood tasted bitter on his tongue the second time around.

Eventually the cramps stopped and he spat one last time, trying to get rid of the bad taste. He wiped his mouth with the sleeve of his hoodie. He'd have to do something about his appearance before leaving. His pants were drenched in blood as well.

His stomach felt slightly better now, but he felt feverish, not overheated, but rather as if his body temperature simply didn't match his environment. He felt both too hot and too cold at once. He was cold, the room was cold and his skin was cold, but the blood in his veins was unnaturally hot.

Worst of all, he felt hungry again.

The hollow feeling right behind his ribs was back. With the blood now spilled across the floor, it felt as if he hadn't fed at all. He was dizzy, and his eyesight was growing significantly worse again. His vision was blurry as if his eyes were filled with tears. Looking down at the floor, everything was one big, red mess to him.

He still needed to cut their throats. He needed to gather everything of value. He missed the old times, when everyone still kept stacks of cash hidden across various places in the house. Those little plastic cards wouldn't help him. Even if he'd known the pin code, the accounts would get blocked as soon as the corpses were discovered. Trading jewellery and the like had been easier once upon a time as well. Ansgar assumed there were still plenty of fences out there, but he didn't know where to find them. He wasn't a criminal mastermind, he was just a poor, helpless night creature who had to hide before the sun came up.

With great trouble, he managed to get up. His knees hurt from collapsing on the floor. He used to heal quickly, but his body didn't recover as fast anymore, especially not after all the blood he had just lost. His cheek was still burning violently. He wondered how bad the mark looked, and if it would draw attention on the street. It was impossible for him to check his reflection in a mirror.

He staggered, nearly slipping on the wet floor.

He needed to cut their throats, find the money that was in the house, and change into a set of clean clothes. Then he could leave and find a place to wait out the day. Tomorrow night, he could feed again, provided he made it to an area far enough from here to avoid anyone connecting the two incidents. Once he'd fed, everything else would become easier again.

Ansgar decided to look for the money first. He'd have to ransack the house anyway, make it look like the murders were the result of a robbery gone bad. The impression wouldn't be all that wrong. Since he was about to steal from them, that technically made it robbery.

He went over to the desk, opening the drawers and going through them carelessly, leaving a mess on purpose. He didn't really think anything of value was kept in here. He had to find a wallet, that was where these modern humans kept all their money.

He walked past the dead man on the floor, wondering where he might have kept his wallet. Ansgar knew that they had been friends, that they had been close. He had a hard time recalling the man's name, though. Surely it would come back to him eventually.

He went out of the living room, leaving bloody footprints on the floor of the corridor. He hadn't realised he'd walked through the puddle of blood, but he was spreading it everywhere. His socks were soaked. The feeling was unpleasantly sticky and the blood still felt warm. But it didn't matter anymore; the place was already a mess and he'd have no time to clean up before sunrise.

There was a dresser in the corridor, close to the front door. On top of it, he found a black leather wallet. He opened it and went through its contents. The cards were all assigned to Richard. That had been the man's name, he remembered now. Ansgar couldn't pocket the whole thing. If someone searched him because he looked suspicious, having the ID of an identified murder victim on him would cause trouble.

Ninety dollars, that was all he found. Living had turned so expensive and still humans barely carried any cash money on them anymore. It didn't make sense to Ansgar.

He pocketed the money and put the wallet back onto the dresser. There had been a girl, too, a girl with curly hair, the daughter. She must have had money on her, too.

Ansgar remembered that her body was out in the garden, but for a moment, he was confused about which door would lead him there. He'd definitely been to this house before, but he didn't know the place very well.

He had to get the money. He'd have to cut their throats, too. There had been a third thing he needed to take care of before leaving, but he couldn't remember what it had been.

He picked the door on his left and it led him into the kitchen that looked out onto the small garden. He gave a sigh of relief as he went over to the backdoor. The lock was tricky; he had to fumble with it for a moment before he figured out how to open it. The handle was weirdly slippery, as if it'd gotten wet earlier.

He expected the air to smell clean and fresh outside, but instead it reeked of stale blood even more intensely than the kitchen. Dried blood stuck all the way down the girl's side. Ansgar's stomach turned again as he bent lower to pat her down for a wallet. He feared he might be sick again.

In one of her jeans pockets he found a small wallet, not meant to hold more than the bare essentials. He had to struggle to get it out, because the angle was inconvenient with her lying down. Her body was already stiff.

He opened the wallet to find about thirty dollars inside. That wouldn't get him far. A night at a hotel to shower maybe, though they usually required an ID at the check-in, or a set of new clothes, that was all he was going to get out of this. Luckily, he didn't have to pay for food and housing was unaffordable for him anyway. Things had been easier back in the old days, especially during the war, everything had been chaotic anyway and people tended to look the other way.

Before he returned to the house, he cast one last look at the girl. He felt woeful and guilty, though he wasn't sure why. He had killed countless times before.

He also felt like he was supposed to do something about the corpse, but he couldn't recall what his intentions had been. He'd just have to leave her. There was no time to bury her before sunrise.

Back in the kitchen, he considered checking the bedrooms for valuables. It used to be where people kept their jewellery and other prized possessions, but he wasn't sure if he'd find anything useful. He assumed the bedrooms were upstairs, but he didn't want to risk checking and getting lost. It was difficult for him to stay on track and he didn't want to waste any more time. The early morning hours were approaching quickly. There wasn't enough time left to search a stranger's entire house. He had to go out and find a hiding spot while he still remembered the task at hand.

He went to the front door. He remembered coming in through here earlier. The girl had brought him in. He was sure that they had known each other. But she should have known better than to trust him. He wasn't an average person. He was a creature of the night, scarier and more powerful than any of these mortals. He was happy with that.

He stepped outside and closed the door behind himself. There would be no going back now; he didn't have a key. That chapter of his life, whatever it had been, was closed for good.

He walked down the stairs. He wasn't wearing shoes. Apparently, he hadn't brought any.

He assumed that it was cold outside, but he didn't really feel it. The smell of the Nachtluft in the city was disgusting, though, filled with smog and fumes. The vehicles on the streets were noisy even at this time of night, and he knew that the morning rush hour would start soon. He'd have to find a place to sleep before then.

He wished that he could just break into one of the houses and drain its owners to have a place to sleep. But he couldn't enter without an invitation, and these days missing persons were noticed too quickly. During the glorious days of the long war, it'd been different. People had gone missing all the time and he had fed freely, up to three or four times per night.

He would need to feed again soon. He vaguely remembered that he'd fed very recently, but he'd thrown it all back up. He'd probably drained them for too long, having upset his stomach with dead blood. But it didn't matter, he'd find another meal soon enough. He used to drain several humans every night. If only he embraced that side of himself, he would be alright. If he kept feeding well enough, no one would be able to stop him, even if they caught on to him. Of course, he still had to be careful. Being a creature of the night wasn't easy, everyone was out to get you: the police, hunters and survivors. That was why you always had to be thorough and kill everyone you fed on. And if you stuck to that rule, life was really quite simple.

He started walking, his body weak and hollow with hunger. The noise all around and the bright city lights were wearing him out. When he'd first been turned, the nights had still been darker and lonelier. He remembered his Heimat more vividly than anything that had happened tonight, the clear night sky above and the unevenly paved roads beneath his feet. Time was like a circle, and the beginning seemed closer to the end than anything else. It was quite confusing. He might have to feed before going into hiding for the day after all, just to fix his memory.

He only hoped that he wouldn't get lost along the way. The neighbourhood looked a lot different from the way it used to be.

Aurora

by Mark Mackey

Another place and time, unreachable from Earth was where Seraph existed. It was a magic world ruled by dragons, vampires, and witches. The legend says, Seraph was created by magic itself, acting on its own accord.

Chapter One

For the past several months Aurora, eldest daughter to King of the Fae, Laurment and his wife Queen Abigaila had the same pleasant dream. She found herself placed in a world unfamiliar to her and saw the most perfect boy approach in a motorized carriage of some sort. She had no interest in wherever this dream placed her; she was only interested in the boy. Aurora knew she had to have him at all costs, if only she knew the name of this world or how to reach it, but she didn't, which disappointed her.

She pushed this thought from her mind to focus on what she and her fifteen-year-old sister Everlista, the only one she confided in about these dreams, were about to do: hunt down a Corter-Dragon. They were significantly smaller in size compared to the fire breathing dragon or the rare Silver Dragon. But with their poisonous saliva and razor sharp, talon-like claws they were just as deadly.

A Corter-Dragon was not more than a nuisance and a threat to Seraph's livestock and Fae alike.

"So, do you think luck will be on our side and we'll be able to dispatch a Corter-Dragon today?" Aurora asked as they traveled through the dense gloomy forest where this particular creature was known to exist. The two of them were armed with crossbows and beige cloth arrow cases filled with steel-tipped arrows strapped on their backs.

"Oh, there's no doubt in my mind," Everlista replied in confidence.

"I've had another one of my handsome stranger dreams last night," Aurora said as they traveled along.

"You mean the one of the handsome stranger in an unfamiliar world?"

"That's the one. I wish I knew what world it is and why I always have it and who he is. Everlista, I'm so certain he and I are supposed to be together. He's so much more attractive than any fae male I've seen or been involved with in Seraph.

"Well maybe you can ask a dark witch to use her magic to find this world and handsome stranger, Aurora?" Everlista suggested.

"Come on, let's go find what we're out here for," Aurora said instead.

As she and Everlista continued on, it wasn't long before their ears picked up the sound of rustling foliage close by.

"Okay, I think we've just found what brought us out here," Aurora whispered. She reached into her case to retrieve an arrow.

In no time, Aurora had her crossbow loaded and pointed straight in the direction of the rustling.

Then they saw it, the hideous dark gray skin with its blackened teeth dripping with deadly saliva. Its appearance forced Everlista to grab an arrow and raise her bow.

"Ready to put a vile Corter-Dragon out of its misery," Everlista asked.

"Just say when," Aurora easily replied as the Corter-Dragon began charging to infect them with its poisoned saliva and make a tasty meal out of them. Of course, the skilled hunters they were, it never had a chance. She and Everlista put it out of its misery in no time.

"And yet again, we've made our section of Seraph safe and took out yet another Corter-Dragon!" Aurora yelled in victory. "So Everlista, are you up for searching out and killing another?"

"No, you know what, its growing late, come on let's get home. Inform our father we were successful in killing this pathetic Corter-Dragon," Everlista replied.

***

During the entire trip back to the castle she and Everlista called home, Aurora felt just one thing, gladness. After all, she and her sister successfully managed to end the life of a dangerous Corter-Dragon. The thought of this caused her to smile ever so slightly.

"I can tell by that smile you're pleased by the outcome of our little evening hunting trip," Everlista commented, taking notice of this.

"You can't expect me to feel any other way, can you Everlista?" Aurora asked.

"No, I sure can't," Everlista replied.

***

It wasn't long before she and Everlista arrived at the place they called home; a monstrous gray brick stone castle placed on a cliff overlooking a magnificent clear blue ocean. An impenetrable black wrought iron gate protecting it, as well as two strong male fae guards armed with sharp Daklin swords dressed in the required uniform—red coats and black slacks.

"Home sweet home at last," Aurora said(,) a pleased look building on her face. She knew the guards' names to be Alston and Kallan. They were by far two of the best guards her father had.

"Welcome back Aurora and Everlista," Alston greeted them, a pleasant look growing on his face. "How did your hunt to rid our section of Seraph of the nuisance Corter-Dragon go?"

"Our section of Seraph is one Corter-Dragon less Alston," Aurora replied and smiled.

Chapter Two

Over the course of the past few days, Laurment had come to a certain decision regarding which one of his daughters would be elevated into the role of princess of Seraph.

"Abigaila, I think it's time we decide on which one of our daughters should become princess," he suggested to his wife. The two stood on the castle throne room balcony staring down at the raging black sea. The evening air chilled them ever so slightly.

But he wasn't about to just give one of them the role; that would make Aurora and Everlista think he favored one over the other. Laurment couldn't afford to have that happen; he'd rather die first.

"I think that's a wonderful idea since Aurora is less than a year away from turning seventeen, Everlista almost sixteen." Abigaila wasted no time in answering him. The sound of her voice indicating she approved of this, "So which one of our daughters do you intend on blessing with it?"

"Oh, come on Abigaila in my mind it wouldn't be fair to either Aurora or Everlista! I'm certain naming one of them princess would only make the other one jealous thinking I favored one of our daughters over the other!"

"So, what do you have in mind to help decide which of them is to become princess?"

"Our daughters should be given a task to compete against each other, with the winner receiving the reward of princess."

"Now I think that's an excellent idea," Abigaila said, her voice maintaining approval.

"Now the question is what should the task be for Aurora and Everlista?"

"You've wanted the head of a rare Silver Dragon to mount on one of these gray brick throne room walls for a long while now Laurment," Abigaila informed him.

"I have," Laurment said. "Very well, it's settled. Whichever one manages to bring me a Silver Dragon's head will be named princess."

***

Accomplishment dominated Aurora as she and Everlista moved effortlessly through the gray brick hallway which lay before the castle throne room. In her opinion with remarkable painted portraits of her sister's and her ancestors decorating the walls.

***

"Once again we survived and yet another Corter-Dragon is no longer a threat to Seraph," Aurora informed her parents, excitement dominating her face as she and Everlista made their arrival into the throne room, seeing Laurment and Abigaila still hovering at the balcony.

"You and Everlista being as gifted hunters and warriors as you are, that comes as no surprise," Abigaila answered.

"Well I can't speak for Everlista, but I'm exhausted," Aurora said, starting to turn away and distance herself from her sister's side so as to make an exit out the door.

"Aurora wait, before you depart there's something I need to propose to you and Everlista," Laurment called out to her; the tone of his voice indicated whatever it was he had to say was of great importance.

"What is it you have to tell us," Everlista asked with sudden interest as Aurora returned to her side.

"My daughters, I've been thinking the past few days," Laurment replied. "And I believe it's time to name one of you Princess of Seraph."

Almost instantly with this filling her ears, Everlista was struck by excitement. Ever since she was a child it had been her dream to become Princess of Seraph, and now she was about to receive the chance.

"So, which one of us are you going to choose," Everlista asked.

"To make things fair and not pick a favorite, I've decided to place a challenge before you," Laurment replied.

"Yes, I agree that's an excellent idea for Everlista and me to compete to become princess instead of one of us just being handed it," Aurora said in an approving voice. "So what's the challenge you have for us?"

"Aurora, with you and Everlista being such gifted hunters, whichever one of you is able to bring me the head of a rare Silver Dragon shall be named Princess of Seraph," Laurment said.

"Something we've never done before, sure I'm okay with that," Aurora replied in full enthusiasm; "Everlista, how about you?"

"Yeah,sure, I'm perfectly fine with it," Everlista replied.

"Now you should get to bed so you won't have a problem heading out as soon as first morning's light fills the sky," Laurment said.

CHAPTER THREE

A few minutes later she and Aurora traveled side by side down another gray bricked hallway. This one containing their bedchamber for some much needed sleep for tomorrow's important challenge. While engaging in this, she came to one specific conclusion; her dream of becoming princess had to be realized at all costs. This meant she would have to do something to ensure her sister was disallowed the opportunity.

"Okay, well I wish whichever one of us whose destiny it is to be named princess much luck tomorrow," Aurora said as they arrived at the tan door to Everlista's bedchamber.

"Yes, and I wish the same for you," Everlista replied.

***

The answer to how she could ensure Aurora was removed from tomorrow's competition struck Everlista hard the moment she entered her bedchamber. His name was Victors, vampire, prince of the section of his world, lover; and so far, Everlista had been successful in keeping their relationship a complete secret from her family. Just the sight of him being there was enough to fill her heart with excitement and bring a smile to her face.

"I'm glad to see my being here brings a smile to your face," Victors said.

"Oh, I was happy even before I made my arrival in here," Everlista replied as she moved towards him, eagerly wrapping her arms around his neck. "Seeing you just elevated that feeling."

The next thing Everlista knew she was connecting her lips to his, the feeling of his icy cold lips pleasantly comforting.

"And why's that?"

"My father's just informed Aurora and me, come dawn tomorrow she and I are to head out and compete against each other for the title of Princess of Seraph."

"Now, you must be excited about that, Everlista."

"I would be, but I don't have much of a chance of winning since Aurora's always been a better hunter than me," she said. "And that's where you come in; I need you to do something short of killing my sister to remove her from tomorrow's competition."

"You know I love you so much not to deny you that request, Everlista," he replied. "Sure, I'll make sure Aurora's taken out of this little competition set for tomorrow."

Seconds later, Victors transformed himself into mist, one of the vampire's best attributes and floated out to take care of this.

***

Despite him saying to the girl he desperately loved he wouldn't kill Aurora, truthfully Victors wasn't sure he'd be able to do so. After all, he hadn't fed since last night, causing him to feel a strong, pulsating desire for blood. *Should he drain Aurora bone dry*, Victors wondered. But if he went ahead and did so, there was no doubt in his mind it would cause Everlista to hate him, and he couldn't have that. With that Victors decided to take just enough of Aurora's blood to weaken her and then drag her to some hidden place until tomorrow's competition was over and done; allowing Everlista to claim the title of Seraph Princess.

***

Once he drifted into Aurora's bedchamber, Victors returned to solid form. Standing positioned over Aurora, her neck and shoulders exposed, his pulsating craving for blood returned; and once again he considered defying Everlista and draining her sister bone dry. But then, like the first time he thought about doing so, it would earn him the ire of his great love, and he quickly dispatched this idea from his mind. Willing out powerful, sharp teeth, Victors moved his head forward rapidly to bury them into Aurora's flesh.

***

Sleeping lightly, Aurora was awakened out of it by booted footsteps creaking against the floorboards towards her. This alerted Aurora to the fact a terrible danger was heading her way.

Just as soon as her eyes fluttered open, Aurora became aware there was an actual vampire standing over her. Long, sharp teeth exposed.

There was no doubt in Aurora's mind what he wanted, and that was to feed on her blood. A look of pure disgust and nausea filled her face as a result.

Before this vampire possessed even a single chance to perform his vile act, Aurora raced off the bed. She shoved him hard—backwards and away from her—before he could even lift a finger to react. She was fast enough to arm herself with her favorite sword. She pointed the blade of it dangerously close to his throat.

"Who are you?" she cried, pressing her forearm tight against his throat.

"Forget it. I'm not telling you a thing," he said in full defiance.

"All right fine, but don't say I didn't warn you," Aurora said, pushing the sword's blade even closer to this throat.

"One more time, who are you," Aurora repeated, this time with more force to her voice.

"I said I'm not telling you a thing!"

"Fine then, I guess Seraph's going to be blessed with one less vampire," Aurora taunted.

Chapter Four

Despite instructing Victors to do whatever it took to ensure Aurora was taken out of tomorrow's competition, Everlista was beginning to have second thoughts. For all she knew, her sister might very well be having every single drop of blood drained despite Victors saying he wouldn't kill her. After all he was a vampire. If not, Aurora had used her fighting skills against him to prevent whatever he had in mind from being carried out.

Oh, how could I have been so stupid and let my desire to become Princess of Seraph send Victors after Aurora?

Now she was going to lose one of them. Or maybe it hadn't happened yet, and she still had a chance to correct the terrible mistake she made. This sent Everlista rushing from her bedchamber.

***

"This is your last chance vampire, talk or lose your head," Aurora warned. Her eyes and voice filled with seriousness.

Instead of receiving another refusal from the vampire, Aurora watched Everlista rushing like mad into her bedchamber.

"Aurora stop, please you'll kill him," her sister pleaded.

"He's a vampire Everlista, you and I both know they're enemies of Fae, he should be eradicated," Aurora said.

"Yes, but I love him!"

Aurora couldn't believe what Everlista had just said to her. Her sister was in love with an actual vampire.

"No please don't say it's true," Aurora said in pure disbelief, snapping attention onto her sister. Her eyes matched the way she felt over Everlista's revelation.

"I'm sorry but I can't," Everlista said. "His name is Victors and he and I have been deeply in love for the past seven months. Now please, if you care about me at all, you won't kill him."

"You're lucky I do Everlista," Aurora said. "So, what was he doing in my bedchamber?"

"I'm not going to lie to you, Aurora," Everlista replied. "I sent Victors in here in an attempt to prevent you from taking part in our competition tomorrow morning."

Shock and disappointment combined with the disbelief Aurora felt. Her own sister had sent her vampire lover after her.

"I don't believe you, Everlista. How could you do such a thing to me, your own sister?"

"Aurora it's been my dream to be princess for so long-"

"No save it Everlista," Aurora said, rage darkening her face. "And just wait until our parents hear what you've done; there's no way they'll let you become princess now."

"You're right. I don't deserve it now after the horrible thing I did," Everlista replied, hanging her head down in shame. "But please, you can't kill Victors! He means the world to me. My life's going to suck more than you can imagine without him in it!"

"You're lucky we're sisters and I have a forgiving heart, Everlista," Aurora said, lowering the sword. "Now get out of here, Victors."

"Aurora, I'm sorry," Everlista said as they watched Victors race out. "So, do you think our parents will be harsh on me?"

"You sent a vampire to kill me Everlista," Aurora replied. "If I were them, I would be."

***

"You really disappoint me, Everlista," Laurment said, his face flush with pure anger as she and Aurora stood before Abigaila and him seated on their thrones. "The punishment for sending your vampire lover to try killing your own sister is that Aurora will be named Princess of Seraph. Now, get out of my sight. You've caused enough problems tonight."

CHAPTER FIVE

Ever since Aldrich, current king of the vampires had made a promise to Ravinger, ruler of a particular set of witches who practiced black magic, it would have to be fulfilled—and with the two of them standing face-to-face in his throne room, his lovely daughter Arleigha present at his side—sooner rather than later. The details of this promise were to have his son Victors marry Arleigha. Not that Aldrich had any problem with it; in his mind his and Ravinger's offspring would be perfect together.

"I swear your daughter Arleigha looks absolutely beautiful standing there, Ravinger," he admitted. "I can't wait for Victors and her to be married."

"That's the reason why she and I are here," Ravinger answered. "So where is your son? Arleigha's quite eager to meet him."

"Victors should be in his bedchamber. Come, allow me to introduce you to him."

※

On his return home, Victors had one thing on his mind, Everlista—the girl he was desperately in love with. He couldn't wait to see her once again.

Thanks to being unable to relieve Aurora of some of her blood to weaken her, Victors was in desperate need of blood. This made him move quicker to get home, where some would be waiting for him.

Arriving, Victors started to make his way through a hallway lined on either side with bed chamber doors. Victors was caught by surprise. His father, along with a man and a girl his age, the two of them clearly witches, emerged from his personal bedchamber.

"We were just looking for you, Victors," Aldrich said in a pleased voice.

"Yes, and I'm pleased to meet you as well," Arleigha said with a smile.

"What's the reason?" Victors asked.

"This is Ravinger and Arleigha, and as you can see, they're witches."

"Why are they here?" Victors asked.

"Victors, before you were born I made a promise to Ravinger."

"What sort of promise?"

"I promised him when you both turned seventeen Arleigha and you would marry."

Victors could not believe what he had just been told. His father had made a promise before he was born requiring him to get married when he was seventeen; and worse, it wasn't the girl he was desperately in love with.

"No, I refuse to marry her," he said flatly.

"Why, is there something wrong with Arleigha?"

"It's not that," Victors replied. "Father, I'm in love with someone else."

"Victors, you're marrying Arleigha, and that's all I want to hear about it."

Victors felt anger course through him over this. He was being forced to marry someone he didn't even know or care about; there was no way he would do it.

"I'm sorry. I refuse to marry Arleigha," he said in full defiance.

"Because of this other girl you're in love with?"

"Yeah, that's exactly it."

"Well, you can just forget about this girl, whoever she is," Aldrich ordered. This caused the anger he felt to increase.

"No, I will not forget about her, and there's no way I'm marrying Arleigha."

"Let me put it to you this way, Victors," Aldrich said, his voice growing with rage. "If you don't marry Arleigha, not only will I disown you as a son, but you will no longer be welcome in this castle."

"I don't care. I'm not about to give up the girl I love because of some promise you made a long time ago."

"Get out. I can't stand the sight of you, Victors," Aldrich yelled in a rage.

"You've got it," Victors said, turning and heading away from them.

"Ravinger, I'm sorry. I don't know what to tell you," Aldrich said once Victors disappeared around a corner.

"Arleigha, you know what you have to do if you want Victors to be your husband," Ravinger informed his daughter.

"You're right. I do," Arleigha said.

✳✳✳

As he headed down yet another hallway with more bedchambers, Victors felt relief in knowing he would not have to give up Everlista. And as for losing his home and being kicked out of his family because of this, so what. At least he'd still have the girl he was in love with.

The thing he wasn't expecting, hearing Arleigha call out for him to stop.

"Look Arleigha, I'm sorry you and your father came here for nothing, but you already know I'm involved with someone else."

"I have no interest in coming between you and whoever this girl is you love," she replied reaching him. "That's just not who I am."

"Hey, don't worry about it, I just need to get the heck out of here, I'm starving."

Instantly hearing this, a sudden and genius idea filled Arleigha's mind. She would use Victors' hunger for blood to make him hers forever.

"Victors, there's no need for you to head out for blood, you have some right here flowing in me."

Victors couldn't believe what Arleigha suggested he do—use her blood to nourish his hunger.

"Now, I know you might not approve of the idea," she continued. "But I'm feeling guilty for you being told to leave this castle and getting disowned by your family because you love someone else."

Due to the desperate need for blood, Victors considered taking Arleigha up on her offer.

"Victors it's all right," she said. "And I did say I won't come between you and the girl you love."

Focusing his eyes on her bare neck and shoulders, Victors felt his desire for blood grow even stronger.

"Are you sure?" he asked in an uncertain, nervous voice.

"Uh-huh, you need this, Victors," she said in a soft, compassionate voice.

Before he knew it, Victors was pushing out long, powerful teeth, grabbing hold of Arleigha's shoulders and burying them into her bare flesh. His tasting of Arleigha's blood surprisingly filled him with pure desire for her. His ears filled with her pleased moans.

What the heck's the matter with me, Everlista's supposed to be the one I'm in love with, he thought. Yet for some unknown reason Victors only felt this emotion for Arleigha.

"What did you do to me?" he managed.

Even though having sharp vampire teeth inserted was painful beyond belief, it was worth it. "I placed a spell on myself. So, when you tasted my blood, it made you fall instantly in love with me. You must understand Victors, I'm going to have you, and there's not a thing anybody can do to prevent it."

Victors couldn't believe the thing he'd just heard. He'd been tricked into falling in love by drinking Arleigha's magic, witch blood.

"But I'm in love with someone else."

"She'll get over it. And if she tries something to prevent our upcoming marriage, she'll pay with her life."

Victor felt overcome with enough rage to kill her. Not only had he been manipulated into marrying a witch, if he didn't, Everlista would pay the price.

"No, you can't hurt her."

"I promise I won't, if you agree to forget about her and commit your heart to me."

"I don't have any choice but to agree to that, do I?"

"Not if you love her, whoever she is, like you said."

"Fine you win, I'll forget about her," Victors replied. He hoped all the while Everlista was able to find it in her heart to forgive him when she found out he had to marry someone else.

***

"So, I guess you've come to your senses and agreed to marry Arleigha after all," Aldrich said with their return.

"I have. Thanks to her setting my head straight about it," Victors replied.

"You've made the right decision," Aldrich said, his face filling with approval.

I'm so sorry Everlista, but I have no choice, I have to marry Arleigha. There's no way I'm letting you get hurt or killed because of my refusal to do so.

Chapter Six

Opening her eyes the next morning, Aurora felt instant excitement. She couldn't blame herself for feeling this way, after all, just last night she had been named Princess of Seraph. As far as she was concerned, her life could not be any more perfect.

The next thing Aurora knew, she was overcome by a strong desire to head out and fulfill her father's request—

bring him the head of a rare Silver Dragon.

Emerging from her bedchamber and starting down the hallway, Aurora decided to check on Everlista's well-being. After all, not only did she lose against her in becoming princess, but the vampire she was in love with almost had his existence ended last night.

Setting foot into her sister's bedchamber, the first thing Aurora laid her eyes on was Everlista, lying on her side, back facing her.

"Are you okay?" she asked.

"Please just go away. I'm really not in any mood to do any amount of conversing with you, Princess Aurora."

"Everlista, I'm sorry."

"Yeah, that's easy for you to say. You're not the one who isn't able to call herself Princess. Now please, Aurora, honor my request and leave my bedchamber at once."

Staring at her sister, Aurora could not believe being named Princess was causing a rift between them. Well, she didn't have to stand there and take Everlista's telling her to get out. Especially since it was her sister's own fault she lost her chance.

"Everlista, I'm sorry to say this," she began. "But if it wasn't for you and your vampire boyfriend conspiring to keep me out of our competition, you never would have lost the chance being named Princess."

Keeping her eyes focused on her sister, Aurora realized saying this was a huge mistake.

"Get out!" Everlista screamed. She grew animated and sat up to glare at her sister, rage darkening her attractive young face.

Fine Everlista you don't have to tell me a third time, Aurora thought. She didn't waste a second obliging her sister's demand by racing out.

Lying back down, all Everlista could think about was Victors and how she needed to be with him, now more than ever. She was going to go to the one person she knew wouldn't let her down.

***

Miraculously, Everlista was met with no opposition traveling to the section of Seraph ruled by vampires. It wouldn't have mattered if she had been since she had enough confidence in her skills as a warrior to deal with anything that got in her way.

This was maintained as she made her arrival at the Castle's entrance and seeing no guards in front of it allowed her to enter with no opposition.

Not one bit of a surprise to her, given this castle was home to vampires, the windows were blackened to prevent the sun from getting in.

Continuing towards Victor's bedchamber, it was just minutes before she stood in front of it. Just as she prepared to make her entrance, Everlista was caught by surprise at the sudden arrival of a woman. Not a vampire, but awitch, and judging from the expression on her face, she wasn't at all pleased by her being there.

"Something tells me with you standing in front of Victors' bedchamber, you must be his secret love," the woman taunted.

"Who are you," Everlista asked as she turned to face her.

"I'm the woman who's replaced you in Victors' life, and I'm just days away from becoming his bride."

Everlista could not believe what this woman had dared say to her. No, it just wasn't possible.

"I don't believe you."

"Yeah, I thought you might say that," the woman said. "Come on inside, and Victors will confirm it."

Setting foot into Victors' bedchamber, the first thing Everlista saw was Victors, standing at the window, his back turned to her.

"Victors, this woman I just ran into says she's replaced me in your life," she said. "Please don't tell me it's true."

"I could if I was able to Everlista," he replied without turning to face her.

Hearing Victors confirm what the woman just told her caused sadness to fill her face.

"I don't understand why you would do something like that to me?"

"Because if I didn't, she, her name's, Arleigha was going to use her magic to hurt or kill you," Victors said finally turning towards her, depression and misery dominating his face. "I couldn't allow that to happen."

"But I love you."

Instead of replying, Victors once again turned away from her and resumed staring out the window.

"I'm sorry Everlista, but that's the way it has to be."

"But I can't live without you in my life! It's going to be miserable if we're not together!" Everlista cried. Tears stung her eyes.

And then she heard a feminine voice fill her mind.

"My name is Alisa. I'm Arleigha's younger sister, and I don't want them to get married, either. If you don't want to lose Victors, I can transport the two of you to a place called Earth where nobody will ever find you."

"Yes, please do it," Everlista pleaded.

Seconds later, she and Victors disappeared from sight.

***

Everlista's face grew bright with excitement. She and Victors managed to escape Seraph—and his being forced to marry Arleigha—to this new world thanks to Alisa's magic. The fact she was about to lose Victors and the love they shared was almost too much for her to handle.

Studying the vicinity of the unfamiliar world Alisa sent them, Everlista instantly fell under the impression she would enjoy residing here, or better yet, become its princess. Yes, she'd show Aurora and her parents. She was going to be princess of this world, have Victors rule it along with her. There was not a thing anyone could do to stop her.

"So, what do you have in mind to do here?" Victors asked.

"Simple, Victors," Everlista said. "Since I was denied being named Princess of Seraph, I'm going to become it here. At the same time, you and me, we're going to take over this entire world."

"You should do that, Everlista," Victors said in approval.

"Of course, you'll rule with me," Everlista said. "So, are you starving for blood?"

"Beyond belief," Victors replied.

"Well, let's go find you some," Everlista said.

***

Traveling a while, Everlista realized full well she wouldn't return to Seraph. She'd make this world named 'Earth' her home. Indeed, she'd rule it with Victors. Of course, his being a vampire, the first thing she'd do—convince him to make a vampire army. Putting him in charge, in turn it would help them take over.

It wasn't long before she and Victors ran into the first resident of this world. The thing that surprised Everlista about him was the bizarre… *something* he rode on. It didn't matter, she was a warrior; Victors was a vampire. They wouldn't have any difficulty overtaking him.

"Him, Victors, satisfy your craving for blood," she said.

Watching Victors race straight for him, she felt excited that the first vampire soldier for her army was about to be created.

Chapter Seven

Frost, a fae who never knew parents—only that her mother's name was Rosewind—had been the property of a well-to-do fae woman named Cambrosia ever since she was born. She didn't have a problem with the life of a servant girl; Cambrosia, who so far hadn't married and as a result didn't bear children, treated her with the utmost respect and was like the mother she never had.

On this particular morning, she and Cambrosia were out and about in the village in a part of the fae section of Seraph. The reason was so Cambrosia could purchase life's necessities for the two of them.

Frost so enjoyed these morning village trips—the pleasant smells which streamed out from the various shops and peddlers.

"This day sure is perfect. Wouldn't you agree, Frost, my close, dear friend and faithful servant girl?" Cambrosia asked as they traveled along.

"Oh, without a doubt," Frost replied as they continued.

As she and Frost continued through the village, Cambrosia came up with the sudden idea. She should show her appreciation to Frost for all the dedication over the years.

"Frost-"

And then she saw it step from the long stretch of forest named Weeping Misery which lay on the other side of the village she and Frost faced. A monstrous, gray skinned Darkmore Gargoyle and in an instant, fear began to race through her heart; it didn't help these creatures craved fae flesh or that his entrance caused the other fae who were out about taking care of their business to run for their lives.

And then he focused his eyes on them.

"Cambrosia run!" Frost cried, grabbing hold of her hand. The next thing she knew, her beloved, faithful servant girl rushed them off and away from the Darkmore Gargoyle. Cambrosia felt her heart start to beat wildly in her chest as they did so.

Out of the corner of her eye, Cambrosia saw the Darkmore Gargoyle give chase after them.

No, Frost and I can't become a meal for this vile creature!

As they neared the street, Cambrosia's eyes widened in a combination of fear and terror. A succession of horse drawn carriages came out of nowhere and traveled by at a slow pace.

Worse, out of the corner of her eye, Cambrosia saw the Darkmore Gargoyle put on a sudden burst of speed. He managed to catch up to them and the next thing she knew, she felt a powerful, crushing sensation grip her shoulder and was yanked hard backwards out of Frost's grip. She spun around so she and the Darkmore stood face- to-face, and again out of the corner of her eye, she saw Frost turn and stand beside her.

And then Cambrosia heard the words she wished she hadn't.

"I only want that beautiful young fae girl beside you."

"You can't have her! She's my property and friend!"

Cambrosia realized saying this was a tremendous mistake on her part as the Darkmore Gargoyle responded by reaching out one of its powerful claws and wrapping it around her neck, snapping it.

For Frost, hearing the neck of the woman who raised her from birth snap was the worst thing imaginable.

"Now, unless you want to suffer the same death as your owner, servant girl, you'll come with me," the Darkmore Gargoyle said, releasing Cambrosia's corpse where it dropped, deflated and lifeless, to the ground.

Frost didn't know which of her parents she inherited it from—her deceased mother, or the father she never knew—but whenever she sang, it put dragons in close vicinity to sleep.

Would it work on a Darkmore Gargoyle as well? Well, there's only one for me to find out.

Opening her mouth, Frost released a beautiful, harmonic song.

It didn't put the Darkmore Gargoyle to sleep.

"Enjoyable melody, songbird," he taunted, and he gripped her bicep and started to drag her off towards the forest.

***

Making her departure from the castle, Aurora knew perfectly well where to go find the elusive creature she was seeking. An unfortunate thing, since the woods where the species resided also held vile, vicious gray-skinned Darkmoor Gargoyles.

These creatures loved nothing more than to travel from their woods home and abduct unsuspecting males and females of her fae species to feast upon.

Aurora wasn't afraid of these gargoyles. She'd gone up against one of them in the past, thanks to him making the stupid mistake to try and abduct her.

Despite all his best efforts, the gargoyle was no match for her. She didn't come out of this battle unscathed, receiving some minor scratches to her arms and face, courtesy of its claws.

They weren't deep enough to cause her to bleed much, healing up weeks after the incident.

Aurora's successful victory against the Darkmoor Gargoyle was the reason she had no fear of the species or to enter its woods home now.

It didn't take long to arrive at the border of the woods, located in a section of Seraph nicknamed 'Weeping Misery,' thanks to the sky above permanently dominated by depressing gray clouds.

This didn't stop Aurora from venturing into them to start her task of obtaining the Silver Dragon head.

She wasn't at all fearful of its immense size and length, six feet tall and a hulk. Given her strength and history as a powerful warrior, Aurora didn't have a single ounce of nervous fear over what she was about to engage in.

She started to move through the woods. It was dominated with dead, lifeless trees, black as night, brown grass, wilted plants. Feeling a slight chill in the air, she brought her guard up. After all, Aurora realized, there was just no telling what awful thing she might run into.

Continuing forward at a steady pace for several minutes, Aurora was struck by surprise. Her ears caught the sound of a branch being stepped on a distance away.

Hearing it brought Aurora's guard up even further. She wasted no time in removing her Alicktors Sword from out of her sheath strapped to her back. The fact she was about to release immense anger over the way her sister treated her earlier and see a bit of action this morning excited her.

Standing in wait for whatever was responsible for the branch, Aurora had a sudden, hopeful desire: it would be a Darkmoor Gargoyle. She'd use her sword to slice its disgusting head clean off its neck.

Only a single minute of standing there, eager anticipation growing over whoever or whatever stepped on the branch to arrive, Aurora was filled with sudden surprise. A light, delicate feminine voice screamed out in clean terror. Never one to abandon a single soul in their time of need, Aurora rushed off to intercept and assist whoever she was.

***

Heading to do so, Aurora's mind was invaded by a certain thought. The idea her arrival at this woman's side might bring her right into danger.

This caused her to wonder if she made the right decision to travel forth and assist this woman, whoever she was. But of course, Aurora continued anyway.

In under five minutes of continued journey through the woods, Aurora arrived at the woman's location.

Almost instantly, Aurora saw the reason why the woman was forced to release her scream. She had her right arm clutched by just what she'd hoped it would be.

"Just what I hoped I'd run into," Aurora said in full amusement, bringing the Alicktors sword up to an attack position.

"There's not a chance I'm allowing you to come anywhere near me with that sword, fae woman," the Darkmoor Gargoyle hissed in anger.

"Yeah, we'll just see about that," Aurora replied, the amusement maintained in her voice.

Charging forward in a furious manner, she hoped it would cause him to release his prisoner and rush to meet her.

Sure enough, it was just as she suspected. He released his hold on the woman to deliver what Aurora was positive would be quite a painful attack.

Reaching her, he didn't waste a single moment in doing it. She was ready for it, both mentally and physically.

This just wasn't enough to deliver a successful counterattack against him. He tore the Alicktors Sword from her hand, tossing it far out of her reach.

Her face grew with tremendous pain, and she was forced to let out chilling screams as he dug his claws straight through her outfit. It filled her blood stream with numbing poison in no time.

"It fills me with tremendous pleasure knowing I was able to overpower you so very easily," the Darkmoor Gargoyle taunted in a snarling growl as he harshly forced her to her knees. "I've always wondered what it would be like to experience the taste of a lovely young fae woman such as you. Now it looks like I'm about to receive the chance to do so. It's a good thing I'm starving and didn't get a chance to devour the prey I managed to get my hands on, thanks to your interference."

Aurora was barely able to wrap her mind around the fact she was about to be turned into a meal for this vile creature and the realization that the end was on the horizon for her.

Before Aurora knew it, he dragged her back up to her feet, his claws instantly ripping the buttons to the portion of her outfit that protected her torso. In such a weakened state, there was no way she could prevent this from happening.

"I'm going to take such great pleasure in devouring your beautiful young flesh," he taunted, starting to move his claw in an ever so gentle manner against the left side of her face. His doing so caused Aurora's face to grow with pure disgust and sorrow.

That was until Aurora's eyes caught sight of the woman he abducted for the purpose she was now situated in. She'd bravely picked up the sword, causing Aurora to be filled with a strong sense of hope.

Whoever she was raced forward with strong energy, using the sword to slice off his head with a single swipe

This allowed Aurora to drop back to her knees, feeling incredibly thankful she had survived.

"That's for Cambrosia!" The woman screamed.

"I'm glad you're well gifted in using a sword," Aurora said before she passed out.

Chapter Eight

Aurora came out of unconsciousness to see the woman kneeling beside her; the sword next to her; the now decapitated Darkmore gargoyle a few feet away.

"I'm glad you're awake. I thought for sure that Darkmore Gargoyle had killed you."

"He would have if it weren't for you and the talent you have with a sword."

"If you hadn't responded to my scream, I would have been the one that Darkmore Gargoyle devoured instead. I found a river close by and used some leaves to clean up your shoulder."

"Thanks for that," Aurora said as she started to stand up. "So, tell me your name, and just how did that vile creature manage to get his claws on you?" Aurora next asked.

"I just go by the name Frost. As for how that gargoyle managed to get his hands on me, was as a result of murdering the woman I was a servant for up until just a little while ago; which means I now belong to you in servitude."

"But don't you have any family?" Aurora asked.

"Tragically no, at least none that I'm knowledgeable about; the woman I was a servant for raised me from birth and never once bothered to mention just how she came in possession of me."

Despite having a deep respect for this woman named Frost for helping save her life, the truth be told, Aurora was in no need of a servant, having enough of them back home.

"Truthfully, I have no use for a servant since I have an overabundance of them back home, thanks to my being the eldest daughter of the Fae royal family of Seraph," Aurora said.

"Well, there has to be something I can do for you. I have no one now," Frost pleaded in a despondent voice.

Feeling sorry for Frost's plight, Aurora started putting considerable thought into a role she could be used for.

It came to her out of nowhere.

With the two of them being closer in age than she and Everlista, as well as her having no one and being pretty much a loner herself from a friendship standpoint—having none at all—this was what Frost could be to her.

"Frost, I have the perfect role for you," Aurora said. "A close friend to advise and give me opinions on issues; it's time I developed a friendship with someone closer to my own age and not of the same blood."

"I'd be honored to be that for you," Frost replied.

***

The desire to present her father with the Silver Dragon's head left Aurora. She needed to return home after the attack that was too close for comfort.

My father would understand, she thought as she and her new self-appointed friend and life advisor Frost continued moving through the woods towards home.

"So, tell me the reason for you being out here?" Frost asked.

"I was in search of a rare Silver Dragon, to bring its head to my father for naming me Princess," Aurora replied.

"You must really feel proud of that," Frost admitted.

"I would be," Aurora replied, a slight sadness in her voice. "If not for the fact my younger sister Everlista was quite upset she didn't receive the role. "

"What was the reason behind that?" Frost asked.

"It was all thanks to sending the vampire she's in love after me." Aurora replied. "You see, she wanted to ensure I was taken out of the contest—we were supposed to compete against each other for the role."

"Vampires, I so despise them, just as much as gargoyles," Frost spat in disgust.

"Yeah, I do as well," Aurora admitted. "It sickens me to know my sister is involved with one."

"You could try and kill him," Frost suggested.

"No, it'll break Everlista's heart," Aurora said

Continuing forward in their journey home, Aurora's ears picked up the sound of a sudden bizarre howling off in the distance.

"It's what I'm out here for," Aurora said, and she smiled.

***

Minutes later, sure enough, she and Frost ran into a Silver Dragon.

"So, I suppose that's the Silver Dragon you were seeking," Frost said, her eyes and voice filled with amazed nervousness over its immense size.

"Yeah, that's it," Aurora replied. "No matter how weak a condition I'm in, we need its head; I really want to obtain it for my father."

Raising her sword, Aurora began to charge for the silver dragon. The thing she didn't count on, collapsing suddenly before she could reach it.

No, I have to get up and kill it! My father needs a Silver Dragon's head!

"Damn you, gargoyle!" Aurora screamed, as she tried to stand and again collapsed to the ground.

"Aurora, I have a confession to make," Frost said. "I'm not just an ordinary servant girl."

"Okay?"

"Aurora, my voice has the power to put animals into a state of sleep. For some unknown reason it doesn't work on Darkmoor Gargoyles, since I tried it against the one who abducted me and murdered my lady master."

Aurora felt a high degree of excitement hearing this. Thanks to the unique ability Frost had, it was a certainty her father was going to receive what he'd long been seeking.

"Frost, put your blessing of a gift to good use."

As she kept her eyes on Frost, Aurora was treated to the most beautiful, harmonic song ever. Exactly like Frost said, it caused the Silver Dragon to stop in its tracks and its eyes to grow drowsy. It dropped to the ground.

After a while, Aurora had strength enough to stand up and perform the task which brought her out there.

CHAPTER NINE

"So, tell me Aurora, are you involved with someone, you know, like your sister?" Frost asked as they neared the castle and home.

"It's not for lack of trying," Aurora admitted, slight sadness building on her face. "Whoever it is I'm supposed to share my life with hasn't shown up yet. I'm beginning to think my life is to be a hunter, princess, and remain single the rest of my days."

"You shouldn't give up hope. The right companion will come, Aurora," Frost replied. "You're still in your youth, so there's plenty of time to worry about that sort of thing. In the meantime, like you said, you should concentrate on being a princess. Continue growing into the best hunter possible."

"You know you're absolutely right, Frost," Aurora replied, her face growing bright with excitement.

***

Aurora could tell Frost was impressed at the sight of the castle. Her eyes and face grew bright with excitement.

"This is the place I call home," Aurora said in a proud voice, the look growing on her face matched that of her new friend and self-appointed life advisor.

"It's really beautiful," Frost admitted. "I'm sure going to be honored calling it home as well."

***

As the two made their way through a castle hallway, its walls dominated with the most beautiful artwork imaginable, Aurora could tell the sight of it impressed Frost.

Reaching the end of this hallway, allowing them to enter yet another one, Aurora was struck by surprise. She saw her and Everlista's parents standing not too far off with a pair of men and two girls her sister's age. The thing alarming her about this, one of the men was a vampire, and the other one and the two girls were witches.

"Father, mother, tell me, what's the reason behind three witches and a vampire standing with you in our home?" Aurora asked in alarm as she and Frost hurried over to them.

"I have a bit of bad news to reveal, Aurora," Laurment replied in a grave voice. "These two men are Aldrich, the King of the Vampires, and the father of that boy, Victors.. The other is the King of the Witches, Ravinger and his two teenage daughters, Arleigha and Alisa."

"Well, just what are they doing here?" she asked, concerned.

"Thanks to Alisa wanting to prevent her sister from marrying Victors, she used her magic to send your sister and him somewhere nobody will ever find them," Laurment replied, "Arleigha fully intends on traveling to wherever this place is to kill Everlista and take Victors back."

Overwhelming dread dominated Aurora upon hearing this. Thanks to that pathetic vampire her sister was in love with, it was going to cost Everlista her life.

"Arleigha I'm begging you not to take my sister's life," Aurora pleaded, positioning herself so they stood face to face.

"And just why shouldn't I, newly titled Princess of the Fae?" Arleigha asked. "After all, your sister stole what's rightfully mine."

Arleigha certainly brought up a valid point, Aurora was quick to realize. She knew full well if she'd had someone she intended to marry ripped from her life, she'd want to kill the one responsible as well.

"I promise you, Arleigha, if Alisa sends me and my friend Frost to wherever she sent them, I'll bring them back," Aurora replied. "Not only that, but I'll make my sister understand she and Victors just aren't meant to be."

"And just how am I supposed to believe you'll do just that and not disregard your promise instead?" Arleigha asked.

"You can't, I suppose. You'll just have to take my word for it," Aurora said. "In the end though, like I said, I guarantee you'll have Victors back, and my sister convinced the two just aren't meant to be."

"Fine. All right," Arleigha said in exasperation. "You have exactly seven days to get it accomplished, and after that, I'm sending something your worst nightmare can't even begin to conjure to get Victors back and kill your sister."

"Now reveal just where you sent this Fae Princess' sister and Arleigha's future husband, Alisa," Ravinger ordered his daughter.

"But father-" Alisa pleaded.

"I mean it Alisa," Ravinger demanded.

"Fine. All right," Alisa said, disappointment building on her face. "The place I sent them to, a strange planet which my magic identified as 'Earth'. I never knew it existed until I sent Everlista and Victors there."

"Give me a few minutes to prepare," Aurora said.

"Ten minutes is all you have," Arleigha said.

"It's all I need," Aurora replied. "And father, I successfully managed to obtain the Silvers Dragon head for you." Placed securely in a blood red sack, she handed it over to him.

***

Despite informing Arleigha she and Frost would travel to this strange world she'd never heard of until now, Aurora realized she should have asked Frost if she'd have interest in going in the first place.

"Frost, I realize I should have asked if you'd be interested in accompanying me to Earth before I said you would," she said.

"No, don't worry about it," Frost replied. "I'd be honored to go along with you. And who knows, you might be able to find someone to fill the role of your prince in this strange new world."

***

"A suggestion, Frost," Aurora said as they arrived just outside her bedchamber. "It might be a good idea to change into one of my outfits."

Judging from Frost's pleased facial expression, Aurora could tell Frost was impressed by her bedchamber.

"Come on Frost, let's choose an outfit for you," Aurora said, taking her by the hand and leading her over to the closet.

"So, what about you Frost, have you ever been involved with someone romantically?" Aurora asked as the two stood in front of the now open closet.

"To tell you the truth, I haven't," Frost admitted. "The reason for it, up until tonight being a simple servant girl disallowed me from even considering such a thing."

"Well, not anymore, you aren't," Aurora said, reaching a hand in to remove a black-as-night dress.

Holding it up to Frost, a pleased expression filled her face as she saw the dress matched her height perfectly.

It's a perfect fit," Aurora said, a smile accompanying the pleased expression.

"Tell me if you want to," Aurora said sitting on the side of her bed, her feet connected to the floor, watching Frost get changed.

"Do I want to what?" Frost asked.

"Oh, don't be dense Frost, be involved in a romantic relationship," Aurora said, her face growing with disbelief. "You can have it now you're no longer a servant girl. So, what do you say, want a bit of companionship in your life?"

That sure would be something for me to have, Frost thought as she finished putting on the dress. There was just one problem she saw with it.

"It sure would be something if I had it, Aurora," she admitted. "The one problem I see, it'll prevent me from fully performing the role you've given me."

"Frost, you've spent almost your entire life in servitude to one person or another," Aurora said. "I seriously think it's time to move away from that. Sure, I want your friendship and advice, but not obsessively, meaning you should have a life as well. Look, why don't you think about it while we travel to Earth and make your decision when we return to Seraph?"

"All right, you have a deal, Aurora," Frost replied.

***

"So be sure to take care of yourself when you arrive on Earth, Aurora," Laurment said just as soon as she and Frost made their way back.

"Rest assured I will father," Aurora replied. "And when I do return, I promise you, Everlista will be back, and the idea she and Victors have any amount of future together flushed from her mind."

"Now, what are you waiting for, Alisa? Send Aurora and her companion to Earth so she can fix your mistake," Arleigha ordered. "And I promise you Fae Princess, after seven days, if you haven't gotten the task accomplished, it'll be one of the greatest mistakes of your life."

Instead of responding verbally, Alisa used her magic to create a blue amulet connected to a pure gold chain; she handed it over to Aurora.

"Aurora, take this, it'll allow you to locate your sister and Victors," she said. "I've installed my magic in it to help you along."

After it being taken from her hand, Alisa used her magic to send Frost and Aurora to Earth, to find Everlista and Victors.

The last thing Aurora saw before they vanished from sight was her parents, a nervous concern on their faces.

Chapter Ten

With a flash of brilliant white light, Aurora and Frost arrived on Earth. It was night. Gold dots of stars and a half-moon dominated the sky.

Studying her immediate surroundings, Aurora saw they were standing on the outskirts to a populated townFrom her point of view, she could actually see herself residing in this world named Earth. But of course, as the Princess of Seraph, this idea was pretty much out of the question for her.

"Come on Frost, let's start our search for my sister and Victors before the seven days are up," she said. "We need to prevent Arleigha from making good on her threat"

"I won't argue with that idea," Frost replied.

Heading towards the town off in the distance, Aurora held out the amulet Alisa gave her to track down Everlista and Victors' location. It indicated they were hiding out in the same town the girls were heading to by changing into a brilliant shade of red.

"There, Frost," Aurora said, her face growing pleased with slight excitement. "My sister and Victors are somewhere in that town."

As she and Frost continued, Aurora was marveled by the sights this Earth-world had to offer.

"So, tell me, Frost; what do you think of this world 'Earth' so far?" she asked.

"No offense, Aurora, but Seraph is the only place I'd like to spend the rest of my days living," Frost replied.

"Yes, what I've seen so far here on Earth looks remarkable, but Seraph is my home," Aurora said. "I wouldn't dare give that up for a hundred thousand, silver Copperstone coins."

Traveling in silence for the next few minutes, Aurora began to wonder what sort of individuals called Earth home. So far, she or Frost hadn't seen any life, which was impossible. Someone had to have been responsible for creating that town Everlista and Victors were hiding out in.

Continuing forward for the next couple minutes, Aurora was hit by surprise. A pair of bright lights suddenly appeared behind her. Alarmed, she almost found herself reaching around to retrieve her Alicktors sword. She would have done this too, if not for being amazed and turning to face whatever was responsible for the lights.

It was like nothing she'd ever seen in her life, a motorized carriage of some sort, containing two of Earth's inhabitants.

As it neared them, Aurora had an idea. "Let's stand aside and allow that strange, motorized carriage to pass," she suggested to Frost.

In no time, she and Frost were on the side of this road so the motorized carriage could pass.

Keeping her eyes focused on it as it approached, Aurora was struck by even more surprise. Contained inside were a male and female around the age of Frost and her.

What she didn't expect was the feeling as she lay her eyes on the male.

The attractive way he looked made her realize in an instant he was the one she wanted to share her life with.

He was unlike any male she'd ever seen in Seraph. Unfortunately, Aurora realized with the female seated beside him, he was probably claimed by her, and there was no possible chance for her. Besides, she was only going to be in this world until Everlista and Victors were found. It was best she not grow attached to any of this planet's inhabitants.

"Come on, Frost, let's continue to that town," she said as the motorized carriage headed from them.

***

Continuing, she and Frost were caught by surprise with yet another motorized carriage approaching.

"Let's stand aside and let it pass just like the first one," Aurora instructed.

Unlike the motorized carriage, this one contained two males, also the same age as she and Frost. It came to a sudden stop next to them.

"Hey, you pair of hot looking babes! my pal Thomas here and I are out in search of a good time," the one closest to she and Frost called out to them.

Almost instantly, Aurora realized she wanted nothing to do with this pair.

"Come on, Frost, let's go," she said in an urgent voice.

It was while she and Frost resumed their journey o the town, Aurora just happened to notice the vehicle was pursuing them.

Given the way the two males acted, Aurora felt anger course through her at an alarming rate. There was no doubt in her mind now, whoever these two were, they had nothing but vile, perverse intentions for she and Frost.

I'll be damned if I allow you two to force your sickening desires on Frost and me, Aurora thought in pure, fiery rage.

"Look, you two lads, I strongly suggest you leave us alone," Aurora warned, turning to face them. The motorized carriage came to a sudden stop before Frost and her.

This caused the pair to burst into uproarious laughter.

"She called us lads, Eric!" Thomas cried out, hilariously.

"Hey sweetheart, I know a few ancient ass words," Eric called out to her in an equally hilarious voice. "Get thee ass into thy vehicle so Thomas and I can pillage and plunder you two sweet, wholesome, chaste bitches!"

Aurora felt the anger steadily increase as a result. On top of these two disgusting, perverse males' sexual intentions for Frost and her, they made fun of the language she'd used.

I swear you two perverted louts have just made the biggest mistakes of your lives, Aurora thought as the rage blossomed even further in her.

Aurora raced to move her hand to her back in an effort to retrieve her Alicktors sword and chase them off. The reaction of her doing so caused the two shock and surprise.

"I suggest you two get out of my sight or I swear I won't hesitate to use this against you," Aurora ordered in a deeply serious voice. She pointed the sword straight at them.

This seemed to do the trick. They raced to speed away and were out of sight in just a few short minutes.

"Frost, the sooner we find Everlista and Victors, the sooner we can leave this Earth and return to Seraph," Aurora said, feeling quite thankful Eric and Thomas weren't able to execute their perverted goal.

CHAPTER ELEVEN

Nicholas Warstone just knew picking up his girlfriend, Savannah Rosefield— who he'd dated since freshman year at Midnight Lake High—something bothered her.

The way she was acting so dismissive, forced him to realize one thing. By the end of the night, he was certain she would break bad news to him.

What could it be? Nicholas wondered as they drove to their all-time favorite restaurant, 'Frosters.'

Halfway to it, what he didn't expect to see were two of the most unusual women ever. He swore the pair looked just like the fae characters in those books Savannah and his sister Leanna loved reading.

What stood out about them, the one with frosty blue hair and wearing a navy blue dress reaching to her feet was a hundred times more attractive than her friend. Heck, she was even prettier than Savannah who didn't miss the mark when it came to beauty. Adding to this was the unusual fact she had a sword strapped to her back.

Nicholas could see himself getting involved with her if he weren't dating Savannah. He was though, so he pushed this and her from his mind. Besides that, he didn't even know her.

*****

It was while he and Savannah sat around a table that Nicholas continued to sense something was wrong with her.

"Okay, what's bothering you?" he asked.

The response Nicholas received, a simple, quiet, "it's nothing."

Nicholas wasn't buying it for an instant. He knew this wasn't the case; something bothered her but what?

"I know you, Savannah, there's definitely something wrong."

"I promise you, there isn't," Savannah replied.

He knew she was lying, that much was clear. The question was, about what? It had to be important, or else she wouldn't be keeping it from him.

"You're keeping something from me Savannah," he said. "Come on. Talk to me; tell me what it is."

Instead of replying, all Savannah did was let loose with an exasperated sigh.

"Fine, all right, I was hoping to tell you just before you dropped me off back home," she said. "Nicholas, Chris Cannerman asked me to be his girlfriend a couple days ago, and I said yes."

Disappointment grew on Nicholas' face. He just found out his girlfriend had been cheating on him.

"Dinner's off," he said, anger building on his face. "And so is our relationship."

"Nicholas I'm sorry," Savannah said.

"Just save it, Savannah," he replied bitterly.

***

Stepping from the restaurant, Nicholas felt as cold and miserable as the cool, late-October night air. With Halloween right around the corner, everywhere he looked there was an abundance of decorations.

Moments before climbing into his car with her for the last time ever, Nicholas again received yet another "sorry," out of Savannah.

She could apologize all she wanted, but it wouldn't change the fact it was over between them.

***

"Are you going to be okay?" Savannah asked as he drove her home for the last timer.

Nicholas couldn't believe the nerve of her; Savannah had just broken up with him, and now she was acting like everything was all right between them.

"Why should you care, you'd much rather be with Chris?" he said.

"Oh, come on Nicholas, don't be that way," she replied.

Continuing to stare out the windshield, Nicholas felt anger rising in him.

"Look Savannah, you already said there's no future for us, and you'd rather be with Chris Cannerman," he said trying to keep the anger in check. "I'm just going to drive you home, and after that, we're over. And that includes being friends."

"Fine, if that's what you want," Savannah said.

***

Driving Savannah home, once again, Nicholas spotted the two fae-obsessed women walking aimlessly down a street. ith his relationship at an end, Nicholas wondered if he should pull over and ask the more attractive one if she was single. I would really piss Savannah off big time by that, he thought, smiling.

"What, you like one of those girls masquerading as fae?" Savannah asked, slight anger darkening her normally attractive face.

"Why should you care? You've got what you wanted—

we're over and done with so you can be with Chris."

"Sure, go right on ahead," Savannah replied in disgust. "She's way too beautiful for you and will tell you to go take a hike just as soon as you say the first word to her."

"Let's go find out," Nicholas said, starting to maneuver his Bronco over to them.

"Uh-uh forget it. I want to get home," Savannah replied. "Now watch some hot, fae-obsessed girl humiliate you for trying to hook up with her."

"Whatever you say," Nicholas said. "I just want to get you out of this Bronco and forget we ever were involved."

***

The rest of the drive to Savannah's house was spent in silence, suiting Nicholas just fine. He truthfully didn't have anything further to say to her.

"So, what are you waiting for Savannah, take a hike," Nicholas said pulling up to her house.

Not saying a word, Savannah simply climbed out and headed towards her house.

Staring after her Nicholas couldn't believe he and Savannah were over; life really hated him at the moment. He started to consider trying to find the fae women and ask the more attractive one if she was involved. *No, she's probably involved, and if not, she'll tell me to go take a hike,* he thought. Starting up the engine, he drove home.

Heading to her house, the only desire Savannah had was to call Chris and tell him she and Nicholas were over. Then head over and celebrate being together.

Chapter Twelve

Stepping into the living room, Nicholas met his fifteen-year-old sister, Leanne, seated alone on the sofa watching a Blu-ray DVD of her favorite movie, 'Disturbia'.

Starting for the stairs and having no interest in conversing with his sister; Nicholas was caught by surprise by Leanne's asking "hey, what's wrong?"

"Nothing's wrong," he said.

"Oh, don't give me that," Leanna replied. "I can see it on your face, something is."

Putting a bit of thought into it, Nicolas realized since it was going to be all over Midnight Lake High by morning, he should just come out and tell her.

"I called it quits with Savannah," he said.

"Why would you do that?" Leanna asked, alarm brightening her face.

"That would be thanks to her wanting to be with Chris Cannerman," he replied. "Now, if you don't mind, I'd like to head up to my bedroom and spend the rest of the night feeling depressed, so goodnight."

"Yeah, sure whatever," Leanna said, unpausing the DVD.

***

Entering his bedroom, Nicholas wasted no timethrowing himself down on the bed. He wanted to lay there and continue to feel depressed.

Like Savannah and Leanna, he too had an obsession for fae. Not that he had a feminine bone in his body. He could always be found catching live sports on a regular basis, was a star player on the football team alongside his close friend Shane Masters, exercised regularly. On top of that, he could be found outside at an ungodly early morning hour running for miles.

No, the type of fae he was obsessed over were the violent, kick-ass warrior type, a rarity since most fae were far from that. At least the ones his former girlfriend or sister read about like they were going out of style. He always had a secret affection for tough, kick-ass heroines. They were the major theme of his fantasy writing, which he hoped to publish sooner rather than later.

Taking his mind off this, he glanced at his watch, seeing it was eight forty-five. Knowing full well there was a party going on over at Crystal Water Beach, he decided maybe his best friend in the world, Shane and his sister Alison could help cheer him up.

Yeah, that's exactly what I'll do, Nicholas thought, racing off the bed.

***

"Couldn't sleep huh?" Leanna asked as he raced back downstairs.

"No uh-uh," Nicholas said, heading straight for the front door. "I'll see you later. I'm heading over to that party over at Crystal Waters Beach."

***

Exiting his house, Nicholas raced toward the bronco, jumped in, and sped off.

Driving through Midnight Lake, Nicholas once again passed by the two women dressed just like fae Just like before, the thought he should drive over to them and ask if the more attractive one was available invaded his mind. She did, after all, resemble the type of fae woman he was obsessed about.

Yeah, it would really piss Savannah off if I showed up with her at school tomorrow, prove to her a beautiful girl could find interest in me. He'd reveal to her he could bounce back and wasn't depressed about her no longer in his life.

The fear of rejection prevented Nicholas from doing so. He couldn't afford to receive any more heartbreak from females tonight.

Chapter Thirteen

Staring out into nothingness, Shane Masters wondered just one thing. When was his only sibling, Alison, going to get up the courage to reveal to her crush that'd started last spring, Adam Ferners, she was interested.

"I can tell you're deep in thought about something, mind filling me in on what that is?" Alison asked.

"Alison, I think it's high time you let Adam know how much of a serious crush you have on him, since we both know he's still single," Shane said, glancing at her. "You want him still, don't you?"

Alison couldn't help but push out a pleased smile over this subject and Adam in particular. Each and every time she thought about him, she was overcome with an excited, blissful feeling. This intensified by several degrees whenever she was near him.

"More than anything," Alison replied, a smile filling out her face.

"So, what are you waiting for? Step up to the plate and tell him, unless you're too scared," Shane said.

"Yeah, I'll show your ass how much of a serious, fearless bitch I am," Alison smartly remarked, turning to face Shane. "First thing tomorrow morning, I'm marching right up to Adam and spilling my guts about how I feel."

"Now that's the spirit," Shane replied in amusement.

Staring forward, Alison started wondering who, if anyone, her brother was interested in. Shane never revealed whoever she might be to either Nicholas or her. It made her constantly wonder the name of the girl, if he had one in mind, he wanted to be with.

Well, she wasn't going to be kept in suspense about it any longer.

"So now it's your turn ,Shane, which girl in all of Midnight Lake are you most interested in?" Alison asked.

There's just one single answer to that, Shane thought continuing to stare forward. A single name, Madeline Waterfield, she was one of the smartest girls attending Midnight Lake High, a brain. He was certain she wouldn't give him the time of day. Sure, Shane got decent grades, but he was no genius. His strengths lie in sports and athletics. It was for that reason, Shane was certain Madeline wouldn't be interested in him. They came from completely different worlds and had different interests.

"Uh-uh, there's no girl I'm interested in yet," he said.

"Oh, come on Shane, there has to be someone! As a matter of fact, I'm not going to rest until I get it out of you."

"You'll be waiting forever, since there's no way she's interested in me," Shane replied.

"So, there is a girl you like!" Alison cried, turning a sudden beaming face to her brother. "Well, you have to tell me who she is!"

"She'd never like me back," Shane admitted.

"You don't know that Shane," Alison replied. "Maybe if you reveal who she is I can give you my opinion on if she'll say yes or no."

Continuing to stare forward, Shane saw Nicholas approach them in his Bronco. *It sure would be something to know someone's opinion if Madeline and I are compatible despite my belief she wouldn't even look at me for a date,* he thought.

"Madeline Waterfield," he said as Nicholas grew even closer. "And there's no way she'd like me; the reason why, she's a genius and I'm not. My interests are in sports, not academics."

Alison's opinion about this came in an instant. She knew why Shane was nervous about keeping his feelings towards Madeline a secret. She was one of the smartest girls at their high school. Alison knew Madeline. However, she didn't come off as the type who thought anyone was beneath her.

"I know Madeline," Alison said. "She doesn't come off as the type who thinks anyone's beneath her. "You should ask her if she's interested."

"You really think so?" Shane asked as Nicholas closed the distance and parked.

"I do," Alison admitted. "So, are you going to grow a pair and ask her if she's interested in you?"

If Alison has the guts to tell Adam her feelings, so can I, Shane decided.

"Yeah, you know what? That's what I'm going to do," Shane said.

"Now that's the spirit, Shane," Alison replied.

***

Spotting Shane and Alison seated alone on the bumper past Crystal Water's parking lot, Nicholas pulled up in front of them. Shane wore a black sweatshirt, blue jeans, and Alison was in cut-off blue jean shorts, a navy blue work shirt tied mid-torso, revealing a perfect, firm stomach. Like Savannah, Alison was part of Midnight Lake High's cheerleading squad, the Warriorettes

Not that he was attracted to her. He considered Alison a friend more than anything. Besides, she had her heart set on one Adam Ferners.

Approaching them, Nicholas saw they were excited about something. It made the depression over he and Savannah calling it quits fade, slightly.

"You two sure look excited about something," he said.

"We have every right to be," Alison replied as he sat next to her. "Unlike you, I might add. I swear you look absolutely miserable, Nicholas."

"Yeah, why so glum chum?" Shane asked.

Realizing the end of his and Savannah's relationship would be news sooner rather than later, Nicholas decided to inform his two closest friends. After all, enough people at Frosters witnessed it. Unless they were deaf, dumb, and blind; it was probably being spread all over Midnight Lake even as he sat there.

"Bad news, Shane and Alison. I just broke up with Savannah," he replied.

"But you two have been together forever!" Alison exclaimed, concern building on her face.

"You can thank *her* wanting to date Chris Cannerman behind my back for it," Nicholas replied.

"Now that sure sucks," Shane said.

"Yeah, you're telling me," Nicholas replied.

"Nicholas I'm sorry and you don't need her," Alison said.

"Alison's right," Shane said. "You'll find someone new in no time."

"Sorry you two. I think I'm taking a break from romantic relationships for a good long while," he informed them. "As a matter of fact, let's change the subject. Tell me, what made the two of you so excited? I could sure use some good news."

"We have every single right to feel that way," Alison said, managing a smile. "Should I go first, or you, Shane?"

"You go first. We've all been waiting for your good news longer than mine," Shane said.

Alison felt the excited blissful feeling she had whenever she thought about Adam or was around him start growing. So large in fact, she felt ready to burst out and reveal her decision about Adam and how she felt about him.

"First thing tomorrow morning, I'm marching right up to Adam to finally reveal how I feel about him," she announced. It brought a large smile growing on her face.

"It's about time you mustered up the courage for it," Nicholas said. And with it, he felt the depression decrease even further.

"So, Shane, what's your good news?"

"Nicholas, Shane finally told me the girl's name he's secretly in love with," Alison said.

"One of the world's biggest mysteries is about to be solved," Nicholas replied in amusement. "Who is she?"

"Go ahead and tell him Shane," Alison said.

Staring out into the empty parking lot, Shane felt excitement grow. His fears over whether he had a chance with Madeline were brought to rest, thanks to his sister. He could barely wait for tomorrow to tell her how he felt.

"Genius girl Madeline Waterfield," Shane said. "Nicholas, you think I have a chance in hell with her, being I'm not as smart as her?"

"I know Madeline Shane," Nicholas replied. "She doesn't come off as someone that shallow; she wouldn't look down on those not as intelligent as her."

"So, you're saying I should tell Madeline I'm interested?" Shane asked.

"Yeah, sure go for it, Shane, since I know she's currently single," Nicholas said. "It's long overdue—you enter the dating scene."

"It's on my agenda for tomorrow," Shane said, managing a smile.

Glancing all around, Nicholas felt the excitement over this evaporate and heartbreaking depression return. Savannah had wasted no time in moving on with her life. She was further down the beach hand in hand with Chris.

In an instant, Nicholas came to one realization. The two being here meant there was not a chance he wanted to remain.

"Shane, Alison, it was a mistake for me to show up, so I'm just going to take off," he said.

Looking around, it was just a second before Alison saw the reason why he was in such a hurry to leave.

"Yeah, I don't blame you," she said. "Let's go and hang out somewhere else."

***

"Where should we hang out?" Alison asked when they were away from Crystal Water Beach driving on a stretch of road free from any sign of life—long stretches of woods on either side.

"My parents are out for the night. We can head over to my house," Nicholas suggested.

Shane and Alison weren't able to reply as out of nowhere, something landed on the back end of the roof with a powerful thud.

It caused Nicholas to come screeching to a sudden halt.

"Damn it to hell and back!" Nicholas cried, "Shane, be a buddy and let's go check if there's any damage."

***

"Come on Shane, give me a boost up," Nicholas said as they arrived at the back of the Bronco.

Stronger than he was smart, Shane cupped his hands together, managing to do so with little effort. Relief filled Nicholas as he saw whatever landed on the roof had left minimal damage in the form of a slight couple dents. Still, it was going to cost him at least a couple hundred dollars to repair.

"What do you see?" Shane asked.

"A couple hundred dollars of damage, that's for sure," Nicholas said in a displeased voice.

"It's a good thing you and Savannah have called it quits," Shane said lowering him back down to the ground.

"Yeah, you're sure telling me," Nicholas replied.

"So, I know you said you were turned off from dating for a while," Shane said. "But you shouldn't allow Savannah happiness while you're miserable. There has to be a second choice."

Again, the thought about the mystery girl dressed like a fae returned. Despite not knowing a thing about her—including her name—there was something appealing. Not to mention she was gorgeous beyond belief.

"I saw a pair of girls dressed like fae twice earlier tonight," Nicholas replied. "One who actually held my attention longer than a minute."

"There you go," Shane encouraged.

"Oh, come on Shane, I don't even know her name!" Nicholas said. "And what if she's involved with someone?"

"Only one way to find out," Shane replied. "When we return to town, try and find her again. Drive up and introduce yourself to your mystery girl. If she doesn't just walk away, you know she's interested. So, are you going to do it?"

"I'll have to think about it. That's the best answer I can give," Nicholas replied. "Although Savannah proclaimed there wouldn't be a chance in hell a beautiful girl would be interested in me."

"So, prove her wrong, and take my suggestion," Shane encouraged.

"It sure would piss Savannah off if I show up with the girl with a serious fae obsession tomorrow at school," Nicholas replied.

Glancing around, he saw nothing. "Well, I don't see what came crashing down. Let's get back in the Bronco before we find out what caused the damage."

***

Little did Nicholas and Shane realize, but they were being watched from afar. By whom? Adam Ferners. The same Adam Alison had a serious crush on.

It was during his routine nighttime bike riding he ran into one heck of a surprise. A strange looking woman side by side with who he swore was a male vampire. They appeared out of nowhere in front of him, causing him to make a sudden stop to not crash into them. This was a mistake as it allowed the vampire to rush at him and do what he was best known for, transforming him as well.

In life, Adam had a huge secret crush on Alison Masters just like she did him. Also like her, he was always too afraid to reveal it. It wasn't the same now as a vampire.

Arriving at Crystal Water's beach party, and seeing the damn hot Alison was dressed, Adam couldn't wait to reveal his feelings for her. Perfect stomach exposed, sexy legs pouring out of the blue jean cut off shorts she wore. His plan was to abduct her to some secret location make her his immortal girlfriend.

Just as he was about to make his move, she, her brother Shane, and Nicholas Warman, who he knew was involved with Savannah Rosefield, took off.

So, he followed them. It wasn't hard given what he was.

Continuing to watch them, Adam came up with a sudden genius idea. Grab either Nicholas or Shane and threaten to kill whichever one unless Alison agreed to go with him. Yeah, that was what he'd do to ensure she was his forever.

Rushing towards them, Adam had his hand gripped around Shane's throat.

***

Standing there, Nicholas couldn't believe his eyes. First, earlier tonight he'd seen the two girls with an obsession for fae, and now he was face-to-face with Adam Farners.

He had never known Adam to be obsessed with vampires, but now there he was, with a genuine authentic vampire appearance. Worse, he had Shane gripped tight around the throat.

"Hey Adam man, what's up with you, I've never known you to act violent or have an obsession for vampires?" Nicholas asked, his face growing with sudden nervousness.

"Yeah, that was the old me," Adam replied. "Now I'm a real life immortal, bloodsucking creature of the night."

"He's not kidding, Nicholas," Shane managed. "His skin's damn ice cold."

"Come on Adam, let him go," Nicholas said.

"Sure, just as soon as Alison gets her ass out of the Bronco," Adam replied. "You see I've had a serious crush on her for the longest time and want her to be my immortal girlfriend. Not just that, I want her to be the first human whose blood I taste."

Chapter Fourteen

Sitting there, windows wide open, Alison received an earful of every single word going on outside. Shane was being held tight by her longtime crush, Adam's, grip. Worse, he admitted to being an actual vampire. She felt shock race through her.

Adam's being what he was now made her realize one thing. She could no longer have a crush on him. She felt sick to her stomach. Adam was now a corpse who had to survive by drinking human blood, and she was first in line to suffer this horrible fate.

What frightened Alison almost to death, his wanting her to be his immortal girlfriend. And it didn't help the situation Adam's plan for her would entail inserting long, sharp teeth into her flesh, her blood being drained from her body, getting turned into a walking corpse who craved human blood. She felt her stomach do somersaults of disgust.

The pained expression she saw on her brother's face told Alison, sickened, and frightened to death, she had no choice but to do as Adam demanded. She felt depression combine with sickening disgust. She had no choice but to hand herself over to him to save Shane's life.

Climbing out, she approached the group-all the while, icy cold terror gripped her heart. Adam's skin was chalky white. She couldn't believe it; vampires really did exist.

For a moment, Alison wondered if it really was such a good idea to hand herself over to Adam so he'd free Shane. In saving her brother's life, she'd lose hers, become immortal, and crave blood. The idea of it caused the sickening, disgusted feeling to increase.

"You okay, Shane?" she asked, her face dominated by nervousness.

"Get the hell out of here, Alison, and don't let this bloodsucking son of a bitch get what he wants!" Shane shouted, his eyes growing large with fear and anger.

Staring down onto the ground, Alison wasn't surprised to feel the cool fall air making her shiver a bit. Or maybe it had to do with the fact she would have to hand herself over to a real, true to life vampire.

"Okay Adam, you got me out here. Now, let Shane go," she ordered.

"Uh-uh, no, not until you promise you'll let me transform you into my immortal girlfriend," Adam said.

Staring down at her feet, she felt the depression, and sickening disgust increase. If she didn't agree, it would be Shane who paid the price. She couldn't have that.

"Fine you win. I'm yours," Alison said returning to staring at him.

"You sure have a loving sister Shane," Adam said, pushing out a victory smile. "I mean, damn, she's willing to give up her life and become a vampire so you won't."

Heading towards him, Alison watched as his face grew wide with excitement. Still, she headed forward like a fearless trooper.

"Shane I'm sorry, but I don't want to see you die knowing I could've prevented it," Alison said, her face growing heavy with sadness. "So, what are you waiting for, Adam? Let go of my brother. I'm yours."

Once Adam shoved Shane away from him, Alison finished her trek. She felt an icy coldness as her bicep was grabbed. Before Alison knew it, he raced them off into the woods.

***

It was less than a minute before they stood face-to-face deep in the woods. Oh, how he wanted her, to touch and kiss her, and if he lucked out, see her naked tonight.

"I want you so much Alison," he whispered, reaching out a hand and connecting it to the left side of her face. His touch made her feel a desperate need to vomit. She didn't, however.

Staring at him, Alison felt anger race through her at a mile a minute. She was about to be turned into a vampire who she used to have a serious crush on.

Alison was surprised by the idea filling her mind. She'd use Adam's desire for her to her advantage. She'd talk him out of making her a vampire—the most horrible thing imaginable. In exchange, sickening as the thought was, she'd agree to be his mortal girlfriend.

"Adam, please, if you care about me like you said, you'll let me go and not transform me into a vampire," she pleaded, staring at him with nervous eyes. "To tell you the truth, I'm not so keen on the idea, and I promise I'll still be your girlfriend. It's what I've wanted since last spring, when I developed a serious crush on you. Please, if you care about me as much as I do you, cut me a break and let me keep my mortality."

"You're lucky I do," he said. "Okay, look, Alison, I'll tell you what, if you're able to escape these woods without me catching you, I won't make you immortal."

"And if I can't?" Alison asked.

"You'll have to agree to have sex with me here in these woods and be turned into a vampire right along with it," he said.

She felt the sickening disgust blossom one hundred percent at the thought of having sex with a corpse, it touching her bare flesh. And so much worse, have sex for the first time ever. It caused the sickening, disgusted feeling to bring on a serious need to vomit. Still, she realized she had no choice in the matter if she wanted to try and escape the worst death imaginable.

"Fine. All right, it's a deal," she said.

"You have five minutes," Adam replied.

***

Racing through the woods, her heart beating a mile a minute, Alison had just one thing on her mind, escape. Her life and virginity depended on it. Just the thought of having sex with a corpse, having her virtue stolen in the process, and being turned into a vampire filled her with dread to the core.

Continuing forward, Alison felt a blast of horror by Adam's, "come out, come out wherever you are!"

It sent her racing faster than ever, the sickening disgust growing worse than ever.

Alison realized it did her little good. Adam was there out of nowhere. He forced her to the ground, driving tremendous pain through her until she had no choice but to push out the loudest scream ever.

Damn it, I'm so dead, she thought, *I'm about to become a sickening vampire. Have sex with a freaking corpse!*

Alison started to feel stinging tears in her eyes. Shutting them tight, she had no desire to even look at him.

Keeping them closed, she felt a blast of sudden surprise when Adam's weight was lifted off her. Re-opening her eyes, they widened upon seeing a pair of girls her age in fancy dresses.

They were made up as fae, one more incredibly attractive than the other—she was armed with a sharp sword. It was this which she used to slice off Adam's head before he even knew what the hell was going on.

It sent relief racing through her. She'd just been saved from having to suffer the most horrible thing imaginable.

"You two showed up at just the right time," she said, jumping to her feet, her face bright with relief.

Standing, Alison felt alarm as neither of these women seemed interested in saying a single word to her.

"Hey, there's nothing to be worried about from me," Alison said.

"Can we trust you not to humiliate us?" The more attractive one of the pair asked, bringing the sword up and pointing it at her.

"Trust me, that's the farthest thing from my mind," Alison said, staring at the sword with nervous eyes.

"I'm sorry. My friend Frost and I were just insulted by two perverted males named Eric and Thomas," Aurora said.

"Yeah, they're real creeps, and I know that from personal experience," Alison admitted. "It was smart of you to stay the hell away from them at all costs. Those two are desperate for sex like you wouldn't believe. So, I guess the way you're dressed, you have a serious love for all things fae, in addition to having skill in using a sword and killing vampires."

Aurora felt comfortable being around his girl she saved.

"I was taught how to use a sword at an early age," Aurora admitted, pushing out a smile. "Frost and I are actual fae, believe it or not."

Alison Masters," Alison said, extending out a hand in friendship towards Aurora. "And up until a few minutes ago, if you and Frost hadn't shown up, almost Adam Ferner's immortal girlfriend."

Aurora felt guilt over this. If it weren't for Everlista and Victors, Adam would never have become a vampire. Alison's life wouldn't have been put in danger.

"Aurora," she said, accepting Alison's handshake. "Alison, it's my sister Everlista's and her vampire boyfriend Victors' fault Adam became what he did. The two of them escaped to Earth from our world, Seraph so he wouldn't be forced to marry a powerful dark witch named Arleigha."

Alison couldn't believe it, not only were Aurora and Frost real fae, but came from another world.

"I've just been named Princess of Seraph, and my mission here on Earth is to bring my sister and Victors back there before Arleigha uses her magic to do so using a much harsher method," Aurora said. "I can't have that happen to my sister, and hopefully, at the same time prevent Victors from making any more vampires."

"You must feel damn lucky to be princess of your world Aurora," Alison said. "That doesn't happen in real life. So where are you and Frost staying while you two are here?"

"Actually Alison, I want to continue my search for Everlista and Victors until I find them," Aurora replied. "I need to drag the two back to Seraph before Arleigha makes good on her threat."

"No one should go without sleeping, not even a fae princess," Alison admitted. "Look I have a spare bedroom at my house. You two are more than welcome to crash there for the night. Besides, I seriously doubt Victors will be out for blood tonight, since he already took from Adam."

"She has a point, Aurora," Frost said. "I don't know about you, but I'm really exhausted."

"All right, we'll resume the search for my sister and her vampire boyfriend tomorrow night," Aurora replied. "Truthfully, I'm feeling exhausted as well."

"You should be, Aurora, given what you went through prior to our arrival here," Frost said.

CHAPTER FIFTEEN

Shane felt depressed as he stood next to Nicholas. So much in fact, he no longer had any desire to tell Madeline he was interested in her tomorrow. If it weren't for him, Alison would still be there and alive, not dragged off to be turned into a vampire's girlfriend.

"My life really sucks like you wouldn't believe," he admitted, his voice growing with despair. "I don't know just how the hell I'm going to explain it to my parents— Alison's in the hands of a vampire with a crush on her."

"Shane, I'm sorry," Nicholas replied, the same despair building on his face. "Come on, we'd better get out of here before Alison returns with a serious craving for blood."

Starting for the Bronco, the despair on Nicholas' and Shane's faces were replaced by excitement. They were taken by surprise as Alison made a sudden appearance. She wasn't a vampire, and amazingly she was with the two fae women. There was no sign of Adam anywhere in sight.

"So, are those the two fae women you saw before?" Shane asked.

"Yeah, that's them all right," Nicholas replied.

"So, what are you waiting for? Go ask her if she's single so you can prove Savannah wrong and piss her off majorly tomorrow," Shane encouraged.

"Shouldn't we make sure Alison's okay first?" Nicholas asked. "I mean she appears to be all right, but she was just abducted by the vampire who she used to have a crush on."

"Right, stupid me. Where's my brain?" Shane replied, offering a slight smile.

Reaching Alison and the two womenit was clear a miracle had happened tonight. Alison had been spared being turned into a vampire by Adam.

"Forgive me for not expressing thankfulness much sooner," Shane said embracing her as tight as possible.

"Thanks to these pair of women beside me," Alison replied quietly.

"You two sure showed up at the exact right time," Shane said, pulling away from his sister and staring right at Aurora and Frost.

"Nicholas, Shane, this is Aurora and Frost," Alison said.

"Have any last names to go with those?" Shane asked, gazing right at Aurora.

"We don't use last names where we come from," Aurora replied, returning Shane's gaze.

"Right, okay," Shane said uneasily. "So, thanks for taking time out of whatever requires you to dress like fae."

Turning to look at Aurora, Alison saw she was offended by this.

"Aurora's the real thing believe it or not, Frost and her both." Alison said.

Nicholas was caught by eye-widening surprise at this. He could barely believe that fantasy creatures like fae actually existed. He wasn't much surprised, since he'd also seen a fictional monster, a vampire, just a few minutes ago. It was just too bad Leanna wasn't there. She'd love to see a pair of fae in the flesh.

"I just wish my sister Leanna was here," Nicholas said. "She would have loved to see an actual pair of real, live fae."

"There's no reason why she can't," Alison replied. "Aurora and Frost have nowhere to crash for the night, and I know you have a spare bedroom, Nicholas."

"The idea's great Alison, but the problem's my parents," Nicholas said. "You and I both know there's no way they'll allow Aurora and Frost to crash under any circumstances."

Staring at Nicholas, that feeling of desire for him once again invaded Aurora's heart. Because of this, she wasn't surprised that the solution to this problem filled her mind.

"Nicholas I've been given a magic amulet," she said. "It should dissuade your parents from their decision."

"What do you think of that Nicholas?" Alison asked.

"I'm sure he won't have a problem saying yes to you, Aurora," Shane said.

"Oh, I don't know, I barely even know Aurora and Frost," Nicholas said, nervously eyeing her sword. "What if she's dangerous?"

"I promise you Nicholas. There's not a thing for you to be afraid of from me," Aurora replied, staring at him with trusting eyes.

Nicholas almost expected Aurora to reach a hand and connect it to his face. She didn't, however.

"So, are you going to have a heart and let Aurora and Frost crash in your spare bedroom for the night?" Alison asked.

"It's lucky I'm in a pretty good mood, probably due to Adam not turning you into his immortal vampire girlfriend," Nicholas replied. "Yeah sure, Aurora can use her magic amulet to manipulate my parents' minds. But just for one night."

"I promise one night is all it'll be," Aurora said, a truthful look on her face.

Chapter Sixteen

Staring at Aurora through the rearview mirror, Nicholas wondered if she was single.

No longer feeling the depression over breaking up with Savannah, he wondered if he should take Shane's suggestion and ask her if she might be interested in him. It sure would be something if he showed up at Midnight Lake High with her tomorrow to show Savannah she was dead wrong that a beautiful girl wouldn't even look his way.

Also that he'd gotten over his ex-girlfriend and was involved with someone. He wasn't dwelling in misery and begging her to take him back. Not that she would, replacing him with Chris.

"So, what exactly are you here for Aurora?" Nicholas asked, coming to a sudden stop at a red light on Waterstone Street and Classers Avenue.

"My sister, Everlista, also a fae, and her vampire boyfriend Victors are hiding out somewhere in your town," Aurora replied. "Frost and I are here to take them back to our world named Seraph. Hopefully we'll be able to find them before he creates more vampires like poor Adam."

"So, I guess that means once you find Everlista and Victors, tomorrow night, you'll be returning to Seraph?" Nicholas asked.

"There's no way around it, Nicholas," Aurora replied softly. "If I don't, the young witch who wants to marry Victors will use her dark magic against my sister. That's the reason why they fled here."

"But what if you're not able to find them by tomorrow night?" Alison asked.

"Thanks to the magic amulet, it's not going to be a problem," Aurora replied in slight relief. "That's how Frost and I found you and Adam. It told us a vampire was in the vicinity."

"Don't worry, I'm sure you'll be able to find them by tomorrow night," Alison encouraged. "As a matter of fact, Shane, Nicholas, and I won't mind helping you with that. Right you two?"

"It's the least we can do for you saving my sister's life, Aurora," Shane replied.

"Yeah sure, we'll help you find your sister and her boyfriend," Nicholas said, despite feeling sudden disappointment. The emotion growing on his face.

"So, tell us, Aurora, were you involved with anyone back in Seraph?" Shane asked, catching this.

"Unlike Everlista, I'm not," Aurora replied. "My interests are hunting and to continue becoming the best warrior I can, not romance."

"Oh, come on Aurora, there's more to life than that, even for someone from Seraph," Shane said.

Staring at Nicholas, Aurora once again felt the stirring desire for him, the first male ever she felt this way for. But he was probably involved with the female in the motorized vehicle she saw earlier. That pretty much meant there wasn't a chance for them. Besides, tomorrow night, after she found Everlista and Victors, she'd no longer be on Earth.

"I now have another role to add to warrior and hunter," she said, proud confidence building on her face. "My father's just named me Princess of Seraph."

"Congratulations on that, Aurora," Alison replied.

"What do you think of that Nicholas?" Shane asked. "The girl you want to replace Savannah with is a royal princess in addition to being a warrior and hunter."

"I thought you said you were taking a break from romantic relationships for a good long while?" Alison asked.

"I was until your brother talked me out of it," Nicholas replied. "I want to show Savannah I'm not feeling miserable about breaking up with her for cheating with Chris."

"Well in that case, I think you and Aurora would be perfect together," Alison continued. "It's just too bad she'll be gone after tomorrow night."

"Yeah, it really is a damn shame," Shane said in disappointment.

"Tell us what you think about Nicholas being interested in you, Aurora," Alison said.

It's the one thing which will make me want to stay longer than tomorrow night, Aurora thought.

"Nicholas, I'm honored you feel that way about me," she replied in slight sadness. "I'm sorry you had to break up with your girlfriend for being unfaithful. But even if I return your feelings, tomorrow night I'll be gone, and it just wouldn't be fair to you. I seriously doubt you'd want to leave Earth and your family and two friends here."

Aurora was sure right about that. His whole life was here in Midnight Lake.

"Yeah, there's pretty much no chance of that," Nicholas admitted, slight disappointment brightening his face.

***

"Thanks again for saving my life tonight, Aurora," Alison said as Nicholas pulled up to the front of her house.

Aurora felt herself grow with excitement over this. The thought returned. She was thankful. Unlike the first Earth citizens she met, Eric and Thomas, Alison, Shane, and Nicholas showed her nothing but respect.

"Like I told you before, Alison, I'm glad you, Nicholas, and Shane didn't treat me like Eric and Thomas," she replied.

"They're dicks, and it's a good idea to stay clear from them at all costs," Shane said.

"My brother's right, like I said before, they're nothing but perverted pains in the ass," Alison said.

"Yeah, you should know ,Alison," Nicholas replied with a smile.

"Catch you tomorrow Aurora and Frost," Alison said. She and Shane made a quick exit.

CHAPTER SEVENTEEN

"So, what's Seraph like?" Nicholas asked, driving down Starlake Avenue.

"It's the most wonderful place imaginable," Aurora replied, her face growing bright. "Seraph is split up into four sections, each one ruled by dragons, vampires, and witches, and of course fae."

Nicholas' face brightened with excitement. Seraph certainly sounded like a place he'd like to visit, especially with his desire to become a fantasy writer.

"So, why don't you have wings?" Nicholas asked.

"I do, but I seldom have use for them and rarely grow my wings out," Aurora replied. "Besides, it hurts to do so like you wouldn't believe, and wings are weighty and strain my back."

"I have the same problem as Aurora," Frost admitted. "Wings are nothing but a hindrance."

"That's a good enough reason not to keep them out at all times," Nicholas replied.

***

"It sure would be something to visit Seraph for a little while and write about the fantasy beings calling it home," Nicholas said, pulling into his driveway.

Studying Nicholas' home, a three-story beige and white house placed in the middle of others with similar designs and appearances ,Aurora's eyes widened with amazement. It sure is beautiful.

"Is that what you intend to do in life, become an author?" Aurora asked.

"Creative writing teacher Anne Newman says I have talent in it, so maybe," Nicholas replied with hopefulness as he shut off the engine. "Are there books in Seraph?"

"We don't have printed books but scrolled parchments," Aurora said.

"It's a form of literature," Nicholas said. "Unique at that. Now come on, let's go meet my parents and sister."

***

"Your house is sure beautiful," Aurora admitted quietly. As they closed the distance, her eyes filled with amazement.

"It's probably nowhere near as attractive as what you live in," Nicholas said. "It's probably a castle, since you've been named princess, meaning your parents are king and queen of Seraph."

"Yes, my home is a castle, and one of the most magnificent ones imaginable," Aurora replied, offering a proud smile. "You'd love it if you ever saw it, Nicholas."

"I probably would," Nicholas said.

***

"Leanna told us the bad news that happened tonight," Jamie Warman said, her face marked with deep concern as soon as they set foot into the living room. She, her husband Christers, and Leanna were seated on the sofa staring at them.

"Don't worry, I'll get over it," Nicholas replied. "Mom, Dad, Leanna, this is Aurora and Frost."

"One thing's for sure, they're obsessed with fae," Leanna said, a glint of excitement developing in her eyes.

"Mom, Dad, I know your rule is no girls not related to me in the house without supervision under any circumstances," Nicholas said. "But Aurora and Frost just arrived in town and helped Alison deal with a situation. She has nowhere to crash for the night. Could they stay in the spare bedroom? It'll be one night I promise."

"Nicholas, that rule's in place for a reason," Christers informed him in a serious voice. "We never allowed Savannah in your room when you two were dating. There's no way we'll let two complete strangers stay the night, even if it is the spare bedroom."

"Oh, come on, they have nowhere else to stay," Nicholas pleaded.

"I'm sorry, Nicholas, but the answer's no," Christers replied.

Before Nicholas had any opportunity to turn and tell her to put her magic amulet to good use, Aurora held it up and pointed it at his parents' faces.

A brilliant blue light flashed, causing Christers' and Jamie's faces to gloss over with a momentary blankness.

"Wait, on second thought, we're not going to have a problem with Aurora and Frost spending as much time as they want here," Christers said in a sudden, easy-going voice.

"I'm okay with it as well," Jamie said. "Young ladies, I'm sorry my husband said you couldn't stay."

"Come on Aurora and Frost, let me introduce you to the spare bedroom," Nicholas replied.

Turning to the stairs, Aurora and Frost following, Nicholas was caught by surprise, making him stop dead in his tracks. Leanna called out, "Stop, you have a bit of explaining to do, Nicholas."

I should have expected it, Nicholas thought, facing his sister.

"Leanna, I think it might be a good idea if you come upstairs with us," he said.

***

"So, start explaining what your brand new fae-obsessed friend Aurora did to our parents with her amulet?" Leanna asked in a demanding voice once inside the spare bedroom.

Despite her love for all things fae, Nicholas wondered how she would react if told the truth about Aurora and Frost. Still, he decided to tell her anyway.

"Leanna, Aurora and Frost are the real deal. They're actual fae."

"Yeah, sure, whatever you say," Leanna replied with a disbelieving smile.

"He's telling you the truth, Leanna," Aurora said.

This caused the smile to melt off Leanna's face.

"Yeah, BS," Leanna replied. "As much as I've loved fae ever since a child, I'm mature enough to realize they aren't real."

"Should I prove it to her, that fae are real?" Aurora asked, glancing at Nicholas, wanting approval from him.

"Sure, go on," Nicholas replied.

Reaching to the back of her dress, Aurora started unzipping it.

"Wait, stop, maybe I should leave first?" Nicholas asked, a deep nervousness on his face.

"There's no need, I have undergarments on," Aurora said.

"You'll have to excuse my brother, he's never seen his ex, Savannah, in her underwear or as you put it Aurora, undergarments," Leanna taunted, the smile returning. "He's probably crap-your-pants-scared over seeing the first girl ever in her underwear."

"Yeah, I'll show you scared," Nicholas replied in sudden bold confidence.

Keeping his eyes on Aurora as she resumed unzipping her dress, allowing it to drop to the floor, Nicholas once again felt his desire for her grow. This time it was stronger than ever, nothing like he'd ever felt for Savannah. "It's really too bad you'll be gone tomorrow night Aurora; I can really see us getting together."

Seeing Aurora with her dress removed, a first for him, since he and Savannah never got this far, filled Nicholas with a serious desire to reach out and touch her.

Aurora's face grimacing in sudden tremendous pain shoved this right out of him. He knew how she intended on proving fae were real.

"Aurora, wait, you don't have to do it," he cried in alarm.

"Nicholas, relax. I'm fine!" Aurora yelled, tears of pain starting to glisten in her eyes.

Icy dread filled Nicholas' heart, and he just knew Leanna felt the same way as nervousness grew on her face. This was nothing compared to what happened next as Aurora let loose with a bloodcurdling scream and long, frosty blue wings, the same color as her hair and three or four feet in length sprouted from her back. He swore they were by far the most beautiful things ever.

"Proof enough for you Leanna?"

"Yeah, I'm convinced," Leanna whispered, her eyes glistening with pure amazement.

"So now you know why I hate growing them out," Aurora said, the pain on her face and tears subsiding a bit.

"So, where are you from and why are you here Aurora and Frost?" Leanna asked, excitement building on her face.

"Leanna, I come from a world named Seraph," Aurora said. "It's where vampires, witches, dragons, and fae reside, and I'm the current princess of it. My sister Everlista and I were supposed to compete for the role, but she sent her vampire boyfriend, Victors, to attempt killing me. It backfired on her, and I almost killed him in the process. The reason Frost and I are here now is to find the two of them, since they fled to Earth to escape a dark witch named Arleigha, intending to marry Victors. She's going to use her magic against my sister if Victors doesn't return with her in a week. Nicholas and his two friends, Alison and Shane, have pledged to help find them before it's too late."

"If it weren't for Aurora and Frost not showing up when they did, Alison would have been turned into Adam Farner's immortal girlfriend," Nicholas said.

A thought flooded Leanna's mind. With Everlista and Victors here on Earth, and she losing against her sister for role of Seraph princess, what if Everlista tried to become Princess here, on Earth?

"Alison's sure lucky you did, Aurora and Frost," Leanna said in relief. "So, you don't think Everlista might try and become princess of Earth, convince Victors to build an army of vampires, starting with the citizens of Midnight Lake?"

Oh, why didn't I think of that from the start? Aurora thought. *If Everlista intends on doing that, this town and all the residents are in terrible danger.*

"Leanna has a point there, Nicholas," Aurora said, turning an alarmed face to him. "What if that's my sister's plan? I think it might be a good idea if we go out and make sure Midnight Lake's citizens aren't turned into vampires. I'd never forgive myself if they were. Maybe at the same time find Everlista and Victors?"

"But you're in no shape to go anywhere," Nicholas replied in protest. "At least rest for an hour before we head back out. Can you do that for me?"

"Yeah, sure," Aurora said.

"Come on Leanna, so we can let her do that," Nicholas replied, grabbing his sister by the hand to lead her towards the bedroom door.

CHAPTER EIGHTEEN

The soft bed comforted Aurora as she lay flat on her stomach. "Are you starting to feel better, Aurora?" Frost asked, lying on her side on the other bed and facing her.

"I'll be fine by the time we go out searching for Everlista and Victors," Aurora replied. Out of nowhere, tremendous hunger pains grew in her stomach. "Frost, do you think Nicholas will show his hospitality and offer us something to eat?"

"There's only one way to find out," Frost replied. "But I don't see why not. Nicholas doesn't seem like the selfish type, as made evident by allowing us to reside in his home."

***

"So, tell me what you think of Aurora and Frost?" Nicholas asked as he and Leanna sat face-to-face around the dining room table.

There was just one answer Leanna had for this. She was beyond excited over seeing—with her own two eyes—two fantasy beings up close.

"Never in my life would I believe such beings as fae were real or for that matter actually meeting a pair of them," Leanna replied as excitement grew on her face.

"That look tells me you're pleased to finally see real life fae," Nicholas said.

"Beyond a doubt," Leanna said. "So, now what's your opinion of our two houseguests for the night?"

"I'm just glad they showed up before Adam received his greatest wish ever, turning Alison into his immortal girlfriend," he said.

"Yeah, it sure would have sucked if one of your two closest friends developed a craving for blood," Leanna said. "So, are you going to be able to handle school tomorrow seeing Savannah with Chris?"

"I'll find out first thing in the morning," Nicholas replied. "I did have this idea to try and talk Aurora to accompany me to school tomorrow, to show Savannah her theory that no beautiful girl would give me the time of day was wrong. Piss her off and show I'm over the breakup, but I don't know."

"Forget it, Nicholas," Leanna said, seriousness building on her face. "That's exactly what you should do, and as a matter of fact, we should head upstairs and do all we can to convince Aurora into it."

***

Standing near the entrance to the dining room allowed Aurora to hear every word of the conversation between Nicholas and Leanna. It made her smile knowing Nicholas wanted her to accompany him to school tomorrow, whatever that was. He thought she was beautiful and wanted to prove to his ex-girlfriend a beautiful girl would be interested in him.

"Frost, I want to do that for Nicholas, help him out and travel to this place called school," she said.

***

"I don't have any problem attending school with you Nicholas," Aurora said, her face dominated with excitement as she and Frost set foot into the dining room. "Disprove Savannah's claim a beautiful girl wouldn't be interested in you.

Aurora could instantly tell Nicholas was pleased by this as he turned an equally excited face to her.

"It sure would be something if Savannah was put in her place and proven wrong," Nicholas replied in appreciation. "So come join us Aurora and Frost."

Starting to head for the table, Aurora wondered if it was all right to bring up to Nicholas if he would offer Frost and her something to eat.

"So, are you feeling better Aurora?" Nicholas asked once she and Frost joined them.

Shooting a glance at Aurora, anticipating an answer, Nicholas instead saw a bothered look on her face. This caused him to feel incredible nervousness over the possibility something might be wrong with her.

"Are you doing okay?" Nicholas asked, concern building on his face. "Something bad didn't happen from showing your wings?"

"Nicholas, it's not revealing my wings that's the problem," Aurora replied as if she was afraid and embarrassed of revealing she was starving.

"Okay, so what's wrong?"

"Nicholas, I don't want to be a burden on you, since you've already shown me more than enough hospitality," Aurora said, staring at him with nervous eyes.

"Aurora, you saved one of my closest friends from being turned into a vampire's immortal girlfriend," Nicholas replied. "If there's anything I can do to help you out, it's okay to let me know."

Aurora felt the nervous embarrassment over having to beg Nicholas for something to eat start fading with this.

"Nicholas, I could stand to eat something," she said.

The immediate thought that jumped into Nicholas' mind, he wanted to introduce Aurora to his favorite restaurant. He had to admit he was kind of hungry himself, since the only thing he did at Frosters was dump Savannah.

"Aurora, I want to introduce you to my favorite restaurant, since I didn't get to eat—thanks to dumping Savannah," he said, excitement replacing the concern on his face. "It's a place where you sit and eat, and I guarantee it'll take care of your problem."

"Nicholas I'm sorry you had to break up with Savannah," Aurora replied. "And like I said, I'm more than willing to attend school with you tomorrow. You just need to explain to me what it is."

"Aurora, it's where Leanna, Alison, Shane, and I go to get smarter and an education," Nicholas said. "Is there something like that in Seraph?"

So that's what school was, Aurora thought.

"There isn't a separate place where Everlista and I travel for an education," she said. "We have a personal tutor who instructs us in mathematics, reading, writing, and history."

"Okay, you should fit right in tomorrow," Nicholas replied with a pleased smile.

Chapter Nineteen

Heading for her house after climbing from Nicholas' Bronco, the only thing Alison wanted to do was shower. She had every right to want this. She could wash off Adam's putting his dead hands on her.

"I know you're thankful Aurora showed up when she did," Shane said as they made a slow pace towards their home. "Otherwise, you'd be the princess of darkness by now."

"You'd better believe it," Alison admitted, pushing out a smile. "I can't wait to get inside and shower off Adam's ands on me."

"I can't blame you for wanting that," Shane said, returning the smile.

She and Shane's setting foot into the living room was met by their parents, William and Mary, seated on a pricey sofa watching the latest episode of CSI on a giant HD television, beautiful artwork adorning the walls.

The Masters had the best that money could buy, thanks to her father being a successful merchandise planner. Mom was a business technology analyst.

"How was the beach party?" Mary asked without breaking her attention away from the show.

"Great as always," Alison said, wasting no time in starting for the stairs.

Stepping into her bedroom was a cheerleader's dream. Everything about it screamed obsession, and each time it made her excited beyond belief to enter it. But not tonight, with her almost being turned into the Bride of Dracula—high school edition.

Alison felt sick to her stomach just thinking about it. A corpse daring to put its hands on her body and wanting to have sex with her – it made her seriously want to vomit up chunks.

She was sure glad Aurora showed up in the nick of time to prevent it from happening. It made her breathe out a sigh of relief.

The thought of Adam's intentions for her was so grotesque that Alison raced to clean up, get her former crush, now headless vampire's, DNA off her.

Immediately entering the bathroom Alison felt something churning in her stomach, an incredible need to vomit. It came so fast and sudden in her, that for a few frightening seconds, she honestly believed she would upchuck all over the damn floor.

Her quick cheerleading reflexes prevented it and allowed her to get the toilet open, kneel down, and let loose. She tasted sour bile after doing so. Remaining in this position, her ears were filled by Shane's sudden entrance.

"Adam sure did a number on you, judging from the evidence you just left in the toilet," Shane said. His sister stuck up her middle finger in response.

Remaining in her kneeling position, unsure if she would let loose with upchucking more vomit, Alison wasn't surprised what happened next. Her eyes began to sting with tears.

"Are you going to be all right?" Shane asked.

"No damn it. I'm not all right!" Alison screamed. "I almost became my former crush-turned-vampire's immortal mate! I was nearly raped by a freaking corpse! Do you realize how many years of head-shrink therapy I'll need to have because of it?"

"At least it didn't happen. You should be thankful for that," Shane said.

Still kneeling, Alison realized Shane was one hundred percent right. Right now, she could be dead. A walking corpse who craved blood and needed it to survive. She wasn't; she was alive and breathing. She truly was blessed.

After another two minutes passing without letting loose with anymore vomit, Alison realized she was okay.

"Yeah, you're sure right about that," she admitted, returning to her feet and turning to face her brother.

"You'll survive, now go take your shower," Shane said.

Standing in the shower a few minutes later, Alison started feeling better. The disgusted feeling about being touched and almost violated by a walking corpse began to fade. It was replaced by a serious appetite for some Frosters.

"So, feeling better now?" Shane asked once she exited the bathroom.

"One hundred percent," she replied, pushing out a smile. "I could sure go for some serious Frosters though."

"Yeah, you and me both," Shane said, returning the smile. "Go get dressed and we'll drive on over there."

"You don't have to tell me twice," Alison said.

Returning to her bedroom, Alison raced to get dressed. She was filled with an incredible eagerness to head on over to Frosters. A deep thankfulness she still had her life and her virtue intact overcame her.

Just as she threw on a faded black Sainters University sweatshirt and blue jeans, Shane made his return.

"Come on, let's go," she said.

And they would have, if not for the sound of Shane's cellphone soothing classical music ringtones.

"It's Nicholas," Shane said, checking the number. "Hey, Nick, what's up? Yeah, sure Alison and I are more than willing to help you out with that. We'll be right out."

"What's going on?" Alison asked, sudden curiousness growing on her face.

"Nicholas wants us to help in the search for Everlista and Victors tonight," Shane replied. "He's on the way here now."

"There's not a chance in hell I'm saying no to that after Aurora's saving my life from the worst thing imaginable," Alison said. "Come on, let's go, Frosters will have to wait."

Chapter Twenty

"Aurora, I think it might be a good idea if we stop by Shane and Alison's house and fill them in on what's going on and get their help," Nicholas said as he was driving them to Frosters. "Yes, I completely agree with that idea," Aurora replied in approval.

***

Pulling up to the front of the Master's house, Nicholas raced to get out his cellphone.

"Change of plans Shane," Nicholas said with relief on his face over his friend answering. "Aurora and Frost are with me. We're driving over to your house. We plan on searching for Everlista and Victors tonight and could use Alison's and your help."

***

"Why tonight and not tomorrow evening?" Shane asked as he and Alison climbed into the back of his Bronco.

"It was Leanna's idea," Nicholas replied. "She thinks Everlista might want to become princess of Earth and convince Victors to make Midnight Lake's citizens into her vampire followers."

"Now that sure would suck," Alison said.

"Yeah, you're telling me," Nicholas replied. "That's why after I introduce Aurora to Frosters we're going in search of them. Hopefully we'll be able to put a stop to them if it's the plan."

"What do you think of being introduced to Nicholas' favorite restaurant Aurora?" Alison asked.

"I'm actually honored by it," Aurora said with a pleased smile.

"So, fill us in on the sort of foods you love," Shane said.

"Oh, come on Shane, she's a hunter. Aurora probably loves meat first and foremost," Alison exclaimed. "That means she'll love what Frosters has to offer."

While it was true, she craved meat, Aurora also had a taste for other things such as wild brown grain rice and crunchy Ickmore celery, Blue crest nuts.

"I enjoy a variety of things, Shane," Aurora admitted pleasantly. "But like your sister said, yes, first and foremost I enjoy the meat of dragons."

"To each her own," Alison replied with a smile. "I'm sure you'll love Frosters' food."

"Changing the subject, Aurora's agreed to attend high school with me tomorrow to disprove Savannah's claim no beautiful girl would be interested in me," Nicholas said.

"I can't wait to see Savannah's face when she receives an eyeful of the two of you," Alison replied, her smile growing larger.

***

"Well, I'm not seeing any sign of vampires," Alison said, staring out the window with eagle eyes as Nicholas drove at a slow pace through downtown Midnight Lake.

"Yeah, I'm sure that's going to change if we don't find Everlista and Victors tonight," Nicholas replied.

"It'll break my heart if I end up having to kill innocent Earth citizens like Adam, if that's my sister's plan," Aurora said.

"None of us want that," Alison said.

"They're called humans by the way," Nicholas replied.

***

The pleasant smell of restaurant food filling her nostrils as they stepped into Frosters told Aurora she would enjoy the food it offered. It caused a pleasant expression to blossom across her face.

"Yeah, I can tell you're seriously going to love the food here with that look, Aurora," Alison said, managing a smile.

"Alison, whatever this food is I smell, I know I'm going to like it," Aurora replied, returning the smile.

"Come on, let's get seated at a table so you can have your first taste of Earth food, Aurora," Nicholas said in an encouraging voice.

In Aurora's mind, she wanted nothing more than to do this.

***

Almost immediately after entering Frosters and seeing Madeline tending to another customer, Shane wondered if he should inform her how he felt now instead of tomorrow.

"I know what you're thinking," Alison said once they were gathered at a booth. "You want to break the news to Madeline right now instead of first thing tomorrow morning."

"You know me too well, Alison," Shane replied with a smile. He felt comfortable Madeline was too far away and preoccupied with a customer to hear this conversation.

"So, since you have no idea of the food Froster's offers, or the names of them, you want me to suggest something I like, Aurora?" Nicholas asked.

"I'd appreciate it Nicholas," Aurora replied, flashing him an approving smile.

Despite picking up the laminated menu, Nicholas already had the item he wanted Aurora to try.

"Get ready to learn what my favorite meal is, Aurora," he said with a smile.

"So here comes the girl of your dreams, Shane," Alison said, producing a smile. "It's the perfect time to reveal just how you feel about her."

"Yeah Shane, why wait until tomorrow, when she's right here heading our way," Nicholas said.

"That's exactly what I intend to do," Shane replied.

Madeline Waterfield's biggest, most closely guarded secret was that she had a secret crush on Shane Masters. She was so hesitant to tell him because she felt he'd be too embarrassed to be seen dating a brain. After all, he was an athlete, and they came from completely different worlds.

From time to time, she considered going up to Shane and telling him just how she felt. But then the thought invaded her mind, if she did, he'd laugh right in her face and tell her to take a hike.

And now she was heading towards the booth Shane was seated around. He and his two closest friends, fellow jock Nicholas Warman, and his cheerleader twin sister, Alison. With them were two girls she'd never seen before, the surprising thing about them was that for whatever reason, they were masquerading as fae.

"What'll you and your two fae obsessed friend have?" she asked, reaching their table and smiling at the sight of Aurora and Frost.

"Aurora, Frost, say hello to Madeline Waterfield," Nicholas said.

"Otherwise known as the girl guaranteed to be named valedictorian when we all graduate," Alison added. "Meaning she's one of the smartest girls in Midnight Lake."

"Have any last names to go with those, Aurora and Frost?" Madeline asked.

Thinking fast, Nicholas came up with a response.

"Madeline, Aurora and Frost prefer to just go by their first names, you know like Madonna or Pink."

"Right gotcha, well at least they have somewhat exotic sounding names, since I don't know anyone named Aurora or Frost," Madeline replied with a slight smile.

"Yeah, those are unusual names all right," Alison admitted.

"So, I overheard what happened between you and Savannah earlier, Nicholas," Madeline said, sudden concern growing on her face. "You were in the absolute right to cut her ass loose for looking elsewhere for love."

"Thanks for the vote of confidence in me, smartest girl ever," Nicholas replied, flashing a slight smile.

"Yeah, that's me for you," Madeline said, returning the smile. "So, I suppose you want the usual Nicholas?"

"Uh-huh, and the same for Aurora and Frost," he said.

"Alison, Shane?" Madeline asked.

"I think I'll have a veggie burger and a side salad," Alison said.

"Great way to maintain that gorgeous cheerleader figure," Madeline replied. "Shane?"

Should I tell her? Shane wondered, staring in silence at the tabletop.

"Is there something wrong, Shane?" Madeline asked. "You're usually racing to order."

"Shane has something he wants to ask you," Alison said.

Continuing to stare in silence at the tabletop, Shane could just imagine the reaction Madeline would give when he told her how he felt.

"No sorry Shane, I'm not interested in jocks, especially ones who only have half the intelligence I do. Why don't you go find a cheerleader to bang?"

"Cheeseburger sub special," he said.

"That wasn't it, Madeline," Alison said.

"No come on, don't Alison," Shane replied.

"I'm sorry Shane, but it's just as I feared, you're too scared to say it yourself," Alison said. "Madeline, my brother wants to ask you out on a date, but he's too chicken crap to do it."

Madeline was hit in an instant with pure excitement. Alison just admitted that Shane felt the same way she did towards him. Or maybe it was just a prank to hurt and humiliate her, the smart girl.

"Look, I'm just going to take your orders and forget I ever heard the last bit of this conversation," she said, slight hurt in her voice.

"He's serious Madeline," Alison said. "Trust me you're the one he wants. It's why my brother's single at the moment. He's never got up the courage to say how he feels about you."

"Come on Shane, now's your chance, don't blow it," Nicholas encouraged.

Nicholas and Alison are right, now's my chance, it's now or never, Shane thought lifting his head to stare at Madeline.

"Madeline let's go on a date sometime."

There I said it, Shane thought, feeling relief.

Staring at Shane, Madeline saw a truthfulness in his face. Still, she couldn't shake the feeling this might be a jock prank to embarrass the hell out of her.

"Shane, I want to say yes to you, I have for a while now," she admitted. "But how do I know this isn't just a trick to hurt and humiliate me, the brain?"

"You can't, I suppose," Shane said. "You'll just have to take my word for it."

"Yeah, don't worry Madeline, if he does anything to hurt you, I'll make sure he'll physically regret it," Alison said.

"So, what do you say Madeline, tomorrow night?" Shane asked. "I promise to show you the greatest night of your life if you say yes."

Continuing to stare at Shane, the genuine expression remaining on his face, caused Madeline to make her decision.

"Pick me up tomorrow at seven," she said.

"I promise you aren't making a mistake Madeline," Shane replied.

***

Heading from the booth, Madeline felt nothing but the highest degree of excitement. The world could not get any more perfect as far as she was concerned.

***

Aurora knew in an instant by the smell it gave off she'd enjoy whatever the meal was that Madeline brought them. She'd never smelled anything like it before, making the desire to taste it grow.

"What sort of food is this?" Aurora asked, looking at Nicholas with sudden interest in her eyes.

"It's called a cheeseburger and fries," Nicholas said. "Go on, try it and tell me what you think."

Picking up the item wrapped in bread off the ivory white platter, Aurora moved it towards her mouth.

Shooting a glance at Nicholas, Aurora could see in his eyes that he was eager for her to taste it. Moving it a bit faster, she took her first bite, and it was delicious.

"So, what do you think?" Nicholas asked.

"It's something I wouldn't mind eating in the future," Aurora admitted with a smile. "So, are you excited Madeline's agreed to accompany you somewhere tomorrow night, Shane?"

"More than you know Aurora," Shane replied. "I kept myself single on purpose, hoping she'd say yes, and now she has. My dream girl knows I'm interested in her."

***

While attending to another customer, Madeline managed to overhear the exchange between Shane and Aurora. He was telling her the truth and was interested in her. He seriously wanted them to go on a date tomorrow night. Her dream was realized. It made her feel excited beyond belief.

"So how are you going to handle seeing Savannah with Chris tomorrow?" Madeline asked as she returned with the bill, wrapped in a coat which indicated her shift was over.

"Don't worry. I have it covered," Nicholas replied in confidence.

"See you all tomorrow," Madeline said, placing the bill down.

"Catch you later smart one," Alison called out to Madeline as she started off.

"You too, cheerleader, and Shane, I'll see you alone in less than twenty-four hours," Madeline called back.

"You have your dream girl, Shane," Madeline heard Alison say as she made her departure.

Chapter Twenty-One

Setting foot from Frosters into a cool fall night, Madeline rushed to her car, desperate to get home. She felt a combination of excitement for Shane's asking her on a date and exhaustion from working her butt off all night. Home for her was in the opposite direction of the former Arkston residence, a year and two months ago it'd been turned into a writer's retreat.

***

Before long, Madeline was driving on a desolate stretch of road. In the middle of this, her eyes start growing heavy with drowsiness, blurring her vision.

As a result, she was forced to pull over to the side, not wanting to get into an accident.

Remaining seated there for a minute, Madeline felt the drowsiness grow to the point she had no choice but to rest her head against the back of the seat. Doing so led to her dozing off.

***

Madeline was brought out of this by a knocking on the window closest to her ear.

Once her eyes adjusted, she turned to face the window. What she saw caused nervous shock to dominate her face. It was Eric and Thomas, and they loved nothing more to cause trouble. Not just that, but try and coerce females her age into having sex with them. So far, Alison and the girls she knew hadn't been stupid enough to fall for this ,and she wasn't about start to either.

Moving her hands towards the ignition key, Madeline breathed a sigh of relief over knowing she was going to escape the threat presented by these two perverts.

Or so she thought.

Nervous fear grew on her face as her engine wouldn't start.

"Damn it, not now!" Madeline yelled in angry frustration.

It was just this morning that she filled her tank; no it was impossible. Her car just had to start.

Trying it again procured the same results, frustrating her even further.

Madeline was struck hard by terror as Eric and Thomas now her car door. Given the pair's reputation, there was no doubt in her mind they intended on fulfilling their sexual desires with her. There was no way in hell she'd let them put their perverted, sex-craved hands on her.

"Wow, look who we have here, Thomas," Eric said with a smile. "One of the girls who thought she was too good for us."

"I say we show her how hurt we were by it," Thomas replied, hi-fiving Eric.

"Yeah good idea! Now out of the car, smart girl," Eric said.

"The hell I will," Madeline replied in a bold voice.

Madeline felt the fear increase as Eric started reaching in for her.

Damn it, I'm not going to be the first girl who's forced to fulfill your sexual needs, Madeline thought in sudden anger.

It caused her to grab hold of Eric's hand, and pulling it straight towards her mouth, and she bit into it.

"Try that again shit again and I'll make you regret it," Eric warned, his eyes glowing with sudden anger.

"She likes it rough, that's for sure," Thomas said with a smile.

"Yeah, I'll show her rough," Eric replied, ripping his hand from her grip, his face darkening with rage.

Real, genuine fear grew on Madeline's face as Eric and Thomas ripped her from the car.

"Is your hand okay?" Thomas asked in concern as they were about a foot away from Madeline.

"Yeah, I'll be fine," Eric replied. "Madeline won't be though, once we get done with her."

"You came up with a great idea to drain her car while she slept to keep her trapped here," Thomas said as they started moving closer to her.

Madeline's face grew large with fear over the realization she was about to fall victim to them and their sexual wants. Even if she was able to get back in her car, thanks to Eric and Thomas, she wouldn't be able to drive it anywhere.

Out of nowhere, making her feel relief, an idea filled her mind; she'd try and apologize for the way she treated them.

"Guys, I'm sorry," she said with sudden pleading eyes.

A sinister smile built on Eric's face. It filled her with an icy cold chill.

"Sorry, smart girl," Eric taunted. "You already had a chance to say yes to Thomas and me and you blew it. Now we're going to have you, and trust me it won't be a pleasant experience."

The terrible thought she was about to have her first sexual encounter at the hands of Eric and Thomas as they moved closer to her.

"I'm sure going to enjoy having my way with you, smart girl," Eric said, placing the palm of his hand against her face.

Madeline felt nervous terror race through her as Thomas got behind her and started slowly removing her coat.

Uh-uh, there's not a chance in hell I'm going to be violated by these two sex obsessed perverts!

With all her strength, Madeline forced her elbow into Thomas's stomach.

There, that should teach you to touch me son of a bitch!

This caused Thomas to cease disrobing her coat and grab her hair in anger, pulling her back towards him in a rough manner.

"Bitch we're going to teach you a lesson you'll never forget!" Thomas screamed in a rage. "Come on Eric let's get this bitch down on the ground."

I won't let you perverts touch me without a damn fight! Madeline thought in a rage as Eric moved closer to her.

Before she was able to move a hand against them, Thomas released her hair, and together he and Eric started forcing her flat on her back down on the ground.

She started struggling, using her legs to try kicking out of this frightening situation.

"We sure have a wild one here on our hands," Thomas taunted, a smile rapidly growing on his face.

"Not for long, I'll tame her ass," Eric said.

What he meant by this caused Madeline's eyes to widen with absolute terror as he removed a sharp, hunting knife from the inside of his coat.

"Calm it the hell down bitch or your face gets sliced," Eric warned, pointing the knife dangerously close to her face.

A deep expression of terror grew wide on Madeline's face. If she didn't cease struggling and allow Eric and Thomas their way with her, her face would receive a ghastly makeover. Madeline felt sadness swell in her as she realized she had no choice but to let them do what they trapped her here to do. There would be no she and Shane sharing their first time together. It depressed her deeply, realizing this.

"Okay you win," she said, relaxing her struggling.

"Good idea smart girl," Eric replied, placing down the knife and squatting at her waist.

Madeline knew at that moment, rape was about to happen and to *her*. Her first time wouldn't be with Shane like she desperately wanted but with these two perverted losers. It made the depression grow even stronger.

Or so she thought.

Madeline felt sudden surprise as she heard a girl's voice— it sounded not much older than hers—come out of nowhere.

"We've found three more, Victors."

She looked up.

Standing behind Eric and Thomas was a girl who looked just like a fae, same as Aurora and Frost earlier.

The alarming thing was that she had a vampire standing beside her, her hand gripped in his like deep, affectionate lovers, Hopefulness started racing through Madeline as the thought invaded her mind—they could help her out of this horrible situation. The depression started fading. Especially since whomever she was had a sharp sword with her.

"Please I'm begging you, don't let them do this to me," she said with pleading eyes.

"Get the hell out of here!" Eric yelled, his face revealing he wasn't at all pleased; more so he was damn pissed off by whoever this pair was.

"I'm more than willing to do that for a price," the girl dressed as a fae said, pushing out a bit of a smile.

"Please, yes anything!" Madeline cried, hopefulness increasing that she would get the hell out of this situation unscathed.

Staring down on this poor girl she'd just saved, Everlista had just one thought on her mind. She'd be perfect to have as a close, personal friend and life advisor.

"Victors please remove them off her," the fae girl instructed.

Madeline felt deep excitement inside her as the vampire who she now knew was named Victors moved forward. He grabbed Eric and Thomas by the necks with no effort, holding them up in front of him.

"My name is Everlista, and my price for freeing you from this terrible situation, I'd like to have you as a close personal friend and life advisor,"

Everlista said. "Of course, my boyfriend Victors is going to need to transform you into a vampire first."

Fully knowledgeable about the tremendous powers vampires possessed, a thought invaded Madeline's mind, *it sure would be something to have them*. Teach Eric and Thomas one hell of a serious lesson for daring to put their perverted ass hands on her. The fact she'd be immortal wasn't bad either.

But do I want to give up being able to step out into the daylight ever again? And how would Shane react when he finds out I'm dead?

She stared at Thomas and Eric, now held in Victor's grip, and thought about what she almost had to endure because of them and almost losing the thing she wanted Shane to have.

No, who the hell am I kidding? I want to kick their asses to hell and back for what they almost did!

"I'm about to give the two of you an ass kicking you'll never forget," she said, boldness dominating her face.

"You deserve that," Everlista replied in complete approval, removing her sword and pointing it at them. "Victors, release them, and I advise you two not to make a move against me. I'm excellent when it comes to using this sword."

The terrified looks building on her two would-be aggressors' faces over this made Madeline seriously want to burst into laughter.

"This is going to be the worst night of your lives and then you'll die," Madeline taunted.

"Oh, come on damn it. Madeline, give us a break!" Eric cried.

"I meant what I said, Eric," Madeline replied, starting to move towards Victors. "What the hell are you waiting for, make me a damn vampire!"

"You heard her, Victors," Everlista said.

"And what Everlista says goes," Victors replied, pushing out lengthy, strong, sharp ivory white teeth.

There was not a single amount of fear in Madeline's heart over being transformed into a bloodsucking creature of the night. What she did feel was excitement. She was about to receive the ability to kick her would-be rapists asses clear into next year. Moving her hand to the collar of her sweater in a rush, she slid down, exposing her bare shoulder.

Madeline felt an icy coldness as Victors gripped her biceps, sinking his teeth into her flesh. As much as it caused pain, it was well worth it to make Eric and Thomas pay.

"So, is it like I've seen so many times in the past?" Madeline asked. "You know where I have to drink your blood mixed with mine?"

"That, I'm not so sure about," Victors said in an unsure voice as he slid out crimson stained teeth. "I suppose we could try. Here Everlista, cut into my hand."

"Yeah, good idea," Madeline replied.

Holding it out for her to do so, Everlista wasted no time in fulfilling this request. It was just enough for a small amount to start flowing.

"Here goes nothing," Madeline said.

Taking hold of his hand, she put it up to her mouth. Even though her face grew sour by the rancid bitter taste, it was well worth it, and Madeline began feeling the transformation within no time.

It clearly wasn't like she'd been led to believe, where days had to pass before the change into vampire took effect.

Starting to grow lightheaded and dizzy, Madeline had no choice but to collapse to the ground. Lying on her side, she could feel her heart slow to a crawl, then stop completely. The same for her breath; it was clear death was on the way and she closed her eyes.

This was just for a second.

They flew open in a flash. Shooting back up into a sitting position, legs splayed out before her, the first thing Madeline felt was a strong need to vomit. No, not need, did, projecting out a sickening stream of her blood onto the ground.

Madeline couldn't react as excitement accompanied this. A smile was pushed out on her face as she began feeling the strength that came with what she'd now been transformed into. She was an actual vampire and now had the ability to kick Eric's and Thomas' asses straight into damn next week!

"Are you all ready to teach them a lesson they'll never forget?" Everlista asked.

"Damn it, Madeline, cut us some slack. We didn't ever rape your ass!" Thomas shouted.

"Run," Madeline ordered returning to her feet.

"What the hell—"

"I said run!" Madeline screamed.

"I suggest you do as she ordered," Everlista said. "Otherwise, I'll have no choice but to decapitate the two of you right here and now."

This sent Eric and Thomas racing away for their lives into a long stretch of woods.

Chapter Twenty-Two

The only thought Eric had as he and Thomas raced for their lives was, they were good as dead. No, he didn't think, he knew. Madeline was now a fucking vampire, a creature who drank blood, and worse, the two of them had made the dumbass mistake of trying to violate her.

"Damn it, Thomas, she's going to kill our asses for sure and fucking drain us bone dry!" Eric yelled.

"Yeah, I won't argue with that," Thomas said. "That's why we need to get the hell out of here pronto!"

Sudden, hard fear was pushed out on Eric's face as his breath grew labored from the running.

"Damn it to hell ,Thomas, I'm tired and out of breath!"

"Fucking move it Eric or our asses are dead!" Thomas screamed.

"I'm on the way fucking would-be rapists!" They heard Madeline scream somewhere in the distance. "And when I reach you, I'm kicking your asses straight into next year and killing you!"

Eric's fatigued condition grew worse, as the running continued. His legs became tired. It forced him to come to a sudden stop.

"Fuck Thomas, I can't go another damn step! You go the hell on and save your own ass and I'll try to fight her until you're home free!"

"Hell no, it's both of us leaving together or not at all!" Thomas said, coming to a sudden halt as well. "Let's go out fighting that bitch."

"I don't know how good I'll be at doing that, but yeah, smart idea," Eric replied, and together they turned to await Madeline's arrival.

***

Racing after Eric and Thomas, Madeline was overwhelmed with desire to teach them one hell of a serious lesson for what they almost did.

Continuing after them, the idea invaded her mind she should treat Eric and Thomas the same way they did her. The thought of her returning the favor and forcing them to experience the same horrific feelings she had made her smile tremendously. Another brilliant idea came as she started racing even faster, she should force them each other.

Now, with having tremendous vampire strength, Madeline realized she wouldn't have any difficulty in forcing Eric and Thomas to perform this act.

Madeline felt a sudden hunger strike in the pit of her stomach. She knew perfectly well the cause-the appetite for blood had commenced. This could not have come at a better time, since it meant she'd be able to use Eric and Thomas.

Finally catching up to them, Madeline felt a strong need to burst into laughter. They actually planned on fighting her to save their own worthless ass lives.

"It won't do you a damn bit of good fighting the inevitable you sons of bitches," she informed them.

"Damn you, bitch, give us a fucking break. We didn't even end up doing anything to your ass!" Thomas screamed.

Madeline felt rage replace the strong need to burst into laughter. After the hell they put her through, Thomas had the damn nerve to say this.

"Why the hell didn't you give me a break when I begged you not to violate me?" she asked, fury glowing in her eyes. "I felt so humiliated and sickened by the things you two assholes were about to do to me— touching me with your disgusting hands like your own personal whore!"

"You deserved it bitch for rejecting Eric and my asking you for dates!" Thomas yelled. "You and all the rest of those stuck-up assed sluts of Midnight Lake High!"

Again, the thought—if she should force Eric and Thomas to experience what they were going to do to her invaded her mind. *No*, who the hell was she kidding, not only were they about to rape her, but threatened to slice her face if she didn't calm her ass down.

"Strip your asses down to your underpants," she ordered.

"The fuck we will. You're not the boss of us bitch," Thomas smartly remarked.

"I'm not damn kidding asshole!" Madeline yelled. She projected herself straight forward, so she and Thomas stood face-to-face. The rage grew so strong in her by the time she reached him that she started moving her hands for his pocket containing the knife.

"Back the hell off me you bitch," Thomas warned.

"I'm not damn kidding," Madeline said, grabbing the hand that tried to prevent her from removing the knife.

She was so angry over what he and Eric did, she had no problem using her brand-new vampire strength to break it and get her point across. She wasn't surprised by Thomas swinging his other hand in an attempt to smash her face.

The hunger for blood had increased to the point she decided to skip showing them how she felt over what happened a few minutes ago.

Pulling Thomas straight towards her, it took Madeline just a second to get her long, sharp vampire teeth out for the first time ever. She had them buried into his shoulder. The blood was so delicious in her mouth, she had to have more. Grabbing his head, delight filled her as she felt his neck snap in her hands, harshly twisting it from side to side.

"Bitch you fucking killed him!" Eric screamed.

"He deserved it loser and so do you," Madeline taunted.

Dropping Thomas to the ground, Madeline rushed at him, desperate to have his blood in her as well.

"Bitch, stay the hell away from me!" Eric warned.

She didn't, latching her hands onto his biceps, racing to drive her still exposed teeth into his shoulder. Her impact against Eric was powerful enough to knock his ass to the ground beside Thomas. Unlike his friend, Madeline just kept going and going until the hunger for blood ceased.

CHAPTER TWENTY-THREE

Returning to Everlista and Victors, Madeline started wondering why they were here in such an out of the way town like Midnight Lake. *I wonder if I should ask them,* Madeline thought. *Well there's only one way to find out.*

"Were you able to teach Eric and Thomas a lesson?" Everlista asked as she made her way back to them.

"Hell yeah, I taught them a lesson they'll never forget," Madeline replied, pushing out an excited smile. "And not just that, but I killed and feasted on their blood."

Keeping her eyes on Everlista, Madeline felt a sense she'd done something wrong by killing Eric and Thomas as disappointment grew on her face.

"Did I do something wrong?" she asked.

"No, of course not," Everlista said, shooting a nervous glance at Victors. "Madeline, the reason Victors and I are here is we're on the run from a dark witch named Arleigha who wants Victors for herself."

"Now that sure sucks," Madeline admitted.

"I swear Madeline, whatever it takes I'm not going to let Arleigha get her hands on Victors. I'd rather die than let that happen."

Madeline felt excited that Everlista was willing to run away from wherever she and Victors came from to make sure they remained together.

"So, where did you and Victors come from Everlista?"

"It's a place called Seraph," Everlista said. "The four parts of my world are sectioned off and ruled by fae like me, vampires like Victors, witches like Arleigha, and dragons."

The fact there was a world like this excited Madeline.

"Wow, it sure would be fantastic to visit such a world, Everlista," she said in amazement.

"Yeah well, I'm not feeling that way at the moment," Everlista replied.

"Why's that?"

"My sister Aurora and I had a falling out over her being named princess of our section instead of me. Actually, it was my fault our father chose Aurora to fill this role, since I sent Victors to try taking her out of the competition. That act failed horribly."

Everlista 's revealing this caused Madeline to remember the girl also named Aurora who was with Nicholas, Alison, and Shane back at the restaurant. Given Aurora looked just like a fae, she couldn't help but wonder if this was Everlista's sister.

"Everlista, earlier tonight, I saw a girl named Aurora with some friends of mine and she looked just like you," Madeline said.

Everlista felt instant alarm over Madeline's revealing this.

There was no doubt she saw Aurora given the appearance. So why was her sister here? To force her into returning home, warn her of something horrible Arleigha intended to commit against her for Victors?

This possibility made Everlista realize she seriously needed to start building her vampire army without delay.

"Victors, there's no doubt it's Aurora who Madeline saw, and that means she knows about the problems with Arleigha," Everlista said in nervous urgency. "I just know she's here to convince us to return to Seraph, and once we do, I'll lose you forever. I refuse to let that happen, and we need to start doing what we agreed to when we first arrived."

"I won't argue with that," Victors replied.

Madeline felt a ping of sadness hearing this, even though she barely knew Everlista and Victors. Thanks to a dark witch with a serious affection for Victors, Everlista's relationship with him was in danger.

"Everlista damn it, you can't let this Arleigha bitch come between you and Victors," she said. "There has to be a way we can prevent it from happening."

It was with Madeline saying this that Everlista realized now was the perfect time to reveal their plan.

"There is a way, Madeline," Everlista said staring at her with serious eyes. "We need your help with it, but I'm not so sure you'll agree to it."

"You never know I might, especially since you saved me from those rapists, and I did say I would accept the role of being your close personal friend and life advisor," Madeline replied.

"Madeline, I want to make Earth a vampire world and to rule as princess with Victors at my side, Everlista said. "It'll go a long way in helping prevent Arleigha from coming between us."

"Yeah, that'll do it all right," Madeline admitted, producing an approving smile. "I guess that means you want to start with Midnight Lake's citizens?"

"With your help," Everlista replied.

"Like I said, you helped me out against those now stone-cold dead, pathetic predators," Madeline said, her smile not going anywhere. "In my mind, I owe you big time for that. So yeah sure, I'll assist you in it."

"I promise Madeline you aren't making a mistake by agreeing to it," Everlista said, returning a smile.

"That's for damn sure," Madeline replied. "Now come on, let's get started making Midnight Lake a vampire only town."

CHAPTER TWENTY-FOUR

Madeline had a single thought on her mind as the three of them headed through Midnight Lake. She wanted to get home and turn her family— mother, father, and identical twin sisters April and Mary Elizabeth into vampires. The way she saw things, Everlista needed as many vampires as possible on her side when and if Arleigha, the wicked dark witch, showed up for Victors.

"Everlista, I've just come up with the perfect idea," she said, a pleased smile growing on her face. "I nominate my parents and identical twin sisters Mary Elizabeth and April to be the first vampires created."

A sudden nervous idea invaded Madeline's mind while the three of them headed to her home.

How's Shane going to react when he discovers what I now am? She wondered. *It sure would be a real downer if being a vampire was the reason he called off tomorrow's date and no longer wanted to have anything to do with me.*

The thought of this made Madeline consider the fact it might not have been such a great idea to allow Victors to transform her into a vampire in the first place.

But then she would never have had the ability to put Eric and Thomas in their place and make the female teenage population of Midnight Lake safe from them once and for all.

What, with the hated reputation the pair garnered, Madeline hoped this wouldn't cause Shane to turn his back on her before their relationship even got off the ground. Given how he desperately wanted to have a relationship with her, even gave up the chance to be with someone else hoping she would say yes, Madeline figured it wouldn't be a problem.

***

By the time she reached her house, the nervousness over the idea Shane would reject her for being a vampire was gone.

"So, here's home sweet home for me," Madeline said as she, Everlista, and Victors arrived at its door.

Reaching into her jean pocket, Madeline took the key out and had the door open in less than a minute. What she discovered, much to her relief, the rule about vampires not being able to enter a house uninvited was disproved.

With Everlista and Victors following behind her, Madeline stepped inside and saw her two sisters, Mary Elizabeth and April, seated side by side on the sofa.

As usual, Mary Elizabeth and April, being obsessed fans of television, had their eyes completely glued to the expensive hi-definition television. It was placed in the back of the living room a few feet from the door.

"Mom and Dad were invited out by friends for the evening," Mary Elizabeth informed her without breaking her eyes off the television screen.

Both she and her sister had their eyes so glued to the television that it prevented them from seeing she was now a vampire, and her two Seraph guests.

That was, until their show cut to a commercial break and they both shot glances over at her. Almost immediately, shocked, surprised expressions brightened her sisters' faces over seeing what she'd become. Or maybe it had more to do with Everlista and Victors standing beside her.

"I don't believe what I'm seeing. No, it's just not possible," April said, slight excitement building on her face.

"Yeah, I didn't expect you to return from work masquerading as one of April's and my favorite supernatural creatures," Mary Elizabeth said. "That or drag two teens with a clear obsession for creatures of the night and fae right along with you—handsome vampire by the way."

"I'm not masquerading as a vampire and neither are they," Madeline said. "Mary Elizabeth, April, say hello to Everlista and Victors. In fact, he was the one who transformed me, out of my own free will of course."

"Hey," Mary Elizabeth greeted.

"I can't believe it," April said in a low, almost whispered tone.

"It's true, April," Madeline said, heading for the sofa and sitting. "I'm officially immortal."

"Okay, now that is like the coolest thing I've heard today," Mary Elizabeth said, producing a smile. "So do Everlista and Victors have last names?"

Should I tell them Everlista and Victors come from an actual fantasy world? Madeline asked herself. *It sure would surprise and amaze the hell out of them if I did.* In the end though, she decided to ask Everlista to cover this subject.

"Everlista, maybe you should fill my sisters in on you and Victors' story," Madeline said, shooting a glance over at them.

"Mary Elizabeth, April, Victors and I have no last names," Everlista said, starting to move towards them at a slow pace. "Where he and I come from, is a place with four kingdoms named Seraph. These kingdoms are ruled by fae, vampires, witches and dragons, and Victors and I are on the run from a dark witch who wants him for herself."

"And what's the reason for making Madeline into a vampire?" Mary Elizabeth asked.

"Just as soon as Victors and I saw her, I knew Madeline was who I wanted to fill the role as my close friend and personal life advisor," Everlista replied. "You see, my plan is to prevent Arleigha from getting her hands on Victors by creating a vampire army."

"And you agreed to such an insane plan, Madeline?" April asked.

"It was the only way to prevent Eric and Thomas from trying to rape me," Madeline said. "I owe Everlista and Victors in a major way for it. If they hadn't shown up…Eric threatened to slice up my face with a hunting knife."

"Damn them to hell," April spat. "I sure hope you killed their asses, vampire style."

"Guilty as charged," Madeline replied with a smile. "Midnight Lake's seen the last of Eric and Thomas, thanks to my hunger for blood."

"I'm sure glad that's part of the benefit of being what you are now," Mary Elizabeth said. "And those two pricks, desperate perverts have finally been put out of their misery."

"I won't argue with that," April said, raising her hand and high fiving her twin in excitement.

Her sisters' excitement compelled Madeline to reveal her other good news before she explained the reason why Everlista and Victors were here. They deserved to know Shane's heart belonged to her.

"It's not the only good news of tonight," Madeline said, flashing yet another smile.

"I don't see how much better it can be then the miracle of Eric and Thomas no longer being part of the world's population," Mary Elizabeth replied.

"It's just as," Madeline said.

"Well don't keep us in suspense, Madeline," April said.

"Mary Elizabeth, April, I just found out Shane's single, and he's been that way because he feels the same way I do toward him," Madeline replied.

"I swear, tonight is one of the most perfect nights ever," Mary Elizabeth said.

"Yeah, you're sure telling me," April said. "So have you two set up a date?"

"It's for tomorrow night," Madeline replied, her face glowing with excitement.

"I take that back, it's not one of the most perfect nights ever, it's the best," Mary Elizabeth said, managing a smile.

The thought of Shane not wanting anything to do with her caused the excitement to melt from Madeline's face. Even though the way he felt about her made her believe he'd accept her, once again she couldn't be sure about this.

"Okay, what's the dilemma?" Mary Elizabeth asked, sudden nervous concern blossoming on her face.

"Mary Elizabeth, April, what if Shane doesn't accept me the way I am now, dead and a vampire?" Madeline asked, the same nervous concern building on her face.

"Yeah, that could be a problem," Mary Elizabeth admitted. "Madeline, if he cares about and wants to be with you, Shane should be able to look past that fact. Just don't try and use him as a source of blood; that'll put a serious dent in things."

"So, you're saying I shouldn't worry about it?" Madeline asked.

"Uh-huh, things will be fine just as long as you stick to my suggestion and think of Shane as your boyfriend and not a food source," Mary Elizabeth replied.

Madeline felt a rush of tremendous relief over this.

"So, changing the subject, tell us who's first on the list to become part of Everlista's vampire army?" April asked.

The answer Madeline gave was to stare nervously down at her feet. *How would Mary Elizabeth and April react when I tell them I want them and our parents to be turned into vampires?*

"Why do I have the sudden feeling it won't be good news?" Mary Elizabeth asked.

"Mary Elizabeth, April, I want you and our parents to be turned first," Madeline said, lifting her head to stare at her sisters.

"Well, at least you care enough about us to want your family to be first in line," Mary Elizabeth said, flashing an amused smile.

"Look, I'm not going to ask Victors-" Madeline began.

"Why can't you do it?" April asked. "You're a vampire now and it might be a good learning experience to know how to make other vampires."

"So, I guess that means you're interested," Madeline replied.

"It's for the right reason, to help Everlista prevent Arleigha from getting her hands on Victors," April admitted. "And besides, if it weren't for them, you'd have been assaulted, possibly dead or your face all fucked up and disfigured."

"She's right, and there's no way you get to be the only Waterfield sister who gets to have immortality and vampire powers," Mary Elizabeth said. "But I call dibs on Victors turning me."

"You can have him for all I care," April replied. "Like I said, I want Madeline to experience how to create vampires."

"Come on April, let's take over the love seat so Mary Elizabeth and Victors can have the sofa," Madeline suggested.

Just as soon as Victors replaced Madeline and April on the sofa, Mary Elizabeth moved her hands to the top button of the navy blue work shirt she had on. She loosened it up just enough to allow Victors access to her shoulder.

While doing so, she kept her eyes focused on him, watching as he produced long, sharp teeth from his mouth.

Even though she knew his teeth penetrating her flesh would hurt like hell, Mary Elizabeth slid down the collar of her shirt, exposing bare flesh. Sure enough, just as she thought, there was pain—biting, sharp, pain. Accompanying it, she felt streams of her own blood race down her back.

At least I'm letting it be done for the right reason, she thought, shooting a glance over at Madeline, long, sharp teeth growing out as she prepared to transform April.

CHAPTER TWENTY-FIVE

Stepping outside following the transformation, Madeline had the perfect idea of where to go to continue increasing the number of vampires for Everlista. With the party still happening over at Crystal Waters Beach, there'd be more than enough candidates. The fact it was a long distance off didn't matter, all of them save Everlista had vampire speed.

"Everlista, Victors, there's a party over at a place called Crystal Waters Beach," she informed them. "It has a lot of perfect candidates to make into vampires. It's a distance away, but we should get there in no time if we put our vampire speed to good use."

"That's an excellent idea," Everlista replied with a smile.

***

Sure enough, thanks to this they reached Crystal Waters Beach in no time. Madeline was sure glad they did since she was certain Mary Elizabeth and April's hunger for blood had commenced.

"Since I'm sure the hunger for blood has started, it's a good thing we made it here this fast," Madeline said.

"Yep, it has," April replied, her eyes growing bright with excitement as she surveyed the crowd of unsuspecting teens, clueless as to what was about to head their way.

"So, there's so many to choose from. Who do you want as your first official victim, Mary Elizabeth?" Madeline asked.

Surveying the crowd as well, almost instantly, one particular girl took Mary Elizabeth's interest, Savannah Rosefield. She never really liked her to begin with, after all.

"Actually, I wouldn't mind sinking my teeth into Savannah, even though she and Nicholas are currently dating," Mary Elizabeth admitted with a smile.

"Not anymore. She dumped him for Chris Cannerman earlier this evening," Madeline said.

"What a real live bitch," Mary Elizabeth spat in disgust. "Well, it's a good thing she's out of his life. Nicholas could do so much better in my opinion."

"That's sure the truth," April replied, producing a smile.

"So, what do you think Madeline, should Savannah be used to take care of my increasing hunger for blood?" Mary Elizabeth asked.

"It sure would be great to pay her back for breaking Nicholas' heart," Madeline replied.

"Savannah it is," Mary Elizabeth said, her eyes glistening with excitement over it.

"This I can't miss," April said.

"You and me both April," Madeline replied.

***

"I'm so glad Nicholas is finally out of your life," Chris said as he and Savannah continued walking hand in hand.

"Yeah, so am I," Savannah replied.

"So, are there any regrets about booting him out of your life in favor of me?" Chris asked.

"I already told you; Nicholas and my relationship has grown way beyond stale," Savannah said. "So, in answer to your question, it's a no."

As she and Chris continued, Savannah felt comfort thanks to the cool fall breeze stroking her face. Glancing around, she wasn't at all surprised to see Nicholas climb from his Bronco. His two closest friends Alison and Shane did the same.

What caused Savannah alarm was seeing the two girls masquerading as fae climb out as well. This made her realize Nicholas had managed to convince the one he expressed interest in that they should get involved. She stood at his side as he scanned his eyes everywhere. Not that she was upset over it. She felt glad Nicholas had found someone to move on with.

"So, it looks like Nicholas has moved on from you in less than two hours," Chris said, catching sight of this as well.

"Yep, it sure appears that way," Savannah said. "I saw that girl while he and I drove to and from our last official date. He admitted to me he could see himself getting involved with her."

"And you weren't even the least bit jealous?"

"No, because I have you in my life," Savannah admitted, managing a smile. "I'm just glad he was able to convince her they should get involved. Nicholas deserves to have someone in his life."

Again, shooting a glance over at Nicholas, Savannah wondered if she should head on over and find out the name of the girl.

"Have any interest in going over to find out the name of Nicholas' possible new girlfriend?" she asked.

"No, we should just let Nicholas get to know her a bit first," Chris replied. "And besides, he might still be upset over you two just breaking up earlier. Don't worry, there's plenty of time to find out who she is."

"Yeah you're right about that," Savannah said. "Hey, you want to take off and hang at Frosters? I'm starving."

"You don't have to tell me twice," Chris said, managing a smile as well.

Turning so they could get to Chris' car, Savannah was struck hard in the face by an enormous surprise. Another girl with a fae obsession and an oh-so handsome guy next to her stood a few feet away. The problem with him, he bore a remarkable resemblance to an actual vampire. Hell, if she didn't know any better, she'd actually think he was one. But of course, such things just didn't exist, just like fae didn't, even though she heard the story about what happened in the neighboring town of Black River countless times in the past.

Three sisters, Madeline, April, and Mary Elizabeth Waterfield stood near them. Like the guy, they looked like vampires, a little too much in her opinion. It really didn't matter, getting dinner in her stomach was far more important. This was the thing which took precedence above all else.

"Come on Chris, let's go," Savannah said with urgency, grabbing his hand to lead him past them.

So Savannah thought she'd do this. An alarmed surprise grew on her face as Mary Elizabeth attached a hand tight around her bicep. Her touch felt icy cold.

"Damn what's wrong with you, Mary Elizabeth?" Savannah yelled. "And why the hell are you so damn cold?"

The near immediate answer Savannah received was Mary Elizabeth's sudden pushing out of long, sharp teeth. It was quite clear by this her belief that vampires were not real was in error. The icy coldness, the teeth, damn it— they were real after all.

"Damn it, I can't believe it," Savannah whispered in a shocked hush.

"Yeah, my two sisters and I are vampires now," Mary Elizabeth said, raising up her other hand to grip Savannah's left bicep. "And guess who I've chosen to be the first human whose blood I taste."

Savannah's face grew wide with genuine fear as Mary Elizabeth released her left hand. She used it to reach out and slide down the collar of her bright red sweatshirt, exposing her shoulder.

"Hey damn it, just back the hell off, or I swear you're in for a serious ass-kicking like you've never experienced before," Chris threatened.

Madeline and April were at his side in an instant, grabbing his arms and holding them tight.

"Hey what the hell is the matter with you cold-ass bitches?" Chris yelled, his face flushed with rage.

Despite Chris struggling hard as he could to try breaking free, he was unable to shake Madeline and April off.

This furthered the idea in Savannah all three Waterfield sisters were now vampires. And then, she felt the sharp points of Mary Elizabeth's teeth press urgently against her shoulder.

Chapter Twenty-Six

No luck came as they drove through Midnight Lake in search of Everlista and Victors, or any newly created vampires.

"Well, it sure looks like we're not going to find Everlista and Victors tonight," Nicholas said as they came to a stop at a red light on Blue Street and Silvermore Avenue.

Glancing over at Aurora who was riding shotgun, Nicholas realized just one thing. She was bothered by not being able to find her sister tonight.

"I promise we'll find your sister and Victors before they're able to create more vampires," he said in a genuine voice.

"I believe you, Nicholas," Aurora replied in a trusting voice, pushing out a bit of a smile.

While waiting for the light to turn green, Nicholas was surprised by a sudden thought that invaded his mind. The party was still going on over at Crystal Waters Beach. If there was any place to create a whole lot of vampires, that would be it with all those teens having a great time.

"Wait a second, there's one more place we should check out," Nicholas said. "Crystal Waters Beach. It's the perfect place for a vampire to create more vampires."

"That's the perfect place all right," Alison admitted.

It's a good thing we're heading in the right direction," Nicholas said as the light switched to green.

***

It took less than ten minutes after Nicholas had this idea for them to reach Crystal Waters Beach and pull into the parking lot.

Climbing out, while the rest of his passengers did the same, Nicholas immediately went into action, surveying the crowd of teens for any sign of a vampire.

"I don't see Everlista or Victors," Aurora said, standing at his side.

For the next couple minutes, Alison and Shane joining them as well, all signs pointed to this being yet another dead end in the search for Everlista and Victors.

"Come on, let's get out of here. We'll try again tomorrow night," Nicholas said, slight disappointment in his voice.

Continuing to keep his eyes focused on everything going on, Nicholas suddenly caught sight of Savannah and Chris walking hand in hand together. Again, the urge to get the hell out of there invaded his mind.

"Nicholas, I'm sorry you had to see them together," Aurora said in an apologetic voice.

"No, it's all right," he replied. "Look, I just want to get out of here."

Again, shooting a glance over at Savannah and Chris, Nicholas was caught by sudden surprise. Madeline and her two sisters Mary Elizabeth and April were approaching the couple. They weren't alone, a female dressed quite similar to Aurora, a sword connected to her waist in a sheath was nearby.

"Nicholas, it's my sister and Victors," Aurora said, sudden excitement filling her eyes.

Even though Nicholas knew Aurora would be heading back to Seraph once she filled Everlista in on Arleigha's intentions, he didn't want to see Savannah and Chris turned into vampires.

Racing over to them, a strong sense of dread as to the reason why Madeline, Mary Elizabeth and April were with Everlista and Victors. Just like Adam, they were now vampires. This was made quite clear by Mary Elizabeth attempting to make Savannah her victim, her two sisters managed to prevent Chris from interfering with no effort by grabbing his arms.

"It looks like we're about to lose three more of our closest friends," he said.

"Nicholas I'm sorry," Aurora said as she whipped out her sword to decapitate the three sisters just like Adam earlier this evening.

***

Everlista felt great satisfaction watching the start of her vampire army commence. This was until she glanced around, catching sight of Aurora, the woman from Seraph she knew as Frost, and the friends she'd made here on Earth tonight.

Damn it, she would have to arrive and ruin my plans, Everlista thought as her face flushed with anger. Well, she wouldn't stand for her sister, once again, preventing her from becoming princess. Racing to remove her sword, Everlista turned to face her rapidly approaching sister.

"Stay back Aurora, I'm not going to let you ruin my chances of becoming princess of this world!" she cried. She raised her sword to an attack position as they came to a sudden stop a couple feet from her.

Aurora couldn't blame her sister for this sudden outburst and wanting desperately to become princess of someplace. But thanks to the danger presented by Arleigha, no, she wasn't going to lose her sister.

"Everlista, I realize you really want to be a princess, and I don't blame you for it," Aurora said, genuine concern filling her eyes.

"So why don't you let me remain here on Earth and do so, unless you're jealous of me being a princess as well Aurora?" Everlista asked.

"You know that's not the case. I just want you to be happy," Aurora replied. "And as for your question, Arleigha's fully intending on using her dark magic against you if I don't convince you to return home to Seraph. Everlista, I'm not going to lose you and am willing to fight you to get that point across."

Everlista realized Aurora was right. Still, she was going to lose Victors.

"The reason I want to create a legion of vampires is to protect my relationship with Victors," Everlista said. "I can't lose him, Aurora."

Placing her sword back into her sheath, Aurora started for her sister.

In the middle of all this, Aurora came to the decision she was going to do whatever it took to make sure Everlista was happy.

"Everlista, I promise to do whatever it takes to make sure Arleigha doesn't marry Victors and he remains part of your life," she said.

"Even though he is a vampire, you don't approve of our relationship, *and* he tried killing you?" Everlista asked.

Despite knowing full well she shouldn't, given these reasons, Victors was the one who made Everlista happy. And with her dream of being princess on Earth and ruling over a world of vampires taken from her, it was the least she could do.

"Victors, do you love my sister as much as she apparently does you?" Aurora asked.

"More than you can possibly know Aurora," Victors replied. "That's why I agreed to marry Arleigha, so no harm would befall your sister."

This caused Aurora to realize one thing. Despite it being against her better judgment, she would have to forgive Victors for what he did.

"Everlista, I forgive Victors for what he tried to do to me," Aurora said.

"Thanks Aurora, so are you ready to get out of here and return to Seraph before Arleigha has a chance to make good on her promise?" Everlista asked.

Shooting a glance over at Nicholas, a sudden look of sadness filled her face. For the first time ever, Aurora found someone she was interested in, and now she would have to give him up to keep her sister safe.

"That look tells me something's keeping you attached to Earth," Everlista said.

"Everlista I've found who I want to be with for the rest of my life," Aurora replied, keeping her eyes focused on Nicholas. "His name is Nicholas Warman, and I don't care that he's not a fae or from Seraph. He's the one I want to spend the rest of my life with."

"You should remain here then, use the few days before Arleigha sends her dark magic against us to convince Nicholas the two of you belong together," Everlista said in an understanding voice. "Hopefully you can convince him to return to Seraph and have your heart's desire, Aurora."

That's exactly what I'm going to do, Aurora thought, managing a smile. *I just hope I can convince Nicholas before Arleigha sends the nightmarish thing created with her dark magic our way.*

Hearing this and realizing Aurora wanted him instead of a fae male, all Nicholas could do was smile as well.

The Vampires Artemesia and Lonnigan

by R. C. Mulhare

"I'm clean, I tell you. I'm not tripping. I know what I saw," Jenny Driver insisted, her hands quaking as withdrawal set in. The track marks and sores from itching her arms visibly indicated use, though given the signs of healing, she likely hadn't shot up in the last few days. She had curled in on herself as she lay on the hospital gurney, quivering from chills and from fright. A pad of gauze covered the side of her neck, blood slowly soaking into it.

Dr. Devi Muktahar, the triage doctor, read off the girl's pulse: too fast, but understandable given her condition and the assault that brought her to the emergency room of St Joseph's Hospital in Portland, Maine. "That's a wild story, Jenny. Are you trying to get a psychiatric admit? Because I'm not sure this story would work."

"I saw what I saw. I felt what I felt. I saw Ned Lonnigan. He pinned me down. He bit me. He tried to drink my blood."

"Can you turn over onto your back and tilt your head so I can examine your neck?" The girl shifted as requested. Dr. Muktahar carefully removed the bandage. Fetching more gauze and antiseptic, she carefully wiped the wound clean. Just below the jugular vein, someone, likely a human with outsized canines, had bitten into the girl's neck. The bite went deep but had stopped bleeding. It looked as though Lonnigan, or whoever, had had a pair of high-quality veneers implanted, or he had somehow sprouted a second set of canines larger than typical human teeth. Even still, the high-grade veneers she'd seen on Gothic and vampire lifestyle people did not leave marks this deep. If she knew anything about Lonnigan, who had shown up as a frequent flier in Emergency with his own substance abuse problems, she doubted he had even dabbled in that, let alone committed to dental modifications.

Dr. Muktahar looked Jenny in the face. "You say Ned Lonnigan did this to you? I thought he'd disappeared back in January."

"That's what I've been trying to tell you. He's still around. He's still alive, and he's worse than before."

"Do you want me to call law enforcement?"

Jenny widened her eyes and pulled back. "They'll lock me up."

"Do you have any illegal substances or weapons on you?"

"No. I told you. I'm clean and I want to stay clean, but I know how it goes. Too many cops act like people like me are just trash."

"I can report what happened and make it clear that you want to remain anonymous."

Jenny said, curled up on herself again. "All right."

A half hour later, a uniformed officer who introduced herself as Royse and a detective named Bellocq approached Jenny's bedside. "You feel comfortable talking about what happened?" Royse asked, kneeling by the bed.

"I was down on the docks, trying to make some cash so I could get a fix, just one last fix… but I changed my mind," Jenny replied.

"Had to be something pretty bad to make someone like you change their mind that fast about a fix," Bellocq said with a "let's hurry this up" sigh.

Royse threw a look at Bellocq, then turned back to Jenny. "What happened to make you change your plans?"

"I'd finished with a guy, a merchant sailor in town. He'd only given me twenty bucks, but the night had just started. I went looking for another client, but it got really cold all of a sudden. I started running toward the Angry Crab for shelter, but I'd been banned from there for getting into a fight six months ago – and it wasn't even a fist fight, I was just yelling at someone who owed me money. Then Ned Lonnigan jumped me out of nowhere. He knocked me down and pinned me on the pavement. That's when he chomped me right on the neck." She pointed to the bandage on the side of her throat, then fell silent as if gathering her thoughts.

"How many vampire movies has she watched?" Bellocq asked.

"Hush," Royse said, giving her colleague another look. "Jenny, if you need to take a break, that's understood. You need anything? Water or something?"

"Orange juice. I could use some orange juice."

Royse looked at Bellocq. "Could you find the nurse and get her some orange juice?"

"Now I'm a delivery boy or a waiter?" Bellocq said. He left the room and sought out a nurse.

"I'd tell you to ignore Bellocq and say he's old and stuck in his ways, but it's a bit late for that now, isn't it?" Royse said.

Jenny shrugged her right shoulder. "I've heard worse."

A moment later, the nurse returned with a small bottle of orange juice , Bellocq following him. Once Jenny had had a drink and settled down as best she could, she continued.

"It hurt. Hurt like hell. The bite, I mean. Then the creep started sucking on it, then it felt weird. But then he let me go and just stood over me, glaring at me. He said, 'You damn bitch. You ain't had a fix, have you?' Then he vanished."

"You mean he ran out of sight?" Bellocq asked.

She shook her head. "No. He *vanished*. Like, I don't know, a wizard or a magician. Just poof!" She spread one hand. "Gone."

"That's weird. That's so weird it's like something out of a Stephen King novel," Bellocq said.

"You're not talking about *Salem's Lot,*" Royse said dryly. To Jenny, she asked, "Do you mind if we take photos of your injuries?"

"No, go ahead, whatever it takes to get him off the street."

"In the meantime, is there anyone we can call? I don't want you to be alone during all this."

"My brother, Jared. He's still talking to me, but our parents won't even return my calls." She fumbled under her pillow and pulled out her phone, pulling up her brother's number.

"We'll get him here as soon he can," Bellocq said. "But are you seriously going to tell him this vampire shit?"

Royse hit the call button on the phone. "Vampire nonsense or not, Jenny needs family at a time like this."

***

Jared's phone rang as he patrolled the corridors of an office tower in downtown Portland. The tenant he wasn't allowed to talk to or about had just left for the night after a long work session, and he had the floor to himself. He pulled the phone from his pocket and unlocked it. "Hello?"

"Jared Driver? This is Officer Alisa Royse with the Portland Police Department. I'm calling about your sister, Jenny."

Jared paused in his tracks, wondering if this might be The Call He Dreaded. "Speaking. Is she alive?"

"Yes, though she's in ICU at Northern Light Mercy Hospital. She claims Ned Lonnigan attacked her on the docks."

"Ned Lonnigan? I thought he was the guy who disappeared back in January. Cousin of ours works security on the docks. Said he'd been seen OD'd on the dock."

"Yes, and by the time EMTs showed up, he'd somehow disappeared. My brother took the call. It appears he's back and even worse, since it seems he's got some kind of vampire fetish."

"Vampire fetish? Do I want to know?" Royse described what had happened to Jenny. "Geez. It's either someone who looks like Lonnigan, or he got his hands on some of that bath salts stuff that made that one guy in Florida chomp on a homeless guy's head."

"Whatever it is, Jenny could use some family near her at a time like this."

"I'll go see her as soon as I get off shift," Jared said. "I appreciate the call."

"She'll appreciate your coming."

Later, as Jared left work, he passed by the cleaning crew finishing up for the night. "You're in a hurry," one crew member called.

"Can't stop to chat... My sister's in trouble, bad trouble," he replied. "Some goon beat her up."

"I'll be praying for you both. I'll get my church to raise the roof for you," the cleaner called back.

"Much appreciated. She'll need it," Jared replied. He'd stopped putting stock in praying, but someone offering to keep him and his sister in their thoughts warmed his heart. Maybe the Old Man Upstairs would listen to someone else.

***

The sun had fully risen by the time he pulled into the visitor parking garage at Northern Light Mercy Hospital. Entering, he found his way to the emergency room, checking in with reception and asking after Jenny, then finding his way to the ICU. He found her room easily: a young police officer stood outside the doorway. Jenny lay huddled under the bed covers, her hands clasped loosely under her chin, her index fingers crossed one over the other.

"Hey, Jenny. Hey, Jen-Jen."

He nudged her arm gently. She jolted awake with a small cry, her bloodshot eyes flipped open as she stared up at him. Whimpering softly, she reached up and pulled him into a hug. He leaned down, kneeling beside the bed, pulling her close and letting her cry on his shoulder.

"Jared, are you real?"

"Yes. I'm real. I'm here for you. You're safe. I got ya," he said. Pulling back while still holding her, he asked, "What the hell happened to you?"

"You remember Ned Lonnigan?"

Jared felt his throat constrict and he willed his fists not to tighten at the mention of that name. He wished he'd caused Lonnigan's disappearance and made sure he stayed gone. "Of course. Did he do this?"

She nodded and pointed to the thick bandage on her neck. He let her go. Rising and perching himself on the bed, he pulled her close and onto his knees as much as he could with her buried under the covers. She broke down crying and buried her face in the side of Jared's neck again. "I got you. I got you. I won't let him near you," he repeated over and over like a mantra or a protection chant.

She told him about the attack, like something from a vampire movie, though she'd never watched those much. "Oh Jared, I'm going clean after this. I don't care what it takes, I'm not going back to that dark place."

One part of him, the part that had listened too long to their father's unforgiveness and the lack of compassion and understanding which had eroded Jenny's self-esteem in the first place, wanted to let these words blow past him. But the better part of him, the part that had stood up to their father when he had railed at Jenny, heard the fear and the resolve in her voice. "Whatever it takes, I'm here for you. I got your back, wherever you go."

She pulled back, looking him in the eye. "I mean it this time. I'm not relapsing, so help me God. Even if you have to chain me to a radiator or put me in a box in your storage unit, I'll do what I have to."

He snorted gently. "I don't think that'll be necessary. I think I'd get kicked out of the townhouse and we don't have any radiators, just the baseboard units."

She shook her head. "You still might need to hide me in a box. I don't know what's going to happen. He bit me on the neck and then he vanished. Doesn't that mean I'm going to turn?"

"Turn how?"

"Turn into a vampire. Nobody just vanishes like that after biting someone and drinking their blood. He's a vampire, I tell you, a blood-sucking vampire."

Even in her most messed-up times, even during the previous detox that had failed, Jenny had never given way to rambling or flights of fancy. He wanted to believe what she told him, but a part of him wanted to credit her observation to shock or fear, her mind framing the attack as the work of a vampire to give it a palatable explanation. The terror of the moment could have shaken the already fragile wiring in her head and created this image.

"A vampire. You're serious about this?"

Her grip on him loosened and she pulled back. "You don't believe me either?"

"It just sounds so wild to me. You're sure of what you saw after he bit you?"

"I swear on Grandma's Bible. I saw him disappear."

"All right." She could have had some kind of perception lapse, but something in her face and her tone spoke from experience, that she had seen it and felt it.

"You believe me. You really believe me?"

"Yes, Jenny." He slid her off his knees and lay her back onto her pillows before pulling the blankets up around her. "You look like you need a rest, though."

"I feel like I need it." She settled herself and closed her eyes. "Just stay till I fall asleep?'"

"I will, Jenny." She settled down quickly. Before long, she had fallen asleep. He rose carefully and tiptoed out to the hallway.

"Is she still talking about the vampire stuff?" a nurse asked quietly.

"She's pretty insistent. She wasn't into that kind of stuff before, addiction or not. She even scoffed at the vampire novel fad back in the day. I think there's some truth to what she's saying."

The nurse wrinkled her lower lip, incredulous. "Are you sure about this?"

"As cliche as it probably sounds, I know my sister."

Once he drove home to the townhouse he shared with two college chums and a friend of theirs, he called his boss, Costas,, informing him that he had a family emergency and would need the paid time off he had accrued. Costas hemmed and hawed for a moment, but he agreed to it. Next, Jared called the police chief to shed more light on what happened.

"From what I can tell, it's a run of the mill case of one junkie fighting another junkie. If we catch Lonnigan, we'll clap him into the drunk tank overnight and leave it to the court. Since she's pressed charges, that means he'll end off in detox at Second Spring or somewhere else and the cycle will start again. Maybe we'll get lucky, and he'll tick off one of Sal Massimo's goons or whoever is sneaking drugs in through the harbor, and they'll feed him to the fishes. If they do, I feel bad for the fishes," Dennis LaChase said, clearly done with the whole case.

"I doubt it's that easy. Who knows, but Jenny saw exactly what she saw."

"You don't mean to say you believe this vampire bullshit?"

"I'm not sure I believe the vampire stuff, but I believe her."

LaChase scoffed audibly. *"I get it, you love your sister, and you want to cover all possibilities, but vampires? Come on. You been reading too many Stephen King novels late at night."*

"Still. What if she's right? What if she saw what she saw?"

"I'll answer that if we start finding blood-drained corpses in the harbor." Before Jared could argue, LaChase excused himself and hung up.

Later, while Jared was cooking a can of soup for himself, his phone rang again. Seeing LaChase's number, he answered.

"All right, maybe there's something true about your damn vampire theory," LaChase said.

"What happened?"

"Same dock where your sister was attacked, the one with the conveniently busted security camera, where Massimo's boats load and unload? I can't let out all the particulars, but someone tripped on a corpse in an alley. Medical examiner says it's drained of its blood, or most of it, anyway. Get this — there's a bite on the DB's neck and another on the leg, with two different sets of teeth marks, but don't say you heard it from me. And don't go saying 'I told you so'."

Jared's heart jumped. "I wasn't."

"You better not. Don't get cocky. I haven't time for that when I've got a pair of blood-drinking lunatics who think they're Dracula and his bride on my hands."

"Wouldn't dream of it. I'm busy helping my sister get her life back on track." Once he and LaChase had exchanged goodbyes, Jared started looking up dry shelters, finding one that looked likely.

"Good Shepherd Transitional Living, this is Sister Maryam speaking, how may I assist you?" a woman's accented voice answered.

"Sister, this is Joe Driver, I'm looking for a place for my sister, Jenny to stay?"

"Oh, that's good to hear. She stayed with us for a time last month, and we'd wondered what had happened to her."

At least she would have people who knew her around her. "She's in the hospital." He continued with a brief account of the attack. Sister Maryam listened, quietly outside of an occasional "hm" of acknowledgment and understanding.

"That's horrible. We have a bed open, and we'd be willing to have her stay here when she's discharged. I'd told her when she moved on two months ago that our door was always open if she ever needed a safe, quiet place."

"I was hoping you could, but I was wondering if I could stay with her? She's freaked out her attacker might come after her. I'm worried she might relapse. I'd take her in, but I already share a place with three other people."

"We can arrange that. No one should be alone or be among strangers after what she went though. But did I hear that right? Did you say that Lonnigan tried to drink her blood?"

Before he could stop himself, the words dropped from his mouth. "Yeah, she's got a bite on her neck and the doctors found she lost a bunch of blood. Not enough to kill her, but enough to mess her up."

A pause on the other and Sister Maryam spoke, *"I know it sounds crazy, but I wonder if something preternatural is at work. My grandmother warned us about gholes, creatures that hide in cemeteries and eat corpses, though they also attacked the living if a person wandered into their territory. My nephew saw something in a graveyard near Kandahar that matched the creature from those stories. He had been in a firefight with insurgents, and during a night patrol a few days later, one of the men they know they had shot and killed appeared again, hiding among the tombs, but he didn't look right. Gholes can take on the form of the last person they devoured, and this could have been the ghole who'd eaten the insurgent."*

"Weird. I've seen some tweaked-out people who didn't seem right, outside of them being higher than a kite. Now I'm starting to wonder what I'd seen" He paused. "Where do you start trying to find out what's going on?"

"Let's focus on getting your sister to a warm, safe place first, and once she's settled, we can work from there."

"I appreciate this, Sister. Pray for us both, will you?"

"I will, Jared."

He went into the office to pick up his paycheck. Out of habit or instinct, he had a look around to make sure his colleagues had it covered, ending up on the floor of the tenant he could not speak to. The floor looked fairly normal, outside of the framed horror title dust jackets and covers on the walls and the name plates on some of the office doors: "Castle Rock Realty", "Miskatonic University Alumni Association", "Umbrella Pharmaceuticals". As luck would have it, he arrived just as the tenant let himself out of the one marked "Castle Rock Realty".

"Hey there, Jared," the tenant said, friendly enough.

"Hey, I know it's against policy to talk you up, but I'm off the clock and I wondered if you had a minute," Jared said. "You wrote the book on what makes scary stuff scary. What do you know about vampires? Just made upor is there some truth to the stories."

"Every culture has their own vampire stories, though the details vary from place to place," the tenant replied. "But truth be told? The reality is more weird and complex than the folklore or fiction."

"So there really are blood-sucking fiends out there?"

The tenant looked around them, then looked Jared in the eye. "Don't let it be known that I told you there are." Breaking eye contact, they sauntered to the elevator. In the meantime, he continued, "Gotta ask, what prompted the question?"

"My sister got jumped and bitten on the neck the other night. She's convinced the guy who did this to her is a vampire, and not just the human lowlife she knows him as. She isn't exactly sprouting fangs and wandering around at night in a gauzy white nightgown, so I'm not sure what to make of it."

"That's the thing - just the bite doesn't turn you. The vampire has to drink from a human and then have that human drink some of the vampire's blood. "But you didn't hear any of this from me. You want to know more, go to Salem, Massachusetts, to a restaurant called Stregoi. Ask for someone known as The Contessa. She might speak to you, she might not. If she isn't up for it, she won't talk to you. Don't try to beg, she hates that."

"Do I want to know how you know all this?"

"I went to Salem for some research since I heard the vampire lifestyle people congregated there. Went to that restaurant specifically and she introduced herself. I asked her a few questions and she answered them, even the goofy ones. No, she didn't ask to drink my blood. She probably won't ask for yours, either."

The elevator dinged and the doors opened. "Why do I have a feeling 'probably' is the operative word?" Jared asked, as he followed the tenant in.

The tenant grinned, just showing the tips of his teeth. "Maybe because it is."

***

That evening Jared brought Jenny from the hospital to Good Shepherd Transitional Living, a converted Victorian that had the look of recent renovation, the windows warm with lamplight. "You don't have to go to all this trouble," Jenny said, hanging onto a bag of new clothes and toiletries Jared had picked up for her.

"You want a new start, figured that included new clothes and things." Jared pulled into the small lot beside the building.

Jenny chuckled. "Looks a little like something Morticia and Gomez's normal siblings would live in."

"I think Morticia had a sister who wore flowery dresses and blonde pigtails. Of course, it was Carolyn Jones dressed like Little Bo Peep," Jared said, cutting the engine.

Jenny laughed. "Seriously? I guess I need to watch more of that show."

"I watch a lot of old TV episodes between security walks. You'd be surprised how many older shows you can find online," Jared admitted, getting out and opening her door before walking alongside her to the front door.

A tall man built like a Ukrainian wrestler and clad in a brown monk's robe met them at the door. "Peace be with you. I'm Brother Daffyd," he said in a melodious bass baritone with a lilting accent.

Jenny and Jared introduced themselves, showing their IDs. "You're from Wales?" Jenny asked.

"Oh, God bless you and your good ears, Jenny. Most people ask me where I come from in Ireland," Brother Daffyd said, taking Jenny's bag and grinning at her as he walked them inside.

Sister Maryam met them in the entryway, leading them into the combination dining room and common area, where a couple small family groups and a few unattached had started to gather, the attendants setting up the small buffet style dinner.

"Welcome back, Jenny. Jared told us about what happened," Sister Maryam said. "How are you feeling?"

"I'm all right. I'm exhausted, but I think I'll be okay. I have to go into the clinic for rehab, but I'm managing," Jenny replied.

One older woman in a heavily mended cardigan looked Jenny up and down, her beady eyes settling on the bandage on the younger woman's neck. "Helluva hickey from your john, girl."

Jenny looked away, pursing her lips to keep them from trembling, then took a seat at the table. One of the mothers reached over and covered her youngest kid's ears. Her older, teenage son giggled, but Sister Maryam shook her head and Brother Daffyd threw the older kid a "Really?" look.

"Gertrude, we don't talk about people that way, especially not at the dinner table," Sister Maryam said.

"Why not? The kids are gonna learn about it soon enough," Gertrude grinned, showing her worn teeth.

Jenny dropped the fork she had taken, breathing hard but keeping them deep. Jared reached out and put an arm behind her back. She leaned slightly into his touch. Jared tossed a glare in Gertrude's general direction. "The guy who beat her up also bit her."

Gertrude gasped and shuffled a few steps backward, making a large Sign of the Cross in Jenny's general direction."You'd better put *her* out! She's a goddamned vampire now!"

Jared blurted out, "It doesn't work that way"

An attendant approached Gertrude, putting a hand on her shoulder. "Gertrude, could you please take your plate and come with me to the kitchen?" she asked, gently but firmly steering the older woman toward the kitchen door.

"Gertie's gonna sit in the corner for telling whoppers," a male client, clad in a worn Army fatigue jacket, joked.

Sister Maryam put a comforting hand on Jenny's shoulder. "I'm sorry about that, Jenny. Gertrude has a big imagination at best."

Jenny smiled gently at Army Jacket Guy. "Thanks, Barry, but she's not wrong. The guy who bit me…. He moved too fast to be anything human."

Brother Daffyd approached Jenny. "I'm not using my office at the mo. You and Jared care to have your supper in there?"

Jared looked at Jenny. "It's your call."

Jenny nodded. "I'd like that. It'll be quieter."

Brother Daffyd took their plates and led them back to a small room at the rear of the ground floor. Jared kept his arm behind Jenny's back as he walked with her. Brother Daffyd set the plates on the uncluttered desktop, moving his computer keyboard and the one stack of files to make some space before pulling a second chair closer to the desk. Jared led Jenny inside and helped her toward the large desk chair.

"Sister Maryam told me about what happened. We weren't expecting Gertrude tonight, but it's getting colder at night," Brother Daffyd said.

"Isn't Gertrude some kind of stereotypical old lady name?" Jenny asked with a wry, shaky laugh.

"And too often, she lives up to it. D' ya want anything more?" he asked.

"I think we just need to be alone together," Jared said, glancing at Jenny.

She nodded. "I'll need to change my bandages after supper, but I'm good otherwise."

Brother Daffyd nodded. "I'll bring you the necessary items when I check in on you." With that, he excused himself and left the room, shutting the door behind him to give them some privacy.

"Miserable old hag, I bet she has sand where the sun doesn't shine," Jenny muttered.

"How much you want to bet she's watched the old black and white *Dracula* movie on the late show one time too many when she was a teenager and wanted to be one of Dracula's brides?" Jared quipped.

"Maybe she saw it in the original run in the Great Depression." She paused, pulling her plate closer to her. "All right, that was mean, but are you saying she's jealous of me? Because if she knew the reality, if she knew how bad a bite wound itches and how bad it hurt getting it, she'd have another dark desire coming."

Jared pulled his chair closer to the desk. "I was trying to make fun of her noise, but you might be on to something."

An hour later, Brother Daffyd came to check on them and to collect their dishes, bringing with him a first aid kit. "Anita Reyes, the lady with the kid who giggled at Gertrude's rude mouth, is worried for you. She's even offered to talk to her mom who works the occult store in Portland. Says she knows a few protection charms." He said this with a bemused look, as if he appreciated the concern, but didn't know what to make of the offer.

"That stuff doesn't work, does it? The garlic and stakes and silver bullets?" Jared asked.

"I thought silver bullets worked on werewolves?" Brother Daffyd asked, assisting Jenny with changing the bandage and cleaning the wound. "The only vampires I've ever seen are the kids in black wearing plastic fangs, whose parents kicked them out of the house, or in the Hammer movies my brother used to bring home from the corner rental near our flat in Cardiff. You rather I kept watch outside the door?"

"Window would be wiser," Jared said.

"We've got a camera on the back of the house, but if you'd rather cover the window, I'll be right outside the door to cover you if there's trouble," Brother Daffyd said.

"We'd appreciate that," Jenny said.

They settled down at ten PM, with lights out at eleven.

"You going to Anita's grandmother's shop about her ooga-booga stuff?" Jared asked as he put a few pillows on the couch under the window rather than bunking down on the other twin bed in the room.

She put her phone onto its charger. "I wouldn't call it that, but you never know: it might work. It might be one of those things you can't know will work or not unless you try it."

"All right, if nothing else, I'll get a few books on vampire stuff, if they got them." He settled on the couch as she crawled under the covers.

She sat up, leaning on her elbow. "You just saying that to humor me?"

"Nope, this situation is so weird, I'll try most anything."

She smiled and, pulling the blankets around her, nestled into the pillows. "Thanks...for believing me and bringing me here."

"Anything to help you. Want me to put the light out?"

"Yeah, I got an early appointment tomorrow. Good night, Jarry."

Jared smiled as he got up. Hearing her old nickname for him warmed his heart. "Good night, Jen-Jen."

She turned over and settled down. Jared read on his phone for a while before putting it on its charger and pulling a blanket over himself. The skill of sleeping with one eye open came back to him from his time in Iraq and he fell into a half-sleep.

Ten minutes or two hours could have passed. Something scratched at the window, awakening Jared from a sound sleep. He bolted to his feet, digging in his pocket for his keys. A shadow passed across the glass, something human shaped. It returned, darkening the window.

The figure lunged at the window, hard enough to crack the glass. Jared sandwiched his keys between his fingers, ready to stab the intruder in the face. Instinct prodded him to open the window and attack the would-be intruder. He ordered himself to hold back and give the wretch enough rope to hang himself through breaking in and entering.

The figure smacked into the window again, shaking it, roaring *"I know you're in there!"*

The door flew open and Brother Daffyd ran in, roaring like a bull and brandishing a cricket bat. The shadow at the window fled.

"What was out there?" he asked. "I heard a loud bang."

"Someone hit the window," Jared said. Jenny shook under the covers and sat up. "Jen, you awake?" Jared asked.

"I am now. What in hell is going on?" she asked.

"Thank God for double-pane glass." Brother Daffyd beckoned them to come with him. They followed him out into the hallway and then to his office. He woke up his desktop, pulling up the feed on the outside security cameras, selecting the one trained on the back wall of the house.

The feed showed a human shape vaulting over the fence surrounding the yard, clearing it with more height than an Olympic pole vaulter could achieve. The shape slunk through the yard to the back wall. They closer they got, the clearer they could see the face: a white male in his early fifties, rail thin, lank hair, clad in a canvas shirt over a tee shirt, worn jeans and work boots.

"That's Ned Lonnigan all right," Jared said.

"I told you," Jenny said.

Brother Daffyd paused the feed. "I thought he was dead or vanished."

"He OD'd, but no one ever found his body. The cops figured he somehow came to and wandered off before he fell off a pier and drowned," Jenny said. "My friend Lucia was with him that night. She went to call for help."

"Hope she didn't try the ice cube trick," Brother Daffyd winced.

"She used to go to nursing school. She knows better," Jenny said.

"Please tell me you never partied with him?" Jared asked.

Jenny gathered her face in a squidge of disgust. "Hell no. He's a creep. Was a creep. Whatever fits since he's a vampire now."

"Well, we've got video proof he's still alive and kicking, if the police will give half an ear and half an eye," Brother Daffyd said.

She looked from the screen to Brother Daffyd, then to Jared. "You aren't going to kick us out of the shelter, are you?"

"That's the last thing we would do to you, especially at a time like this," Brother Daffyd said. "Especially when there's a vampire in the mix."

Jared put an arm behind Jenny's back. "Let's get you back to bed."

Jenny let him lead her back to their room. "I just hope I can back to sleep after all this."

***

INTERLUDE 1

FEBRUARY 14TH 20 --

"This why you turned me? Some do-gooding notch on your fangs?" Lonnigan muttered, the shakes running down his arms to his hands.

Artemisia, his sire, leaned over him, her pallid face close to his. "Because you amused me, because of your uncommon taste."

"Tasted me enough. Did more than taste me - ate every bit of me."

"I remade you to enjoy life eternal."

"Wasn't enjoying life that. I'd take a stake through the heart. I need a fix. Anyone thinks becoming a 'chylde off thee nyght'," he waggled his hands airily, "cures you of needing a fix, got another thought coming."

"Perhaps on this night for lovers I can make amends." She licked his mouth before kissing it. Then she vanished from their cellar nest, out the broken panes of the north-facing window. He pulled a tarp over himself, hiding from urban explorers wandering inrather than keeping out the winter chill or the last daylight.

***

Late that night, his sire's voice called deep in his mind. Lonnigan climbed out the window and up the warehouse wall to the roof, leaping to the next. He scrabbled from one roof to another, taking longer leaps as the warehouse gave way to shops and houses. Her voice sang louder, guiding him.

He landed on the roof of a restored Victorian mansion. He scrabbled down the wall, to the sill of one open upper-story window. Within, a young woman lay sprawled on a four-poster bed. Syringes, spoons, lighters, and baggies lay scattered on a nearby rosewood nightstand. Artemesia sat beside the girl.

"I had an eye on this pretty one."

"May I enter?" Lonnigan asked.

"What? Who's… this?" the girl asked.

"Londarian, my childe." Artemesia replied. Lonnigan smirked. Pretty words for an ugly bastard. "He cannot enter 'till you invite him."

"Sure." He dropped over the sill, hobbling to the bed.

"You wish for death, sweetling? You can leave this world of hateful men. Your heart can never break; you will never see another lonely Valentine's night."

Lonnigan knelt over the girl, smelling the chemicals in the fresh needle mark in her leg. Saliva moistened his fangs. Taking her arm, he bit her wrist. Her blood flowed over his tongue, bitter but within a few swallows, his nerves trilled. Images, voices flooded his mind as if he lived them: a guy in a designer tee-shirt over artfully torn jeans saying, "We're through.", breaking glass, a tree looming before a sports-car's windshield, someone tossing a small, blue box into a pond…

Lonnigan broke away, halting the images. He dropped the girl's body to the mattress. Artemesia smirked. "And how does it feel?"

"Crazy. Know how they say your life flashes before your eyes when you die? Saw 'er life."

"What did you see?"

"A brat with everything I never had got dumped by her dumb-fuck boyfriend. Did her a favor."

"Could you find him if we sought him?"

"Sure. Need t'give you as good a Valentine in return."

***

The following morning, Jared and Jenny came down to breakfast late. Gertrude, likewise, had come down late.

The old woman stopped in her tracks and pointed at Jenny. "That one's dangerous: - she lured a vampire here." The clients at the table stared, looking from Gertrude to Jenny, who stood with head bowed, her face going red.

"Gertrude, shut your trap. You are not helping the situation," Jared snapped, staring her in the eye.

Sister Maryam turned from speaking with Anita and her kids. "You're on your third strike for causing commotion, Gertrude. Cold weather is coming, and I don't want you to be without a warm place to stay."

Gertrude pursed her lips, glaring at Jenny before making a rude comment regarding 'pretty young things" and members of the religious life. Jenny broke down and ran from the room crying.

Sister Maryam frowned at Gertrude. "That was your last strike. Come with me." She and an attendant approached her, leading her from the dining room.

"You can't toss an old widow woman out! I got nowhere else to go! You don't care! You just want to make money!" her voice yelled, bouncing off the painted walls.

Anita stared in the direction of the noise, then looked to the attendants. "Yeah, you people are just rolling in cash."

Jared managed a nervous laugh, then collected himself. "I'd better go check on Jenny."

He found her curled up on the bed, face buried in her arm. "Hey, Jen, you all right?"

"No, but I'll manage," she murmured.

"Come on, let's get you to the clinic," he said, gently helping her sit up. "I'll get you some McDonald's hot cakes on the way."

"I'm not exactly six anymore, but….that sounds good about now," she said. "Don't let me be alone, will you? Outside of the therapy session, I mean."

"I get it, and I got ya. Want me to go full Secret Service wannabe and check bathrooms for you?"

She managed a shaky laugh. "People might get suspicious if you went to those lengths. But I appreciate the thought."

He drove her to the rehab clinic connected to St. Joseph's, then called Dr. Mukhtahar's office. A few minutes later he sat in her office, a small but well- lit room with a number of potted plants on the windowsill. He sat across from her, her desk between them.

"We'd swabbed your sister's wounds and also took some photos of the bite for law enforcement. They sent the swab in to the FBI. They've matched it to a suspect in some drug trafficking cases, a guy who'd gone missing in January. Not that he's been missed by many people. There have been blips on the radar since then, but no one's been able to substantiate them."

"Pretty solid blip if you ask me."

"Do you feel safe where you are?"

He tried not to think of the attempted attack on the previous night. "Yeah, there's good people around us."

"I'm just concerned there may be another attack."

Jared snuffed. "You want to carve some wooden stakes?"

She gave him a hard look. "I trust you're joking?"

He shrugged with his hands, palms turned up. "I'm not about to rule out the possibility. It's the only explanation why a guy would come back after an overdose."

"He could have recovered and returned."

"It doesn't explain why he bounded over a fence like a pole vaulter without a pole."

Once he came out of the consult, he left a message on Jenny's phone, then drove to the downtown area and the psychic shop. The place looked like something out of Salem, Massachusetts - pentagrams and mystical sigils painted in gilding on the black exterior walls, colorful scarves festooned like curtains across the windows. Jared let himself in, stepping into a shop space sweet with incense and making his way around and among tables covered in boxes and bowls of crystals and bags of herbs, tarot decks in boxes and bundles of incense sticks.

The clerk behind the counter looked up from jotting in a journal. "Welcome to the Enchanted Cottage. May I guide you in your journey through the wondrous?"

"Yeah, could you point me in the direction of the books on vampires and things like that?"

The clerk pointed to a shadowed corner toward the rear of the shop. "You should find them on those shelves

"Thanks." Finding a shelf of vampire books, he flipped through several. A few he put back due to the edgy. "dark of the dark darkity darkness dark" tone they carried, but he selected a few for sounding more level-headed.

He paid for the books and drove back to the hospital. Once there, he checked his messages, finding a text from Jenny. *I'm in the hospital cafeteria. Food's actually good. Come meet me here?*

He smiled and texted her back. *I'm in the hospital parking lot. I'm on the way, Love you.*

He found Jenny at a table at the back, close to the counters and the staff members working behind them. Jenny sat huddled in her seat as she poked at the remains of a salad but perked up as Jared approached. He sat down across from her.

"Looks like you got some reading materials," she said, her eye on the bag of books Jared had brought with him.

"Yeah, I found a few books on vampires. Did you know there were vampire scares in New England as far back as the 1700s?"

"Did that grow out of the witch hunts in the 1690s?"

"Maybe. But the last major one involved Mercy Brown in the 1880s, in Rhode Island. There's a lot of indicators Bram Stoker got the idea for *Dracula* from newspaper accounts of what went down. It legit went international."

"That's nuts. And you wonder if some of the more out there vampire lifestylers might be the real deal only hiding in plain sight."

"Except I doubt many of them are attacking people for funsies, otherwise they're likely to get immobilized by a stake to the heart and their head chopped off before they torch the body."

Jenny spat some of her iced tea. Jared took some napkins from the holder, offered her some and blotted the table. "Seriously? They do that?"

"That's what they did in Mercy Brown's case, minus introducing her to Mister Pointy."

"That's creepy and messed up, but I suppose when people get desperate, they'll do weird things." She managed a wry smile and a glance at the fading track marks on her arm. "Or inject themselves with dangerous addicting chemicals."

He reached across the tabletop and put a gentle hand on her wrist. "We'll get you through this."

"If we can deal with Lonnigan."

***

Supper at Good Shepherd passed far more peacefully than the night before. "Find your answers about dark things in the darkness?" Anita asked.

"We'll have to find out what his main weakness is, but I've been clued in to someone else who might be in the know," Jared said. "I broke the rules at the job and talked to the tenant I can't talk to."

"The author with the writing office?" Jenny asked.

"Yep. They clued me in to some vampire expert in Salem."

"Guess you'll have to go down to the flat lands," Barry, the guy who often wore a worn Army jacket, piped in. "Jen, how well did you know Lon?"

Jenny rolled her eyes. "Not well, but I know crucifixes wouldn't work. He used to talk about giving up being Catholic for Lent."

"Crucifixes don't always work in the movies, but maybe since he 'used to be' Catholic, it might work?" Barry asked.

"Maybe him specifically. He used to go off about the Church at any chance he could. Dissed me for coming here the last time I crashed here, said a lot of rude stuff about Sister Maryam and Brother Daffyd."

Sister Maryam approached with a basket of warm rolls, setting it in the middle of the table. "I'd almost keep crucifixes as a possibility. It's been my experience that the louder a person objects to something, the closer it is to being something they truly value, even if that value comes only through hating it."

"Guess I'd better invest in the biggest crucifix I can find," Jenny said.

At lights out, Jenny had her eye on the nightstand between the beds, the tip of her tongue in the corner of her mouth as she did when an idea had come to her.

"Penny for your thoughts?" Jared asked, making up his bed.

"I'd like to push the beds together so we can be closer without being in the same bed, but I'm not sure they'd let us," she said.

"The staff doesn't have to know; we can move stuff back first thing in the morning," Jared said. "It'd be like the times we'd gone camping as kids and we'd all end up piled on each other and Mom and Dad like a family of dogs and puppies."

She grinned impishly and moved the nightstand to the foot of the bed. Jared took the hint and moved his bed close enough for the mattresses to touch.

"Safety in numbers and in proximity." She fluffed her pillows and crawled under the covers. Jared slipped into his side, pulling up his covers. Jenny crept closer, nestling near him.

"Whatever happened to your kid sister who used to puppy-pile with you and draw pictures of princess knights rescuing scared princes?" she asked.

"She lost her way in a dark forest. There're creatures snapping at her heels, but she found some wise owls and a brave bear and some helpful deer to assist her as she finds her way out," Jared replied.

"If she's smart enough to listen to the owls and follow the bear and ride one of the deer, hanging onto the antlers." She paused. "Hm." She uncoiled from her blankets and found first her phone to switch on the lantern and the journal on the nightstand.

"Got an idea?"

"Maybe for a kid's book, if I can find someone to write the story."

"What about the tenant I'm not allowed to talk to?"

"Nah, I was thinking maybe the writer up in Winter Harbor, except that's a ways up there and she might not be glad to see me."

"Once you're cleaned up and healing, she might. If she won't give you a second chance, is she worth working with?"

She smiled at him. "You've got a good point." She drew for a while, then sandwiched her pen inside the journal before tucking it under her pillow and settling down. The phone lantern switched out. He smiled and closed his eyes. Perhaps she had come to a corner and passed it into a clearing in her dark forest.

Late in the night, footsteps pounded past their door. Jared bolted awake. He slid from under the covers and ran for the door to crack it open. Someone screamed in the front of the house. Barry the Army guy ran past the door, turning a corner into the common area.

Jared ducked out, pulling the door shut behind him. He ran to the common area. Another loud scream cut through the night, then cut off. Sister Maryam entered the common area in her terry cloth bathrobe, joining the two men. Barry had a narrowed look in his eyes which Jared had seen with some of his combat buddies.

"The hell is going on?" Jared asked.

"Something horrible out there," Barry said. He strode toward the foyer and the entryway. Jared followed him, past the reception desk and the intake room. The inner and the outer doors of the entryway stood open. Barry grabbed a heavy chair and glanced at Jared. Jared nodded and rushed to the door, opening it wide.

The reek of blood and ammonia blew through the doorway. On the steps, Gertrude's body lay sprawled, her throat torn open, blood soaking the front of her coat.

Two figures grappled with Brother Daffyd. A small woman in a tattered gown had perched on his back, her knees wrapped around his waist, throttling him with her hands. Daffyd wrestled with a roughly-dressed male with lank, gray hair, gripping the shaft of the bat Daffyd wielded.

Barry rushed the figure on Daffyd's back, bashing her on the shoulder with a chair. It cracked but held. The woman shrieked, the sound tearing into Jared's ears. She released Daffyd and hit the steps. Righting herself, she vaulted onto the roof and out of sight.

Brother Daffyd wrenched the bat free and cracked his attacker over the head. The male ducked, stumbled, then fell backward down the stairs. Landing on his feet, he vaulted from the ground to the roof of the house.

"We've only just got started," the male yelled and leaped out of sight, following the woman.

"What in hell goes on around here?" Barry stared after the intruders.

Red and blue lights flashed off the buildings across the way. Two cruisers and an ambulance pulled up before the shelter. Four officers and a crew of paramedics approached, two examining Gertrude while another examined Brother Daffyd.

Some of the clients tried coming to the door, but Sister Maryam stepped out, holding them back, her arms stretched out. "It's bad out here. I don't think you need or want to see this," she said. A female officer approached and asked to speak with Sister Maryam. Another officer took Barry aside, while a third questioned Jared.

"So what did you see?"

"They got Gertrude, I'm guessing. The two people fighting Brother Daffyd. A man and a woman." Jared said.

"I vaguely recognized the guy," Barry said.

"What do you mean, you've met him before?" one officer asked.

"He'd hung out in every homeless camp and shelter, till he got his miserable ass banned from the legit places and driven out of the rest," Barry replied.

"He's stalking my sister. She's cleaned up, but he used to party with a girl she partied with," Jared added.

"By 'partied with' you mean 'used illegal substances with'?"

"Yeah," Jared replied.

"You got a name for this guy?"

"Ned Lonnigan," Barry replied. Jared nodded in agreement, trying to cover the shiver starting to run through his frame.

The officer looked from Barry to Jared. "The guy who OD'd and vanished? He's turned up again?"

"Yeah, it was him. He ran off that way." Jared pointed down the street, roughly in the direction in which the pair had vanished, avoiding the necessity of explaining how they vanished.

"All right, I'll talk to Sister Maryam about the camera footage," the officer said, moving on.

One paramedic approached Jared with a blanket and draped it about his shoulders. "You'll be all right." At one in the same time, he couldn't take it as anything more than a gentle platitude, but also his thoughts clung to it to keep his mind from spiraling downward.

Once the coroner's workers had taken Gertrude's body and the police had left, Jared limped back to his and Jenny's room. He found Anita sitting on her bed, beside Jenny, her arm behind the younger woman's shoulders.

"I should leave. All this is happening because of me. I'm bringing this on these good people. It's like he's gotten inside me and he's using me as a way in," Jenny said.

Jared knelt before his sister. "Jen, if there's any consolation, the cops are on this, though I'm wondering how serious they'll take it, after what the door camera picked up." He snuffed dryly. "I suppose it's no consolation, but Gertrude won't be accusing you of luring in a vampire when she ended up as vamp chow herself."

"Please tell me he didn't bite Gertrude?" Jenny asked.

"'Fraid they did. Didn't think an old bat like her had that much blood," Jared said.

"They?" Anita asked with a concerned frown.

"Looks like Lonnigan brought a lady friend. Guess he figured reinforcements were in order, but I don't think they counted on dealing with an ex-Army guy and a monk built like a rugby player."

***

"You up for a road trip?" Jared asked Jenny after she got out of her next session at the clinic.

"A road trip to where?" Jenny asked, closing the shotgun side door to his car.

"Down to Salem, Mass. Get to the bottom of all this vampire stuff."

She fastened her seat belt and nestled down in her seat. "Yeah, I suppose. I mean, it would do me some good to get away from everything."

He took Route 1 to the nearest exit onto the Maine Turnpike, the better to speed up their travel time. They passed through the tollbooth before the New Hampshire state line, then another before the Massachusetts state line. Once they reached Route 128 and traveled as far as the North Shore Mall, Jenny woke up and uncurled.

"Are we in the Witch City yet?" she asked.

Jared took the Danvers exit. "We're heading into Danvers, or Salem Village, as they used to call it in the Witch Hunt days."

They passed a large cemetery with an iron fence, then drove across a large overpass above the commuter rail tracks. They passed the Witch House before taking a left into the downtown area and a right onto Washington Street. They passed a housing project in construction and pulled up before a restaurant with its windows covered with heavy floor to ceiling deep red drapes and the name "Stregoi" in red LED rope lighting.

They entered just at the evening 'happy hour'. A few patrons, some clad in black, sat along the bar or in some of the booths. A tall, robust woman standing behind the bar looked in Jared and Jenny's direction. Jared approached.

"We're here to see The Contessa," he said and named the tenant who had pointed him in her direction.

The barkeep pointed them toward one of two curtained doorways. Two short, stocky, heavily muscled and hairy guards, one male, one female stood before it.

"She's taking guests but don't be long." the male guard said.

"Tell her there's trouble and it involves Ned Lonnigan," Jenny said.

The guards went still, then exchanged glances. "Hold that thought," the male guard said as he lifted the curtains went inside. A moment later, he returned.

The two guards frisked Jared and Jenny before the female of the pair opened the curtains. "You can see her but don't look her in the eye. She hates that," she said. Jared led Jenny inside.

Within, behind an ornate mahogany table covered in red and black damask, a young woman sat on a carved wooden armchair upholstered in red velvet. Jared had expected the archetypal slim Gothic beauty with pale skin and black hair. Rather, he gazed on a curvy woman with red hair contrasted with a Mediterranean complexion, though she leaned into her cliches with the black velvet gown of a vaguely medieval cut. He paused in his tracks, looking to Jenny, who looked from her brother to The Contessa. Jenny dropped her an awkward curtsy, which brought a small smile to The Contessa's face.

"You needn't stand on ceremony with me," she said in a deep, melodious voice. "So you've seen Artemesia's childe?"

"If you mean some ugly fuck named Ned Lonnigan, then yeah," Jared said.

Jenny related what had happened on the dock, then Jared added what had happened at Good Shepherd House.

The Contessa listened, sitting perfectly still and unblinking, but Jared caught her eyes slowly narrowing. When they had finished, Jenny turned her face to blot her eyes on her sleeves. Jared pulled his sister closer, wondering what their host would make of this.

"I was afraid this would come about," The Contessa said. "For what you've been through, you deserve to hear the whole story. Though it's likely hard for you to believe, Lonnigan is the childe of my childe. Her name is Artemesia, originally Artemesia Gamwell and she is, no doubt, the small woman who accompanied him. She was a society girl in Victorian London, the daughter of a merchant, one of the captains of business who dominated that era, a typical bored rich girl. Her father had worked with me; she had developed consumption, what people commonly called tuberculosis at the time, which she tried to ease with laudanum."

"Sounds like the opioids I got hooked on after a car accident in my teens," Jenny said wryly. She darted a look toward The Contessa. "I didn't mean to interrupt."

"No offense taken. Her father begged me to turn her before he lost her to illness and narcotics. I refused, but he warned me that he knew the kind of people who could end me for the right price." The Contessa paused. "And so, I agreed to turn her. When she came back to full consciousness, she screamed at me and tried to scratch my face. I let her. She ran away as soon as she could. Her father raged at me, but he couldn't fault me for her reaction. He had insisted on this.

"I've kept an eye on her as best as I could, but she is elusive at best, not always the elegant figure most people imagine when someone speaks of vampires. She is…closer to the feral creatures that the vampires of folklore manifest as. I'm not surprised that her childe turned out as feral as she."

"He wasn't exactly a Victorian gentleman anyway," Jenny said.

"She had a taste for lowlifes, for lack of a better term for people who've made certain dark choices. The novelty of the experience likely amused her since she had grown up in the lap of luxury. I'm sure that life bored her."

"So what would take the both of them down? I've been warned crucifixes may not work since he wasn't much of a believer? Would it work on her?"

"That would weaken Artemesia. She has been skulking around this town, trying to harass me by harming the people under my protection, but I've found sanctuary at a local church. As I recall, her childe wasn't particularly religious before he was turned, though he was raised in the Faith. Silver, on the other hand, is something that affected him even then," The Contessa replied.

"So what do we do? Take him down by smacking him to death with a silver spoon?" Jenny asked.

The Contessa chuckled, a human sound. "I would rather you weakened them both. Their hellish joyriding has gone on long enough. It's attracted the wrong kind of attention, from humans with no compassion and from vampires far more dangerous than I." Jenny flinched. "Oh, don't be alarmed. They won't come after you. You're too small and weak by their standards. But there are beings who walked the earth long before the birth of humanity, who may have created the first vampires. They fed on the blood of creatures older than your kind, thus your blood is too weak to sustain them. Thus, they are only able to feed from the descendants of the first blood drinkers whom they created."

"Creepy," Jenny shuddered.

"So, what, they're super vampires which can only feed from other vampires?" Jared asked.

"A simplified explanation, but it will suffice," The Contessa replied.

"So what do you want us to do? Hunt 'em down for you?" Jared said. "Some vampire queen you are or whatever we should call you."

"How would we even do that? Put me out as bait?" Jenny asked.

"There is a police officer in Biddeford, Deacon Taylor. Make contact with him and let him handle the hard work. Don't let him know that you know me but let him know that you have a vampire problem. Do try and avoid letting his colleagues know about this. Too many of them don't understand the situation beyond 'Vampire bad. Staking vampire good'. Innocent until proven guilty still applies past a person's turning. In the meantime, the two of you must find a way to live your life, to heal and move on."

"Don't worry, I'm in rehab and I'm starting to find my way out of the woods," Jenny said.

"I know the 'Kill 'em all and let God sort it out' types too well. I served with people like that in Afghanistan, only substitute 'Middle Eastern people' for 'vampires'," Jared said. "I'll keep my wits about me."

A small, sad smirk crossed The Contessa's impassive face. "I appreciate your shrewdness and your good heart, Jared Driver. Jenny, you have a noble brother."

Jenny started to make an objection, but she glanced his way, trying not to smirk. Jared felt his face grow warm.

The Contessa sat back slightly. "Now, I regret to say our time to speak has grown short. Hopefully, the next time we see each other, we shall be quitting ourselves of these pests."

"I hope so, too. I wasn't sure what to expect, but you're a very gracious person, Contessa," Jenny said. The Contessa beamed.

Back in the car and on their way north, Jenny curled up in the shotgun seat, but her eyes stayed open and almost painfully thoughtful and alert. "You getting the feeling we're getting the runaround?" Jenny asked.

Jared darted his eyes back to the road. "Does feel like we're getting drip fed only part of the story with each person we meet." The evening commuters had thinned out considerably as the September twilight deepened into night's darkness.

"Let's hope we don't have more trouble at the shelter. I don't want us to get kicked out like Gertrude."

"I doubt they will, and even if they do, I will put my foot down with my roommates and let you sleep on the couch or in my room while I sleep on the couch or something."

"Jared, when's the last time I told you you're the best older brother ever?"

"You've told me that almost every day since this all started."

She looked at him, the dashboard lights glowing amber on her tired face. "Is it getting old?"

"No, not at all."

***

INTERLUDE 2
AUGUST 20TH, 20--

Ryan looked at the strings of LED lights Shelly had strung up inside the tent, the inflated king-size air mattress covered with a duvet and piled with green, brown, and tan velour pillows. "This isn't real camping."

Shelly returned from the van with an armload of mosquito nets, about the first practical thing she'd brought along. "They do call it glamping."

Evan poked at the glowing coals in the fire pit, adding sticks gathered from the woods. "We're out in the woods. We've got a tent to sleep in. We're cooking over a fire."

"Could you help me drape the nets over the bed?" Shelly asked. "Have you seen the one for the door, too?"

Evan tossed a small log onto the fire. "Think it's in the van."

"I dunno, I think of camping, I think of something more rugged," Jared said, going to help Shelly fasten the ends of the net to the tent ceiling. "The mosquito nets are about the most camp-like thing I've seen so far, 'cause we used those when I camped with the Scouts. Otherwise, I feel like we're crashing in your living room."

Evan eyed Ryan over their glasses. "She doesn't have trees in her living room."

"But there's cushions and string lights in her living room."

Shelly looked around the edge of the net. "Dudes, let's just enjoy our weekend in the great outdoors?"

"I guess I just wanna let my inner woodsman out to roam when I go camping," Ryan said.

Evan poked the fire with a metal rod before laying the grill over it. "You wanna rough it, I'll go with you some weekend when Shelly's off with her sisters."

A couple hours later, they sat chatting over the remains of veggie burgers and a tossed salad from the organic grocery, and now roasted marshmallows over the fire. A twig snapped nearby. Ryan nearly dropped his bamboo skewer into the fire. "Okay, things in the woods. That makes it feel more like camping."

Evan grabbed a flashlight and switched it on, pointing the beam into the shadows beneath the trees. The light glowed red in the eyes of some creature, too high off the ground.

A short, slim girl glided from under the trees, clad in a ragged white gown spattered with brown and green. "I saw your fire. I hoped I'd come to the edge of the woods."

Ryan propped his stick against his portable canvas chair. "It's not the edge, but we're close to the road out to civilization."

Shelly rose and approached the girl. "You okay? You hungry? Thirsty? We've got food and some drinks. And if you need a ride to the road, we can help."

Evan looked at the bottles in the cooler. "We got drinks if you like wine."

The girl stepped closer to the fire. The light glinted red in her pupils. She grinned, uncovering a pair of fangs nested among her other teeth. "I regret that I need something not so strong."

She lunged at Shelly, grabbing the back of the taller girl's neck and clamping her jaws onto her throat. Shelly screamed, the sound cut off. Ryan rushed toward them. Something lunged from the pines above the campsite, grabbing him by the head and hauling him into the branches.

Evan stared from Shelly with the girl at her throat to the treetops, frozen in place. The girl in white dropped Shelly's body, skin paler than ever, to the pine straw on the ground. "Don't worry, I've had plenty." She glanced down at her stomach, now rounder under her gown. "Don't worry for your friend, either, my childe made swift work of him."

Ryan's body dropped from the tree and hit the ground along with a brackish stream of water. Evan looked into the tree branches at a rat-faced man with lank, dishwater-colored hair, grinning down, with blood dripping from his fangs and mouth.

"Lonnigan, be civilized and wipe your mouth. We are vampires, not wild dogs," the girl vampire said.

"Yeth, mommy." Lonnigan wiped his mouth on his ragged denim sleeve.

"Which-what are you going to do to me?" Evan backed toward the van.

Lonnigan dove from the tree and pinned Evan. "We're used to stowing leftovers." He grabbed Evan's head, twisted it and snapped the human's neck. "Think this one will taste as good, Artie?"

"It's Artemesia, and this one should taste as good as the others."

Lonnigan limped to the tent, lifting the mosquito netting over the door. "Heh. Lookit this."

Artemesia approached the tent. "Have these young people ever truly slept rough that they bring such finery?"

"Or maybe they have and they'd rather not do that again," Lonnigan plopped himself on the nest of pillows.

She ran the mosquito netting through her fingertips. "And this mesh, to keep off the mosquitoes and other biting flies?"

"Didn't do much good to keep off a completely different kind of blood sucker."

**

They pulled into the lot of Good Shepherd Home too late for supper, but just in time for an aide to meet them at the door and lead both of them into Brother Daffyd's office. There they found a tall, dark-haired man in a sheriff's uniform, talking with him and Sister Maryam, who introduced himself as Deacon Taylor.

"We were hoping you'd come home soon," Brother Daffyd said.

Jenny hung her head. "Yeah, I'm the cause of all the trouble." She eyed Taylor's badge. "You aren't going to arrest me, are you?"

"No, not at all. I came here to have a look at the doorbell camera video," Taylor said. "I want to get to the bottom of this as much as you do."

"Do I want to know how you got involved in this mess, outside of the fact that it's your job to investigate these things?" Jared asked.

"I can't really get into it, since it's personal and it's the proverbial long story." Taylor said. "But I am investigating another attack with a similar MO. We've been telling the local news it's a series of animal attacks, but it's hard keeping a lid on this kind of case."

"One of those things you can't tell the details of, because it's an ongoing investigation," Jenny said.

"More or less." To Brother Daffyd, he added, "Now about that footage?"

Jenny shivered and exchanged a look with Jared. "Do we want to see it?" she asked.

Jared tried and failed to suppress a wince. "If it's anything like what I saw the tail end of last night, you might be better off not seeing the rest of it."

Jenny looked at Brother Daffyd. "I feel like since I brought this on, I need to see this through to the end, however bitter."

Sister Maryam put a motherly hand on Jenny's shoulder. "If it gets to be too much, you can step away. You need to protect and care for you."

"All right, it's your funeral, as my uncle the undertaker would say," Brother Daffyd said. He pulled up the doorbell camera feed on his desktop and selected the previous night.

An image in night vision showed the small porch area by the front door, dim except for the lights from passing trucks and the lights on the buildings across the street. No sound and nothing moved for several minutes. At length, Gertrude shuffled into view, looking around her as if keeping watch for a pursuer. She reached in, pressing the doorbell several times, then looking around her again.

First one pair, then another pair of beads of light showed in the gloom beyond the reach of the camera. One pair hovered slightly higher than the other.

A small shadow jumped Gertrude from behind, pulling her over backward. Brother Daffyd paused the video and played it back slower. The replay revealed the shadow as a petite, dark-haired woman in a tattered gown, made up of what looked like layers of torn Victorian-styled dresses. She grabbed Gertrude by the neck, ripping open the older woman's coat and tearing apart her worn shirt collar. Gertrude opened her mouth in a soundless scream as her attacker bit down on the angle of her neck and shoulder.

A figure resembling Lonnigan broke from the shadows and dropped out of frame. Gertrude struggled till something held her still. Brother Daffyd clicked off the mute button.

"Oh God! Oh God! Let me in! Get off me! Save me! Save me!" Gertrude's voice shouted. The small woman shifted over her throat, blocking it from view. Gertrude gurgled and her voice went silent.

Jared and Jenny looked at Taylor, Jenny quivering. Sister Maryam put her arm around Jenny's shoulders. Taylor watched the screen, his face set in a stony deadpan, his gaze dropping from time to time, fear and disgust competing in his eyes.

On screen, a large, dark shape blotted out the camera for a moment. It pulled away, revealing Brother Daffyd's burly figure, wailing on someone with a cricket bat. Something jumped up onto his back, revealing itself as the small woman in Victorian garb, trying to throttle and bite him, but he continued beating someone out of frame. Brother Daffyd paused the video and minimized the window. Sister Maryam crossed herself.

"That was awful," Jared said. Jenny hid her eyes in her hand, concealing her tears.

"I should leave. I should get out as soon as I can stop being such a fucking load," Jenny murmured.

Sister Maryam turned Jenny around to face her. "Jennifer. Jennifer, look at me." Jenny uncovered her eyes. "You aren't a load. You didn't ask for this to happen. You weren't the one who hurt Gertrude. Lonnigan and his strange friend did. Jared and Barry and Brother Daffyd scared them off. Neither of them has come back-"

"Yet," Jenny said. "The night isn't over. God only knows if he'll come back again."

"I can talk with some of my colleagues and have a detail put here to keep an eye on things," Taylor offered.

"They got silver bullets or whatever it takes to kill two vampires?" Jenny asked quietly.

"Hopefully we won't need them, but I know two guys with access to those and a whole lot more," Taylor said.

"Who, some kind of modern Van Helsing?" Jared asked.

"Close, they're with the FBI out of a Boston satellite office," Taylor said.

"I need to crash for the night. I'm exhausted," Jenny said, her face gray and drawn as she started out of the room.

Jared followed her, putting his arm behind her back. She pulled away, going straight for their room.

Once Jared shut the door behind them and Jenny had curled up on the bed, he knelt beside her. "You okay at all, Jen?" he asked.

"Of course I'm not okay." Jenny hid her face in the crook of her elbow. Jared got up and sat beside her. She pulled away. He pulled back from her, giving her space.

"I'm sorry," he said.

"You're sorry, how do you think I feel? My stalker killed someone. I feel like I brought this on a perfectly good place, literally to their front door," Jenny said.

"Jen, did you ask that goon to follow you around?"

"No, but he knows me. He bit me. I can't hear him in my head, but I think he has a hook in me."

"What, like that crazy, bug-eating guy in *Dracula*?"

"No, thank God, but something like it."

"He's not here now."

"Wait till later. Wait till around midnight."

"We will, and if he shows up, we'll deal with him then."

"But we keep dealing with him, and nothing changes."

He reached out and cupped her cheek in the palm of his hand. She allowed him, leaning slightly into his touch. He stroked her cheek with the ball of his thumb. She sniffed, stifling a sob. "We got a bead on him now. He doesn't seem exactly as powerful as Dracula or some other big name vampire. The Contessa certainly does, and I think she likes us, or at least she has a dog in this fight. A bat in this cave?"

"I'd think that would be a bat in this game, but that's probably too silly. I have to ask - why doesn't she just sweep in and take him down herself, if she's so powerful?"

"I have a sense she's giving him and Artemesia enough rope to hang themselves. Or maybe sharpen the stake to a fine enough point to hurt when someone hammers it in. Does that even work on vampires?"

"It works on anything with a heart, so I'd imagine it does on vampires."

"Suppose I should check one of the books I got. *The Science of Vampires* seems the most logical and informative. Guess I better hit them up. You want to read some?"

She made a face and shook her head. "I think I've had enough vampire stuff for now. Maybe forever. It's not as much fun to live it as the books or the movies make it seem."

"Vampire movies too real for you now?"

"Probably." She got up and collected her toiletry bag. "I need a shower badly."

"I'll be here reading."

She headed out to the common showers down the hallway. Jared settled back with a book, skimming through the basics, focusing on the chapters that dealt with methods of catching, containing and dispatching vampires and blood drinkers and life force feeders of all kinds. It seemed every culture and country had their own different vampires and thus their own methods to deal with these supernatural intruders, but some methods seemed to carry across from one tradition to another.

Jenny returned, her hair damp and looking more relaxed. "Found any useful tips? Looks a bit intense, but you do you."

"Looking at vampire containment or killing methods. Remember the Count on *Sesame Street* and how I said he was a poorly done vampire?"

"Yeah, you said he was too cute and vampires are supposed to be scary. But somehow he still creeped out cousin Tina. Remember how she hid behind the couch whenever he showed up on Grandma's VHS tapes?"

"Oh man, yeah, I tried talking her out and she dug in deeper. Well, it turns out that Romanian vampires have a thing for counting stuff."

She laughed nervously. "You're serious?"

"Dead serious. All puns intended. If you lived in Transylvania and needed to keep vampires out of your house, you'd hang a sieve over the keyhole of your door. Before the vampire could turn into a smoky mist and pass through, they'd have to stop and count all the holes in the sieve, which would keep them busy till it got too close to daybreak."

"That's crazy. Okay, never criticizing Count von Count ever again," Jenny said, slipping under her bed covers.

"Another trick - if you're running away from a vampire, stop and toss a handful of seeds onto the ground in front of them. The vampire will have to stop and count them while you're able to make your escape."

"Vampires have some kind of OCD?"

"Who knows? Maybe only vampires in Romania do. Does human psychology even apply to a person when they get turned? Or does it depend on the vampire?"

"It might depend on the vampire and how much they have a hold of their humanity. I think the only way that trick would work on Lonnigan is if someone threw grains of cocaine on the ground in front of him." Jenny put her phone onto its charger and nestled under her covers.

"Want me to shut off the light?"

"Nah. I'm gonna crash to sleep as soon as I get comfortable. The nights have been too busy." She turned over, away from the light.

Jared flipped through more books, till one of the aides tapped on the door, reminding him of lights out. He set the book aside, put out the light and slid under the covers before closing his eyes.

Somewhere nearby, a dog he didn't remember hearing at night before barked several times, then stopped. His mind went right to the chapters on vampires shape shifting into wolves or other animals. Jared stiffened under the covers and sat up slightly, listening. The dog had gone silent. Jared slid himself down again, laying quietly till he finally fell asleep.

For once, the both of them slept through the night, without disturbance; for once, the both of them awoke to someone knocking on their room's door. Jared got up to answer, full daylight shining in the window behind him.

Sister Maryam stood outside the door. "Good morning. Did Jenny and you sleep well?"

"Better than we have till now."

"Oh, thank God. I just wanted you to know, we're clearing the breakfast things soon."

Jenny stirred under the covers and sat up, stretching. "We'll be up as soon as we can," Jared replied

"Are they telling us we need to move on?" Jenny asked, reaching to the floor for her pants.

"Nah, just that we'd better move quick if we want to get some breakfast here."

"I'm on it," she said, slipping into them.

After breakfast and while he waited outside the clinic while Jenny had her appointment, Jared called Blair Moffat, the main leaseholder on the townhouse he shared.

"It'd be easier if Jenny crashed with us till she can get a place of her own. She's working on that with the shelter folks, but she'll need somewhere to stay in the meantime," Jared said.

"How long do you think that will take?"

"She's still going to the clinic, but she's sticking with it. She wants this to work. When she gets a place, I'll move in with her."

"You sure she's not going to bring any business home?"

"I'm sure she won't. She's determined to get the four-hundred-pound gorilla off her back."

"I think we need to talk this over with Micah and Darleen, if we want this to be a long-term thing. But she can at least crash on your couch for a few nights."

"Fair enough," Jared said. Once Jenny had finished with her appointment and came out to join Jared, he relayed this conversation to her.

"Let me pack the little stuff that I have. Brother Daffyd said he knows some guys who'd be willing to collect my stuff from the flophouse I'd crashed at," Jenny said, breathing easier. "Though maybe it's better if I make a complete break with the past."

"'It's only when you've lost everything that you're free to do anything'," Jared quoted.

Jenny darted the Look at him, but she still smiled softly. "*Fight Club?* Really?"

"Brad Pitt's character might be a dick, but that line sure fits the situation you're emerging from," Jared said.

They drove back to the shelter to collect the few things Jenny had for clothes and toiletries, then drove to the townhouse complex in Portland. His college friend and roommate, Blair, met him at the door.

"Hey, Jen. How are you doing?" she asked.

Jenny approached, carrying her tote bag. "I've been worse, but I'm a lot better than I've been."

"Want some help with that bag?"

"Thanks, but no. I can manage it. I feel like I'm imposing, and I need to shift more for myself."

"Nah, from everything Jared described, I'd rather do what I can to help you out. It's better if you're here among people you know and that you're behind a threshold."

"A threshold of...what?" Jenny asked, stepping through the door.

"I've heard vampires and other things, if they exist, can't get at people who live in a home. Apparently, the sense of community and closeness in a home builds up something like a force field that makes anything supernaturally nasty think about going somewhere else. I used to be into occult stuff when I was a teenager, so I remember a few things from it."

"I'm not sure how accurate that information is, but I suppose that creep wasn't able to get inside the shelter, the two times he tried to attack," Jared said, following Jenny to his room.

Jenny set her tote on the futon behind the door before unpacking it. "I thought that had everything to do with Lonnigan and his little friend being cowards and Brother Daffyd being a bad-ass."

They had dinner without incident. Jared went to work, confident that Jenny had settled in with Blair and the others.

His shift passed quietly for the most part. He caught himself bracing for a panicked call from Jenny. *Guess I'm bracing for anything. Guess I've gotten accustomed to weird stuff happening,* he thought during a coffee break. On a security walk past a wall of windows, he saw a wolf-like dog trotting along the sidewalk across the street before it crossed at a crosswalk and trotted along the sidewalk before the building. Probably someone's husky that had escaped from their yard. He chuckled; his contract called for dealing with suspicious humans, not canines, but given the supernatural intruders he'd dealt with in his personal life, he considered adding them. The question remained if his employer would take this seriously.

He arrived home just after daybreak gave in to full daylight, as Micah headed out for his shift at the clinic. "Catch any bad guys?" he asked.

"No bad guys, but I think I saw a bad dog who got away from his yard," Jared said, heading for the kitchen, where he found Jenny making coffee.

"Huh. We heard a dog barking outside late at night," Jenny said.

"Weird." Jared said. The image of the hairy, scary-looking guards at Strigoi came to mind as he dug in the freezer for a box of waffles. Breakfast as dinner, one of the things he liked about working the graveyard shift.

He crashed for the day, waking in the afternoon, when Jenny had arrived home via an Uber, looking tired, but better. "Had a good appointment?" Jared asked her

"Yeah, I'm looking at some job openings. The new Market Basket has a lot of cashier jobs open. I applied for Section 8 housing, but the wait list is a few months out," she said.

"Please tell me you found something better than Market Basket. I know it's an excellent company, but I'd rather you didn't have to deal with nasty customers," Jared said.

"Once I'm back on my feet, I can work on my art on my days off," Jenny said.

"You sure you don't want me to get your stuff from the place where you were crashing before? I can talk to my friend La Chasse-"

She put up both hands. "No. I'd rather throw a bomb on the bridge to my old life than go back to it any way shape or form. Besides, the goons I was crashing with probably wrecked my sketch pads and sniffed my paints before wearing them."

"Did you have any paintings?"

She hung her head. "I sold the few I had to get a fix. That's when I decided I needed to get clean. Before I decided to get that last fix." She went quiet, looking away.

Jared came to her side and hugged her. She put her arm around him. "Thanks." she murmured.

She really has turned a corner, he thought.

***

Two weeks passed without incident. Jenny had settled in and started working evening shifts at Market Basket, a generally slower time and the clientele less prone to showing entitlement complexes. Jared spotted her sketching Darleen as she sat knitting on the couch one Sunday night, the news droning on the TV in the background.

"Working on making my lady into the next glorious mystery woman of art?" Micah asked, passing behind the couch and seeing the sketchpad.

Jenny chuckled. "Just some warm-ups. I'm afraid I got out of the habit of keeping a daily art diary. I hope I can get something ready to sell at the summer art sales."

"How about doing quick sketch caricatures down on the boardwalk at Old Orchard Beach?" Darleen suggested.

Jenny squidged her mouth and wrinkled her nose. "Nah. I tried that one summer in art school. Never again. Too many people ordering a caricature and expecting to get a piece of fine art. It's probably one of the things that dug the last bit of ground from under my self-esteem."

"Oh no, I'm so sorry. I hope that suggestion didn't hit you too hard," Darleen said.

Jenny reached over and patted Darlene's arm reassuringly. "Apology accepted. You mean well."

"Reports of large dogs roving the streets in Portland, Maine have neighbors on edge, in the wake of several animal attacks in neighboring towns..." the anchor on NECN announced.

"That sounds bad," Blair said, getting up and turning up the sound. "Haven't you been seeing odd dogs running around?" she asked, looking at Jared. The report described several people being attacked and bitten, generally on the neck or the arm.

"Hope those folks can get the rabies shot," Micah said.

"Hope they can catch the animals." Jared said, dubious. Jenny stiffened, then drew in a deep breath, letting it out slowly. "You okay?" Jared asked.

"Yeah, I just hope it's only a raccoon," she replied, turning her attention to her sketch diary. "Too bad if it is, though. Raccoons are really cute, like little pandas that catch crayfish and dig through your trash or your compost heap."

"Not so cute when they make a huge-ass mess or they come down your chimney and hibernate in your wall before they wake up in March and run around on your ceiling, shaking your chandelier and scaring your mom," Micah said.

"Ouch, that doesn't sound like fun at all," Jenny said.

"No, it wasn't. I was keeping vampire hours at the time, trying to juggle college and work, but it made it hard to get any sleep at all," Micah said. He glanced at Jenny. "Sorry, wrong word to use."

"Apology accepted. It was just a metaphor. No harm, no foul."

"Thanks."

Jared tossed some papers into the recycling bin, glancing at the chore chart while he did so. "Hey Jenny, it's your night to take the trash and recycling to the dumpster."

"I'll be on it, once I finish up here," Jenny replied.

"Gotcha. You lot be safe. I'll be back before sunrise," he said, grabbing his keys and going for his keys, coat, and taser.

"You be safe yourself," Darleen said.

***

Around three a.m., Jared's phone rang. He let it go to voice mail, as he had a break in a half hour. Whoever called could wait. But something in his gut told him to call it back. He radioed Nylund, a colleague on another floor. "Got a phone call. Can you cover for me?"

"That sister of yours?"

"Not sure, I'd let it go to voice mail." Jared's phone vibrated against his thigh. He took it out.

fget ghome bnow showed on the screen, from his sister's number.

"Nylund, it's her She sent a key smashed text."

Nylund made an insensitive remark. Jared holstered his radio and called his sister back. The connection rang, then went to voice mail. He tried Micah's phone number, which went to voice mail as well. He called Darleen's. It, too, went to voice mail.

They could be sleeping, he told himself. He tried his sister's phone again.

The line rang, then picked up. *"Hiiiii big brother,"* Lonnigan's raspy voice spoke. *"Your sister tastes yummy, even when she's clean. Whatcha let her do a thing like that for?"*

Jared cut the line and dialed 911. *"911 Portland, Maine, what's your emergency?"*

"My sister's being attacked. She's at home, at our townhouse," he said, fighting to avoid babbling in panic as he gave their address. "She texted me in a panic, but when I called back, an intruder in our house picked up. This guy's been stalking her, and I think it's him." *Don't mention the vampire stuff,* he told himself. "The guy thinks he's a vampire and he's tried to bite her before. See if you can call to Biddeford and tell Officer Deacon Taylor. He knows about this stuff."

"Officer Deacon Taylor?"

"Yeah. He's been helping us. He told us if anything else happened to her, to let him know."

"All right. I'm sending a unit over to your address." She read it back. *"But I'll see if I can get through to Officer Taylor."*

"Thanks, I appreciate this," he said. The connection cut out.

Scenarios of what could have happened, what could await him, flashed in his head. He forced himself to breathe in through his nostrils and out through his mouth. Shoving his phone into his side pocket, he grabbed his radio. "Called her and a burglar answered. Called the police. They're sending a unit to my place. I gotta go and see what the hell happened."

"So she had a john get rough with her. You're three hours from the end of your shift. Can't it wait? I can't keep covering your stupid ass while you cover your sister's junkie ass-"

"Nylund. if you ever have a loved one in trouble — and that's supposing you can find a place in the brick you call a heart for a loved one — I hope I can find it in me to cover you when you go take care of them," Jared snapped back and slammed the radio back onto his utility belt before calling their supervisor.

Costas sent Jared home immediately, with a promise to have a few words for Nylund at the end of the supervisor's shift. While driving home, Jared pushed the speed limit, forcing himself to avoid another tragedy. As he approached the drive to the complex, red, blue, and silvery beacons lit up the night, hinting at what awaited him. He pulled onto the shoulder at the mouth of the drive, parking his car. Getting out, he shuffled past the gatehouse with the vigor of a zombie.

Taylor approached, a shadow against the blur of flashing beacons, and ducked under a cordon of crime scene tape across the walkway to the townhouse.

"What the hell happened?" Jared said.

"You don't want to go in there. It's bad. It's terrible-bad."

"Jenny…the others?"

Taylor looked him in the eye, his face grave, then dropped his gaze. Another officer lifted the tape, as two people emerged carrying a stretcher on which lay a black bag. "Micah was found dead, drained. Darleen had her throat bitten, but there's a chance she'll live. Blair was hiding in a closet. But Jenny…" He drew in a breath and looked toward one of the ambulances, where Jenny lay on a gurney, pale as a ghost, an oxygen mask over her blood-spattered face, blood-soaked bandages taped to her throat.

"Oh God," Jared tried not to wail. Taylor put a hand on his shoulder. "Is she…did they?"

"Most of her blood drained, from the look of it. They're not sure if she'll make it."

"You know her blood type?" an EMT asked.

"A-positive, I think," Jared replied. Another crew member fetched a blood bag from a bin and set to hooking it up.

"May I…will they let me go with her?"

"You up for that?" Jared nodded. Taylor led him to the ambulance as the crew closed the rear doors. "Got her brother; he wants to ride with her," Taylor said to one of the EMTs.

The crew member opened the side door and helped Jared in, letting him sit on a jump seat behind the driver. Jared sank onto it. The crew worked over Jenny as the ambulance pulled away. Jared looked away as one of the crew taped an IV into her arm, The lights inside the ambulance grew brighter, then slipped sideways before they crashed into darkness.

An hour or five minutes passed. Jared sneezed and felt his eyes flutter open. "What the hell…?"

"You fainted. You're all right," one of the EMS crew said, holding a jar of smelling salts under his nose. "It's okay, normal even. You must care about your sister a lot."

"Thanks…is she?"

"We're at North East Medical Center. She's in the trauma unit." Jared found himself sitting in a chair in a hospital waiting area with a blanket around his shoulders. He looked past the EMS crew member, down a hallway, watching orderlies and nurses hurrying by. "Everything that happened hit you hard. Can we get anything for you?"

"No, just…make sure they take good care of Jenny. She's been through hell lately," Jared said.

Taylor stepped into his line of sight and knelt before him. "She's in good hands. Meantime, I've called in some heavy hitters."

"What? Vampire slayers? Do I want to know?"

"Those FBI agents I mentioned. I met them at a law enforcement conference on paranormal elements."

"Seriously?"

"There's been an uptick in the frequency of strange things happening and unusual stuff coming out of the woodwork. Helps for LEOs to stay ahead of the trend. Hard enough dealing with typical cases involving plain old humans. Add ooga-booga stuff and things get hairier."

"You got to be kidding. Who are they, Mulder and Scully?"

"Not exactly. They got the know-how and experience. They should be here by the morning. And hopefully the doctors will know what to do for Jenny. Right now, take it easy."

"I'll try."

***

By full morning, Taylor had gone home to catch what sleep he could, and Jared had curled up in his seat. In his dreams, something dark and full of teeth had pounced on him. He jolted awake as a nurse approached and nudged his shoulder.

"Oh."

"It's all right. How are you doing?" the nurse asked.

"Okay. But...Jenny?"

"She's stable. Her blood platelet count had dropped very low, but we gave her a transfusion and it's stabilized her condition. There's a problem, though."

Jared felt his stomach drop into his feet. "What?"

"About ten minutes ago, she dropped into a coma-like state. We tried waking her up, but she hasn't come around. We have a specialist coming to examine her, but we may not have anything conclusive till later this evening." The nurse looked around them, then leaned in closer. "Has your sister been involved with people deep into the vampire lifestyle, or people who claim to be involved in it?"

"She got attacked by a goon who thinks he's into it. Why?"

The nurse drew in a deep breath. "Don't be alarmed if there's a change in your sister. He could have turned her."

A weight crashed down on Jared's shoulders, through his body and into the floor. "I was bracing for that. I was sure the past eight hours were just a crazy dream, but hearing you say it..."

"You were bracing for the worst and now it's happened," the nurse said, her deep voice understanding.

"This specialist you've called in, do they handle vampire stuff?"

"Yes, she doesn't make it very well known outside of medical settings. The public at large might get weird about it."

"Like trying to stake their patients?"

The nurse winced and gave him a small, wry smile. "That or trying to get the patients to bite and turn them. The first group, we can file assault and battery or attempted murder charges on, but outside of harassment or stalking charges, we can't do a lot with the vampire wannabes."

"Oh man, that's…good grief, is this what my sister has to look forward to? It'll drive her over the edge."

"Let's hope she's in a coma only because of the attack," the nurse said.

An hour later, a tall, dark-skinned woman in a lab coat over a modest blue dress approached Jared in the hospital's small cafeteria. "Jared Driver? I'm Dr. Candace Bouthiette, a specialist in Blood Dependency Syndrome who's treating your sister."

Jared set down his second cup of coffee and rose to meet her. "Oh, thank God." He paused with the question on his tongue that he did not want to ask. "Is she… turning into a vampire?"

"She's in torpor right now. She's in a very deep sleep, almost like hibernation. It's a normal state for Blood-Dependent Persons, during the full daylight hours, but she's also in the process of the change. When she wakes up, she'll need blood."

"But she's already had a transfusion."

"She'll need more and need it on a regular basis, to maintain her health and to keep from falling into a death-like state. She'll only need a couple of pints a day."

"She's going to hate that. She'll either try to walk into the sunor find some Van Helsing type."

She gave him a gentle smile and shook her head. "There's people out there who'd harm her, but I'm afraid walking into the sun only works in the movies."

"Guess I'll need to protect her from the goons with the crossbows. Is there anything I can do for her in the meantime?"

"Right now, you'd do best to go home and rest. She'll likely wake up around four this afternoon."

"Except I can't go home. Our townhouse is a crime scene right now."

"Is there a place you could stay?"

"I could try going home to our parents, but once they find out what's happened, they'll likely lose it on me. They pretty much disowned Jenny and I think I'm next because I haven't given up on her." He paused, considering his options. "I could go back to Good Shepherd Transitional Home, where she'd been staying off and on. I'd gone there to keep her company."

"If I know Sister Maryam and Brother Daffyd, I know they'll welcome you in with open arms," Doctor Bouthiette said. "Go get some rest and come back this afternoon."

"I'll be back then."

***

Brother Daffyd looked grave as he let Jared into the home. "You look like the Devil himself stomped you with his hooves."

Jared managed to laugh. "I feel like he has," he replied and explained what had happened.

Brother Daffyd nodded. "You can crash here for the day. We'd heard about the excitement, but we'd thought – hoped, I suppose – it was exaggerated or embellished."

"I'm afraid it's very true. At least…you won't get any intruders during the day."

Jared crashed in the men's dormitory room on the top floor, sleeping as best as he could in a less than familiar place. At three thirty, he got up, showered, took his leave of Brother Daffyd and drove back to the hospital. As he approached the ICU, two nurses hastened past him toward loud crying and wailing. He hurried after them, following them to Jenny's bay.

Jenny knelt on the floor beside her bed, struggling with two female nurses. "Just kill me now! Just end me! Throw me right into the sun! I don't want to be anything like him."

Jared knelt on the floor beside the struggling women, trying to meet Jenny's gaze. "Jenn, Jenn, listen to me. I'm here now," he said, trying to keep the dismay from showing in his voice or his face.

She met his gaze and the despair in her eyes made his heart drop into his feet. She dropped her gaze and pulled her upper lip back from the extra canines newly sprouted from her jaw, then started to raise her wrist. Jared lunged and grabbing her arm, pinned her to the floor. Jenny growled and bucked against him, knocking him back onto his haunches.

Taylor approached, accompanied by two men in black suits, one short and blond, wearing gold-rimmed glasses on his lean, professorish face, the other tall and dark-haired with a build worthy of a reformed

Mob enforcer. Taylor paused in his tracks and looked to his colleagues. "Should we come back at another time?"

Jenny stared up at Taylor and his two companions. "You got silver bullets in your guns? Shoot me now."

"I regret to inform you, but unless you were already allergic to silver, it won't have an effect on you now," the professorish agent said. Reaching into his breast pocket, he took out a black billfold with his credentials. "I'm Special Agent Blake Matherton, the robust gentleman with me is Special Agent Dante Stamos."

The other agent likewise showed his credentials, tilting his head toward his colleague. "He's the Van Helsing type. I'm the dumb muscle who watches his back."

"Would that make you the cowboy fellow in the Stoker novel?" Taylor said.

"Maybe," Stamos said, smirking, his dark eyes glinting. Matherton sighed, though a tiny smirk of amusement crossed his impassive face.

Taylor looked to the nurses. "Could we have some space to talk with her?"

The largest of the nurses looked Jenny in the eye. "Can we trust you not to attack these people or hurt yourself?"

"Does my word even hold any weight now?" Jenny replied.

"It does with us," Stamos said.

"All right," Jenny said.

Matherton knelt before Jenny, close enough that she could have bitten him easily if she wanted to. "Miss Driver, may we speak to you?"

"I don't know what you want to hear or what you can do for me, outside of putting me out of my misery," Jenny said.

"It wouldn't be ethical, and besides, we need your help," Stamos said. "You were attacked by Edward Lonnigan last night?"

"Yes. He started all this, if Officer Taylor has told you anything about this mess," Jenny said.

"He also told us he attacked you last month. That true?" Stamos asked. She nodded, tiredly. "Do you want to talk about last night?" Stamos asked with the warm concern of a father talking to his scared child.

"I suppose you're going to find out sooner or later." Jenny paused and swallowed. "I was asleep last night, in the room Jared's sleeping in, at the townhouse he's sharing with Micah and Darleen and Blair. It was late, I don't know what time, but it must have happened well after Jared left for work for the night.

"I heard a crash in Micah and Darleen's room. Then I heard screams, but they cut off fast.

"I was just crawling under the bed when someone kicked the door off the hinges. I smelled blood. Then he was on top of me. Lonnigan. He pinned me to the floor, grinning at me. And I heard him say 'It ends here and it starts now'. I tried to smack him in the face, but he bit down on my neck. I tried to scream again, so someone, anyone, could hear me, but he pressed on my throat. I felt something pierce my ankle. Everything went gray. Then I saw nothing.

"Then everything snapped into view again and it all looked too bright to look at. I tasted metal in my mouth, and I thought I'd bit my tongue. Everything hurt, starting at my neck and my ankle, and at the same time it all hurt, it all tingled and felt…good. So good. It…scared me, but I felt so good. Like a high, but different. He had his wrist to my mouth; I think he'd bitten it open, dripping his own blood into my mouth.

"That's when my phone rang. He let me go and grabbed it off the charger. I heard him sneering into it. Then the window lit up with blue and red lights. He dropped the phone and dove out the window without even opening it.

"I must have passed out again. I remember people calling out, calling my name and banging at the room door. I think I tried to call out, but I couldn't make a sound louder than a moan. The room got brighter. Someone must have put the room lights on. People were coming in with a stretcher. Officer Taylor showed up. I tried to talk, but I couldn't get a word out. Too much blood in my mouth. The lights are so bright here, too." She closed her eyes.

Agent Matherton reached into his breast pocket and took out a pair of sunglasses, offering them to her. "These might help."

She opened her eyes, staring at the glasses, then accepted them and placed them on her face. "Thanks." She added, dryly, "Please tell me they make me look like an old-time movie star trying to hide from her fans?"

"Yeah, you kinda do," Jared said. She managed a tiny smile.

"Is there more that happened?" Agent Stamos asked.

"There's not much more to say. The paramedics treated me. Officer Taylor tried asking me some questions, but I couldn't. I felt so tired I just slipped into a deep sleep. I felt people prodding me, but I was dead to the world. Or undead to the world. What am I now? I'm here now and I'm awake and alert, but I don't feel like I did before last night." She looked up at the agents. "So, what are you going to do with me? Stake me?"

Agent Matherton shook his head. "No. Far from it. We could, if you wish, bring you down to Salem, Massachusetts to meet one of the oldest vampires in the North East, a woman we know only as The Contessa."

"We've met her, she seems like good people," Jared said.

"She's scary, but she seems all right." Jenny added. "Does that make any sense?"

"Makes more sense than you'd realize," Agent Stamos said. "I imagine it's all a lot to take in right now. But by all accounts, you're changing into a different version of you."

"You sure I won't turn into a monster?"

"Were you a monster before?" Agent Stamos asked.

"It depends on how one defines a 'monster'," Agent Matherton added, making air quotes with his index fingers.

"I was…am…I'm a recovering addict. I've stolen to feed my habit, to medicate myself. I've hurt people, emotionally, physically, especially when I was messed up."

"Doesn't make you a monster by nature. You get off on hurting someone? You hurt someone because you could, and they were there?" Agent Stamos asked.

"No. I hated myself after I did."

"Still doesn't make you a monster. Maybe the self-medicating put you into a dark place, but just because someone or something resides in the darkness, doesn't make them a monster," Agent Matherton said. "Some of the worst monsters are walking in the light."

"So where do we go from here?"

"We'll need to trap him first, then we'll need to bring him to The Contessa and the rest of the Council of Three," Agent Matherton said.

"You want me to help you throw a butterfly net over his head?" Jared asked.

Agent Stamos chuckled. Agent Matherton rolled his eyes. "Maybe you'll get lucky if you use me as bait," Jenny offered.

"I regret to say that's a less than wise idea, but it's better if you came with us when we do take him down," Agent Matherton said.

"Name what I need to do, and I'll be there." Jenny said.

"I have to ask - can you sense Lonnigan's presence?" Agent Matherton asked.

Jenny turned her face away to her left. "It's not like I can hear his voice or see through his eyes or hear through his ears, but…I can tell he's close by. You know how sometimes you can tell someone's in the next room even though you don't see them? It's like that, only more intense."

"Like a weird vampire GPS," Jared suggested.

"Maybe, but it's hard to explain unless you've been there."

"This is too much. I need some air," Jared muttered.

He stumbled from the ICU and down the hallway, his stomach roiling. "Outside, need to get outside," he muttered to a passing orderly.

"I can walk you to the nearest door," the orderly replied, putting an arm behind Jared's back and steering him toward an automatic door which opened onto a green space courtyard.

Jared stumbled to some evergreen bushes, dropping to his knees behind them and retching till his mouth burned. He knelt there not moving for some time, till a tall, lean man with a young face and graying dark hair approached, kneeling beside him.

"Are you all right?"

"No. 'S my sister. Vampire bit her, turned her," Jared muttered, the words falling from his mouth before he could stop them.

The tall man nodded, head slightly on one side, listening without judgment, not even a flicker of wariness or confusion in his eyes, not even a hint of pity for what sounded like the ramblings of a person with a disturbed mind.

"You probably don't believe a word of this," Jared said.

The tall man pointed to the white Roman collar of his black shirt. "Actually I do. I'm Father Martin J. Crowley. I'd come out to pray the Divine Office and get some air."

"Hope I didn't intrude on your prayers."

He shook his head. "Not at all, it's what I'm here for."

"So, what, you believe vampires are a thing?"

"More than just a thing, but a reality which some people are starting to understand," Father Crowley replied. "I'm an exorcist with the Boston archdiocese. We're just starting to figure out where vampires fit into the world between the natural and the supernatural."

"It's something you'd better figure out fast, before more people get turned."

"And there's the rub - not everyone who require blood or energy from other living beings is dangerous or monstrous. For some, it seems. rather, to enhance their sense of protecting or defending others. For others, it seems it heightens an already warped sense of where they belong in the world. We think the condition is caused by a pathogen of some kind which attaches to the centers of the brain associated with the free will and making moral decisions."

"Speaking of religious stuff, you wouldn't happen to have a crucifix I could lob at the damn bloodsucker, if he shows his fangs again?"

"That's where things get interesting - the efficacy of a crucifix as a vampire deterrent rests on the faith of the person wielding it and the faith of the vampire. If the person with vampirism sincerely sees themself as a dark child of the night, the crucifix will affect them; if they think they're a human person with different dietary needs, it won't affect them. You could have an atheist wave a crucifix at the former kind of vampire and it won't affect the vampire at all. I will tell you what is one hundred percent effective against a vampire."

"What's that?"

"Having a Catholic priest approach them with the Holy Eucharist."

"What, like inside the gold pinwheel on a base thing?"

"If you mean the ostensorium, then yes," Father Crowley said, fighting back a smirk.

"Yeah, that thing. Implement. Whatever."

"We call them liturgical vessels, but I can see where you're coming from," the priest said with a smile like he was trying to keep from chuckling gently at Jared's attempts to name the article in question.

"Think you could walk around my sister's room with one?"

"I'm afraid I'd need permission from my superior, but if I could, I would. I've been dealing with a similar case in Salem, Mass., as a matter of fact."

"Anyone I know?"

"A fellow priest was bitten and turned. I'm still working out the details, but I suspect he got too close to someone and let his guard down. A priest may have the seal of Holy Orders fixed onto his soul, but he's still a human, he's still capable of falling on his flaws."

"Ain't that the gospel truth," Jared said. He tried to laugh, but he shuddered into crying.

Father Crowley put a fatherly hand on Jared's shoulder. "Go on. Cry it out. Let it go," he murmured. For a long moment, Jared heard only his own sobbing, until he heard a soft humming from the man kneeling by his side, a melody Jared vaguely remembered from Mass forever ago.

"Be thou my vision…" Jared ran out of tears to cry, but the priest beside him continued to hum softly.

"Father, I'm not a praying type, neither is my sister. You think this is why this is happening to us?"

"It's happening because these particular vampires have lost their way in their own darkness. They lost themselves to their own appetites. And if I'm not mistaken, there's a judgment coming to them soon, for the things they've done."

"I certainly hope so, but I'd need assurance from a party who can handle them. I hope this Council of Three can do something."

"From everything I know about them, they're more than capable of containing these two nuisances."

***

INTERLUDE 3
BEHIND THE ANGRY CRAB, KENNEBUNKPORT

Talk about a stakeout, Special Agent Dante Stamos thought, dropping the cigarette he wasn't supposed to be smoking to the grimy pavement behind the dive bar and grinding it out under his heel. "You sure this technique is going to work?"

"I'm positive," replied Mathertonfrom his perch atop the lid of a nearby dumpster, the scant light from the kitchen door glinting off his night vision goggles and the loaded crossbow he hefted. "This particular vampire says attacking the intoxicated is the only way he can get drunk any more. And according to Miss Driver, he frequented this place, trawling for dates or a fix, whichever came first."

Stamos looked down the alleyway. "Doesn't explain why he'd attack a senior citizen in her own yard. He wanted a taste of Grandma's home cooking?"

"For all we know, that's what he had in mind," Matherton said.

"So why would he turn her?"

"That's what we're trying to find out. Now stop chattering; you'll give away our position."

Stamos suppressed a snort. "I could be talking to someone on a Bluetooth earpiece or be a drunk mumbling to myself. You're the one giving your own position away."

Matherton grunted a small, dry laugh as if to say, *Point taken.*

Stamos shifted the beer-soaked denim jacket on his shoulders. *And I might actually be drunk by the time this guy shows his fangs. Could be worse, could be summer and I could be getting a whiff off that dumpster.*

The latest rendition of "Achy Breaky Heart" emanating from the bar jukebox clanked to its conclusion. Stamos hoped the barkeep had had words with the lonely heart who'd kept feeding that song into the machine for the past half hour. After a pause, the opening riff of Creedence Clearwater Revival's "Bad Moon Rising" started playing.

Stamos breathed out his next breath as a plume of mist and the silver-studded collar piece around his neck burned against his skin. "Dante..." Matherton murmured, in warning.

Something with pointy teeth lunged out of the darkness, roaring toward Stamos. Matherton leveled the crossbow, aiming below the attacker's heart. The vampire stumbled, falling over backward.

"Hunters!" the vampire cried.

"You've got the wrong side of the law," Matherton replied, and jumped from the dumpster, pinning the vampire to the pavement. "The stake hit your pancreas; you're not going to turn to dust. We're only holding a suspect who can jump onto a roof without hurting his ankles. Drinking from drunks and addicts and old ladies and then turning them without their consent, Lonnigan? That's low even for you."

"I only turned three of them. I bet none of them have the guts to hunt," Lonnigan sneered, looking daggers at the two agents. "Who told you Feebs about me, anyway?"

Matherton shifted to allow Stamos to flip their prisoner onto his side, then shackle him with silver-plated cuffs linked to a set of silver-plated shackles. "Lots of tips, anonymous and otherwise, plus you've been spotted all over the area. And there's nice little clinics that ask no questions that you could have utilized."

"Funny, soon as I learned people with vampirism exist, I thought of them getting transfusions, like my aunt taking her insulin shots," Stamos said. "Didn't expect that to be so close to the reality."

"Where's the thrill of hunting? Getting blood from a needle's not much different from when I was a junkie shooting up," Lonnigan snapped. Matherton reached into his coat, drew out a muzzle and strapped it into the lower half of Lonnigan's face, Stamos fastening the back straps.

"Lon, you still *are* a junkie - you get high from terrorizing the mundanes," Matherton said, rising. They guided their prisoner out of the alley and across the street to an unmarked van parked on the other side.

***

In the van, Taylor sat in the front seat, while Jared sat in the shotgun seat with Jenny crouched in the floorboards between them. A second van, just as battered, parked diagonally down the street from them

Jenny lifted her head, gasping. "He's coming closer."

"They got him?" Taylor asked.

"I think so."

Dogs howled nearby. The rear door of their own van opened from outside, and someone opened the gate of the silver-plated containment cage in the back of it. Someone roared and shouted, turning the air blue with foul language. Jenny flinched. Jared put a protective hand on her shoulder.

A shadow fell across the open rear of the van. A small figure sagged between the pair of agents. Compared to their suspect, Matherton looked taller. "You! You ratted me out, you little bitch!" the figure yelled. Matherton and Stamos lifted him into the cage and shut the doors behind him, locking it.

The vampire Lonnigan. The ghost-like figure who has stalked us the past month and more, Jared thought. Out loud, he said, "Seriously? This little guy? I was expecting someone taller and skinnier, like that bald guy in the silent movie."

"Charles Manson wasn't very impressive either," Agent Matherton said.

"Yeah, Manson would make Matherton here look like Tom Hopper," Agent Stamos said, closing one door. "I suppose it would be mean to stuff this jacket through the mesh for our guest to chew on?"

"Even if it could fit," Matherton said.

"Damn you, damn the lot of you," Lonnigan snarled.

"Is that the worst you have to say?" Agent Matherton drawled before shutting the other rear door and joining his partner in the rear seat.

"Let's do this," Stamos said, nodding to Taylor, who followed the van in front of them as it pulled away, heading for the exit to the Maine Turnpike.

Lonnigan uttered a threat against Matherton, involving Matherton's proclivities, and threatening the collective blood of every human in the van. Jared covered Jenny's ears. Taylor's face went pale in the dashboard lights, but he kept his eyes on the road ahead.

Something slammed into the top of the roof. Jared yelped. Lonnigan laughed. Jenny grabbed Jared, pulling him into the floorboards and covering his torso with hers. Agent Matherton sighed and unholstered his sidearm.

Something scraped at the edges of the roof, seeking a seam or a crack in the metal. "Mommy's heeeerre," Lonnigan said in a creepy, drawling sing song.

Taylor jerked the wheel back and forth, weaving the van while keeping in the same lane. Something slithered backward overhead. Jared poked his head up to peer over the seat back, looking ahead. The back hatch of the lead van opened. One of the hairy guys riding in it hefted a crossbow and fired at the roof of Taylor's van.

Something slithered over the edge of their roof. "Awww, you hurt Mommy," Lonnigan sneered.

"Your mommy looks young enough to be your daughter," Agent Stamos said.

Jared peered past the cage and out the back window. The van behind them had stopped, the headlights growing smaller as it fell into the distance. He thought he saw a heap of rags laying on the road.

"Is that…did they just…" The words caught in Jared's throat.

"The main reason we got the assistance of the werewolves," Matherton said. "The Contessa offered them to make sure this went without a hitch, and they wanted a piece of Artemesia and Lonnigan."

"Did your supervisory agent sign off on this?" Taylor asked.

"Locke deputized them. Not the oddest thing she had done," Stamos replied. "And from what you were saying, this isn't your first time at the vampire horse race either."

"Why do I *not* want to know what is the oddest thing she's done? Or what the first vampire horse race would be?" Jared asked.

"I do," Jenny said.

"Besides the fact that you're the real Mulder and Scully, and your higher ups take your work seriously," Taylor said.

Matherton sighed patiently. "The Contessa sent along her security team-"

"Her self-described wolfy goon squad," Stamos cut in, grinning.

"Her security team. She has a personal stake – no wordplay intended. Also, vampires exist in a twilight area between-"

Stamos giggled. "You said Twilight."

Matherton sighed. "Vampires exist in a gray area between human society and the realm of the supernatural. The Federal government or any other human government body can step in only when a member of the vampire world infringes on the rights of a member of human society."

"In other words, the humans don't tell the spooky folks how to spook. Spooky folk don't hurt the humans. But if they do, the humans reserve the right and duty to defend themselves and push back," Jared said. "How come we don't know about it or knew about it sooner?"

"It's getting harder to keep the genie in the bottle, but we try and keep the matter low key to avoid a public blow-out," Matherton said. "It's bad enough humans can barely tolerate variety in their own species; you can imagine the outburst if people knew for certain that vampires and werewolves existed. There's too many humans who'd find a way to start a war with the preternatural or turn into those toxic allies who harass and annoy they very people they support."

"Like the teen girls who shove some random guy to their gay friend telling him to kiss the poor mook because the girl thinks it would look cute, and neither the random guy nor the gay friend has any interest in snogging each other," Stamos said.

"So there's people who bug vampires to turn them, or people who try and fight werewolves on purpose?" Taylor asked.

"Not that some of us would mind," Lonnigan muttered.

"Only because it would give you an excuse to harm more humans. Or other vampires, for that matter," Stamos said. "Now not another word, since you're only undermining your own case."

"But to answer your question, unfortunately, there are, and they've been known to get in over their heads. I've seen the results more times than I care to count," Matherton replied.

Well on toward midnight, the small convoy pulled behind the Hawthorne Hotel before parking close to a loading bay near the rear door, which stood open as if waiting for them. Two tall, dark figures stood flanking it.

Taylor unlocked the rear van door as Stamos and Matherton got out. Matherton unlocked the cage. Between the three of them, they carried Lonnigan toward the hotel door. The doors in the van that had followed them opened and several agents emerged, two female agents carrying a smaller figure in a tattered white gown, a wooden crossbow bolt protruding from her torso.

"You want to see this going down?" Jared asked Jenny.

"I think it's right that we do. We'll know it ended," she said.

They descended via a service elevator, emerging into a short hallway which in turn gave way to an open sitting area, the walls lined with bookcases. In the center of the floor lay a silvery containment circle. In the center stood three carved wood armchairs on which sat three elegant figures in black: The Contessa, a tall blond male in a suit, dark glasses covering his eyes, and a dark-skinned person of indeterminate gender, their head shaven and their tall, willowy form clad in a loose, black robe.

Jared started to step closer to the circle as the group entered the space. "Thus far and no further," Matherton said to Jared, who paused in his tracks. The agents brought the small woman and Lonnigan across the silver arc and set them before the three, Lonnigan turning the air blue with curses while the woman remained silent.

"You two don't have to stay," Stamos said, looking at Jenny.

"I need to see this through. I want to see what happens," she replied.

"We can allow that," the blond man said. "That way, when you see what happens in the silver circle, you're less likely to end up there," he added with a dangerous smirk which made Jared shudder.

The Contessa sat up taller. "Artemesia Gamwell and Edward Lonnigan, you are called before the Council of Three to have your fates decided. You have manifested your nature openly to mortals. You have attacked, drunk from, and in some cases, turned the unwilling. You have attacked innocents and the impaired. You have fed indiscriminately, draining people to death, including feeding upon the elderly, those suffering from addiction, even children and a Catholic priest."

Lonnigan made a rude noise. The bald council member turned their face to Lonnigan slowly, fixing their dark eyes on him. Lonnigan uttered a slur against the council member's ethnicity.

"You are only digging more ground from under whatever defense you may have," the bald vampire said.

Lonnigan piped down. Artemesia hissed. "If I could pull out this stake..."

"Have you something to say?" the blond vampire said.

"You should never have turned me," Artemsia snarled.

"I agree," The Contessa replied.

"Then what are you going to do about it?" Artemesia sneered.

"You will not like the answer," The Contessa replied. The werewolves around the circle gathered themselves, some snarling softly and crouching like dogs bracing to attack.

Lonnigan peered around them. "Hey, call off the literal dogs."

"We're wolves, bat boy," one of the werewolves snipped.

The Contessa gave the werewolf a hard look, at which they fell silent.

"And what do you plan to do about this? Pull our fangs?" Lonnigan sneered.

The blond vampire smirked. "You have said it."

"Not like it would hurt me much," Lonnigan muttered.

"Sounds to me like the best course would be to let them live in some kind of vampire jail," Jared said.

"At times the worst punishment to receive is the one the subject has suggested," the bald vampire said.

The blond vampire rose to his full height and, reaching into his breast pocket, took out a pair of medical pliers, something straight out of an old-time doctor's office. In one stride, he reached Artemesia and knelt over her.

"You are *not* pulling my fangs," Artemesia hissed.

"Unfortunately, I am." the blond vampire replied.

Putting the thumb and forefinger of his free hand into her mouth and levering her jaws open, he reached in with the pliers, tugging on one of her fangs, pulling it free. He did the same with a second, then a third, then the fourth. Releasing her, and letting her slip to the floor, he licked the blood from the roots of the teeth and, producing a small plastic zip bag, he dropped the fangs into the bag, pocketing them. Turning to Lonnigan, he prepared to repeat the process.

Lonnigan managed to turn his head and clamp down his jaws on the blond vampire's ankle. The elder sighed and lifting his other foot, pinned Lonnigan's torso. The dark-skinned vampire rose and held down Lonnigan, a serene look on their face while the blond vampire proceeded to pull and bag Lonnigan's fangs. The blond vampire held up the bag, turning to Agent Matherton, who stepped up to the edge of the circle and took it. "I believe you'll be wanting to hand these to Madame Edna Gilhooly?" the blond vampire said. "Unless you'd prefer to give them to Madame Jennifer Driver." He turned his face toward Jenny.

She put up her hands, shaking her head. "Ugh, no. I wish I could put this time in my life behind me. I appreciate the thought, but I'd rather move on from this."

"I don't say this easily, but I don't blame you in the least." Matherton handed the baggie off to Taylor.

"Let's hope that Edna's more into the notion. Doubt she will, but who knows?" Taylor said, accepting the bag.

The bald vampire reached into the air at their left and traced the shape of a doorway. The very substance of reality shimmered, then parted, opening a portal which led into a space lit by a strange, unearthly light. The blond vampire approached the two defendants, taking Artemsia under the arm. The Contessa took her by the hand, lifting her up and pulling out the stake before leading her across the threshold of the portal. The blond vampire drew out the stake and started to lead Lonnigan toward the portal. Lonnigan reached across the line of the containment circle, despite the burns rising on his skin, and smacked Jared across the face, sprawling him onto the floor across the circle. Lonnigan sneered and started for Jared. Jenny roared and, despite her own burns, lunged across the circle and floored Lonnigan. Baring her own fangs, she stooped and clamped her jaws onto Lonnigan's throat, tearing it out. Blood spewed across the circle, spattering the blond vampire. Lonnigan stared at her, fear glazing his eyes.

She dropped her sire, standing over him "You can't hurt me anymore, but you don't hurt my brother. Whatever happens to you now, is the only thing you deserve for everything you've done."

The blond vampire smirked at her. "Remind me never to cross you." He gathered up what remained of Lonnigan, the smaller vampire's head lolling as the weight pulled on the strands of flesh, sinew, and veins which held it on and carried Lonnigan through the portal. The bald vampire nodded to the gathering, then stepped through the portal. Reaching back, they took hold of the sides of it, and pulled the fabric of reality back together, sealing it behind them. Before the portal shut, Jared glimpsed a vast space, an open barren wilderness amid a circle of standing stones, in the midst of them a massive shape formed of toothed mouths, looming over the procession approaching.

"The hell was that?" one of the field agents asked.

"The hell were those people?" Jenny asked.

Matherton stepped forward, taking up a section of the circle. "The three vampires? They're the guardians of the vampires dwelling east of the Mississippi."

One of the werewolves went out reluctantly, returning with two mop buckets full of water and a clean mop. "One of you humans want to mop this up? 'Cause I ain't getting singed crossin' that circle."

Agent Stamos looked at the youngest agent in the room. "It'll make a crazy story later when you get to be our age." The older agents laughed, and the werewolves hooted, while the young agent took the buckets and the mop from the werewolf, who handed them over, bowing exaggeratedly like a stereotyped British manservant in a *Downton Abbey* parody.

"But what the hell was that thing beyond the portal?" Jared asked.

"The mother and father of all vampires. It has a name, but it's unpronounceable by human mouths," Matherton said.

"If you can call them that. It…they looked into me," Jenny said. "It saw what I am and what I've become."

"Some kind of eldritch queen of the vampires, only she doesn't look like Aaliyah?" Jared said.

"The source of all vampires, but even that is too simple an explanation," Jenny said.

The agents and the werewolves had started filing toward the elevator. Jared put a comforting arm behind Jenny's back as they stepped into the moonlight. "Let's get you home. This is getting too weird and too much to take in. Where do we go from here?"

"Right now, I just want to go home and sleep, though I guess that's not happening until daybreak." Jenny looked up to the sky. "I guess I'll need blood, too."

"You could get some at the clinic in Biddeford for a few days, but you'll need a regular supply after that," Taylor said.

"And the question remains where home is, since I won't be able to carry the rent on that townhouse on a security guard's salary," Jared said.

"You could stay here in Salem and help us work security for The Contessa. We always need waitstaff in the restaurant and bouncers for the basement club," one of the werewolves offered.

"That's a good offer, but I'll need to think on it. I mean, I am mortal, after all. Wouldn't that put me at a disadvantage?"

"Not at all; we need mortal co-workers. Keeps us humble," the same werewolf said.

"Seems I'm starting a new life as well," Jared noted.

"I hope that…being turned cleans out the last of the poison of the past," Jenny said.

"'The poison of the past'. Good way to put it," Jared said.

"Maybe the title of my vampire memoir someday," she said as they climbed into Taylor's van.

"You're off to a good beginning," Jared said, climbing in beside her and pulling the door shut.

THE DRAGON LADY AND THE LITTLE SPIDER

BY G K LOMAX

And now abideth faith, hope and love, and the greatest of these is love. I first heard those words from my father as he read from the Good Book each evening. It was long before I understood their full meaning, however. Love is indeed great – but it is great for both good and ill. What will a man not do for love? What will a man not forgive for love? What man will not imperil his liberty, his life – his very soul – for the sake of love? This I have done. That the object of my love is a monster and an abomination I know only too well. I know it, but it matters little when set beside my love. For the greatest of all things is love.

***

They waited until morning before they came for my Lady.

She'd been expecting them of course. There wasn't a soul within fifty miles who didn't know that the King had ordered Palatine Thurzo to arrest my Lady, and few that didn't tremble at the prospect, myself included. Indeed, I trembled with more reason than most, for I was the one who knew the truth. I was the one who'd be called upon to bear witness, who'd be summoned before the court and, with my hand upon the Bible, made to swear at the peril of my soul, to tell all I knew of my Lady's crimes. And of my own.

They arrived a little after sunset in the dying days of the year. A few flakes of snow were lazily falling to add to a landscape already white and there was a sharp frost in the air. They met with no challenge at the castle gate, nor did they announce themselves with any flourish. Everyone knew their errand and wanted it over and done with. Everyone except me.

My Lady and I looked down from our high window as they dismounted. Their horses steamed mightily as they were led off to the stables. They'd clearly been ridden hard – possibly in a vain attempt to reach the castle before sunset. The men themselves stamped their feet and stretched away the cramps of their ride. A few of them glanced up at where we stood. I don't know if they could perceive us in the dark, but even from a distance, it was plain that they dreaded what was to come.

Some of them crossed themselves. Then the steward appeared and beckoned them into the Great Hall.

"Twelve," my Lady said, having counted them. "So few? Surely they fear me more than that?"

I made no answer. I was in no mood for jests, even of the grimmest sort. Instead, I turned to my Lady with a pleading expression on my face. "You must flee," I told her. "It's not yet too late. There are quiet ways out of the castle and you may get far whilst hidden by the darkness. And then – there are those who would grant you a safe refuge. The Lord Gabriel your cousin, perhaps. He surely will not turn you away."

"Peace, Ficko," my Lady said, holding up a hand to silence me. "How many times already have you urged me to flee?"

"Without number my Lady," I admitted.

"Without number. And my answer has always been the same. Yet you urge me again?"

"I am concerned only for your safety, my Lady," I mumbled.

"I know it well, and am touched," my Lady said. "But I say again, I will not flee."

"No, my Lady," I said. In truth I'd expected no other answer. Whatever else may be said about my Lady, no one can accuse her of lacking courage.

I drew my dagger and turned to face the door. It occurred to me that if I was struck down in my Lady's defence, then I would at least be spared the ordeal of appearing before the court. It seemed the best outcome I could hope for. Besides, I'd been a soldier in my time. I'd make at least one of them pay.

"Patience, Ficko," my Lady said. "We have time yet. A little time, at any rate. A night, in fact. They will make no move against us when the world is in darkness. They dare not." I asked her how she could be so sure, and she answered with a smile. "I know what sort of men they are. Have I not ruled over them these many years?"

I acknowledged my Lady's wisdom with a bow. She ruffled my hair affectionately. "We have a night, as I have said. How shall we use it?"

I looked at her in surprise. "Come, Ficko," she said. "Would you rather waste these last few hours? Besides," she said, as she took me by the hand and led me into the bedchamber, "I have a long-promised gift for you."

***

My Lady is the Countess Elizabeth Bathory. The Bathorys, of course, rank among the noblest families in Europe. For nearly two centuries they have ruled Transylvania where my Lady's cousin Gabriel is the current Prince. Some say that King Matthias has ever been suspicious of my Lady for this reason and would have found some other reason for her overthrow had he had not learned the truth about her. He's distrustful of Transylvania and those that have ties there. With reason perhaps. It's true that we in Hungary can never be sure whether Transylvania will side with us or with the infidel Turks, but this is not, my Lady insists, the fault of Prince Gabriel. Rather it is because Transylvania is so situated that it ever risks being caught between the hammer and the anvil and must needs deal with both — but such matters of high politics are far beyond my comprehension. I only know my Lady's loyalties are not to be questioned, and that I am her most humble and devoted worshipper.

I first beheld my Lady seven years ago, at the funeral of her husband and my Lord, the Count Ferenc Nadasdy. Though I am a person of little account, I should perhaps explain that, as a youth, I foolishly left my father's farm and enlisted in Count Nadasdy's army, believing that the life of a soldier would be more exciting than an endless round of ploughing, sowing, and reaping. This youthful folly was soon bitterly exposed. I was a soldier for three years, during which time I marched uncounted miles in all weathers, slept under the stars as often as under a roof and considered myself fortunate if I got a hot meal once a day. Our pay was irregular, our food was poor, and we were subjected to many cruelties in the name of discipline. I was present at the sieges of two fortresses whose names I can no longer remember — if indeed I took the trouble to learn them in the first place. For that matter, I can't even remember whether these sieges were successful or not. I think one was, but such things had ceased to matter for me. What I mostly remember was digging a seemingly never-ending succession of trenches and reflecting that this was not so different from the work I'd left behind. Well, there was one difference, I suppose: a soldier plants nothing but corpses. Disease kills many more soldiers than swords or muskets.

It's a wonder I didn't desert. I think the only reason I didn't do so was because I couldn't face the shame of going home and admitting to my father that soldiering hadn't turned out to be the carefree life I'd expected. That and the friendship of Stefan — another prodigal like myself but who always seemed to have something cheerful to say, no matter the situation.

I finally got all the excitement I could've wished – and more – at the battle of Brasov. According to the histories, Count Nadasdy had joined with Radu Serban of Wallachia in order to overthrow Mozes Szekely, who had usurped throne of Transylvania and allied himself with the Turks. I'd long ceased caring about the whys and wherefores by that time, and care nothing still. I only know that the battle was fought under a blistering sun, and that, for a time that seemed very long indeed, I and my fellows had to grip our pikes and stand shoulder to shoulder, rank on rank, whilst the enemy blasted our lines with their cannon. I believe our cavalry had some success on the flanks during this time, but I saw nothing of this.

At length, the order came to advance. The enemy had lashed a row of wagons together, and as we got nearer, musketeers behind them poured fire into our ranks. My bowels were like water and I wanted to turn and run. I wish I had. Beside me, Stefan spoke words of reassurance to keep up my courage – and his own, I dare say. The last thing he said to me was, "We're nearly there. A few more steps, then we'll show…"

Then a musket-ball struck him in the eye. His blood and his brains bespattered my coat.

Rage seized me and I surged forward with my comrades. When we reached the wagons and climbed over them, there was some bitter fighting. I killed three men. I wondered afterwards if they'd also thought that the life of a soldier would be exciting. Then with a suddenness that astonished me, it was all over. I was weary beyond measure and lay down among the dead and dying. I didn't move for a long time. They tell me that Brasov is accounted a victory for Hungary and the Empire. It didn't feel like a victory to me.

There were some Turks among the prisoners. Mercenaries. Thirty, forty, I don't remember. I do remember that the day after the battle, we were all called on to witness their fate. We stood in our ranks as, one by one, they were stripped naked and beaten. After this, they were impaled on stakes. They say Radu Serban copied this practice from the tales of Vlad Dracula, who ruled Wallachia in years gone by, and whose name is still used by mothers to frighten their children into behaving themselves.

They were brave men I don't doubt, but there are limits even for the bravest. Their shrieks and screams were piteous to hear. Their prayers and imprecations, though delivered in an uncouth tongue, were easy to understand. Some of them claimed that they were Christian, a few even producing crucifixes by way of proof. This was no great wonder as many

Christian lands lay under the Turkish yoke, and many boys were taken from these lands to serve the Sultan. Myself, I felt sorry for them.

Serban, however, did not. He was in no mood to grant anyone mercy. Indeed, he declared that those who professed the true faith were particularly guilty, as they had served an infidel master. For them, he decreed that the stakes should be deliberately blunted which, I was told, increased the agony. One, the most outspoken, was impaled through the fundament, and the stake driven in until the tip came out of his throat. Serban expressed disappointment at this – he was hoping to see the stake exit the victim's mouth.

Afterwards, the stakes were planted in the ground so that they formed a macabre forest. There were some who exulted at the sight. Count Nadasdy told us that such was the punishment that should be meted out to all those who did not follow the true faith, and many believed him. I, however, felt sick beyond telling – yet I found that I could not look away. There was one poor fellow, I remember, who remained alive and twitching for a horrible time before death finally took him.

***

Six months after the battle, Count Nadasdy died. Quite suddenly, it is said. Murdered, it is said. Whether that's so, I still don't know. I only know that he marched his men hard, provided them with meagre commons, and never mourned the death of a single one.

As befits a man who was both a noble and a general, Count Nadasdy's funeral was conducted with great pomp and ceremony. My regiment was selected to line the route down which the cortege passed – and I might add that more money was lavished on making us look presentable than had been spent on feeding us for the previous year.

The Count was interred in the family vault at Csejte Castle – high on a crest in the Lesser Carpathians. I was stationed just outside the main gate and stood for hours as the cortege slowly wound its way through the village and up the steep road to the castle. It was a bitterly cold January day. It had snowed heavily the night before, and though with much labour – our labour – the way had been cleared for the cortege, we stood ankle-deep in snow as we lined the route. I began to wonder if I'd ever be able to feel my fingers or toes again. When at last the bier passed before me, I bowed my head, as was proper. After it had passed and I looked up, I beheld my Lady for the first time.

My Lady Bathory – she kept her own name after her marriage as her family was higher in prestige than her husband's – rode a palfrey whose coat shone as white as the snow. Beside her rode one who bore her personal standard – a green dragon coiled about a row of bone-white teeth, all upon a field the colour of fresh blood. I'd seen many banners in my time, of course, but never one to stir the spirit as much as my Lady's. I had only an instant to consider it, however, as my gaze was swiftly drawn to my Lady. Beautiful she was, and far younger than I had expected, knowing the age of the Count. She was dressed in mourning black and was the epitome of poise and dignity. The sight of her made me gasp. Possibly she heard me do so, for as she passed before me, she turned and looked into my eyes.

I will never forget that look, though it may take me a lifetime to find words adequate to describe it. It was as though she saw right through me, reading my heart and soul as if they were open books. All my hopes, my fears and my dreams she perceived at a glance. I felt like a tankard that was being emptied. But there was something else, too. A feeling that she approved of what she saw, together with the whisper of a promise. Overwhelmed, I went down on one knee and was rewarded with an enigmatic smile. Her teeth were even whiter than the snow.

"Taken with the Dragon Lady, are you?"

The man to my right had spoken. I only knew him slightly. Carl something – an Austrian who'd been in my regiment since the wars had begun. I got back to my feet and stared at him stupidly.

"You'd better steer clear of her," Carl said, speaking out of the corner of his mouth. "She eats lads like you for breakfast so they say. Murdered her husband, too."

"That cannot be," I said. "He died on campaign whilst she was managing his estates."

"Believe that if you want, lad," Carl said. "But some of us know different. I spoke to a man who saw the Count die."

"You did?"

"I did. One of those messengers who are always galloping about. Like most of his kind, his two favourite things were wine and gossip, so I shared a bottle with him and heard his tale. One moment the Count was in the saddle, giving orders to some flunkey; the next – 'As God's my witness,' the man said – he'd fallen from his horse and was writhing in agony on the ground. Frothing at the mouth he was, and dead within the hour."

"He was known to be ill," I said.

"Known to have pains in his legs, aye. But painful legs just make you walk slow. They don't kill you."

"And you suspect what? Poison?"

"Poison, aye, that's one possibility. But another's witchcraft."

"Witchcraft?"

"Not so loud lad, but yes, witchcraft. Or worse. There are tales told about the Dragon Lady. Dark tales." What these tales might've been, Carl never had a chance to tell me, for at that moment the trumpets rang, and we were marched off to other duties.

I kept the memory of my Lady's glance close to my heart. I had no hope of more from her, though I knew that my deepest wish was to be her slave for the rest of my days.

***

Once when I was small, I was walking with my uncle when he beckoned to show me a strange sight. I looked where he pointed and saw a spider at the centre of a web. I thought this unremarkable, but watched as my uncle urged me. After a moment I saw a second spider, much smaller than the first, on the edge of the web. "That's the male," my uncle told me. "The larger one is the female, with whom he wishes to mate." As a farmer's son, I knew about animals mating and was curious to see how spiders managed it. Slowly, hesitantly, the male approached the female, until they touched. The actual mating was quite brief, but it was what happened afterwards that has stuck in my memory. After she had received what she needed from the male, the female ate him.

"Does that always happen?" I asked my uncle, horrified. He said that it did.

"Then why does the male not avoid the female entirely? It would be far safer."

"True," my uncle said, "but the female had power over him. Though he knew what was coming, he had no choice in the matter."

I often think about that little male spider when I am with my Lady. I think I know how he felt. I both love and fear my Lady and her power over me is beyond description. Of course she has not eaten me – or at least, she has not eaten me yet.

***

They came, as I said, in the morning. My Lady rose early to be ready to receive them. She took care to array herself most magnificently until she looked as beautiful and as terrible as the sun rising over the mountains.

She also gave me strict instructions so that when they pounded on the door I kept my dagger sheathed and opened to admit them as though they were welcome visitors. Hesitantly, they entered. All twelve of them, wearing cuirasses and helmets, holding pistols and drawn swords. My Lady sat facing them, silent and unmoving. They halted before her, cowed by her magnificent defiance. It seemed to me that they huddled unnaturally closely together, as if they grew comfort from the press of bodies.

"Welcome, gentlemen," my Lady said eventually. "How may I be of service to you?"

"You know full well demoness," replied a gruff voice. From the midst of the intruders, one man pushed his way to the front. It was the Minister Stephen Magyari. The man who had railed against my Lady from the pulpit and petitioned the King for her arrest. He alone held no weapon, though he did grip a large cross suspended from his neck. His knuckles were white.

"Ah, Minister," my Lady said. "May I offer you some refreshment?" She rose and crossed to a small table where there stood a flagon of wine. She poured a glass. She did so slowly and it seemed to me that every eye in the room was drawn to the red liquid which sparkled in the bright morning sun. My Lady put down the flagon. A drop of wine remained on its lip. She wiped it away with a finger, which she licked with obvious relish. Then she offered the glass to Magyari.

He dashed it from her hand. "I'll touch nothing that has been sullied by you, demoness," he said. No doubt he intended us to hear contempt in his voice, but I heard something else. I heard fear. He was afraid of my Lady. A muscle in his cheek twitched. I'm sure that if she'd said "Boo" to him at that point he would have turned and fled.

No doubt my Lady read him as well as I, but she remained calm. "It's a pity to waste such a good vintage," she said, "but you have not stated your business."

"Your arrest, demoness." Magyari produced a roll of parchment. He hesitated for a moment, as he was not able to unroll it with one hand. After some indecision he reluctantly let go of his cross and used both hands on the parchment. In other circumstances, I might have found it comic, but there was no laughter in me that day.

Magyari cleared his throat noisily. "To the esteemed Georgy Thurzo, Palatine of Hungary, greetings," he read in a self-important voice. "It is my command that you are to oversee the arrest of the Countess Elizabeth

Bathory and to arrange for her to be closely examined by competent judges with regard to the murders and other unholy crimes of which she stands accused. Given under my seal this twelfth day of December in the Year of Grace 1610, Matthias, by the Grace of God, King of Hungary." Magyari held the letter out to my Lady, so she could read it for herself.

She didn't take the letter; didn't even glance at it. She said nothing. Instead she smiled slightly and ran the tip of her tongue slowly around her lips. Magyari recoiled a pace. An expression of stark terror crossed his face and he looked as though he was on the verge of soiling himself. But then what can one expect from a Lutheran?

No-one spoke for some while. At length, my Lady asked, "Did the good Palatine Thurzo not see fit to run this errand himself? It would seem from the wording of that letter that the King commanded him to do so."

Magyari looked uncomfortable, and at least one of the men he'd brought with him started to back towards the door. "My Lord Thurzo," Magyari began, then had a coughing fit. "My Lord Thurzo," he began again, "was ordered to arrange your ladyship's arrest and questioning. He will no doubt be present at the latter, but would you expect him to personally attend the arrest of every common criminal?" Magyari clearly wished that Thurzo had not delegated the task of performing this particular arrest, but Thurzo was a coward. He would not have dared to face my Lady, even with eleven armed men at his back.

"Am I a common criminal?" my Lady asked. No one answered her. Two more men shuffled nearer the door.

"I don't think I am," she said. "I'm sure that after due – examination, was that the word? That after a due, even a thorough, examination, Palatine Thurzo will be able to confidently declare that I am no criminal. But there needs to be no examination to discover that I am anything but common. I am the Countess. Elizabeth. Bathory."

My Lady did not raise her voice, but the quiet firmness with which she'd named herself was as devastating as if she'd screamed at the top of her lungs. She honoured her would-be captors with a graceful smile, though I doubt that they saw any humour in it.

Magyari struggled to compose himself. "I am commanded to apprehend you, and apprehend you I will. Will you come willingly, or must you be compelled?" I looked at Magyari's men. Most of them looked as though they'd rather compel a viper.

"Most willingly," my Lady said, stepping forwards. They parted before her as she swept from the room. As he turned to follow her, Magyari glanced at me. "You too, Janos Ujvary," he said. "You are to be examined as well." I started, being unused to hearing my true name spoken. My Lady never uses it. I summoned all the courage I could muster and followed her.

***

After the Count's funeral I returned to the quarters allotted to my regiment, where we jostled each other as we tried to get as close as possible to the small fire. There were the usual complaints and ribald jokes together with more speculation about Count Nadasdy's death. Carl the Austrian told his tale again. The fact that the Count had been struck with a sudden sickness and had fallen from his horse was no great marvel, but Carl added his darker hints. I'm not sure how many believed him. I know old Samson didn't. He'd been in the regiment longer than most of us had been alive, and liked to say that he'd visited so many whorehouses in his time that the chances were that he'd fathered at least a couple of us. His hair and moustache were white and he always complained of a pain in his knee when we marched; but his wits were still sharp.

"I once heard a man say that he'd heard a man say that *he'd* heard from a man who'd seen a dragon with his own eyes," he said, "and so such nonsense spreads. If you listen to every rumour you hear you'll end up believing that there's a type of bee that makes gold instead of honey, or that the Earth goes round the sun."

A sensible attitude, I thought. Others were less ready to let the matter rest. It seemed that Carl wasn't the only one who'd heard 'dark rumours' and were there was some discussion of them. The problem was that no two men had heard the same rumour. Various scraps were chewed over, various theories were put forward, various misdeeds attributed to my Lady. I shan't list any of the accusations, not least because I can now say with certainty that none of them were true. I can also say that if witchcraft *was* involved in the death of Count Nadasdy, it was none of my Lady's doing. If she'd wanted to murder her husband, she would've had no need to stoop so low.

Samson let us prattle on for a while then, with a loud oath, told us, "You all believe in dragons, I see. There's only one dragon to be seen round here, and that's on the Countess' banner."

"It's a dragon that Janos here will follow to the ends of the Earth," Carl said. There were laughs, for others had seen me taking a knee. "She smiled at him, too," Carl went on. "Now, I wonder what she could want of so young and handsome a fellow?" I blushed.

"In love, are you?" Samson asked. Then, in the fatherly voice he uses when he dispenses wisdom born of long years of soldiering, "Loyalty's one thing, and a man should be loyal if he's paid regular. But don't think any of those great ones care a copper for you – or any of us. We're useful to them, but only in the way that sheep and cattle are useful. They won't weep if we end our days in the slaughterhouse. Mark me well, lad; if she smiled at you it's for her own amusement." Then he bent close and said in a low but serious tone, "If she wants to amuse herself further, you'd better desert. Desert and run from here as fast as you can. The worst they'll do to you for deserting is hang you."

Several of my companions fell silent at this and looked thoughtful. Carl, however, was still in a jesting mood. "Never mind what the countess wants, Janos, what do *you* want?"

I blushed deeper. "I w-would serve my Lady," I stammered.

More laughter. "Serve or service?" Carl asked. "Either way she'll eat you for breakfast."

I said nothing further, though for the remainder of the day I thought much about the little male spider.

***

For the next few days I was kept busy doing very little. When great persons gather they like to see castles well-staffed by guards looking smart and standing very still, and many such persons had gathered for the funeral. After it was done they lingered for a while in order to consult, confirm friendships, renew alliances – and to plot, I don't doubt. Prince Gabriel was there, of course, and Radu Serban as was only proper. Most of the local nobility paid their due respects, and there were representatives from Moldavia, Russia, Venice, and I know not how many other places. There were two persons I particularly remember, however. One was Matthias, now King of Hungary and the man who later ordered my Lady's arrest. There was much gossip to the effect that Matthias and his brothers were conspiring to have their uncle, the Holy Roman Emperor Rudolf, declared mad so that one of them could succeed him. The other was Gyorgy Thurzo, newly-appointed Palatine of Hungary. I make no claims to be a seer, or to possess any great degree of foresight, but the moment I laid eyes on Thurzo I detested him. He was too smooth and too arrogant, and ambitious beyond acceptable limits. Even when he spoke to his betters (those whose duty it is to hold a spear and stand motionless see and hear a great deal) he was at pains to demonstrate his learning and intellectual superiority. I wish I'd known then that, for all his scholarship, he was a physical coward. I might've saved my Lady much pain.

***

The chief afflictions of those standing sentry are boredom and the weather, but these did not bother me on this occasion. The first was banished by the vision of my Lady which filled my every thought – her grace, her nobility, her bearing. The way she'd held her head, the way she'd gripped her reins, the way she'd kept her mount under control with so little apparent effort, the whiteness of her smile. If I'd tried to explain these thoughts to Carl or Samson they would've mocked me, and advised me to relieve my frustration by visiting the stews, but I swear that there was nothing impure in my thoughts. When I'd said that I wished to serve my Lady, I meant just that: to serve her. Honestly, faithfully, honourably. As for the weather, it troubled me not at all. The land was still in the grip of winter, but where others complained that they were near frozen to the spot as they stood atop a tower watching for supposed foes, I only had to think on the way my Lady had honoured me with the gift of a smile, to feel warmth within.

***

After three days or so, the great ones started to depart, having presumably forged their alliances and plotted their plots. My only reaction was that of relief at not being required to be so visible and so still for quite so long. I also hoped that my regiment would be allowed to spend the rest of the winter in the castle, where we'd be sheltered from the worst the sky could throw at us. When, therefore, I returned to the guardroom one evening after another turn of duty, I was annoyed to find that instead of being allowed to partake of the supper which was my due, a serving woman was waiting for me with a summons. Though I questioned her as she led me towards the heart of the castle, she would tell me nothing. I detected a measure of nervousness in her manner but put it down to the natural reaction of one who is entrusted with an errand by a person of high rank. To be entirely honest, I was more than a little nervous myself. I worried that I might have offended in some way and was being called to account. I couldn't have been more wrong.

The woman led me to that part of the castle where the choicest chambers were located and knocked at a certain door. On receiving a reply from within, she turned to me and said "Enter." Then she fled as though a pack of hounds was after her. I shrugged, opened the door, and stepped through. That was possibly the last thing I ever did of my own free will.

The chamber was that of my Lady. She was sitting in a high-backed chair, close by the fire. At her elbow stood a small table upon which was a glass filled with what I took to be red wine. She'd set aside her mourning attire and wore instead a crimson gown of the finest silk, which shimmered and danced in the flickering light of the flames. "Welcome," she said. I cast myself upon my knees and bowed my head.

"What is your name?" my Lady asked. I made as if to answer but I could not – my tongue seemed too large for my mouth.

"No name?" my Lady asked, teasingly. "Very well then, I shall call you Ficko. It seems fitting – my lad, my Ficko. From now on, you will answer to no other name in my hearing. Do you understand me?"

I nodded. That at least I could still manage.

"Good. Stand up, Ficko, let me look at you properly."

I obeyed. My Lady gazed on me for a long time. I felt naked. From time to time she sipped with evident relish from her glass.

"You tire of the soldier's life, do you not?" my Lady asked me at last.

"Y-yes, my Lady."

"So, you do speak? So much the better."

Close to her – alone with her – I was overwhelmed. My head spun as though I was drunk, though I'd touched nothing more than ale that day, and then only a flagon or two. It seemed to me that with every breath I took I was inhaling her very essence. I wondered if this was what love felt like. If it was, then I understood why the poets make so much of it.

My Lady rose and walked slowly around me, as if appraising me from every angle. I kept my eyes facing rigidly forward even when she was behind me, though I could feel her gaze boring into me.

At length she seated herself again and took another sip from her glass. She licked her lips. "I think you have the qualities I'm looking for," she said. "Suppose I were to ask the commander of your regiment to release you to my service. Would you like that?"

"Y-yes, my Lady." This seemed an inadequate response, so I accompanied it with a deep bow, which seemed to amuse my Lady.

"Good," she said. "You may go. You will learn of your new duties in good time."

***

Four days after that, I learned what sort of services my Lady had in mind. I was allocated a small sleeping chamber and was permitted at the senior servants' dining table three times a day. I seemed to have no actual duties though. I did ask the other servants what might be expected of me, but they pretended not to have heard, or pointedly changed the subject.

After supper on the fourth day, I was approached again by my Lady's serving woman. As before, she seemed nervous. "The Lady calls for you," she said, then hurried off. I took a moment to make myself as presentable as possible then made my way to my Lady's chamber.

When I knocked, the door was opened by an old woman whose dress suggested that she was something more than a maid. "You are Ficko?" she asked.

I nodded.

"The Countess awaits."

I entered and was once more struck dumb. This time my Lady wore a gown of green – the green of woods in springtime. She smiled at me. "You may go, Ilona," she said. The old woman left.

"That was Ilona Jo," my Lady said. "She was my nurse when I was small, and now she is my – well. Let's say that she knows most of my secrets and I know all of hers. But sit."

I obeyed. For all its cushions, I'd never experienced a more uncomfortable chair.

My Lady had two glasses of wine already poured and handed one to me. I stared at it stupidly. "Drink," my Lady said. I sipped at the wine. It was a heady vintage, far superior to any I'd tasted before.

I found that I was unable to meet my Lady's gaze and cast my eyes downwards. If she sensed my discomfiture, my Lady ignored it. The floor was richly carpeted.

"Have you guessed?" my Lady asked. "Have you guessed why I have chosen you?"

I made no answer.

"The late Count, my husband," she began, "was not a bad man. Not entirely, anyway. He was loyal to his King and Emperor, courageous in battle, obedient to the church, just to his subjects, generous to the poor. He was, however, not a very good husband. He was inattentive and dull. He could only speak two languages, and them only coarsely. He could barely write his name. He got drunk more often than a man should, and for the last few years performed his marital duties poorly, if at all."

I was shocked by the way my Lady spoke. I dug my nails into the palms of my hands, and

prayed for the interview to end.

"I was quite pleased when I was chosen to be his bride," she said. "I didn't love him, nor did he me, but it's the curse of the high-born to marry for reasons of policy rather than any tender feeling. Nevertheless, I was glad — or relieved, at least. Many such a one as I has found herself shackled to an old man, twenty or thirty years her elder. I counted myself fortunate that Count Ferenc was only five years older than I. But then he aged so quickly. One year for him was three or four for anyone else. And he became infirm. Those painful legs that everyone knew about? They were the least of it. He was at least seventy when he died, even though he'd been on Earth for only eight and forty years. Dying was the kindest thing he'd done for me in many a year."

I became aware that my Lady was standing directly in front of me. Appalled at my lack of manners, I leapt to my feet, though I kept my eyes downcast. My Lady put her finger under my chin and raised my head so that I was looking at her face. Her eyes were dark, yet brilliant. They spoke to me of sorrow and great wisdom, of longing and otherness. They were intoxicating.

"I do hope you're not naïve, my Ficko," she said. "A great responsibility has fallen to me. I must govern in my late husband's stead. Well, that task will not be beyond me. But I need diversion as well. I will wear widow's weeds in public for the prescribed period, but in my private chambers — well."

I struggled to gather what few wits I possessed. Surely my Lady couldn't mean..?

My Lady seemed to find my confusion amusing. "There is no need to fear, my Ficko. I will never harm you. Indeed, I may decide to give you a great gift."

"A g-gift, my Lady?"

"In due time, if you prove to be as loyal as I believe you will be. As loyal and as amusing."

Then my Lady raised herself on her toes and kissed me on the mouth. She smelt of spices and nobility. She tasted of something I could not name.

We held — my Lady held — that kiss for a long time. When she released me, I was astonished to find that there was blood in my mouth. My Lady had bitten my lip, though I hadn't felt it.

My Lady read my expression. "No, Ficko, I have not bestowed the gift yet. It takes somewhat more than that."

I didn't know what she meant. Not then. I could only stare stupidly as she smiled at me. There was a trace of my blood on her upper teeth, which she licked off.

Then she took me by the hand and led me into her sleeping chamber.

I was nineteen then, not much more than a boy. I had experienced of the pleasures of the flesh, of course, but my hurried couplings with the whores who followed the army and who would spread themselves for a few coppers seemed poor preparation for what my Lady presumably had in mind.

And yet, like the little spider, I could not resist. Also, like the little spider, I found myself overmatched. Hitherto, my Lady's behaviour, though beyond my understanding, had struck me as meek and demure. Now she suddenly tossed aside all restraint. With surprising strength, she threw me onto the bed and knelt astride me. She wrenched open my doublet and ripped my shirt to shreds with her bare hands. She clawed at my chest. Her nails were exceedingly sharp, and I felt a thrill as she dragged them over my ribs. Then my Lady bent over me with her mouth open wide. She hissed like the most vicious cat that ever walked on four paws, then bit me. She bit my neck, my shoulder, my chest, drawing more blood, I was later to discover, though I never felt any pain from her bites. Her teeth were as sharp as her nails, and her tongue flickered between them like that of a serpent. She was astonishingly strong. I struggled in her grip, though whether I was trying to escape her clutches, or was transported with ecstasy the like of which I'd never imagined, I cannot say.

Then – and I don't know quite how it happened – she was disrobed. She said nothing, but her desire was clear. Trembling like the little spider, I did my Lady's bidding – and I realised that the camp whores had known – or cared – nothing. Stars exploded in my head.

Afterwards, I dreamed. I dreamed that I stood on a high mountain, with the whole of creation spread out below me. I saw Hungary, France, Italy, and the land of the Turks. I saw Africa and Russia, and beyond them India and Cathay. In the other direction I saw the mysterious New World. Above me, the sun shone dazzlingly.

"Everything you see can be yours."

My Lady was standing by my side. "Everything you see can be yours," she repeated. I took her in my arms and kissed her, inhaling her hot breath into my own lungs. We were enveloped in a shower of gold.

It was only much later that I understood the message of my dream. In Matthew it says that Satan took the Lord Jesus to the summit of an exceeding high mountain and showed him all the kingdoms of the world...

By the time I understood my dream, however, it was too late.

***

For the next three days, I saw nothing of my Lady. Perversely, I began to miss being a soldier. Standing sentry was tedious, marching was hard, battle was terrifying – but to have these taken from me and to have absolutely nothing to take their place did not improve my lot a great deal, I thought. A couple of times I looked in on my former comrades who, though they didn't throw me out, were cold and unfriendly. Carl refused to talk to me, and Samson shook his head sadly. Each time I tried to talk about my Lady, someone loudly spoke of something else. I realise now that they were afraid; possibly even afraid of me. All I knew at the time was that I was no longer of their regiment. After the second visit, I left quietly and did not return.

At the end of the fourth day, Ilona Jo entered my chamber unannounced. She had a pile of clothes in her arms. "Put these on," she said. "If you're going to be the Countess' puppy, you should at least look the part."

She folded her arms, making it plain that she expected me to dress in front of her. I felt oddly self-conscious.

There were three shirts of good linen ("Wash your face each morning and change your shirt every second day," Ilona told me. "They will be laundered and returned. The same goes for the drawers. The Countess appreciates cleanliness." I tried to conceal my blush by pulling one of the shirts over my head). There were britches and a coat, each of green wool, the coat having some decorative piping in white. There was the best pair of boots I'd ever worn. There was a wide hat with, I think, an eagle's feather in it. There was also a cloak, though Ilona told me I wouldn't be needing it that night.

"You're not the first," she told me as she led me briskly to my Lady's chamber, "and I don't doubt that there'll be others after you. The last one lasted almost a month before the Countess tired of him. She says you have more promise than most, however, so perhaps you'll last. I wouldn't get your hopes up, though. That said, she can be generous if you please her, however briefly."

"She said…" I began.

Ilona stopped abruptly and turned to face me. "What did the Countess say?"

"My Lady said… she said something about a gift. I didn't understand her. I don't think she meant money."

Ilona Jo looked at me sternly. "No," she said, "the gift is not money. It's less than that, and much more. She's never given it to anyone to my knowledge. You must please her very much if she's even hinted at it to you. If you value your skin, however, don't probe the riddle. You'll find out if you find out. And don't mention the gift again; not to me or to anyone. Certainly not to the Countess."

She turned on her heel and walked on. I followed, even more confused than before.

My Lady was reading a book when I entered her chamber. She has a great many books – perhaps as many as fifty – and has read them all. I stood there in silence until she had finished the page she was reading and set the book aside.

"Ficko," she exclaimed. "My, you look almost the gentleman." I tried to bow in the courtly fashion, flourishing my new hat. My Lady laughed. "You might want to practise that," she said. "But that can wait. Come sit by me and drink wine and talk to me. Tell me of yourself. Where were you born?"

I told her of my father's farm and my decision to leave it. She seemed quite amused when I told her that I'd enlisted as a soldier out of a sense of adventure and asked if I'd found the experience as exhilarating as I'd hoped. I confessed that I hadn't. Quite the reverse, in fact. I told her of Brasov and – my tongue running away with me, I'm ashamed to say – of the awful treatment of the captured Turks. My Lady looked uncomfortable when I mentioned the stakes. I apologised and attempted to change the subject. Unfortunately, the only thing that occurred to my poor brain was Count Ferenc. I praised his military acumen and his steadfastness as an ally. I soon saw that this was not what my Lady wanted to hear, so I trailed off, feeling that I'd failed some sort of test.

"I told you my husband was dull, did I not?" she said. "No matter. I should be able to plant a little erudition in you, given time. For now, it's enough that you are good at one thing."

✳✳✳

Half a year went by. During the day my Lady conducted the affairs of her late husband; administering justice, raising taxes, sending men to the never-ending wars. By all accounts, she performed these duties well and was accounted wise, just, and generous. One incident sticks in my mind. There was a young woman from Sarvar, who'd been raped by a Turkish soldier during one of their many raids. As a result, she'd fallen pregnant. All shunned her, including her parents and the church. As a last resort, she appealed to my Lady, who took pity on her. She gave the woman money and arranged for her to marry a man who lived in Pest. If the man was bribed, he kept his side of the bargain, for the woman and my Lady wrote letters to each other for some years.

I told my Lady that hers was a noble and Christian act. I'd meant to flatter her, but her eyes flashed with anger. "What do you know of rape, Ficko?" she demanded. "What does any man know?"

I wondered what had made her react like that but didn't dare ask.

But matters of rulership were nothing to me. By day I was an empty husk. I did try to improve myself. I practised my reading, for my Lady liked me to read to her. It was hard at first, but I progressed. In Hungarian, at least. I never got beyond a few phrases in Latin.

I also learned a poem or two and cudgelled my memory for the peasant songs of my childhood (my Lady told me I had a good singing voice and said that my songs had a certain rustic charm). These things gave me no pleasure, however. I did them to please my Lady. I lived only for her.

She did summon me every night, but ever and anon my Lady's serving woman – her name was Katarina – would seek me out and give me a brief nod. Then fire would burn in my veins, and I would go to my Lady. She received me as a hostess would. We would drink wine together (at least, I would drink wine. I tried not to think what might be in my Lady's glass). We would discuss the news, and the book I was reading; and sometimes she would call for a song.

Eventually, however, she would take me into her bedchamber. Her passions were vigorous and not easily satisfied. Often it would be nearly dawn before she was spent, by which time I was utterly exhausted. She never failed to make full use of her nails and teeth, and usually drew blood (never more than a trickle, which she would lick off of me with evident relish, telling me that my blood was sweeter than any she'd ever tasted). Sometimes, in addition, she would beat me. Not so as to cause any lasting injury, but smartly enough. My Lady was, as I have said, uncommonly strong. And I will not deny that she aroused within me passions stronger than I'd ever felt before. I learned to derive pleasure from the pain she inflicted (it was only on that first occasion that I didn't feel her bites) and even to welcome it – until pleasure and pain were one and the same to me, and I experienced transports of delight beyond all imagining.

Then came a time when I was awoken from my slumbers on the night of a full moon. Bleary-eyed, I opened my door, to see Ilona Jo standing there. She looked at me in a strange and knowing way, which I found disquieting. Her message was clear, however: I was summoned. I dressed hurriedly and made my way to my Lady's chamber. As I approached it, a strong smell rose to my nostrils. As a soldier, it was a smell I recognised only too well. It was the smell of blood.

I entered my Lady's chamber with some trepidation. The smell of blood was stronger, but she herself was not to be seen. I stood there in some confusion, until I heard her voice calling to me from her bedchamber. Thither I went. As I entered and saw, I froze in horror.

My Lady was lying upon the bed, naked as a babe and liberally bedaubed with blood. At first, I thought that she'd come by some horrific injury, but soon saw that it was not so. On a low table by the bed was a bronze basin, and by the basin lay a bloody sponge.

My Lady smiled at me. "Yes," she said. "It's time you knew the truth. Once a month, when the moon is full, Ilona assists me to bathe in blood. It enables me to preserve the appearance of youth. Do not underestimate the power of the moon. Or of blood."

I could think of nothing to say, so stood there like a half-wit.

"Oh Ficko," my Lady said with a chuckle. "How easily shocked you are. Drink some wine if that will help. It *is* wine, on this occasion," she said, pointing towards the table where it stood, "though mine isn't always."

I drank some wine. It helped a little, but not much.

"Now sit down, Ficko, and listen to me," my Lady said. "Do you know what you should fear more than anything in this world?" she asked me.

"Damnation?" I ventured.

"That is a matter for the next world. I asked you what you should fear most in this."

"Pestilence?" I suggested. "Poverty, famine, bandits?"

"None of those. Ageing is what you should most fear."

"We all age."

"Indeed we do. You, Ficko, are ageing by the moment. Yet you do nothing to prevent it."

"There's nothing that can be done."

"Is there not? Come, Ficko, how old do you think I am?"

"I wouldn't care to guess, my Lady."

"I insist."

I hesitated, thinking that some trap was being laid for me. I suddenly remembered a piece of advice that my father had given me: *Always guess that a woman is younger than you think she really is.* "Perhaps five and twenty?" I offered, eventually.

My Lady laughed merrily. "Five and twenty? Very good, Ficko. A valiant guess, but wrong. I have, by my mother's oath, been on this Earth some three and forty years. A week from now, the total will be four and forty."

I sought to hide my shock but failed to do so. Surely my Lady jested. But no; I remembered that she'd told me that the Count had been only five years older than she, and he had died at eight and forty. My Lady laughed again. "Yes, Ficko, three and forty. My mother was dead at three and forty. I have loftier ambitions."

"B-but," I stammered, "you cannot halt time."

"No," my Lady said, "but you *can* stand aside as it passes. Perhaps I will tell you the secret one day."

"Is this … is this the great gift of which you spoke?" I realised as I asked this that I'd disobeyed Ilona Jo's instruction not to raise the matter of the gift in front of my Lady. I experienced a moment of terror, but my Lady didn't seem angered.

"It is," she answered me. "I was told when I received it that I should pass it on to the one I chose. It is some twenty years since that day, so perhaps I should look three and twenty rather than five, but no matter. I shall just consider you a poor guesser."

My head was reeling. "That blood, my Lady. Is it ..?"

"Is it human? Yes it is. Do you want to know whose veins were opened to supply it?"

"No, my Lady."

"That is wise. Do you fear that one day your veins will be opened in like manner?"

"Yes, my Lady. Forgive me, but –"

"There is nothing to forgive. Also, there is nothing to fear. Though your blood pleases me greatly, a few drops at a time will satisfy. This I swear."

I stood there, silent. I wanted to run, but my legs would not obey me.

"It seems that I shall have to take you into my confidence, young Ficko. You see the crucifix on yonder wall?"

I turned my head. It was there, but it was so common an object that I hadn't noticed it before. "Yes, my Lady."

"Bring it here."

I did so.

"Kneel and hold it before you. Now repeat after me: *I, Janos Ujvary, henceforth to be known only as Ficko, do hereby swear, in peril of the life everlasting, never reveal to any man or woman the things that I am about to hear.* Good. Now kiss the crucifix."

I obeyed and, at my Lady's instruction, replaced it on the wall.

"Well done, Ficko. Know now that if you break your oath, my vengeance will be swift and terrible. I will forgive you much; indeed, I expect to have to forgive you much. But oath-breaking is the one thing I will never forgive. Do you understand?"

I nodded.

"Good. And now I must ask you to forgive me."

"For what, my Lady?"

"A deception. Minor, but unavoidable."

"What deception, my Lady?"

"I bade you swear in peril of the life everlasting, did I not?"

"Yes, my Lady."

"Yes. What I did not make clear to you, is that 'the life everlasting' can be interpreted in two ways. Do you see now?"

"No, my Lady."

"It seems I must be plainer. What do you know about the Bathory family?"

"That it is ancient and noble; that it has provided many Voivodes of Transylvania, and latterly Princes also; that —"

My Lady held up a hand to stop me. "And for what is Transylvania best known?" she asked. I made no reply. "For vampyres," my Lady said.

∗∗∗

The tales I'd heard about vampyres were both true and false. True, in that such creatures existed. False, in that the attributes ascribed to them by folklore are fanciful. They are vigorous and strong and take their sustenance through blood, that's true. But it's not true that they cast no reflection in polished surfaces, or turn to dust if they walk in daylight, or cower in fear at the sight of a cross. As to whether they can transform themselves into bats or other creatures of the night — well, I'll come to that in due time.

From my earliest youth, I'd heard and relished these tales. Gruesome and thrilling tales, which were neither wholly believed, nor wholly disbelieved. What it took me long to realise, however, was that I heard these tales differently to others. To most, the vampyre was evil beyond hope of redemption. He (in all the tales of my childhood, the vampyre was masculine) was to be hunted down and destroyed. His defeat at the end of the tale — leavened as it may have been with dark hints about his ability to return from the grave in a dreadful and blasphemous mockery of our Lord and Saviour, and to weave his wickedness anew — was satisfyingly just. I, however, saw the vampyre as a tragic figure, doomed to live on in this world with no hope of the next. Sometimes I wondered what it would be like to meet one. It was nothing like I'd expected.

I must've looked a simpleton as these thoughts tumbled through my head. At length I became aware that my Lady was smiling at me, and that I was once more on my knees.

"Have you remarked the banner of the Bathorys?" my Lady asked.

"Yes, my Lady."

"It shows a dragon, does it not?"

"Yes, my Lady."

"Know then, that this emblem was chosen with good reason. The first Bathory who received the great gift — and who passed it to me — received it from the one known as the Little Dragon and adopted this banner as a form of silent homage."

"The Little Dragon? You mean Vlad Dracula who ruled over…"

"Over Wallachia, yes. The southerly neighbour of Transylvania, where my cousin now rules. I sometimes wonder why folklore always speaks of Transylvania rather than Wallachia when vampyres are mentioned, but that is a small matter. It is indeed Vlad Dracula of whom I speak."

"But he died long years ago."

"He did and he didn't."

"So he is alive still?"

"The answer to that question is somewhere between No and Yes. Let us say that he is sleeping for the moment. When he will choose to awaken again, I do not know, but were you to go to the monastery at Snagov and open his supposed tomb, you will not find what you expect to find.

"I remember when I first learned about blood," my Lady said, and there was a tone in her voice that suggested that she was talking to herself as much as to me. "I was a girl, seven years old or thereabouts. I was walking in the company of, well, let us say a relative. The Bathorys are a large family, with numerous branches. I was walking, as I say, when I chanced to prick my finger on a thorn. I was about to put my finger in my mouth, as a child does, when I noticed the drop of blood on its tip. Just a single drop, an almost perfect sphere and a deep red. I held it up, and the sun caught it, its rays making the drop shine.

"My relative saw what I was doing. 'What do you think if it?' he asked. 'It's beautiful,' I said. 'Like a ruby.'

"'It's more precious than a ruby' my relative said. 'More powerful as well. May I?'

"I wasn't sure what he was asking, but he put my finger in his mouth, and sucked gently. When he released my finger, the blood was gone, and the skin whole and unpunctured. I was both puzzled and disappointed.

"'Now you try' my relative said. He looked for the thorn on which I'd pricked myself and pressed his own finger onto it. Then he held it out for me to see. His blood was slightly darker than mine; thicker, richer. He gave me an encouraging nod. Hesitantly I put his finger in my mouth. The taste of it was beyond description.

"'Never forget the power of blood' my relative said. 'Nothing is its equal. I think you're capable of understanding that. Not everyone is. When you're a grown woman, I shall explain blood to you more fully, and will pass a deep secret on to you. Until then, say nothing of what has happened here. You won't tell, will you?' I shook my head.

"I didn't tell. I think I enjoyed having a secret. I think I enjoyed being different. And I was different. From time to time, I had visions. Strange visions. The sort that mark a person out for sainthood – or for something else. I never told of these visions, but others said that from time to time I seemed to enter a trance. I was given blood to drink. As a medicine, I was told, though I now realise that I was being prepared for what was to come."

I glanced down at the glass in my hand.

My Lady saw me do so. "No, Ficko," she said. "I have not given you blood to drink. Not so much as a drop secreted in your wine. Not yet, at any rate."

She sighed. "But we are straying from our purpose. I did not summon you to talk to you of such things. Well, not wholly for that purpose. You know what I want from you; and I know that you want it also."

"But not —" I began. I had somehow forgotten that she was besmeared with fresh blood.

"But not while I am like this?" my Lady asked. "On the contrary, I want you particularly while I am like this. I told you: never underestimate the power of blood. I expect your best performance. If it will make it any easier, on this night I shall not bite you. I've had my fill of blood for now."

I felt sick, but the time when I might have resisted was long past. Like a little trembling spider, I approached my mate. Whether I gave my best performance, I don't know.

***

The next morning, I left Csejte Castle. I bundled up my few belongings and passed through one of the lesser doorways. I'd hoped to do so unobserved, but it so happened that Samson saw me go. The rest of my old regiment had been marched off I knew not where, but Samson had persuaded his masters that his bad knee meant that his marching days were behind him, and had wrangled himself as post as a permanent sentry in the castle, meaning that for the rest of his days he'd never be too far from a fire, a kitchen and a roof. The rest of his regiment had held a celebration to toast his good fortune. I'd wanted to join them. I'd even approached near enough to hear the sounds of jollity but had not dared enter within. That chapter of my life had closed for ever.

Samson, I say, saw me depart. I felt that I had to say farewell to someone at least, so I approached him. He shook his head. "I tried to warn you lad," he said.

"I know."

"So, you're finally deserting."

"Not really. I'm not a soldier anymore. I ..."

"Don't try explaining that to the Countess. There are many forms of desertion. I doubt you'll look favourably on yours."

"How much do you know about my – I mean the Countess? I mean *really* know?"

"Too much and too little, both at the same time. Go, lad, while you still can. I hope they hang you."

"You do?"

"I told you before: it's not the worst that could happen to you."

I left the castle. I'd no idea where I was headed; I just knew that I had to but as much distance as possible between me and the Dragon Lady.

I managed a little over five miles.

After this distance I reached a crossroads below the village. As I stood there, uncertain which path to take, it occurred to me that crossroads were the places where those denied proper Christian rites were buried. Suicides, felons, unbelievers. Witches. Possibly vampyres. I wondered whether there were any unquiet souls beneath my feet at that very moment, and somehow this drained me of any will to walk on. That was what I was destined to be – an unquiet soul, doomed to wander the Earth, finding no rest this side of the grave and no peace beyond it. I sat down by the side of the road and wept.

How long I sat there, I don't know. If anyone passed me, I didn't notice them. A black bird circled over my head for a while. I thought about my Lady. It was clear that she was dealing in dark arts. Arts from which a wise man should flee. Arts which an honest man should report to the law, the church, the King. I thought about how my Lady had ensnared me unknowing, about how I should shun her. I thought about how she'd used me, and how I feared her. I thought about blood, and the unknown victims from whom the blood came. I thought about vampyres. I thought about my nights of passion with my Lady. I thought about love. I thought about the little spider, crawling across the web to his doom.

When I'd spent long enough in thought, I rose and made my way back to the castle.

***

It was nearly two weeks before my Lady sent for me again. When she did, she was stern. "You tried to leave me, Ficko, did you not?"

I knelt before her and admitted that this was so. Ilona Jo, who was present, smiled nastily.

"You disappoint me, Ficko. I should be angry with you, Ficko, but I am not. Not above a little, anyway. You did, after all, return of your own free will, so I forgive you. I said that I would have much to forgive you for, did I not? I must know one thing, however. Did you break your oath? Did you speak of that which you should not have?"

"No, my Lady, I swear I did not. I swear by my mother's grave."

"I'm not interested in your mother's grave, nor any grave saving a select few. However, I believe you."

Relief washed over me, but my Lady was not finished. "Be warned, Ficko, I will not tolerate your straying a second time. If you do, I will not receive you back."

I bowed my head almost to the floor.

"No, Ficko," my Lady said, "from this moment on you must be my creature entirely. Any task I set you, you must perform without question."

I glanced at the crucifix on the wall. "No," my Lady said, "I will not demand of you a second oath. I don't think it will make any difference. I will command. You will either do or do not. That is all."

I cowered in terror.

"Do not fear, my Ficko," my Lady went on in a kinder tone. "I have no wish to harm you. But you must prove your loyalty to me. You must bring me a gift."

"A gift, my Lady? I am a poor farmer's son —"

"Not the sort of gift that can be bought with money, Ficko," my Lady said.

"What then?"

She told me.

***

I was three years a soldier, during which time I killed four men — perhaps five. They do not weigh heavily on my conscience. If a soldier follows his lawful Prince as I did, then he's absolved of the deeds he must do on the field of battle. For my Lady, however, I committed murder.

"Never underestimate the power of blood," my Lady said. "I know I say that often, but I cannot say it often enough. Blood has power. I need blood each full moon. And where does blood come from?"

If I'm being completely honest, I already knew the answer to that question. Nevertheless, I'd closed my mind to it. Now I couldn't avoid the truth. The blood in which my Lady bathed had once flowed in human veins. Up until that moment my Lady's victims had been servant girls with no family, procured for her by the old crone, Ilona Jo. Many a girl had been enticed to her doom by the offer of good wages at the castle. But the number of girls that had disappeared had begun to be remarked upon. Servants come and go, it's true, but the whispers were striking too near to the truth.

Girls therefore had to be obtained from further afield. Obtained by me. Two days before the next full moon I was dispatched on my foul errand. I left the castle in a small cart — the sort that fetched supplies every day and passed to and fro without comment. I drove slowly through the village and into the farmland beyond. It was broad day, and I passed many people. In my imagination, each of them saw the guilt in my face and looked on me with revulsion. I drove on for an hour, perhaps two, looking for a victim. My Lady had specified a girl; the younger the better.

Her name was Agnes. She was perhaps twelve. I passed her on the road as she was carrying a basket to her aunt's house. She was barefoot but cheerful and accepted readily when I offered to let her ride with me.

Afterwards, I tipped her body backwards into the cart, covering it with sacking. Then I wiped my dagger, turned the cart, and returned to the castle. Again, I passed many people. Every glance pierced me and seemed to carry an accusation. There was a part of me that would've welcomed a challenge, would've welcomed the discovery of what I had done. No challenge came. The smell of Agnes' blood mingled with the smell of fresh bread that rose from her basket. It rose into the air, also, and attracted a carrion bird — a crow, I thought. It followed me for some miles.

When I passed through the castle gate, the sentry was Samson. He didn't stop me. He didn't even look at me. I'm sure he knew what I'd done. I'm sure he could smell Agnes' blood. I was sure that everyone in the castle could smell Agnes' blood. I was almost choked by it. Nevertheless, I was able to deliver my cargo unmolested.

***

I'd give much to be able to say that that was the whole of the horror, but it wasn't. There was more. More and worse. Under the direction of Ilona Jo, I drained the blood from the body of poor Agnes — how I wish she hadn't told me her name — then carried her pathetic remains up a narrow stair to a room whose existence I hadn't up until then suspected. There were other bodies in the room — perhaps three dozen. All were young girls or had been. Some of the bodies were fairly fresh, some were rotten. Some were alive with maggots, some showed bone where the flesh had fallen away. One in particular seemed to stare accusingly at me from empty eye-sockets. The smell was overpowering. My gorge rose in protest.

That evening, Ilona Jo and I carried the blood to my Lady. Ilona Jo withdrew, and my Lady beckoned me to sit beside her. She dipped a small jug into the basin and poured blood into two glasses. She offered one to me.

I refused it with a shudder. My Lady smiled. "Do not be afraid, Ficko," she said. She might as well have told the wind to stop blowing.

"There is naught to fear," my Lady told me, offering the glass to me anew. "Indeed, there is much to gain. I told you that blood was given to me in preparation."

"Preparation for what, my Lady?"

"Preparation for the receipt of the gift. I haven't wholly decided if I shall bestow it on you, but it is as well to plan ahead."

I was the little spider again. I took the glass and sipped. The blood was warm, surprisingly so, and filled my veins with fire. The room began to spin about my head, faster and faster. I have a confused memory of my Lady handing me a sponge and directing me to anoint her with blood. Anoint her from top to toe. Then the room seemed to melt away completely, until I was floating in a black void. After that I knew no more.

When I awoke, I struggled to remember who I was. I couldn't bring my true name to mind, but eventually remembered that I was called Ficko. A little more effort, and I perceived that I was lying in my Lady's bed. She was lying close to me, still red with blood.

She saw me look at her. "Hush," she said soothingly.

Some confused memories of the previous night came back to me. "Am I —" I began.

"Are you a vampyre?" she asked. "No, not yet."

***

So began the catalogue of my crimes. Does it matter if they were committed for love? Probably not. I brought many girls to my Lady. I helped drain their blood, helped anoint my Lady. And yes, I drank of this blood. Only a sip on each occasion, but that is a poor defence. My Lady said drink, so I drank. My Lady said it was in preparation for the gift. Maybe it was; maybe it was a way for her to emphasise her power over me.

I don't know how many girls I murdered. At the trial, de Szulo suggested that many hundreds of girls had been slain. I'm sure this was an exaggeration intended to stoke up the already bitter tide of feeling against my Lady, but I was never good with numbers. How many full moons are there in six and a half years? I won't give the full details. I told them to de Szulo at my trial and once is enough. Suffice it to say that the horror went on, the murders went on, and the pile of bodies in the secret room grew and grew. And despite it all, my love for my Lady, though it cost me great pain, never diminished. Sometimes when I was alone, I considered confessing all. Sometimes I considered trying to flee. Sometimes I even considered self-murder, which though it is a mortal sin, seemed to me the lesser of two evils. Each time I was in my Lady's presence however, such thoughts vanished. Such is the power of love. Such is the curse of love.

There was talk of course. For one girl to vanish was no great matter, nor for two to do so, or five, or even ten. When the count reached the dozens, however, the secret could not be kept. Even though I took to venturing further and further afield in order to draw eyes away from the castle, people spoke openly of the monster that was stalking the land. Fingers began to be pointed, mostly in the wrong direction. Men distrusted their neighbours, and travelling merchants were viewed with such hostility that many of them decided to take their trade elsewhere. My Lady came to be blamed; not for the murders, but for her failure to apprehend those responsible.

There came a time – this was three or four years after Agnes – when Palatine Thurzo felt that he needed to act. He therefore appointed Minister Magyari to be his special investigator. Magyari was no fool. He received evidence from the parents of every girl who had vanished and noted the position of their homes on a map. This showed that the girls had vanished from a circle of territory which had Castle Csejte at its centre. One evening, Magyari came to visit my Lady. I was present, but Magyari paid me as much notice as he would any servant, which is to say none. He didn't suspect my Lady, or at least he didn't do so then, but spoke of the need for her to supply men to aid him in his investigations. His idea was to search for the bodies which, he was sure, had been collected in one place.

It's good that Magyari didn't notice servants, else he would've seen me start guiltily when he said that. He didn't know that he had but to twitch aside a tapestry to reveal the small door leading to the chamber where he would have found just that place. As I listened to him, I thought I could smell the stink of corruption that came from there, but that must've been my imagination for Magyari clearly smelt nothing.

My Lady, I'm sure, was enjoying herself. Nevertheless, she did what she could to muddy the trail. She freely put a number of men at Magyari's disposal, but where he spoke of apprehending the monster, my Lady planted the idea that there were surely monsters in the plural, for the number of instances made it unlikely that a single individual was responsible. She also cast doubt on Magyari's theory about the pile of bodies. Since not a single body had been discovered, she said, this surely indicated that the girls had been carried off rather than murdered.

Perhaps, she suggested, they had been taken to serve the Turks in what she coyly described as "various ways."

Magyari acknowledged the possibility, but wondered why the Turks would take girls from one district only, and that district not the nearest to the lands hey controlled. My Lady countered (it came to me later that it was a matter of cut-and-thrust, even if Magyari didn't realise it) that perhaps their intention was precisely to spread terror and suspicion in a single district. Either that or there was a local gang who were selling girls to Turkish agents.

Magyari left, a hound resolutely following a false scent. When he was gone, my Lady laughed merrily. I, however, looked up at the sky. The moon lacked some five or six days of being full. It would be time for me to leave soon; and this time I'd have to venture far afield indeed.

***

Another year passed. Thirteen full moons. The terror continued. Magyari's circle grew a little larger. People still mostly suspected agents of the Turks. I got a year older, but my Lady did not.

Then my luck ran out. Twice.

The first occasion came when I'd journeyed two days to the East. I think I'd passed into Moldavia; I'm not sure where the border ran. I'd seen a likely victim. She was gathering berries. I stopped and asked her for directions to the nearest inn. I didn't ask her name.

What I didn't realise was that she was not alone. Nor that she'd been told to be wary of strangers (which ought to have been no marvel, but perhaps I'd become over-confident). When I offered to give her a ride she backed away. I ought to have simply driven on, but time was pressing. It only lacked three days to the full moon, and my journey back to the castle would take two of them.

I jumped down from the cart and made a grab for the girl.

She screamed.

Two men appeared from the other side of the hedgerow. They held hoes. Their faces were grim.

I protested that there'd been a misunderstanding, and that I'd only stopped to ask the girl for directions and had offered her a ride out of kindness.

The men were suspicious, but not certain. They stood there for what seemed a long while, silently staring at me. A black bird came and settled on the cart. It occurred to me that I'd often been followed by such a carrion fowl (I saw now that it was a raven, rather than a crow) after I'd collected a victim – attracted, I'd assumed by the smell of fresh blood – but that I'd never noticed one when my cart was empty. The men, of course, paid the bird no mind, but a thought occurred to me.

The men were undecided. "I assure you, goodmen," I said, "that I am no murderer. I've heard of the disappearances, of course, but those all happened in the district of Csejte, or so it's said."

"Perhaps we'll let the magistrate decide," the elder of the two said, brandishing his hoe. A hoe is no battle weapon, but wielded with intent it can still inflict a grievous injury.

I backed toward the cart. My accuser lunged at me with his hoe. And the raven flapped down from the cart.

Except that it wasn't a raven. There was what I can only describe as a shimmering black blur, and the bird transformed itself into my Lady – but my Lady as I'd never seen her before. First, she seemed considerably taller than her usual self, though that might have been my imagination. Second, she was clad all in flowing black, which billowed about her but didn't impede her movements in any way. Most of all, however, she'd changed from a demure and genteel noblewoman into a spitting, hissing fury. She struck the first man in the chest, and he was propelled backwards as if he'd been kicked by the angriest horse that was ever foaled. The second man swung his hoe at her. She caught it in one hand and snapped it like a twig. She opened her mouth impossibly wide. I saw that her teeth were as brilliantly white as ever, but that two of them had grown until they seemed like fangs, long and needle-sharp. She grabbed the man by his jerkin – her nails had grown into talons – and held him in the air with one hand. He screamed. She hissed, then bent and sank her teeth into his neck. There was a spurt of blood, then he went limp.

My lady tossed him aside as though he was nothing but a rag doll and turned back to the first man. He'd struggled to his feet but now, seeing the fate of his fellow, turned and fled. My Lady let him go or seemed at first to do so. Then, however, moving as swiftly as an eagle flies, she caught him, seized him, and to my open-mouthed horror, tore him limb from limb.

The girl had remained motionless while all this happened. I presume she was too shocked to move. For that matter, so was I. My Lady approached the girl slowly, offering words of reassurance. She seemed to have shrunk back to her usual stature, and her nails and teeth had returned to their usual size. The girl showed no sign of fear. She merely stared into my Lady's eyes, transfixed as if she was in some sort of trance.

My Lady took the girl into her arms. She didn't resist or cry out. My Lady bit deeply into her neck and began to drink – and drink, and drink. I do not know how much blood the girl's body contained, but it seemed to me that my Lady drained every drop.

At length she let the husk fall and turned to me.

"You have grown careless, Ficko."

I acknowledged that this was so.

"You are fortunate that I was close by."

I bowed in acknowledgement of that rebuke as well.

"You had better bury these bodies. It would not do to encourage unnecessary gossip."

I obeyed. It was fortunate that no other traveller chanced down that road whilst I toiled. Then again, if they had, I presume that my Lady would've dealt with them.

When I was done, my Lady nodded at me and turned away. I presumed that she was about to transform herself back into a raven. "My Lady," I called.

She turned back to me. "Yes, Ficko?"

"Will you still be needing..?" I couldn't finish the question, but there was no need.

"Yes, Ficko. I will be requiring a girl to be delivered by the full moon. You must make haste."

My heart sank. "Yes, my Lady."

"And yes, Ficko, I do sometimes accompany you as you run your errands. Not all the time, for I have duties to perform at Csejte. I can travel swiftly when I take wing, but I cannot be in two places at once."

"My Lady...?"

"Yes Ficko, you did see me at the crossroads the day you attempted to flee my service. Are there any more questions?"

"No, my Lady."

"Good. Now you must complete your errand without my assistance."

She raised her arms, which blurred into wings, and away she flew.

I felt sick.

***

The second time my luck ran out, I had to shift for myself.

It was a few months after the episode in Moldavia. Autumn was beginning to turn into winter; there was a bite in the air by day, and frost by night. Once again, I'd travelled far in an attempt to allay suspicion, or at least to make people look in as many different directions as possible. I'd passed through the mountains, south into Transylvania which might be seen as a dark jest.

I'd learned my lesson and had made double and triple sure that there would be no witnesses. The girl I took wasn't one who'd be missed. She was a homeless beggar, friendless and half-starved. If I hadn't taken her, hunger would've caught up with her in two or three more days. I got the impression (or perhaps I was just fooling myself) that she was quite glad to be relieved of the burden of life. As ever (or as ever since Agnes) I was careful not to learn her name. I turned the cart and started for home.

Two hours later as dusk was falling, I began to feel that I was being watched. To be sure, this wasn't the first time I'd felt as much, but on this occasion it was particularly insistent. I scanned the sky overhead. No raven, nor any other sort of bird. I turned in my seat and looked back the way I'd come. There was a rider behind me. Distant enough to be almost invisible in the gloom. Close enough for me to be just visible to him.

I told myself this meant nothing. Roads are for travelling along. I'd passed and been passed by any number of people during my various expeditions. Even so, the feeling of unease wouldn't leave me.

I considered. If I tried to flee, it would be tantamount to an admission of guilt. In any case, I in my cart couldn't outpace a man on a horse. I could continue on my way, but an honest man would hardly fail to stop during the hours of darkness. Indeed, my horse was telling me in not so subtle ways that it was time to turn aside from the road and camp for the night.

I decided to do just that, and to trust to bluff if I was challenged. To my left was a meadow that sloped gently downwards to a small stream. I directed my horse onto it and halted. I unhitched him, and he walked slowly down to the stream to drink. I spread some corn on the ground, knowing that he'd come back for it. I made a fire. During all this, I kept an eye out for the horseman. I didn't see him. He didn't approach, but neither did he pass by, following the road. Had he turned aside a moment earlier? I hoped so, but still my nerves were on edge.

I ate my supper of bread and bacon, then wrapped myself in my blanket and crawled under my cart. I couldn't sleep *in* my cart, given the cargo it was carrying. Lying underneath afforded me some shelter at least.

Sleep wouldn't come. I turned this way and that, trying to get as comfortable as possible. It wasn't the worst ground I'd ever slept on, and I was certainly weary. Even so, the persistent idea that I was being watched wouldn't leave me. I began to wonder if there were vampyres other than my Lady (she'd hinted as much but had named no names) that might've been close by in creature form. I wondered how I'd recognise them even if I saw them.

Eventually, I gave up trying to sleep. I got up and walked up and down for a bit, flapping my arms to get some circulation going. I'd taken to carrying a pistol with me on my travels. It was too large and cumbersome to stick in my belt, so I kept it under the seat of the wagon. I checked that it was there, primed and loaded. I prayed that it would fire if I needed it to – there was a touch of damp in the air.

It was a dark night. The moon was nearly full but was hidden behind heavy clouds. The fire had died away to nothing. More than once I started at some movement in the dark, only to realise that it was my horse, behaving as horses will.

"I told you to run, didn't I?"

The voice came from behind me. I whirled to face it but could see no-one.

"Oh, you poor, stupid boy. What've you got yourself caught up in?"

The voice was familiar. "Samson?"

"Who did you expect?"

"Where are you?"

"Here." Samson stood up. He'd been lying on the ground a mere dozen paces away. He must have approached by worming his way towards me on his belly.

"It shouldn't be so easy to sneak up on a sentry," he said, walking up to me. "You are standing sentry, aren't you?"

I ignored the question. "How long have you been following me?" I asked.

"Since you left the castle, two days ago. Three days, if it's past midnight, as I judge."

"I never saw you."

"Which proves that I'm a better soldier than you. Don't take it too hard. I've been at it almost twice as long as you've been alive. Of course, you made it easy. That cart has to stick to the roads, and you hardly ever look over your shoulder. If all else fails, a copper or two will prompt people who may have seen a cart passing by a few hours before."

I did take it hard, though I wasn't going to admit as much. "So, you've been following me. Why?"

"I can only repeat: you poor, stupid boy. Did you think Samson was so easily taken in? Samson, who has little to do these days but to stand and watch, or to sit and gossip. You drive a cart out the castle gates as regular – well, as regular as moonrise, I suppose I should say. I'm not sure how long you've been doing so, but I worked it out almost a year ago. Of course, carts leave the castle every day, and most of them are on some innocent enough errand. You, however – well, the fact that you almost always returned under the cover of darkness, so to speak, made me wonder."

I cursed myself. Ever since I'd felt obliged to venture so far afield as to be away for more than a day, I'd taken to returning by night. At the time, it had seemed safer. Now it seemed that it had simply aroused suspicion.

"You never set out in the same direction twice running," Samson went on. "I took to watching you. You can see a fair way from the top of the tower. Two months ago, I started leaving the castle a day ahead of you, in order to let you come to me, making it easier to pick up your trail. Of course, I had to guess which way you would set out. Twice I guessed wrong. This time I guessed right. So what are you up to?"

"That's no business of yours."

"No? Do you know why I followed you?"

"Why?"

"So that I could talk to you here, rather than in the castle."

"Why's that important?"

"Because I've noticed something else that happens as regular as moonrise."

"Really?"

"Don't play the innocent, lad. It insults my intelligence and yours. I've noticed that a maid child vanishes almost every time you take one of your little trips. I'd wager it would be every time if it weren't for some disappearances going unnoticed."

I said nothing. I've no doubt that my silence spoke loudly.

"I told you I listen to a lot of gossip," Samson said. "All news comes to the castle in time. And if old Samson has noticed a pattern, then others will have as well. I know there's a man that marks things on a map and compiles a list. Of course, he doesn't know that someone has noted which direction you've set out in over the last year. If the two lists were to be set side by side…"

"What then?"

"Aye, what then?"

"Tell me, Samson, why are you here? Truly."

"Truly? I told you that a long time ago. I hope they hang you." His tone suggested that he wasn't jesting this time. "There are those who wish a worse fate on – on whoever is behind these deaths. There are those who think that impalement is too good for him. And for her."

"For her?"

"I told you not to play the innocent. Everyone knows the Countess is behind all this. I'm surprised you haven't heard the whispers, but I suppose you're too close to her." He sighed. "Do you remember, the day of Count Nadasdy's funeral, Carl spoke of dark rumours about the Countess?"

"I do. I also remember that you called them nonsense."

"I did, to my shame. I've since repented of my error. Tell me the truth, lad. All of it."

"The truth? For that you'll need to look in the cart."

Samson took me at my word. He walked over to the cart. I walked a step behind him. As he pulled the layer of sacking behind, I reached under the driver's seat.

The pistol was not too damp.

The moon came out from behind the clouds and I saw Samson's face quite clearly. His expression was that of disappointment.

"Oh, you poor, stupid boy," he said, and died.

***

I'm having trouble remembering which events happened in which year. Everything seems jumbled up when I try to arrange matters in order. I'm almost certain that I shot Samson in November 1609 – that is the year before last. Of course, I told my Lady what had occurred. Told her that the net was closing in. She didn't seem concerned. Was that over-confidence? I don't know.

I also took to watching those around me a little more and keeping an ear out for gossip. Samson had been right about one thing. I was too close to my Lady. I realised that for almost a year I'd spoken to no-one in the castle except my Lady, Katarina, and Ilona Jo. What I hadn't noticed was that this was only partly because I'd withdrawn so far that my Lady was my world entire. It was also because others actively avoided me. I was rarely spoken to in the servants' hall, for example. This hadn't bothered me; indeed I welcomed it as I had no longer had any wish for company other than my Lady's. But in welcoming it, I had failed to see what it betokened.

That wasn't all. The more I thought things over, the more I saw things that should've been plain. My Lady still held her court once a week, for example, but fewer and fewer cases were being put before her. Some weeks there were none. This wasn't because we'd become a much more peaceful and law-abiding people; it was because people feared to bring their pleas to her. They feared to appear before her, or even to be noticed by her. Similarly, the army, such as it was, no longer reported to her. Of course, as a woman she'd never been expected to lead her men in the field, but more and more our men had fallen under the control of Palatine Thurzo, even of King Matthias himself. No longer being a soldier, I'd foolishly failed to notice this.

At one point, I explained my fears to Ilona Jo (there was no point speaking to Katarina. She was weak of intellect and terrified of Jo, who beat her). I said we needed to persuade my Lady to flee before it was too late. Ilona Jo had never liked me. She'd been disappointed that I'd remained in my Lady's service so long, and that my Lady cared for me far more than she did for her, who'd served her for many times as long. All she would say to me was that if my Lady chose to leave, she would leave, and that if she chose to stay, she would stay.

Of course, this was folly, but Ilona Jo would never see it as such, or never admit that she did, which meant that I would have to do something drastic.

Which is why when my Lady next gave me an order, I said "No."

This, to my eternal shame, was the thing that caused my Lady's downfall.

***

Why did it take so long before my Lady was brought to – well, I suppose I must call it justice? I've had long to ponder that question. I believe it must be because she was a Countess. Had she been the wife or widow of a humble cottager the law would've come pounding on her door readily enough. But a member of the nobility? No-one of humble stock would dare to move against her; those of an equal stature were reluctant to do so, for fear of implanting the idea in the minds of the people that the high-born weren't above the law.

Of course, it helped that the whispers (and whispers there were, now that I listened for them) were confused and contradictory. Some said my Lady lured the girls to her castle with offers of employment. Some said she ensnared them by magic. Others that she had a network of agents who sold her the girls. Still more that she roamed the country in disguise.

As for the fate of the girls, most thought they had been murdered, mostly for obscure reasons associated with my Lady's magic; but the idea that they'd been sold to the Turks convinced some. I actually heard one woman (this was while I was sitting in a roadside tavern, some three months before my Lady's arrest) say that although her daughter had been taken, she hoped she was still alive somewhere, and remembered her family.

But my refusal: I told my Lady that it was dangerous to continue to take girls too regularly. That sooner or later, someone would put the pieces of the puzzle together. I expected her to be furious. I expected her to dismiss me, as Ilona Jo had long predicted. I was wrong. She didn't dismiss me, and if she was angry, she concealed the fact. All she did was to say, "Very well," and ask to be left alone.

Katarina didn't come for me until the day after the next full moon. I found my Lady regarding herself in a looking-glass (the first I'd ever seen). She turned to me.

"Tell me truly, Ficko. Do I look a month older than I did the last time you beheld me?"

"No, my Lady." This was truth. She looked the same as ever.

"Are you sure?" She turned back to the looking-glass. "I believe I do. There are some lines that were not present last month. They are small, to be sure, but they will grow. They will spread. Month by month, year by year – until I look as old as Ilona Jo. Is this the fate you would wish for me, my Ficko?"

"No, my Lady." I looked at her again. It occurred to me that that although I could see no diminution of her beauty on the surface, there was a perhaps lack of vitality about her. Maybe that was what she felt.

"Are you sure, Ficko? Do you want to see my beauty fade?"

"No, my Lady. But the risks?"

"Risks, Ficko?"

"The risk that someone will discover what you – what we have done."

"You fear for yourself, Ficko?"

"No, my Lady. I am yours, and always will be."

"I believe you. But you will run no more errands for me?"

"No, my Lady. Not if it brings Stephen Magyari to your door with a writ in his hand."

"I see. In that case, I shall have to run my own errands."

This my Lady did.

***

At each of the next three full moons, my Lady, in her own words, ran her own errands. How she left the castle, and how she returned, I do not know. I assume it was in the form of a raven. Indeed, she later hinted that she'd sometimes flown during other phases of the moon, and that the girls I procured for her were not the only ones from whom she drew sustenance. When I thought about it (and I had much time for thought during these weeks) she'd told me she'd been given the gift years before I'd entered her service. Had some previous Ficko or Fickos been running her errands during this time, or had she shifted for herself? How many deaths did lie at her door?

During these weeks, my Lady didn't summon me, nor send me any word. I didn't lay eyes on her, nor on Ilona Jo, nor even Katarina. I had never felt lonelier.

At last, I could bear it no longer. I went to her chamber and banged on the door as if I wished to stave it in. I had to bang for a long time, but eventually Ilona Jo opened it, a look of triumph on her face. I entered and threw myself on my knees before my Lady.

"Ficko," she said. "This is a surprise. What service may I perform for you?"

"Forgive me, my Lady, and receive me back into your service."

"I told you before that I expected to have to forgive you much, did I not?"

"You did, my Lady."

"Well, I do. As for receiving you back into my service, you never left it."

"But my Lady —"

"There are no buts, Ficko. But tell me, are you ready to resume the undertaking of my errands?"

"Yes, my Lady."

"And you will speak to me no more of risks?"

I was miserable, I was trapped, I was doomed. I was a little spider. "No, my Lady."

***

A few days later, I learned that my Lady had made a mistake.

Her name was Anna Liptay. She was thirteen years old and had been born in Trencsen. My Lady had encountered her, killed her and presumably anointed herself with her blood. But she had been unable, in raven form, to carry off her body, and had been obliged to bury it. Presumably she did not bury it deep enough, for it was discovered and identified. It soon became clear that my Lady had made an unwise choice, for Anna Liptay was shortly to take holy vows. She'd been accepted as a novice at the nunnery of Stary Sacz – that one where St Kinga, daughter of Bela IV, famously retired to.

This gave Stephen Magyari the opening he'd been waiting for. I now know that he'd pieced together the puzzle some time before, but had feared to act without some sensational evidence to back up his accusation. Anna Liptay was what he needed. Despite having spent so long concerning himself with secular politics that people had almost forgotten that he was a priest, he mounted a pulpit (I forget where) and delivered a thunderous sermon of denunciation. Never mind that he was a Lutheran and Anna had been a Catholic. She was a child who'd wished to dedicate herself to God, and who'd been cruelly slain by the unholy monster that had terrorised the land for too long. He screamed for vengeance; and he named my Lady.

This caused a sensation. Copies of his sermon (some more accurate than others) were widely circulated and eagerly read. How much they were believed is not clear, but if a castle can be put under siege by people shunning it, then Csejte castle was besieged. Everyone, however, waited for someone else to make the first move.

That someone was King Matthias. He'd come to distrust the family of Bathory. In particular, his attention was drawn to Transylvania and its unreliable (in his view) ruler, the Lord Gabriel, my Lady's cousin. If a scandal could be proved against one Bathory, Matthias would have the pretext to replace Gabriel with someone more amenable. Never mind that this would do nothing to alter Transylvania's situation between hammer and anvil, but that's how the game of politics is played.

It took some months. I resumed my grisly duties, and procured three or four more girls for my Lady, but all the time I was waiting for the blow to fall.

It fell in December of the year 1610.

✳✳✳

They took me to a room deep below ground and put me to the torture. I won't speak of pincers and hot iron. I was a lost soul already. My only thought was to remain loyal to my Lady. During our last night she'd told me what to say and what not to say, so I told the truth. I told the truth, and nothing but the truth. My examiners did not believe me, so they put me to the torture again. I told them the truth again.

They told me that Ilona Jo and Katarina had confessed fully. I believed them. I knew they'd been tortured as well, for though I never saw them, their screams carried to the place where I was held. I told them that Katarina was simple and asked that she be spared. They were surprised at that.

They told me that they'd found the room with the bodies and confronted me with some of the things found there. I told them the truth. They tortured me again, and I told them the truth again.

They asked me for names. I told the truth, that I knew but one. They did not believe me and put me to the torture again.

I told them the truth. I told them nothing but the truth.

I did not tell them the whole truth.

They put me to the torture again.

***

The trial of my Lady was held in the second week of January 1611 before a panel of judges presided over by Theodosius de Szulo. He was an old man, learned but bitter. He'd clearly decided on his verdict beforehand – or, at least, it had been made plain to him what verdict was expected. He often glanced at Palatine Thurzo, who sat in the front row of the spectators. Beside him sat a churchman. I did not recognise him, but later learned that he was Melchior Klesl, a former Lutheran who'd become a bishop of the true church. He was King Matthias' principal advisor – both spiritual and temporal. From time to time, he spoke in Thurzo's ear, and to judge by the way the latter nodded, it was clear who ranked above who.

It was also clear that the trial was merely a piece of theatre. In my mind's eye, I saw a hierarchy of puppets. De Szulo's strings were being pulled by Thurzo, his by Matthias in the person of Klesl, and those of Matthias by – did this ascend all the way to the Pope? I still don't know the answer to that question.

Puppet theatre or not, de Szulo put on a show of being thorough, and spun things out over many days. He called dozens of witnesses and heard much testimony, not all of it true.

For example: Twelfth witness, the noble Andras Somogy. Sworn and interrogated, he testified that the Widow Nadasdy had travelled to Trencsen and that with his own eyes he had seen two girls, both of whose hands were burned so badly that they could not touch anything. He said that the Widow Nadasdy had burned their hands.

Twenty-fifth witness, the honourable Gyorgy Hladny. Sworn and interrogated, he testified that at the wedding celebration of Lord Homonnay, the Widow Nadasdy had whipped and tortured two girls so much that they died.

These accusations were baseless lies. My Lady did not use the torture. Indeed, she had told me more than once that she wanted her girls to die as swiftly and as painlessly as possible.

I also noted that the name Bathory was not uttered during her trial. She was referred to throughout as the Widow Nadasdy.

Much of the testimony was of no value. Example: Sixteenth witness, the honourable Janos Mezar. Sworn and interrogated, he said he knew nothing about the cruelty of the Widow Nadasdy, except for that which was known by hearsay, namely that she had abused living girls and that these naked girls were made to roll on a floor covered with nettles.

Twenty-second witness, the honourable Janos Hlavach. Sworn and interrogated, he said that he had heard from different people what the Widow Nadasdy did to girls. Namely that she stuck needles under their nails and submerged them naked in ice-cold water. He had also heard that she had killed some girls.

Thirty-second witness, the honourable Ladislas Holechny. Sworn and interrogated, he said that he knew nothing, except what he had heard from many; that the Widow Nadasdy would perpetrate cruel deeds.

In my head I heard Samson's mocking voice: I once heard a man say that he'd heard a man say that *he'd* heard a man say…

Lies, half-truths, rumours. If this was the way that courts went about their business, I thought, then it would be a miracle if anyone ever received justice. Little by little, however, a terrible picture was painted.

Unsurprisingly, the trial proved immensely popular. Those with money or influence packed the small court-room. Others crowded outside, eager to hear news of what had been said. After each witness, someone rushed outside to relay to the curious a summary of what that witness had said. A crude summary of second-hand rumours, half-truths and lies. I'm told that crude summaries of these summaries were distributed as popular pamphlets. I doubt that de Szulo would recognise them as originating in his court.

Much grisly evidence was displayed, some in the court-room, some outside. Had I been asked – which I was not – I could've said that not all of these gory exhibits were genuine. No-one else seemed to doubt their provenance, however. Indeed, people came from many miles around to gaze on them and be shocked. Afterwards, the bodies were buried. In a mass grave, I heard, though they were given a semblance of due rites by two priests – one Lutheran, one Catholic – who tried to out-do each other in outrage and mock piety.

At least, most of the remains displayed to the curious and the credulous ended up in a mass grave. I also heard (it's surprising how much gossip reaches those behind bars, but gaolers have little else to do to pass the time) that a number of macabre souvenirs were taken. Why people would want such things, I can't begin to guess, though my gaoler did relay to me, with relish, a juicy tidbit from Trencsen, namely that three separate people claimed to have secured the skull of the would-be nun, Anna Liptay, and that various churches were seeking to obtain them. A hundred years from now they'll probably make Anna a saint.

Throughout the proceedings, my Lady sat calm and impassive. She wasn't asked if she wanted to question any of the witnesses herself, nor did she seek to intervene when falsehoods were spoken or fraudulent exhibits presented. She merely waited patiently. The only thing she insisted on was to have her banner displayed over her chair. She would remain the Dragon Lady to the last.

***

We servants were made in to testify last. As co-defendants with my Lady, we'd been made to sit on the accused's bench throughout the many days of the trial, but I found it curious that de Szulo (or Thurzo, or Matthias, or the Pope) were only interested in what my Lady had done. The question of what I had done, or what Ilona Jo or Katarina had done seemed unimportant.

Nevertheless, we were called to testify. Katarina went first. She said nothing coherent, and de Szulo soon dismissed her, ordering his clerks to strike her evidence from the record, as he didn't want the dignity of his court to be tarnished by the ramblings of a simpleton.

Ilona Jo was next. Her hands were wrapped in blood-stained rags, and one of her eyes was swollen and closed. She seemed to have fewer teeth than I remembered. The evidence she gave was the most coherent of the whole proceedings. She declined, however, to name names. She admitted that girls were brought and that girls were killed, but nothing more. De Szulo pressed her hard to admit that the girls had been brought on my Lady's orders, and that my Lady had killed them, but she refused.

She said only that girls had been brought and that girls had been killed. She didn't name my Lady, and she didn't name me. I don't know why.

She was then questioned about the testimony regarding my Lady's cruelty; whether she had indeed whipped girls, or burned their hands, or did any of the other things that the court had heard. She said that my Lady had done none of these things.

"Only those involved with the law use torture," she said, waving her bloody hands at de Szulo. Then she spat on the floor. I think it was this that persuaded de Szulo that Ilona Jo was more culpable than I.

I testified last. I was brought to stand before de Szulo. He reprimanded me for not standing up straight and showing the court the proper respect.

"I'm sorry, my Lord," I said. "I find it difficult to stand straight. After the torture, I'm not sure that my legs are the same length."

There were some laughs at this, but de Szulo was not pleased to be reminded of torture twice in one afternoon. He moved on to questioning me.

As I have said, my Lady had told me what to say and what not to say. I told the truth, and nothing but the truth. I said that I'd fetched girls from many parts. I didn't say that I'd killed them first, and de Szulo was in too much of a hurry to get things over with that he never asked me a direct question on this point. I described the way a body is drained of blood. I said what my Lady did on the night of each full moon (there were gasps at this – I think I'd gone beyond anything even Thurzo and de Szulo expected).

I also told the court of my nights with my Lady. Long nights of carnal pleasure, of unbridled lust, of animal fury. De Szulo's face was grim, but most of the others present were thrilled. I even heard one voice at the back of the room venture the opinion that a mere three nights with my Lady would've been worth a hanging.

I told the truth. I told nothing but the truth. I did not tell the whole truth.

I did not tell them about Samson.

Nor did I tell the court about was what had passed between my Lady and I on that last night before our arrest.

***

"We have a night, Ficko. How shall we use it?"

"I don't know, my Lady."

"Don't you? How unimaginative. Well, why don't you sing me one of your peasant songs? You know I've always liked them, and it's likely to be a long while before I hear them again."

I sang. An old song I'd learned from my mother; a song that was to be sung in the winter, and which promised that spring was on its way, so that the world would renew itself. My Lady heard me in silence.

"Thank-you, Ficko," she said when I was done. It occurred to me that never before had she actually thanked me for anything.

"That was a fitting song. I wonder if you realise how fitting, but no matter. Sit by me." I complied.

"It is time to speak to you of the gift. I'm sure you've guessed what it is, in broad terms at least, but do you really *know*?"

"No, my Lady."

"It is the gift of life, of youth. It is the gift of enduring. It is the gift of biting one's thumb at time. It is the gift of power. It is the gift of dominion over death. It is the gift of many things – but it does not come without a cost."

"A cost, my Lady?"

"A cost, Ficko. A cost that I shall be called upon to pay shortly."

"You mean..?"

"I mean the cost of being shunned by lesser, envious folk, who do not possess the gift. They cannot, for if the gift is distributed too widely, it will lose its potency. We are of this world, and we are not of this world. We can live in it for only so long at a time, before we have to leave it. But we are able to return."

"Is this what you meant when you said that the Little Dragon was sleeping, and will awaken in time?"

"It is. I'm glad you have grasped the point. I have always known that this moment would come. Oh, I was not so far-sighted as to be able to name the day, nor did I foresee that it would be King Matthias who would ultimately be behind my fall; but I knew that it would come to pass, sooner or later. Knowing this, I have made certain preparations. I shall seem to die, but I shall return. You too will seem to die; but if you place your trust in me, you will return also. Will you place your trust in me?"

"This gift, my Lady. You will make me a vampyre?"

"I will, if you wish it."

"And I will return?"

"I will make sure that you do. A generation from now, or maybe a hundred years."

"I will return, to serve you?"

My Lady laughed. "Is that what you truly wish?"

"With all my heart. My Lady, I must tell you this now. I love you. I have loved you from the moment you smiled at me on the day of the Count's funeral. I would say that my wish is to love you life-long, but if the gift has the power you say, I will be able to love you for longer than that."

"Interestingly put, my Ficko. I take it that this means you will accept the gift?"

"With all my heart, my Lady."

"Good." With that my Lady opened her mouth wide. Her teeth gleamed by the light of our sole candle, and seemed sharper than ever. She bit deep. I felt no pain as she began to drink my blood.

***

Afterwards, we pleasured each other for the last time – or maybe just the last time for a century. My Lady was gentler on this occasion than she'd ever been before.

I fell asleep in her arms. My last thought was that, although I'd declared my love to my Lady, she'd not said whether she loved me in return.

It doesn't matter. Love is pain.

***

The court concluded its business at last. De Szulo decided not to question my Lady directly. I think he didn't dare to. My Lady, I'm sure, was disappointed. She would've enjoyed toying with him. Most of those gathered were disappointed as well, but Thurzo was relieved, and I think Klesl was, as well.

De Szulo made a show of conferring with his fellow-judges (I've not mentioned them up to now. They never said a word during the trial and were clearly just there for the look of the thing). Katarina was ordered to be confined in a nunnery for the rest of her days. Ilona Jo was to burn at the stake. I was to be beheaded.

As for my Lady, she was not to be harmed. Some muttered that the name of Bathory protected her even after the most hideous crimes had been proven against her, but I wonder. I wonder whether her enemies feared to punish her. Had they, perhaps, some understanding of what she truly was, and dreaded that condemning her to death would simply hasten the day when she returned to wreak her vengeance? I don't know. I hope they go on fearing my Lady, however.

Whatever the truth of it, my Lady was merely ordered to be confined to Csejte Castle for the rest of her days. There was talk of having her sealed up in her own chamber, with only a small gap left to pass food and water. If her promise to me holds good, I'll ask her later if this was done.

Tomorrow, they'll march me to the scaffold and strike off my head. I'll die or will seem to do so; but when the time is ripe, my Lady will call me forth, and once again I will be like the little spider, dancing on her web.

HISTORICAL NOTE

Elizabeth (or Erszebet) Bathory (1560 – 1614) is sometimes regarded as the first female serial killer in history, or the first we know about, at least. She was responsible for at least 80 deaths, and possibly as many as 650, depending on which account you read. The lurid tales about her have almost certainly been embellished over the years (did she really bathe in her victims' blood?) but it's hard to believe, as some have suggested, that she was completely innocent, and that the elaborate charges were invented merely to side-line her and her family for political reasons.

Elizabeth Bathory was an intelligent and educated woman, who was fluent in Hungarian, German, Latin and Greek. She was raised a Calvinist, though I seem to have implied that she and Ficko were Catholics. I don't know why. In her youth, Elizabeth suffered from seizures – presumably epilepsy – part of the treatment for which involved the blood of a non-sufferer being rubbed on her lips, and possibly given to her to swallow. She was also rumoured to have given birth to a child at the age of thirteen – the father being a peasant. Whether there is any truth behind this rumour and, if so, whether the child was born of a liaison or a rape, is not known. It's certainly true that in later life, Elizabeth was generous to several destitute women, including at least one rape victim.

Janos "Ficko" Ujvary, Katarina, and Ilona Jo were real servants of hers, and were sentenced as I have stated. Two other servants, Dorottya and Erzsi, were also executed but I've omitted them for convenience. For the same reason I've set the whole tale at

Csejte Castle, though Elizabeth had other homes. Most of the other people named are real, including Radu Serban, Thurzo, Magyari, de Szulo, Klesl, Gabriel and King Matthias. Ferenc Nadasdy's death was indeed sudden and unexplained, but so were a lot of deaths before the advent of modern medicine. He did have pains in his legs, but their cause is unknown. Despite my tale, Nadasdy's army wasn't present at the Battle of Brasov. No account I've read mentions the impaling of any prisoners after the battle, but it was a common practice in the region for many centuries.

I've omitted to mention any of the eight children Elizabeth had, two or possibly three of whom survived infancy and were still living at the time of their mother's trial. The story of the would-be nun is my invention, but the extracts from evidence given at the trial are taken from surviving records.

There are conflicting versions of Elizabeth Bathory's fate, though all agree that she was confined to Csejte Castle (now in Slovakia) for the rest of her life. Some accounts say that she was walled up in her apartments, with food passed through a slot; others that it was more like a house arrest. She died three and a half years after her trial.

Or did she die? Was she indeed a vampyre? Maybe we'll hear from her again.

About the Authors

Richard Beauchamp

Hailing from the lush, verdant hills of the Ozarks, Richard Beauchamp has been spinning tales of horror that take place in the quieter corners of the midwest and other parts of the world since 2017. His debut short story collection "Black Tongue & Other Anomalies" was a nominee for the 2022 Splatterpunk Awards, and his fiction has been placed in such esteemed publications as Cohesion Press' "SNAFU: Dead Or Alive" and Dark Peninsula Press's "Negative Space" anthologies. Readers can find him online at:

http://www.richardbeauchampauthor.com
Facebook: RichardBeauchampOfficial
Instagram: @r_b_author

Francis Verelle

Francis Verelle chose to become a writer because it is a profession that allows you to sleep during the day and stay out of the sun. She has published both short stories and novels under various pen names over the last century. Despite her questionable sleeping habits, she swears she is not a vampire. But if you ever want to buy her a drink, please keep in mind that she prefers blood type A+.

MARK MACKEY

Mark Mackey is a fiction writer who has known only one state as residence and hometown, Chicago Illinois. Mark has co-written an island horror novel with Shawn Davis. His stories can be found in various anthologies, some charity, others not.

R.C. MULHARE

R.C. Mulhare once successfully defended her day-job workplace from zombies, through some judicious use of clearance-rack garden tools and survived a fight with Yog-Sothoth cultists in a hallway of a hotel in Providence; she's also picked up extra work editing the product blog of Umbrella Corporation...

In actuality, R.C. Mulhare was born in Lowell, Massachusetts and grew up in a nearby town, in a hundred year old house up the street from an old cemetery. Her interest in the dark and mysterious started when she was quite young, when her mother read the faery tales of the Brothers Grimm and quoted the poetry of Edgar Allan Poe to her, while her Irish storyteller father infused her with a fondness for strange characters and quirky situations. Between writing projects, she moonlights in grocery retail. She's also fond of hiking in the woods of the White Mountains of New Hampshire and browsing the antiques shops one finds all over New England. A two-time Amazon best-selling author, contributor to the Hugo Award Winning Archive of Our Own, and member of the New England Horror Writers, she has one hundred twenty stories in print through dozens of independent publishers including Atlantean Publishing, Macabre Maine, DBND Publishing, Hellbound Books, Nocturnal Sirens Publishing, FunDead Publications, Deadman's Tome, NEHW Press, Lovecraftiana Magazine, Tales of Wonder and Dread, and Weirdbook Magazine, with more stories in the works. She shares her home with her family, a vintage music-loving baby parakeet, about fifteen hundred books and an unknown number of eldritch things that rattle in the walls when she's writing late in the night. She's happy to have visitors through her page at: https://linktr.ee/rcmulhare

G K Lomax

G K Lomax is a nom-de-internet. Behind it lies a rather strange individual from the fair English county of Essex. He has appeared on several broadcast quiz programmes, is constantly baffled by modern technology, and was once cursed by Sean Connery for the erratic nature of his golf. He writes weird fiction because he hates having to come up with happy endings, and sometimes thinks the end of the world can't come soon enough.

ABOUT THE EDITORS

AARON CROCKER

Aaron was raised in the small town of El Dorado Springs, Missouri and later moved to Virginia where he currently resides. He holds a few degrees, the most applicable being a B.S. in English, Linguistics, and Communications from the University of Mary Washington.

In 2016, he wrote his first piece "Suburban Suicide" which took second place in a national divergent literature competition. From there he picked up a few more national and international awards in short and micro fiction competitions, sat on various short fiction judging panels, and has spoken at several writing events—the most notable being an invitation to address the Library of Congress in 2020 (virtually).

Over several years, Aaron published two moderately successful, limited-edition fundraising anthologies, and this is where he gained an appreciation for and enjoyment of publishing. From there, he dreamed up and founded Campfire Publishing, and although he quickly became aware of the editing skills required of such an endeavor, he is nothing if not dedicated and open to learning.

LINETTE KASPER

Linette primarily writes supernatural fantasy but enjoys dabbling in other styles, especially horror and suspense. She has released three novels from her first series, "Daimon", "Rogue", and "Phoenix", and is currently working on a prequel. She also has two short stories published in anthologies, "What They Did Not Know" in FunDead Publications' *One Night in Salem* and "Undine" in *Rejected*. Linette also enjoys editing, which is not something most authors can say, and has done so with her own novels, as well as others'.